BACK

"[Hickam's] boy . . . . showing again in his fir . . . . . is fiction . . . . Sky' . . . . . . One of the strengths . . . this readable, diverting novel is that th . . . reader . . . isn't absolutely sure who's good and who's bad un . . . . near . . . the end. I like the sharp . . . char . . . ctures . . . . . . and . . . 'sly plot twists.' . . . ."

—*The New York Times Book Review*

"A . . . FASCINATING PLOT . . . A FUN, INTERESTING PA . . . TURNER."

—*SpaceViews News*

"Hickam proves that the meteoric success of his last book, 'Rocket Boys,' was no fluke. The signs and smell of the coalfield life are large in Hickam's latest prose, but there is a compelling pathos in 'Moon' . . . unlike to the bootstrap determination of 'Rocket Boys.' . . . Hickam spins a damn good yarn. . . . '*Back to the Moon*' has a wealth . . . bed of . . . re, legacy and hope for the future that could only be written by . . . . history tale of adventure and pathos . . . ."

—*Bluefield Daily Telegraph (W. Va.)*

"A TIME-BOMB . . . HICKAM'S PACE HEATS UP . . . THE ROCKET RIDE ACHIEVES HIGH VELOCITY."

—*Publishers Weekly*

"[Hickam's] vast knowledge of the politics and hardware of space . . . ining shines through, filling the reader with hope that . . . great things still await us." . . . . ws

"A CLIFFHANGING YARN." —*Booklist*

"[A] novel . . . . in space—with a dedi . . . . heart . . . saga. 'This rocket flies on dreams,' says the hero. 'You better believe it.'"

—*Library Journal*

Also by Homer H. Hickam, Jr.

TORPEDO JUNCTION
ROCKET BOYS

BACK
to the
MOON

A NOVEL

Homer H. Hickam, Jr.

Island
BOOKS

ISLAND BOOKS
Published by
Dell Publishing
a division of
Random House, Inc.
1540 Broadway
New York, New York 10036

Reprinted by arrangement with Delacorte Press
Printed in the United States of America
Published simultaneously in Canada
April 2000
10 9 8 7 6 5 4 3 2 1
OPM

To Linda
and
the women and men of NASA

ACKNOWLEDGMENTS

Unlike astronauts and cosmonauts, no author ever works in a vacuum. A support team is required, albeit ad hoc, to complete any manuscript, especially one that attempts to recreate a reality that never existed. This is especially true of a writer devising a tale of space that occurs in the near future. The space business today is hideously complex. In a way, it inhabits a separate world, complete with its own unique laws, personalities, technologies, bureaucracies, and language. An outsider entering this world quickly becomes lost in the myriad unwritten rules of those who work the space trade, confused by the jargon, bewildered by temporary organizations within organizations that rapidly coalesce then just as quickly fall apart, bemused by managers both cautious and audacious nearly at the same moment, disgusted by the often enormous waste of talent and money and time just to stroke a particular ego, baffled by decisions never decided but realized anyway, and mentally pulverized by a technology nearly impossible to understand because no one has ever written it down in a way that's understandable. Even though I've been a space business insider for three decades, I have had to rely on the assistance of others who work space to make my manuscript as accurate as possible. To them (and you know who you are) I give my heartfelt gratitude, especially Jim Baker, an engineer of great vision and special talent. Clay Terry was also especially helpful in transferring vitally important documents written on one computer platform to another so as to allow me access to them.

Special thanks are also due to Linda Terry Hickam, my first editor, Tom Spain of Delacorte, my final editor, Frank Weimann, my literary agent, and Mickey Freiberg, my Hollywood agent. Finally, for the inspiration they have always given me, I doff my spacesuit helmet to NASA agency and contractor grunts everywhere. God bless them. They toil endlessly for me and you along the pathways to space.

AUTHOR'S NOTE

Coalwood, West Virginia, my hometown, was not a place where children often looked at the stars. The narrow swath of sky between our mountains only allowed us a peek at the heavens, and even that was often blotted out by the dust and smoke coming from the coal mine tipple. The people of Coalwood, dedicated to the industry of coal mining, tended to look down, not up. That all changed for me when I was in the fourth grade. After reading everything on the grade school bookshelves, I started going upstairs to the junior high library and there I discovered the wonderful novels of Jules Verne. I was astonished by his tales, filled not only with great adventures but with scientists and engineers who considered the acquisition of knowledge to be the greatest pursuit of mankind. When I finished everything by Verne in the library, I started to read the modern science fiction writers who had followed in his footsteps: Heinlein, Asimov, van Vogt, Clarke, and Bradbury. These writers challenged me to look up at the sky, and to imagine myself crossing the boundless frontier of the universe. The junior high librarian knew to call me any time a new science fiction book arrived and I would almost break my neck running up the steps to get at it. This distressed my grade school teachers, who preferred that I have a more eclectic library record. To counteract my fixation they prescribed appropriate doses of Twain, Steinbeck, and other writers. I was happy to oblige them because I loved those writers too. But

I was always happy to get back to my literary adventures in science and space.

In the fall of 1957, when I was in the tenth grade, *Sputnik* was launched and a great space race began between the United States and Russia. Because of the science fiction I'd read, I thought I already knew something of spaceflight and began to build and launch my own rockets, much to the consternation of the good citizens of Coalwood. I wrote about what happened in the three years that followed *Sputnik* in the book *Rocket Boys, A Memoir* but the story didn't end there. I eventually fulfilled my boyhood dreams and secured a position as an engineer with the National Aeronautics and Space Administration. I had become, I thought, a man like Verne's men, an engineer dedicated to the pursuit of science and exploration.

The space shuttle era was just beginning when I started at NASA. It was an exciting time for engineers, scientists, and astronauts in the space agency as we learned how to fly and operate a manned heavy-lift spacecraft with wings. The space shuttle proved to be a magnificent machine, capable of accomplishing a wide variety of tasks in space. But as the years passed, I began to notice an increasing frustration among my fellow NASA engineers. The fact was most of us had signed on to explore space, to go to the moon, to the planets and beyond. The space shuttle was designed for the routine task of people and cargo hauling into low earth orbit. It was almost as if after the *Apollo* flights there had been a directive from on high: the moon and the planets were off-limits to astronauts. All they were allowed to do was carve endless loops around the earth in the space shuttle and maybe, someday, aboard an International Space Station. This caused much frustration within the agency. Many of us especially thought we should build on *Apollo*, and go back to the moon.

I began to get together with a few of my NASA colleagues who thought as I did and we worked on ways to get out of low earth orbit, usually in a variety of new spacecraft. One day a paper written by Jim Baker, a Rockwell engineer, fell into my hands. In it was a proposal for modifying an existing space shuttle to fly to the moon, orbit around it, and return to earth. I called Jim and we discussed his idea at length. Yes, he said, it could be done. All that it required was the will to go and do it. Many years passed but Baker's idea stuck with me. I often found myself lurking in the techno-thriller or science fiction area of bookstores looking unsuccessfully for a novel about a realistic spacecraft, maybe even the shuttle, going back to the moon. I never found it. One day it occurred to me that if I wanted to read such a book, I would have to write it myself. About the same time I began to hear about a very special isotope called helium-3. Helium-3, a source of almost limitless energy, is rare on earth but abundant on the moon. I found it both ironic and hopeful that mankind's survival on our relatively lush planet may very well depend on our airless, desolate moon.

And so it was I set myself to the task of writing the book I wanted to read, remembering not only Jim Baker's designs, and the promise of helium-3, but also the strong-willed, inventive men and women who peopled the science and space adventures I read as a boy. It is said that heroes are made by the challenges they confront, by the risks they take, and by the pain they endure. Challenges, risks, and pain are all necessary for the fictional characters of *Back to the Moon* to live up to the book's title. This reflects reality. The *Apollo* missions pushed the edge of the technological envelope and to go back to the moon today would still be difficult and risky. Nevertheless, many of my colleagues at NASA share my belief that we need to go now, without delay. The moon is laden with a vast storehouse of treasure that this country, and the world, will need in the very near future. If we aren't willing to take on the challenge of securing it, we will perhaps doom our planet to a limited and painful future that won't allow spaceflight at all. Then it will be too late. Let's not risk it. We need to go back to the moon. All that is required is the will, and the courage, to do it.

Homer H. Hickam, Jr.
Huntsville, Alabama

BACK
to the
MOON

O fortune like the Moon
you ever want
but to regain
your former circumstance.
Life's equally fain
to decimate
as reinstate
the mind with games of chance
prosperity
and penury
reversing with a glance.

—*Carmine Burana,*
"Fortune, Empress of the World"

PROLOGUE:

The End of the Beginning

Oh, it's home again, and home again, America for me!
I want a ship that's westward bound to plough the rolling sea,
To the blessed Land of Room Enough beyond the ocean bars,
Where the air is full of sunlight and the flag is full of stars.

—*Henry Van Dyke*, "America for Me"

Apollo 17
Frau Mauro, the Moon, December 12, 1972

Gene Cernan was having the time of his life. He tried to restrain himself, but driving the Lunar Rover over the powdery regolith of the moon was simply too much fun not to bust loose now and then. When he hit a bump and the Rover's front wheels left the ground, he let out a whoop. Then he spotted a dune and, rather than steering away, headed straight for it. The Rover dug in, its wheels gaining traction. Cernan, grinning like a school kid, looked over at his partner, Harrison "Jack" Schmitt, who kept his eyes straight ahead, stoic as always. The Rover bounced as it went over the top of the dune, its wire wheels spinning. Cernan spotted a large crater off to the left. He heard Schmitt's voice crackle in his helmet headset. "I want another reading on the traverse gravimeter." Schmitt pointed to the crater. "And I want to go over to Shorty."

Cernan marveled that Schmitt had memorized the name of every crater in the Taurus-Littrow region. "Okay, Jack. We're on our way." He made a quick turn and pushed the joystick throttle forward.

"Be advised you are near red line on consumables, Gene," Houston Mission Control crackled in the headsets of both astronauts.

Cernan switched to crew-only comm. "You heard the man, Jack. We've got just enough oxygen to get back to the Lem."

Cernan heard Schmitt's exasperated sigh. "That's if we had to walk back, Gene, and you know that's not going to happen. The Rover's in good shape. I really need to take a look at Shorty. Make a bunch of geologists happy if I did. It's a bit of a mystery."

Cernan weighed the odds. If anything happened to the Rover, he and Schmitt would run out of oxygen before they could make it back to the Lem on foot. But Schmitt was the only scientist ever to walk on the moon. He needed every precious second he could get for his research. Cernan shrugged invisibly inside his thick suit. It was the last time men were going to be on the moon for many years. Maybe it was time to play the odds. He stopped the lunar "dune buggy" at the base of the steep crater rim. "This do, Jack?"

Schmitt made no reply, not a second to waste. He hopped out and headed up the slope in as near a run as his suit would allow. Cernan detached the television camera from the Rover so he could show Houston the view. He trudged up the crumbling slope. The view up there was by God beautiful! Undulating sand mountains lay like white porcelain sculptures in a vast gray ocean of dust. "Take a look at this, Houston!" Cernan called. After a pan he aimed the camera into the deep pit of the crater. "And this!"

While Cernan enjoyed the view and shared it with earth, Schmitt kept up a one-sided commentary to the boys in the geologists' back room. "The crater named Shorty has a distinctly raised rim and a hummocky floor," he said. "Dark ejecta surrounds it."

Cernan pointed the video camera at Schmitt as he hustled over to a boulder that was coated with black dust. "I'm beside a boulder that has a knobby surface and is covered with hairline cracks," Schmitt reported, and then laughed.

Schmitt's laugh was so unusual, Cernan switched to crew-only comm. "What's going on, Jack?"

Schmitt's voice was absolutely merry. "I've just solved in less than a minute an argument that's been raging in the geology world for years. Some of the boys say that Shorty's volcanic, others say a meteor caused it. Well, I know exactly what it is now."

"Then tell the world, Jack." Cernan chuckled. He worked his way over to his partner and filled the television frame with him. "Hey, Houston, listen up—especially any geologists monitoring."

"Shorty is a fresh impact crater," Schmitt observed succinctly. He went to the crew-only mode. "Hey, Gene—money's going to be changing hands in Houston on this one!"

"Wish I'd placed a bet myself!" Cernan answered, pleased that his partner was enjoying himself.

Schmitt went back to earth comm. "There's an accumulation of basaltic spatter and cinders. Shorty's floor appears to be either impact-indurated soil breccia or the top of the subfloor basalt."

"Copy that," Houston intoned. But Mission Control seemingly had a one-track mind. "You should be heading back to the Lem now."

"I want a soil sample," Schmitt replied stubbornly.

"We got to go, Jack," Cernan told his crewmate as gently as he could, trying not to betray his own anxiety. Hypoxia was not an easy way to die. The Houston training people had been pretty graphic on what it would be like: First there would be a splitting headache, followed quickly by shortness of breath and air hunger. Being astronauts, they'd probably gut it out and still trudge on but they wouldn't get far. Convulsions would soon wrestle them to the ground and then they'd gasp and twitch like caught fish until the black shade of death enveloped them. Cernan guessed that would be a blessing.

Schmitt turned away, clumped down to the Rover, and popped the lid on the aluminum box that held drive tubes and tools. "This is important, Gene, and it's why we're here."

Cernan was the commander. He could order Schmitt back on the Rover, but there was something about Shorty

Crater that made Cernan want to push the envelope. "Make it fast, Jack," he relented.

Schmitt puttered around the site, taking samples and gravity readings. Houston kept calling Cernan and reminding him that they were at the limit of their walk-back capability and Cernan kept replying that he knew it—just another minute more and they'd be out of there.

"Oh, hey—wait a minute—there's orange soil here!" Schmitt's excited voice was an octave higher than usual.

Cernan shuffled through the gray dust to peer at the splotch of color in front of his partner. He briefly raised the shield on his helmet. There was no change in the hue. "He's not going out of his mind, Houston," he reported. "It really *is* orange!"

"I've got to see how big it is!" Schmitt said eagerly.

"I don't know, Jack," Cernan said worriedly.

Schmitt didn't reply, bounded back to the Rover to the storage box, and got out a rake. "Gene, if there ever was something that looked like fumarole alteration, this is it!" he exclaimed. He trudged back to the splotch. "Orange soil is consistent with oxidized iron. This indicates volcanic activity, but everything else about Shorty points to an impact crater. We haven't solved a mystery at all. We've just created one! We've got to get some samples back."

Cernan checked all his gauges and didn't like what he saw. He waited a minute, then another, while Schmitt filled some sample bags. He looked at his gauges again. If the Rover conked out, they were dead men. "Let's go, Jack," he urged. "You got enough, right?"

"Still need a core sample." Schmitt puffed and picked up the drive tube he had brought from the box.

Cernan watched Schmitt bobble the tube. He knew his partner was bone tired. Cernan was also feeling the fatigue of the long day. They had covered nearly two and a half miles of terrain, had made three stops, and gathered more than a hundred pounds of samples. Working on the moon in the pressurized suits wasn't easy. Cernan's hands ached and his forearms felt as if somebody had tightened steel bands around them. "I forgot the hammer," he heard Schmitt say apologetically.

Cernan ignored another call from Houston. "I'll get the hammer, Jack," he said. "Just stay where you are. Rest a little." Cernan moon-hopped to the Rover and opened the box, revealing a jumble of tools all coated in sticky lunar dust. He was glad he wouldn't have to clean them. Everything in the toolbox was scheduled to be left behind on the moon. As he searched, Houston made another call, this one a command to get in the Rover NOW and head back to the lunar module named *Challenger*, their home on the moon and their ride up to Ron Evans waiting for them in the *Apollo* Command Module. Cernan, a Navy commander, had named the Lem after the old wooden sailing ship *Challenger* that had, in another age, explored uncharted seas for the purposes of science. Those old sailors had more time than he did. With both time and air running out, Cernan dug through the tools, still not finding the hammer. He grabbed the next best thing, a cylindrical canister capped on both ends. He had no idea what it was or why it was in the toolbox but he didn't care. He was going to give it a new purpose.

The soil was hard and Cernan had to use the canister to pound the drive tube with both hands. At two feet it refused to go any deeper. He gave it another tap, dropped the canister, and grabbed the sample tube with both hands and rocked it back and forth until it loosened enough to be pulled out. "Even the tube is orange!" Schmitt cried gleefully, reaching for it.

Cernan looked once more at the gauges on the front of his suit. All the needles were pointing south. "Come on!" he said, scuttling back to the Rover. He unlatched the sample box and stowed the precious orange-coated drive tube inside. If the Rover held together, if the oxygen gauges were correct, and if they didn't get lost on the way back, they could make it. There were a lot of *ifs* in that equation, too many for Cernan's comfort. His fingers mentally crossed, he cranked up the juice as Schmitt climbed into his seat. Plumes of lunar dust from the Rover wheels erupted behind them as the last two men on the moon made a desperate run against the clock.

Marshall Space Flight Center, Building 4200, Huntsville, Alabama

Dr. Wernher von Braun was called from a meeting of his designers who were working on the new engines for the proposed space shuttle. He listened carefully to the caller, and went back to his meeting, wrapping it up quickly. He left work early, the first time in decades, and drove his Mercedes up the mountain called Monte Sano, which overlooked Huntsville.

Von Braun, a handsome man with silver-gray hair and a bulldog chin that made him look perpetually optimistic and determined, was actually quite tired. For three decades he had fought bureaucrats, cajoled politicians, and courted the public in his quest to get humankind to the moon. Now, after he had done all that he said he would do, his beloved adopted country was abandoning the triumph of the lunar explorations after a final flight. He had told everyone—the NASA administrator, Senator Vanderheld, who chaired the Science and Space Committee, even the President of the United States—that it was madness to quit, although he had carefully couched his arguments in terms of scientific benefits and simple economics. To help his argument he'd even agreed to transfer to NASA headquarters in Washington, reluctantly leaving Huntsville for the chilly environs of the capital city. But all of his arguments had been turned away, especially after Vanderheld had issued his committee's recommendation to cancel *Apollo*. It was difficult, although von Braun had accepted the challenge, to debate with Vanderheld over the relative merits of spaceflight versus public housing, school lunches, veterans' benefits, and farm subsidies. How was it possible to say that *Apollo* was more important than any of those things? Senator Vanderheld, although polite, was sincerely troubled by von Braun's assertion that *Apollo* was like seed corn for the nation. From it, von Braun argued in his testimony before Vanderheld's committee, many things might be derived, great and noble things, wealth not yet understood, a new world of not only things but possibilities. Vanderheld had sadly refuted point by point everything the great rocket scientist had said. "The business of the federal government is to see to the needs of the people, Doctor," the senator had politely lectured von Braun. "Tomorrow will take care of itself only if wise choices are made today."

Von Braun's supervisors at NASA told him he should try to accept it. The director had even come up to him, put his arm over his shoulder, and said, "Be reasonable, Wernher. We've drunk the wine that has been given to us. And now the glass is empty."

"But there is no reason to break the glass, is there?" von Braun had retorted. The director had shrugged, walked away, muttering. A NASA headquarters directive had ordered von Braun to shut down the *Saturn V* moon-rocket assembly line. Even the tooling that had built it was to be broken apart, sold as scrap. *Apollo* was over. Only the shuttle, now on the drawing boards, was left. By order of NASA headquarters the shuttle was to be designed so that it could only go into low earth orbit. It seemed almost deliberate that the moon had been put out of reach for a very long time.

Von Braun parked in front of a small brick cottage on a bluff that overlooked the city. Ursula Suttner answered the door. Von Braun kissed her cheek. "Are you well, Uschi?" he asked, holding her shoulders and searching her face. Ursula Suttner had come from Germany to marry her husband, Gerhard, von Braun's chief aerodynamic engineer.

She was younger than the other wives, most of whom had been with their husbands through the war. Ursula brushed a wisp of blond hair away from her forehead. "I am quite well, Wernher," she said with a smile. "Please," she said, indicating the living room, "they are waiting for you."

Shouts of greeting from the living room brought von Braun inside. There he found Katrina, the Suttners' ten-year-old daughter, lying on a rug watching the television coverage of the *Apollo 17* flight. As her father beamed proudly, and her mother watched adoringly from the living room door, Katrina got up and ran to von Braun, hugging him around the waist. "Have you heard, Katrina?" von Braun asked her gently. "It wasn't exactly what we plotted, I'm afraid."

"Oh, Uncle, it's even better. I saw what happened. Do you think he will find it? Do you think so, really?"

Von Braun knelt in front of the little girl, gently touching her hair. Katrina Suttner was the kind of child who could light up a room with her bright, optimistic intelligence. Von Braun was certain she was destined for greatness. "Yes, little one. If he is the man you think he will be, I believe he will." Then he let her lead him to a chair so together they could watch the end of the exploration of the moon.

The next day von Braun was on an airplane, flying back to Washington, while his rocket team gathered at the Suttner house to watch *Apollo 17*'s final moments. The crew had made it back from Shorty Crater with their treasure of orange soil and geologists were licking their lips at the opportunity to see what they had actually found. There was a lick of flame at the base of the *Challenger* lunar module and then arcing debris flew away from it as it rose. The video camera attached to the Lunar Rover, abandoned by Cernan and Schmitt, tracked upward until the module and the men in it had disappeared into the black sky. Then it came slowly back to the abandoned lander and stared at the *Challenger*'s truncated base.

Katrina looked around at the old Germans surrounding her. To her amazement many of them had tears streaming down their faces. "Do not be sad, Uncles," she told them. "We will go back. I promise you we will."

"If Katrina says it," her father said, wiping away his own tears, "then it must be so."

All the old men nodded solemnly. *Ja*, it must be so.

At the doorway Ursula Suttner put her hands to her face and turned away. A terrible premonition had reached her, come down as if from heaven, and turned her soul to ice.

30 YEARS LATER . . .

1

Decimation

This I have known always: love is no more
Than the wide blossom which the wind assails,
Than the great tide that treads the shifting shore,
Strewing fresh wreckage gathered in the gales.
Pity me that the heart is slow to learn
What the swift mind beholds at every turn.

—Edna St. Vincent Millay, "Pity Me Not"

Prometheus
MEC Clean Room, Hangar 1-D, Cedar Key, Florida

"NASA is and always has been a subversive organization. Anything else you hear is a public relations lie," Jack Medaris said.

Dr. Isaac Perlman looked at the ceiling of the big hangar and wagged his head from side to side, an indication of his doubt at his companion's comment. "Subversive? Why, Jack, there's never been a more conservative bureaucracy on this planet. It takes polls to see what it should do next. It lets politicians decide technical matters. You forget I went there first for my moon dirt. NASA just laughed at me. That's why I hired you!"

Medaris and Perlman, dressed in clean-room regalia — white one-piece coveralls, puffy plastic hats, and latex gloves — were watching a dozen other similarly clothed men and women ministering to what looked to be a giant robot, two gangly arms akimbo, mounted on a go-cart. The doleful strains of Barber's *Adagio for Strings* accompanied the technicians as they moved slowly and reverently around the machine's oddly shaped pyramid of spheres, rods, and cables. Antennae protruded from each level of the machine. Its "arms" were actually two extendable and jointed booms. At the end of one of the booms was a digger, a rakelike device. The other arm had a grasping claw.

"I'll grant you NASA as a bureaucracy is timid," Jack said. "But what I'm talking about is its charter. NASA is supposed to develop the means to allow American citizens to leave the planet. *Leave*, Doc! What could be more seditious than that? If NASA ever does what it's supposed to do,

Americans are going to be flying all over the solar system. Where there's Americans, there's trouble. It's in our nature to cause trouble, challenge authority, kick up our heels, and be ornery. You think it's going to be any different in space? Just you wait. It'll be a sight to behold!"

Perlman kept shaking his head. "No, no, no, Jack." He laughed. "Nothing of the kind will ever be done. You're talking about Americans the way they used to be. We're too fat and happy now. No American is going to get in a rocket ship and take off into the wild blue yonder. Why, they'd miss *Monday Night Football*!"

Jack grinned. He enjoyed debating with Perlman. None of it was serious, just lighthearted philosophizing to offset the boredom of watching his engineers prepare for the final flight-readiness test of the robotic moon miner—*Prometheus*, as it was called. Jack owned the company that had built it, the Medaris Engineering Company, MEC for short. After the accident that had killed his wife, and the investigation that had resulted in his banishment from NASA, MEC had become the most important thing in Jack Medaris's life. An invention of his called the sling pump, used in almost every liquid rocket tankage system in the world, had made Jack wealthy and MEC a very prosperous company. His people were paid accordingly. WE HAPPY FEW, read a banner over the entrance to the clean room. It reflected the fierce camaraderie of the company and the loyalty of its people to its founder.

As the test neared its critical phase, Perlman became visibly nervous, not surprising since he had paid Jack and MEC over thirty-one million dollars to build *Prometheus*. "Is it looking good?" Perlman worried.

"Very good, Doc," Jack said, concentrating on the sensor data scrolling down a computer screen.

"It's got to work," Perlman breathed, his fingers covering his lips as if he was afraid to let his voice fall on the precious spacecraft.

"Everything is fine," Jack said distractedly. And it was too. Jack and MEC's thirty engineers had spent a year carefully constructing *Prometheus*, borrowing liberally from the proven design of the old Soviet Union's *Lunakhod* series of moon-sample return spacecraft.

"I feel like WET's coming at me like an unstoppable locomotive," Perlman remarked with a groan. Every so often, it seemed, Perlman had to voice a little misery.

Jack ignored the comment. He didn't want to get off into a discussion of WET. The acronym stood for the World Energy Treaty, a United Nations agreement that had been drafted after the breeder reactor disaster in Sorkiyov, Russia. Hundreds of Russians had died, thousands more were going to get cancer, livestock devastated by the score, trees, grass, everything contaminated and dying. An antinuclear frenzy had swept the planet. WET banned all "power plants utilizing fissile and radioactive materials." The treaty had been ratified by every country in the world except France and the United States. President Edwards had signed WET but the Senate, as yet, hadn't approved it.

Jack had known Perlman for five years. The physicist had just turned up on Cedar Key one day, introduced himself in Jack's office, and tried to start an argument. "Do you know what the most important product of our civilization is?" he had demanded.

"No, Dr. Perlman," Jack had replied, amused, "what is the most important product?"

Perlman had raised his finger, his habit when he pontificated. "It's not cars, not television sets, not even computers. It's energy! Without energy Western civilization would not exist. A good portion of the earth—the so-called Third World—struggles in misery and degradation. Those poor people think what they need is money, or a different political or economic system, to rise up out of their poverty, but what they really need is energy!"

To Perlman's disappointment Jack had not seen fit to

argue. "Okay, Doc. Energy. What does that have to do with me?"

Perlman had looked out Jack's office window, to the ocean tide that lapped the nearby shore. "Mr. Medaris, did you know that in a gallon of seawater there is the equivalent energy content of three hundred gallons of gasoline? That's because ordinary water contains deuterium—heavy hydrogen. If deuterium is fused with an isotope known as helium-3, the result is nearly limitless energy. Did you know that?"

Jack remembered Perlman spreading his hands in that effusive way he would come to know so well. "I have come up with a way to use inertial confinement of a quantity of deuterium and helium-3, subject it to the heat and pressure of a rather large laser beam, and release all that energy. Fusion, Jack. Energy from fusion is within my grasp."

Energy from fusion: the commercial application of the same physics as the sun and the hydrogen bomb. It had been the dream of scientists, engineers, and researchers for six decades. The little man had leaned forward. "But I need help, Jack. You are my only hope!"

Sally Littleton caught Jack's eye, releasing him from his reflections. Her eyebrows were raised. She was ready to complete the final test. Jack nodded and his lead *Prometheus* engineer began to call out the next steps.

"If it fails . . ." Perlman worried.

"It's not going to fail."

"There's so little time."

"There's plenty of time. Everything I read says the Senate won't pass WET until July. That's six months away. When we finish tonight, we'll disassemble *Prometheus*, ship him off to Shiharakota. The Indians have already mounted our dog engine to their *Shiva* launcher. Once this payload is stacked, we launch. We'll have your dirt back to you in three weeks."

"It isn't dirt," Perlman grunted, ever sensitive. He could call it that but he didn't like anybody else doing it.

Jack nodded. "Fire beads, then."

"And it's not quite true that I will have it three weeks after launch." Perlman clucked. "It'll still be on a ship."

Jack had explained it to the physicist a half-dozen times. "We could speed things up if we had the freighter dock in Hawaii, lease a jet there. Probably save you a week."

"I'll ask my benefactors," Perlman said doubtfully.

Jack shrugged. It was ever thus, even with a group of heavy-hitting investors like the January Group. Jack assumed at least one of the members of the organization was a bean counter, worrying about spending thousands when they'd already spent millions—hundreds of millions, in fact —to build Perlman's pilot fusion plant in Montana. "Penny wise and pound foolish, eh, Doc?" Jack gently gibed.

"The men and women of the January Group are cautious with their money in their own audacious way," Perlman answered stiffly. "Thank the good Lord for them or I'd not be as far as I am. You wouldn't either."

"Do you even know who they are, Isaac? I know you work through their attorney."

"I do not," he said primly. "It is none of my business. But I've been told they are the movers and shakers in this country."

Jack looked Perlman over. "You haven't told them about me, have you?"

"You asked me not to."

"You didn't answer my question."

Perlman changed the subject, not fooling Jack for a moment. "I still can't believe WET will make fusion energy a crime. It will all be done in the name of the children, of course—what reckless activity in the last decade hasn't? And what is the world going to do for energy? Keep burning fossil fuel! Oil and coal, Jack! Can you imagine the pollution? The degradation to the environment? My technology is clean, cheap, and limitless!"

Sally gave Jack a thumbs-up on the sensor readings, and also a pert smile. She was a handsome woman, that Sally. Perlman was still rattling on, extolling the advantages of his technology. "Doc, everybody's going to see that," Jack interrupted. "We've still got time. You'll get your dirt—fire beads —in a month or so and you'll be able to fire up your plant, show it to the media, demonstrate how safe it is too. After that I guarantee you they'll make an exception in WET for fusion."

Perlman shook his head. "I don't want that damned treaty modified. I want it killed. If we approve it, we might as well pack it in. In fifty years, maybe less, this tired old polluted planet is going to go dark."

"We're doing the best we can, Doc."

Perlman was into it. He stabbed his index finger at the roof. "I don't care about fission energy, Jack. They can shut down every nuclear reactor in the world and I wouldn't give a flying fig. But fusion is not fission."

Jack took a deep breath. "You told them about me, didn't you?"

Perlman slowly lowered his hand. "I had to. The January Group wasn't going to give me seventy million dollars to hire someone they didn't know."

Jack looked at Perlman. "What did they say? I'm sure they dug up everything they could find on me."

"Nothing." When he saw Jack's doubtful expression, he added: "I swear, Jack. They cut the check within two weeks after I told them your plan."

Sally had rolled a computer up to *Prometheus*, plugged it into an interface panel. A graphic display, a thick red horizontal line on a blue background, formed on the monitor. "Ascent stage sim, plus ten," she announced, keying in the parameters of the final stage of the mission.

"Reentry activation, nominal readout," Virgil Judd said, watching the numbers come up on the computer. Judd had been a Cape Ape, laid off by the decimation of the work-force there over the last two years. He was a big, gentle man with a lovely wife and a very sick daughter suffering from the advanced stages of cystic fibrosis. Jack had done every-thing he could to help Virgil, including arranging for tests at the Mayo Clinic. *We happy few.*

"Vector all balls, deceleration nominal," Virgil said. Then, "Bingo deceleration. Switching to reentry mode."

A few minutes later another layer of numbers slid across the computer screen. "Simulating reentry, checking azi-muth, bingo envelope," Sally said. "Readouts on volume." The music, provided by a CD player outside and piped in through speakers in the four corners of the bay, switched to Orff's *Carmine Burana*, placing a triumphant caste on the already exciting moment. "Nominal targeting. *Prometheus* has landed," she concluded, peering at the screen. She looked over at Medaris, her eyes twinkling with excitement. "On the money, Jack. *Prometheus* is ready to rocket and roll!"

Jack joined in the spontaneous applause of the engineers, muffled by their latex gloves. He approached the moon miner, looked over the numbers still running down the computer screen. "Let's pack him up, children. Our boy is ready to go to India." His people crowded in, clapping him and each other on the back. Virgil picked a protesting Perl-man up bodily and waltzed him around the room. The CD switched to "Jailhouse Rock." The dozen engineers in the room joined them in an impromptu shag. *Prometheus* seemed to be thoughtfully watching.

It was several hours later, well past midnight, when Jack finally got to his office to catch up on some paperwork. Virgil was the only other person still in the plant, detailed to finish the inventory of *Prometheus* components, and to ini-tial out the procedures manuals. Since there were only thirty full-time employees at MEC, everyone pulled double, even triple, duty. Jack scanned his desk, determined to make a dent in the piled-up documents, mostly purchase orders for the myriad of hardware required to build such an exacting machine as *Prometheus*. He walked over to the interior window in his office that looked down into the clean room and admired the robotic spacecraft, resting in a cone of light from an overhead lamp. He especially admired the arm with the claw. That had been his addition to the spec. Perlman had asked him about it and Jack had explained that *Prometheus* might need to move a few rocks to get at the fire beads at Shorty Crater. It was an explanation that could be defended but it wasn't its real purpose. That purpose he kept to himself.

Virgil spotted Jack and walked to the squawk box. "Hey, boss, I'm nearly finished down here. How about you?"

Jack looked over his shoulder at the purchase orders and gave in to his fatigue. They could wait until the morning. "Yeah, Virg. I'm ready to pull the plug too. Go ahead. I'll lock up." Virgil, Jack knew, wanted to know who was going to be the last out of the building. The MEC burglar alarm system was cranky, requiring a complicated code to be entered into a box at the exterior door and again at the parking lot gate. It was a time consuming process and about half the time it didn't take and had to be reset and reentered. Everybody hated it. The system had been installed, the cheapest available, when MEC first moved into the facility. Jack depended, more than anything, on the remoteness of the site to protect the company. Trooper Buck, the Cedar Key constable, made routine swing-bys during the few hours the plant was unoccupied at night. Still, having a burglar alarm that might not even work was foolish and Jack knew it. One of the purchase orders on his desk was for a new security system, but there had just been so much to do.

"See you tomorrow, boss," Virgil called.

"Okay, Virg. I'm right behind you."

Jack took a moment to savor *Prometheus*, but memories of his wife flooded him as they often did when he was tired. Looking out over the moon miner reminded him of the time when he had found Kate in their mountain-home sunroom, pensively gazing down on the city of Huntsville and, on the distant horizon, the big rocket test stands of Marshall Space Flight Center. When he'd asked her what she was thinking, she had said, "Jack, if I die, will you forget how much I love you?" He hadn't known what to say. It was such a preposterous idea. She was younger than he, the very picture of health. "Please tell me you won't ever forget." He'd knelt before her, taken her hands, and promised. They'd ended up making love, passionately clinging to each other as if they only had a few hours left together rather than a lifetime. Five months later she and their unborn child were dead. NASA had determined that it had been his arrogance that had killed them. Soon after, he had resigned and left the agency. Ever since, it had seemed that he lived in a different world, one of shadows and pain.

Jack shuddered, pushed away the memory that was beginning to creep into his thoughts, of the bitter night on the test stand, when he had lost all that he loved. What good did it do to think of it now? A lump in his throat, Jack turned from the window, found his briefcase, and was nearly through the door when the telephone rang. It was Sally Littleton, calling from what sounded in the background like a party. "We're getting down here at the Pelican, Jack," Sally yelled over the din. "You got to come on by and live a little, boy. You deserve it."

He felt drained. "It's been a long day, Sally."

"Jack Medaris, you get on over here. Isn't that right, everybody?" Jack heard a chorus of shouted agreement in the background. Sally came back on. "Your people are celebrating and they want you with them!"

Jack looked at *Prometheus*, saw his own reflection in the window. He had been a solitary man for years. He was lonely. There would never be, couldn't ever be, another Kate. Yet he needed the touch and the warmth of a woman in his arms, her breath in his ear, her perfume. . . . "All right, Sally," he said quietly. "Tell them I'm on my way."

"I'll be waiting, Jack," she replied with the emphasis on *I*.

Jack clumped down the wooden steps of the old hangar, set the alarm on the clean room, then moved through the two outer dressing chambers. The old hangar was plunged into darkness except for an emergency light mounted above the main door. He went outside, turning to set the exterior alarm. Compared to the crisp, sanitized air in the plant, the breeze coming off the lapping ocean nearby was rich, heady. Jack took a deep breath. He loved Cedar Key, a bountiful treasure of nature. He had chosen the remote Florida island as the site for his plant because of its isolation. He could hear in the distance the plaintive call of a loon. The Key was a nature preserve, only the old airport where he'd built his company zoned for industrial commerce. Bird watchers the world over came to the island. Fishermen crowded in for saltwater fishing at its best, at all times of the year. A single narrow bridge was all that connected Cedar Key to the Florida mainland.

Jack stepped off the stoop and was surprised to find a big recreational vehicle facing him. He glanced toward the perimeter fence. Virgil had left the gate open, as was common when someone else was following close behind. The RV's lights went on, blinding him. "Hey, mister," an unfamiliar voice called out. "You got any idea where we are?" A man walked out of the glaring light. He was short and stout, had a walruslike mustache, and was wearing a bright yellow shirt and creased tan slacks. He was holding a sheet of paper.

Jack shielded his eyes with his hands. "This is a restricted area," he said. "You need to leave."

The man waved back at the RV. Jack could see several shadowy figures standing alongside it. "Sorry, mister. We saw the gate open and the lights. We're fishermen and we're lost. You got any idea how to get to Stevenson's Fish Camp? I got a map here."

The man appeared innocent but the road was clearly marked as leading to the old airport. If they had ignored the signs, they had to be not only lost but stupid too. "Never heard of the place," Jack said. "If you'll go back through the gate, turn left, that'll take you into town. You can ask there."

"Why don't you just look at the map, mister? I think we're way off here."

The man approached. Jack thought about going back inside, but that would have required entering the code. "Look, fellows, this is a restricted industrial plant. Go into town, ask there."

"You know, you're not an accommodating fellow, Mr. Medaris," the man said, smiling. "I've decided to Milli Vanilli your ass."

"What?" *He knows my name.* Jack was startled by the sound of heavy boots pounding on the asphalt. He didn't have time to react. Someone big, dressed in black, came out of the lights, tackled him, knocked him down, and fell on top of him. Jack landed on his back, his head hitting the concrete stoop. Everything dimmed. He struggled for consciousness. He grabbed the man, pulled at his arm, felt something give way. It was a patch on his shoulder, a piece of black Velcro. There was a flash of gold letters, just for an instant. *Puckett Security Services.* Then he felt himself being rolled over, his hands jerked behind him. Something hot dripped down his neck. Handcuffs clicked shut on his wrists.

"Cut the wires, all of 'em," somebody said.

Jack was blearily aware of men running past him, battering at the door. He heard it tear from its hinges. There was no alarm. The man in the yellow shirt knelt beside him. "Milli Vanilli means I pretended to kick your ass while somebody more qualified did the work." He laughed and then abruptly turned deadly serious. "Take him inside."

Jack was ruthlessly jerked by his wrists, pushed into the hangar, through the doors, all hanging from their hinges. Two men, dressed in black fatigues, clustered at the clean-room door. The yellow-shirted man walked in front of Jack. "The lander in there?"

"I don't know what you're talking about. That's a clean room. We use it to inspect our pumps."

Using a flashlight, the man peered inside, *Prometheus* glittering in the spot of his light like a giant tin man. "Doesn't look like a pump to me, Mr. Medaris."

Jack tore loose from his captor, ran for the door. He had to get help. He was quickly caught, thrown to the floor. His shoulder felt as if it had been dislocated. Jack groaned, kept struggling. "Get him out of here," the man said harshly.

Jack was jerked to his feet again. It felt as if a spear had been stuck in his shoulder and twisted. He couldn't help but cry out, although it shamed him to show weakness in front of these men. He looked over his shoulder, saw men in black fatigues batter down the clean-room door, go inside. Other men followed, carrying sledgehammers and cutting torches. Despite the pain Jack struggled to stop them. He was savagely driven to his knees, then dragged across the concrete, through the halls, out the door, thrown down onto the asphalt in front of the RV, its headlights now dimmed.

Nearly mad with impotent outrage, his head in a puddle of his own blood, Jack listened to the sound of smashing sledgehammers, glass breaking, the hiss of torches, more doors being battered down. The man in the yellow shirt stepped up, knelt down beside him. "Well, thank you, Mr. Medaris. It's been real. By the way, you ought to be more careful with the combustibles in your plant. I'm afraid it's caught on fire."

Jack struggled to raise his head, saw the flames licking

out of the broken windows, an orange glow deep within. "Why?" he cried.

"Don't you know, Mr. Medaris?" the man said softly, his small dark eyes twinkling mischievously. "We did this for the benefit of all mankind."

Jack felt the heat of the flames against his skin. He turned away from it, trying not to think of the time when another fire had engulfed him and all that he loved. He involuntarily groaned, let his face down into his blood. He felt someone taking off the cuffs. He was roughly dragged to his feet. Blood still streamed down his neck. His shoulder felt as if it had been torn to shreds. His wrists were raw and bleeding. The men got back into the RV and drove away, left him standing alone. It turned away from Cedar Key, toward the main highway.

The hangar was an inferno by the time the volunteer fire department arrived ten minutes later. Trooper Buck was with them. Soon afterward the engineers of MEC, Doc Perlman, and the company lawyer, Cecil Velocci, arrived as well. They found Jack sitting in the parking lot, quietly watching the futile efforts of the firemen. When they reached down to help him, he pushed their hands away, then finally stood up under his own power. He growled at anyone who approached not to touch him. He held his shoulder, gritted his teeth against the pain, ignored the steady drip of blood puddling at his feet. The others were certain he'd gone insane.

The glow from the garish flames made the scar on his face and neck look as if it were on fire too. His eyes glittered as the flames reached solvents stored in a back room. The hangar burst apart, buckets of solvent flying into the sky, trailing long torrents of hot liquid fire. Jack said nothing, didn't move at all when everyone else fell back from the resulting volcano. He was thinking.

After the fire had died down, Jack turned to the throng. "Isaac, a word," he said quietly.

Perlman approached him, his eyes wide. "What happened?"

"Men came to destroy *Prometheus*. They knew all about it."

"How did they get in?"

Jack grimaced. "The gate was open."

Perlman was quiet for a moment. He might have been looking at Jack's dripping blood, scarlet in the glare of the burning hangar. "Jack, I'll have to tell my investors the circumstances. They may come after you, want their money back."

"They'll get their dirt," Jack growled.

"How?"

Jack's lip was split. He spat blood while the likely scenario played out across his mind. The company had insurance, but he could see the insurer accusing him of arson. A jury, hearing of his background, might conclude he was guilty. In any case, it would be tied up in court for years before he saw a dime. "Buck," he said quietly. The policeman came to him. "You ever hear of Puckett Security Services?"

Buck was six and a half feet tall in his cowboy boots, a formidable man and a secure presence on the little island. "Nope," he said. "That who did this?"

"Do you still have contacts with the FBI?" Jack asked.

"Sure. You want me to check it out for you?"

"Yes."

Buck leaned into Jack, his big broad face lit by the guttering flames. "I will on one condition. Let the paramedics take a look at you."

Jack relented, walked toward the ambulance. The people opened a lane for him. He kept his head down, not from pain or shame. He was still thinking. A fresh ocean breeze fanned the embers in the hangar and a torrent of flame suddenly roared alive.

Jack turned to watch the blaze and then saw the bloody

crescent of the moon floating through the smoke. *Luna.* The face the moon showed the earth was pocked and scourged, but like many plain women she had a body that could still fill men with lust. Another sea breeze blew the smoke away and the crescent turned from scarlet to gold. Isaac Perlman coveted the golden dust that layered the moon, sifted into her cracked rock, coated her craters, seeped into her pores. He had revealed to Jack the moon's secret treasure: helium-3, blown through space for billions of years by the solar wind, laid down on Luna's airless surface. Perhaps, Jack realized, helium-3 was a threat to someone who might do anything to keep it off the earth. The moon also held another treasure. *Kate.* She waited for him at Frau Mauro. Jack's eyes slowly began to fill with determination.

"What are we going to do, boss?" Virgil asked, holding the door of the ambulance open.

"I'm still working on that, Virg," Jack said quietly as he climbed in. He sat on a bench, looked at the faces of his people, his happy and faithful few. "But I can tell you this much: *We're not going to quit.*"

2

The Launch

She walks in beauty, like the night
Of cloudless climes and starry skies,
And all that's best of dark and bright
Meet in her aspect and her eyes;
Thus mellowed to that tender light
Which heaven to gaudy day denies.

—Lord Byron, "She Walks in Beauty"

Abandoned in Place
Launch Complex 34, Canaveral Air Station, Cape Canaveral, Florida

"You are an arrogant bastard, Jack Medaris!" Isaac Perlman shouted at his back.

"Go back to Montana, Doc," Jack said as he trudged past the ancient, salt-streaked blockhouse.

Perlman struggled to keep up. "Are you so angry that you would kill yourself and others to get revenge, Jack, is that it?" He gasped as his cane sank into the loose sand and he almost lost his balance. "You would destroy your company, put all your employees out of a job? What kind of madness is this? I want no part of it!"

"Who called you?" Jack calmly questioned the little physicist. "Let me guess. Sally Littleton."

Perlman puffed up beside him. "No, but don't ask further. I won't tell you."

That got Jack's attention. He whirled around. "The January Group? How could they possibly know about this?"

Perlman's face was streaming sweat. He leaned on his cane, took out a red bandana from his hip pocket, and mopped his brow. "I told them you were still going to get me my dirt but I didn't know how. They have vast resources, Jack. They investigated. I don't know. Maybe somebody told them. Then they told me."

"Did they tell you to stop me?"

"Oh, no! I think they're quite excited by the prospect! But they don't care about you, Jack. I do. Why didn't you just build another *Prometheus*?"

Jack studied the diminutive physicist. "In less than six

months? Not enough time. We had to come up with another plan."

Perlman leaned on his cane, looked around. "Where is this place?"

Jack started back down the path. "The end of the world, Doc," he said over his shoulder as he walked into the battered refuse of Launch Complex 34, all that remained of the site where men had begun the engineering process that had led to the *Apollo* moon landings. Here, the first three *Apollo* astronauts had burned to death in their capsule while running a simple communications and power check. Jack, as much as anyone who worked in the aerospace industry, knew the engineering required for spaceflight was never simple, always fraught with hidden dangers, small things that added up quickly to deadly things. That's what had killed the men of *Apollo 1*. "This ought to be a treasured site in American folklore, Doc," Jack said wistfully after he had told him what had happened at LC 34. "Instead . . . well, look at the signs."

The weathered signs posted at various locations around the battered pad read ABANDON IN PLACE. NASA had saved money by simply walking away from the old facilities rather than tearing them down. But the signs had a larger meaning too—an unintended, ironic truth. "Doc?"

"What is it, Jack?" Perlman sighed.

"The first time I ever came here, Kate brought me. We were down to supervise a shuttle main-engine test firing and she dragged me here as if it were a holy shrine. You know what she did? See what that sign posted on the blockhouse says? She did that." Jack gazed at the sign with a sad smile, gratified that someone, perhaps a Cape worker, had refreshed Kate's message: ABANDON*ED AND BETRAYED* IN PLACE.

"Betrayed, Jack?"

"That's what Kate thought."

Jack remembered the way Kate had looked that day.

Even though she had a tomboy figure, and a face best described as vaguely elfin—she hated being called cute but she surely was—he had always thought of her as the most beautiful woman he'd ever known. He had simply adored her, had known from the moment he met her that she belonged to him, and he to her. He savored the memory of how she'd stood on her sneakered tiptoes that day to reach the sign with her paintbrush, how she tilted her head, and the way the sun turned her cropped hair into golden straw. He could almost smell her. She never wore perfume but always smelled so clean, of white soap, as if she'd just stepped from a shower of rainwater. Involuntarily, his hand went to the horrible red scar that ran along his jawline and down his neck. When he realized what he was doing, he dropped his hand away. It made him ashamed. She had suffered so much more. He wondered if his unborn child had felt the fire, too, and then, with a shudder, drove their memory out of his mind. It did no good to think of them. Not now.

Perlman noticed the movement to the scar. "Do you hate NASA so much then, Jack," he asked quietly, "for what it did to you?"

"I don't hate anything or anybody, Doc," Jack said grimly, "except for maybe little physicists who follow me from my hotel room when I try to get some time to myself." Jack walked under the huge "milk stool," the massive concrete pedestal on which a *Saturn 1-B* had once sat prior to launch. He carried a coil of rope over his shoulder. Just beyond, the Atlantic Ocean grumbled and groaned, as if providing a perpetual chorus of mourners at the tragic site.

"I forbid this . . . this"—Perlman sputtered—"*madness.*"

"Go home, Doc," Jack replied calmly. "Wait for me to bring you your dirt. Then fire up your machine, show the world what you can do."

Jack had cast off his worry. If the January Group wanted

a return on their huge investment, they needed Perlman to get his dirt. And if they knew about MEC's plan and hadn't done anything about it, they apparently approved. Jack looked up at the milk stool, then stepped back, whistled the end of the rope around, and then threw it up and over the curved track high above. The free end came down and Jack tied it off. He gripped the rope and pulled, took a breath, put one hand up, and heaved with all his might, wrapping his feet around the rope. It swung as he climbed toward the clear blue and the blackened concrete circle in the sky. His shoulder was completely healed. He felt exalted by the effort. When his hand gripped the slick, moldy concrete of the track, he easily pulled himself over the edge and then knelt atop the ring, feeling the sweat run down his chest and his back. The sea breeze blew over him, cooling him. He stood, his silhouette against the clear sky.

He had come to LC 34 to clear his mind, to prepare for the next day's events. But this had been one of Kate's favorite places and he couldn't stop her from flooding his mind. Jack caught his breath, let the memories come. He thought of what Kate had told him very soon after they'd met, of the day when she was only ten years old and had lain in front of the television set in her parents' living room, watching astronauts walk on the moon for the last time. On that same day the great rocket scientist Wernher von Braun had stopped by to talk to her about the wonderful thing he had helped her do. She'd explained what the two of them had done for Jack, a man neither one knew—the man who one cold night would kill her just at the moment of her greatest success.

Jack took a deep breath, smelled the ocean, the musty smell of the wet sand. Close to the beach lay the pad's massive flame deflectors, a tangled heap of curved pieces of corroded steel that looked for all the world as if some ocean beast with gigantic twisted tentacles had crawled up out of the Atlantic and died. To the south were the skeletal remains of the old launch pads abandoned by the Air Force and NASA over the years. They almost seemed to be ancient sentinels standing guard against an unseen enemy. To the north behind a line of low dunes that marked the beach's gentle curve Jack could see the two launch complexes that serviced the space shuttles. Both complexes were active, the shuttle *Endeavour* on Pad 39-A, getting ready to fly up a node for International Space Station *Aurora*. *Columbia* was on Pad 39-B, her primary task a tether satellite experiment. It was just low earth orbit stuff, routine work.

Perlman had stayed back near the blockhouse, the sand too soft for him to try to get nearer. "What do you see up there?" he called.

"Time, Doc."

"Time?"

Jack checked his watch, looked down the beach. "Time!" The klaxon was right on schedule. There was a flash of light at the base of the launch tower a half mile away to the south, then a funnel of smoke. A *Titan IV*, an Air Force vehicle, rose majestically, gathering velocity, a wall of sound moving out from it in every direction until it enveloped Jack as if trying to tear him from his precarious perch. Jack stood up against it, yelled at it as it roared over him, shook both of his fists at it, danced beneath it on the narrow track. The giant rocket, carrying a secret Air Force payload into orbit, lashed him, scourged him of doubt and fear.

For the benefit of all mankind, that was the NASA motto and also what the ugly short man in the yellow shirt had said when Jack had asked him why he'd destroyed *Prometheus*. The man was being snide, Jack knew, but somebody had put that phrase in his head. Jack had gone over it a thousand times, with himself, with his lawyer, with Sally and Virgil, all his MEC people. Jack was certain whoever had destroyed *Prometheus* had done it to stop Perlman. Perlman was right. Energy was the most important product on the planet. Perlman's fusion plant could change who controlled that product. There were probably a lot of corporations and countries that wouldn't like that. It would take a desperate and unexpected act to defeat Perlman's foes, whoever they were.

High above and already a hundred miles out over the Atlantic, the *Titan IV* soared toward space, its bellowing engines receding to a distant rumble. Jack let a grin slide across his face as he admired the *Titan IV*'s exhaust, a grayish wisp across the sunlit sky.

Kate's spirit was so strong here. Jack could almost hear her talking to him. *Go on and do it. You know you will anyway.* She had said that the night she had died. "I am, Kate," he whispered. He was going to complete the circle she and Wernher von Braun had begun. Along the way he was also going to get Isaac Perlman his damned dirt and perhaps change the destiny of the world. Wasn't all that worth nearly any gamble?

Perlman. Jack had forgotten him. He looked over the ring, saw the physicist struggling to get up out of the sand. The *Titan IV* launch had bowled him over. "Hang on, Doc," Jack called. "I'll help you."

Jack went hand over hand back down the rope. His mind was clear. He was ready to do what had to be done. For Kate, for himself, for MEC, for Perlman, *for the benefit of all mankind.*

LAUNCH MINUS 0 DAYS, 5 HOURS, 4 MINUTES,
8 SECONDS, AND COUNTING . . .

The Vulture
Shuttle Mission Control (SMC), Building 3-B, First Floor, Johnson Space Center, Houston, Texas

The flight director for STS-128 was Sam Tate, a thin-skinned results man who accepted nothing but perfection from the people who manned his consoles. He was considered by his console jockeys a walking, talking legend because he was the only remaining active NASA controller who had been on console during *Apollo 13*. Someone back then had called him a steely-eyed missile man for the gutsy decisions that saved the crew of that nearly lethal mission. He'd worked his way up to assistant flight director for the last mission to the moon, *Apollo 17*, and then stayed on to become a full flight for over forty shuttle missions. If it had happened in flight ops, Sam Tate had been there.

Sam used his legendary status to maximum advantage to keep his young troops respectful and in line. He knew discipline was the only way to get them through both the long periods of boredom and the tense moments that occurred during every shuttle mission. When there was a problem, he made a practice of standing so his people could see him, his lanky frame leaning forward, his head thrust out, his eyes sweeping the trenches while one hand pressed a communications headset to his ear. His people described him as "vulturing" when he did that. On the morning of the scheduled launch of STS-128 (which stood for the 128th flight of the Space Transportation System—popularly known as the space shuttle), Sam had been playing the vulture all morning, popping antacid pills like they were candy to coat what he feared was a flare-up of an old ulcer. He switched his video monitor to the Cape. "Aaron, what the hell's going on over there?" he growled. "The cryos should be loading by now."

Aaron Bilstein, the launch director at Kennedy Space Center, leaned back in his chair, grinning. Bilstein gave Sam a cheerful thumbs-up after shaking his head in mock despair. "You're still an old worrywart, aren't you, Sam?" He chuckled. "We've been loading cryos for two hours. Good morning to you, too, by the way. Sorry I didn't call you when we started."

"No glitches?" Sam demanded.

Bilstein shrugged. "Just a Space Camp bus with a misguided driver. Got halfway down the crawlerway before they got stopped. Security's going nuts. The Camp kids are having a ball."

Sam almost smiled, a rare event on the day of a launch. Guards worrying about a bunch of Space Campers or anybody else assaulting the shuttle struck him as amusing. The enemies of the space program were not terrorists who lobbed bombs but bean counters who lobbed budget numbers. Bilstein kept talking, advising Sam that a NASA inspector general team had suddenly appeared and was on the pad. "IG on a launch day?" Tate questioned. "That's damned unusual."

Bilstein sighed. "I know, Sam. It's Mickey Mouse. But I figure if I complain about it, HQ might think we've got something to hide."

Sam knew that Bilstein had another reason to worry. *Endeavour*, carrying a Space Station node, was stacked on nearby Pad 39-A. The reason why shuttles were on both pads at the same time was because of *Columbia*'s primary payload, an Italian tethered satellite experiment called the ATESS (Advanced Tether Experimental Satellite System). ATESS had been delivered late to the Cape and had since proved a cranky fit in *Columbia*'s cargo bay. The *Endeavour* stack had crept forward on its integration schedule while *Columbia* fell behind. Now, both stacks were on the pads and KSC management was under the gun not to delay either launch. Gross amounts of overtime had been the result and it was an open secret that Bilstein's workforce of Cape Apes were exhausted. There was another reason for worry too: this was the last flight of *Columbia*.

Tate munched another handful of antacids. The decision to retire *Columbia* had been made by Vice President Stuart Vanderheld. Since the President hadn't bothered to appoint a new NASA administrator following the last one's death in office, the veep, as the head of the Space Council, had the power to piddle around in NASA's business. Vanderheld had been a thorn in NASA's side for over thirty years, starting when he'd chaired the old Science and Space Committee back in the late 1960s and early 1970s. He'd always been against the space program, took every opportunity to denounce it as a waste of the taxpayers' good money. His surprise vice-presidency in the Edwards administration, and his position as chair of the Space Council, had given him a new lease to bash NASA. Still, Sam had to admit the vice president's reasoning on *Columbia* couldn't be entirely faulted. International Space Station *Aurora* was in a high inclination orbit to accommodate Russia's northerly launch facilities. That had meant *Columbia*, which had been built heavier than the other shuttles, lacked the lift capacity to carry any useful payload up to the station. *Aurora* was eating NASA's lunch. Every available dollar had to be used to support the thing.

Scowling at the thought of the International Space Station, a political program he'd never liked, Sam signed off to let Bilstein get back to his job. At least *Columbia* was going to fly one more time, and, by God, Sam was going to see her and her crew safely into space and back again. Still, it was a crime to turn *Columbia* into a damn tourist attraction. *Damn stupid politicians. Damn stupid Americans who built magnificent spaceships and then just threw them away! They'd done that with* Apollo *too!*

LAUNCH MINUS 0 DAYS, 2 HOURS,
3 MINUTES, AND COUNTING . . .

High Eagle
Operations and Control Facility 302-A, Astronaut Prep Room 1-D, Kennedy Space Center

Dr. Penny High Eagle irritably tugged at the tight rubber neck seal and squirmed in the heavy folds of her launch-and-entry suit. "Shit. Is this thing really necessary?" Because of the heavy public-relations schedule Penny had not had time to properly train in the LES suit, and was unfamiliar with its weight and strangling seals. "I feel like a deep sea diver," she added, fixing her big brown eyes on the suit technician.

"Sorry, Dr. High Eagle," the man replied, fussing with her wrist seals. "If the shuttle loses pressure on ascent, this suit'll keep you alive."

"Quiet, please," Colonel Olivia Grant ordered. Grant, the commander of STS-128, walked down the line of her crew, stopped in front of each of them for a personal word, a quick check of their garish orange suits. She held out her gloved fists and Tanya Brown, the pilot, did the same, thumping their fists together in sisterly solidarity. Grant moved to Betsy Newell, Mission Specialist 1, inspected her, tightened her suit harness, went through the fist routine. She repeated the exercise once more with Janet Barnes, MS-2. Then Grant stood in front of Penny. Penny was a payload specialist, not a real astronaut, as she'd constantly been reminded by the rest of the all-female crew.

Penny took a deep breath and let it out slowly. Grant made her nervous. The woman had never made any secret that she resented Penny's late assignment. She clutched each of Penny's arms with her powerful hands, checked the wrist seals of her gloves, but avoided eye contact. Olivia

Grant, called Ollie by the others, wasn't a bad-looking woman, Penny thought. She shouldn't wear her brown straight hair pulled back so tightly, that was all. She had too much forehead and her ears were too large to be so exposed. And a little blush color on her cheeks wouldn't have hurt either. Penny had brought her own makeup man for most of her expeditions. He could have done wonders for Grant. The astronaut commander darted her gray eyes at Penny as if she'd heard her thought. "You drink plenty of water this morning, High Eagle?" she demanded. "Got to make sure you're not dehydrated."

One of the other three women snickered and Grant shot them a dirty look. "Knock it off."

Penny nodded dutifully. She was determined to be a good trouper on this flight. "Four glasses, Olivia."

"Good." She glared at the others, then beckoned them to follow her. "All right, ladies. Let's go to space." Grandly, she burst through the swinging doors of the suit room and into the hall that led to the waiting crew transfer bus. She nodded to the applause of admiring engineers and raised her hands aloft in a triumphant gesture.

Penny dutifully trudged along behind until she spotted the reporters shouting questions outside. All of them were calling to her, so she stopped and pirouetted as gracefully as the LES suit and the heavy black boots would allow. Playing to the press was such a natural thing for her that she didn't even notice the sour faces of her fellow crew members waiting impatiently at the bus door. She believed the press existed for one reason: publicity. Her job was to keep them interested, keep the publicity flowing. The day before, on the tarmac after the T-38 jet ride from Houston, Penny had shown them a glimpse of the frilly white bra she wore underneath her flight suit. She thought it was pretty funny when a reporter asked Ollie Grant to show what she was wearing under *her* flight suit too. For a moment Penny thought Grant was actually going to coldcock the reporter.

"Dr. High Eagle," a reporter shouted at her, "are you scared?" He was a handsome young man, obviously one of the fluffball anchors on local television.

"Of you?" Penny grinned, her perfect teeth flashing. "Petrified!"

The anchor laughed appreciatively. "No, of flying into space!"

The NASA publicist, a shrill-voiced woman dressed in a severely tailored gray suit, stepped protectively in front of her. Penny wanted to shove her out of the way. "Dr. High Eagle is prepared," the publicist told the reporters in a boring monotone. "She has trained diligently."

"Yeah, right," Janet Barnes gibed from the bus door.

A female correspondent waved her hand. "Dr. High Eagle, how do you justify going into space? According to my estimates it will cost the American taxpayer one million two hundred thousand dollars to send you into orbit. Considering all the problems here on earth, does it make sense to keep spending money on space?"

Penny pushed past the publicist so she was in front of the cameras again. "One million, two hundred thousand dollars is about what Americans spend on cat litter in a week," she said, adding a dazzling smile. The reporters wrote her comment down. She waited—timing being everything—and then got serious. "I am, as you well know, a qualified biologist. I have a series of experiments that I will be performing in the microgravity environment of space that may very well have practical applications in the medical field. My seat on the space shuttle has been paid for by a one of the largest pharmaceutical companies in the world, which is intensely interested in the results of these experiments. I believe the American taxpayer is going to get a good return on the investment of flying me into space."

Penny waved at the excited reporters and correspondents, who were still yelling questions at her as she climbed

aboard. The rest of the crew had grabbed front seats together, so Penny worked her way to the back. The bus stank
like a closetful of wet rubber raincoats because of the LES
suits. "Hey, High Eagle." Astronaut Janet Barnes snickered.
"You know the difference between you and God? I do. God
don't think he's you!"

"Shut up, Janet," Grant snapped, standing as she spoke.
She walked down the aisle, leaned into Penny's face. "High
Eagle, have you got makeup on? Wipe it off. You're not
wearing powder into space. It'll pop off you in zero g and
float around and I, for one, don't want to breathe it."

"I guess I'm one of those women who like to look their
best wherever they go," Penny replied in a reasonable tone.
She didn't want a fight. Not now.

Grant reached above her, opened a locker, and threw her
a box of tissues and a bottle of water. "Where you're going,
honey, all you need is a bag to puke in."

Penny shrugged but complied. She was getting her jaunt
into space, would get her book out of it, hit the best-seller
lists again. On her way to success she'd dealt with a lot
worse than Grant and her pumped-up astronettes. Penny
finished, threw the tissues on the floor, and looked forlornly
out the window as the lush swamp of Banana Creek slid by.
People lined the road, waving. She waved back and then
suddenly felt very alone. Penny had hoped she would be
able to find at least one friend among the women astronauts. It was ironic, she knew, but it was the truth. Her
books and articles about her adventures had made her one
of the most famous women in the world but she had no
friends, just associates, employees, and agents.

The crew bus slowly made its way to the access road that
paralleled the reinforced concrete crawlerway. Pad 39-B
loomed ahead. Penny drank in the sight. *Columbia* was
beautiful. A wreath of surrealistic white mist, the liquid oxygen boil-off, swirled around the huge spacecraft. For a moment Penny allowed herself to savor the adventure ahead.

The guard trucks peeled off as the bus braked in front of the pad, and Penny followed the crew outside to the launch tower. When the elevator doors opened to take them up to the crew access level, Grant and the three other astronauts shuffled aboard. A guard approached Penny, holding an autograph book and a pen. "Would you mind, ma'am?" he asked politely.

"We're not going to wait," Grant snapped at her from the elevator.

Penny had learned long ago she could not be who she was without her fans and they came first, even here in *Columbia*'s shadow. "Go ahead," she said to her grumpy commander. "I'll catch up." More scraps of paper were being thrust at her and she was more than happy to oblige. Neither she nor the excited guards heard the nearly inaudible thump as the pulleys of elevator number one disengaged halfway between the fourth and fifth level where there was no floor structure.

The IG Team
Fixed Service Structure, Launch Complex 39-B, Kennedy Space Center

On the highest level of the tower, where even the pad rats rarely ventured, Jack stood beneath a vast bowl of clear blue sky and savored the salt-laden breeze coming off the rumbling Atlantic shore. He turned as Virgil came up the steps behind him. The big man nodded, took off his hard hat, and wiped his forehead with his sleeve. "I checked the ET, boss. Tribble and Estes did a great job. I couldn't see the seam at all. We're ready to rocket and roll."

Virgil was talking about the inside job two MEC employees had performed in the external tank plant in New Orleans. MEC had contracted with Lockmart, the tank manufacturer, to study the use of the ET as a cargo carrier. It had been expensive but it had gotten Tribble and Estes inside the plant, working all hours of the day. One night they'd put cargo in the base of *Columbia*'s tank, then covered it with insulation, leaving no trace. Then they had gotten the hell out of there.

Virgil was in the white coveralls of a NASA IG (Inspector General) team official, festooned with all the necessary badges, all perfectly authentic, all completely fake. IG teams were feared on the pad. They came looking for errors and could destroy a career with one critical report. "Everything else copacetic, Virg?" Jack asked his engine man.

"As long as my little girl's getting help, I'm happy."

Jack patted Virgil on the shoulder, gave him an encouraging smile. Virgil had put much of the bonus he'd received for the mission into gene therapy for his daughter. The experimental treatment for cystic fibrosis was expensive and medical insurance wouldn't pay for it, but Jack knew their daughter meant everything to Virgil and his wife.

Virgil left and Jack watched the ocean waves marching in and out, line after line, as if translucent blue ranks of soldiers. Then he heard the ringing of another set of footsteps coming up the steel steps. Craig "Hopalong" Cassidy, outfitted in blue astronaut coveralls, leaned on the rail beside him. "Hot damn, Jack," he bellowed over the roar of the surf. "It's gonna be a fine day, one for the books, eh? God, I can't wait!"

Despite his bravado Jack caught a flash of anguish on Cassidy's face. *He's scared*, Jack thought. Captain Craig "Hopalong" Cassidy, the best shuttle pilot on the planet, was scared. Cassidy was blond and blue eyed and looked every bit the part of what he had once been: America's premier astronaut and fantasy figure of millions of women. He had piloted each of the shuttles several times, spent six months aboard the Russian *Mir*, joined a team of spacewalkers to repair the Hubble Space Telescope, and commanded a team of scientists on the *Spacelab XXI* mission. He had flown every high-performance aircraft in both the Air Force and Navy stables and even built his own experimental airplanes, using one to break the civilian altitude record. He could fly anything that had wings and land it on a dime. Or at least, that had once been true. Now, he was another NASA outsider, thrown out for one drunken brawl too many. And he was scared, needed reassurance. Jack gripped Cassidy's shoulder. "This is going to be your day, Hoppy. You're going to show the world you're still the best shuttle jock there ever was."

Cassidy nodded. The wind rustled his blond locks. "Thank you for believing in me, Jack," he said after a moment. "I'll do you proud, I promise."

"You've done that already, Hoppy, just by agreeing to go with us."

"Wouldn't have missed this for the world." Cassidy laughed. "Or the moon."

The two men, outcasts to the community they loved, laughed together, and faced defiantly the constant, unceasing Atlantic wind whistling through the launch complex. Beneath them huge steel pipes grumbled and groaned as an immense wash of super-cold liquid propellants flooded through them into the shuttle's external tank. At launch *Columbia* with her stack weighed 2,250 tons. Eight hundred and fifty tons of that was liquid oxygen and liquid hydrogen. Immersed in the cacophony of wind and propellant Jack felt excitement crawl up his spine. He was ready, tired of waiting, and willed the clock forward. He was supremely confident but he also believed that the day's work would be difficult, and all that followed filled with pitfalls. He didn't care. The clock was counting. It was time to go into the history books or hell. Maybe both. "Let's go do it," he said to his pilot, and together they turned away from the wind.

The JSC Director
**Building 1, Sixth Floor, Johnson Space Center,
Houston, Texas**

Frank Bonner, director of Lyndon B. Johnson Space Center, surveyed each of his managers at the conclusion of the meeting he held every morning in his office. Sullen faces looked back. As was his habit, he'd chewed each of them out by turn. "That's it," he said. "Any questions?"

There were none. His managers had learned over their tenure that to ask a question was to invite a biting retort. Bonner didn't like questions. He wanted action. They also knew today he was in an especially foul mood. One of his shuttles was being retired. That didn't sit well with the director of Johnson Space Center. He needed every shuttle he could get to keep flying his astronauts into space.

Lily Acton, his secretary, came bustling into his office while the managers filed out. She straightened his tie, brushed lint off the sleeves of his suit jacket. "Law, Frank, you can't go down to the press room dressed like a tramp."

Bonner frowned. "I don't need you to look after me, Lily."

"Somebody needs to," she admonished.

When Lily finished checking him, she left, going back outside the heavy oaken doors to maintain her vigil, to keep away anyone other than approved personnel. Bonner still had fifteen minutes before he would go down the six floors and walk across the JSC campus to Shuttle Mission Control. He went to his floor-to-ceiling office window and drew back the curtains. His view was of a grassy park where a giant *Saturn V* moon rocket lay splayed on its side like a beached whale. It never failed to remind him of Huntsville, the city where the von Braun team had built the giant booster. When he'd first come to work for the agency, he'd spent a year as an engineering intern in the Rocket City. He'd enjoyed the work with the researchers and engineers of Marshall Space Flight Center. Most of the Germans who'd built the big boosters for *Apollo* had retired by then but he'd met the daughter of one of them, a vivacious, gregarious young woman named Katrina Suttner. She was a fellow engineering intern in the Propulsion Lab and he'd fallen hard for her, as hard as he ever had imagined that he could. He had doggedly pursued her, wore her down with long phone calls filled with his longing. He went after her as if he were on a campaign, every waking moment dedicated to the question of how to win her. For six glorious months he used logic on her, debated with her the relative merits of being single versus marrying someone such as himself. He was going somewhere in NASA, he'd told her. So was she. Together, they could change the agency and the world. When he'd asked her to marry him, to his astonishment and utter joy she'd said yes. Then she shared with him her greatest secret, what the late Wernher von Braun had arranged for her when she was a child. It was the happiest time in his life and he'd dedicated himself anew to NASA, to make everything she'd wanted come true for both of them. Sometimes, he would just wake up grinning. Every love song that was played on the radio seemed to be for him and Kate. He couldn't get enough of her, ever. Then all his hopes and dreams of romance came crashing down. Someone else had taken his place, an arrogant man named Jack Medaris.

Bonner found himself angrily gritting his teeth. He turned away from the old rocket and the old memories. He left his office, the proud and tough director of JSC, to bitterly watch the last launch of *Columbia* from Shuttle Mission Control.

Automatic Launch Sequence
FSS, LC 39-B

The Fixed Service Structure had the appearance of an unfinished office building, a steel framework holding open catwalks and steel steps, interior elevators, and small corrugated tin enclosures for officials to get out of the wind. A vast complex of tubing and pipes, designed to fuel and provide power to the shuttles, snaked through the structure, giving it the further appearance of a gargantuan boiler room turned inside out.

On the fifth level of the complex, Jack, dressed in astronaut blues, walked to the center of the tower and went behind the gray canvas curtain marked IG TEAM. DO NOT ENTER. As he came in, he kicked a small duffel bag. "Sorry, Virg."

Virgil was sitting behind the curtain on the steel floor, leaning against a vertical support, waiting. He got up, picked up the duffel, and set it beside his console. "Sorry. Just some odds and ends I'm carrying with me."

"Let's go, Virg," Jack said urgently. "We're falling behind."

Virgil nodded, flicked a switch on the console, tapped on a laptop keyboard, and then turned an analog dial as far as it would go. "They don't hear nothing now but a squeal like a hog in heat. You're good to go, boss."

Jack found Cassidy by the elevators. "Come on, Hoppy," Jack said, pointing toward the white room down the catwalk.

"Shorty" Guardino, leader of the ingress team, was standing in the room that led to the shuttle hatch with his headset peeled back, his eyes squeezed shut in pain. His two white room assistants were cursing and also fumbling with their headsets. Jack knew the screech in their ears produced by Virgil's machine was intense. Guardino was reaching for the telephone just as Jack and Cassidy caught his attention. He dropped his hand away. "Hullo, Hoppy!" He grinned, instantly recognizing the famous ex-astronaut. Jack noted the other members of the ingress team straighten at the sight of the famous pilot.

Cassidy squared his shoulders. "Hey, Shorty, you old hoss," he grinned, smacking the man on the shoulder. "Here with some bad news, son. This launch is a scrub. Some kind of a communications problem."

"Yeah? It's screwed up, all right," Guardino said crossly. "Man, a howl in this headset just about busted my ears. But what are you doing here? Thought you retired."

Cassidy pointed at the badge on his pocket. "Consultant for Bilstein," he said easily. "Even old broken-down ex-astronauts got to make a living. Bilstein told me to get out here and run an abort training session. Make the best of a bad situation. We're going to the slides. Come on."

Guardino nodded toward Jack. "Who's this?"

"My assistant. Come on, Shorty. Let's do this and get it over with."

Guardino and his men looked at one another and then reluctantly followed Cassidy down the open catwalk, across the primary tower floor, past the elevators, and to the baskets. Jack followed. The five baskets, each designed to hold two people, swayed in the slight breeze. They were attached to slide wires twelve hundred feet long that stretched from the tower to the ground. Cassidy swung open the gate to one of the baskets. "Come on, Shorty. Let's play the game. Bilstein wants to make sure you guys know how to get in and go."

Jack stood back, still anxious. This part of the script was critical. The ingress crew had always been a question mark, how they'd react. Every move had been choreographed, every word in the script practiced again and again. There was not a second to spare—one extra bit of conversation was all that was needed to cause the entire operation to get behind, for everything to fail. But Cassidy was doing his job well. The men trusted the astronaut.

Guardino and his team climbed aboard the baskets. They creaked and swung against their stays. Gurardino eyed Cassidy. "How come you ain't getting aboard?"

"Do you think I'm nuts?" Cassidy laughed. "I'm just here to make sure *you* do it, Shorty."

"You sonuvabitch," Guardino griped, but he did it with a grin.

Cassidy tapped his headset and turned to Jack. "Damn loops are still down. Keep these guys in the basket until I get back. I'm going to give the long line a try."

Guardino gripped the sides of the basket as a light breeze sent it wobbling. "I'd almost rather be blown up than have to ride one of these damned thangs!" He looked at Jack and scowled.

Jack took the clipboard he carried and nonchalantly made a note. He avoided looking at his watch. The precious seconds were ticking away.

Ground Level, FSS, LC 39-B

Penny stepped inside the second elevator, waved to the departing guards, and pushed the button for the crew level. She knew the way. Although she had missed some of the training for the flight, she had attended the shuttle tower familiarization. The doors opened and she stepped out, turned right, and clumped down the access-arm catwalk. To her right through a chain-link fence, she could see the Launch Control Center, hundreds of cars in its parking lot sparkling in the hot July sun. To the left was nothing but a beach and the Atlantic Ocean. She stopped for a moment and watched a pelican fly over the catwalk, and then stepped through the open door leading inside the so-called "white room," the cramped enclosure where she would be inspected one last time before climbing through the small hatch into the shuttle. A technician in white coveralls, a telephone handset to his ear, turned as she entered. "Well, here I am," she said.

The man, a big guy who looked like he could be one of those wrestlers on late-night TV, stared at her. "Yes ma'am." He gulped. "I can see that." He slowly hung up the phone.

Penny waited. "Can I go inside?" she finally asked, pointing at the circular hatch.

That seemed to knock the technician out of his trance and he helped her strap on her parachute and then guided her to kneel on the wooden step in front of the hatch. She pushed her head inside and crawled through and then stood up on the aluminum plate of the aft middeck bulkhead. She had a moment of disorientation. It was like standing inside a small van turned up on its tail. Two seats, their backs horizontal with the ground, were bolted above her. Her seat was the closest to the curved airlock, which meant it was the farthest from the hatch. There was little room to maneuver, and she felt especially clumsy encased in the LES suit. She ducked under the nearest seat and waited for the technician to help her. He wormed through the hatch, pushing a stool in front of him, and placed it beside her seat. He was built like a little Mack truck. From the look of his nose he'd managed to have a few head-on collisions too. She leaned against him and climbed up on the stool and fell back into the seat. Then she raised her arms while he strapped her in, finishing with a final click of the belts that met in a cross on her chest. "You got a name, sailor?" she asked, keeping it light.

"V-virgil," he said, tripping over his tongue.

Penny was used to getting this reaction from men. She had been described in *People* magazine as "blessed with almost perfect olive-hued skin, sculpted cheekbones, and dark eyes that are like pools of liquid amber." She knew she made a striking impression on people, especially men.

She looked up at the empty flight deck. "Where's the rest of the crew?" When the big lug didn't answer, Penny scooched around in the pool of hot sweat that immersed her butt. The rubber smell of the LES suit was nauseating too. "Well, hell," she said irritably. "Am I supposed to fly this bucket myself?"

He checked her restraints again. "I'll go find out what's holding them up. Sit tight, okay?"

Penny blew a strand of hair out of her eyes. "Okay, Virgil. It's not like I have a choice, is it?" When he plugged her headset into her seat, she heard a loud whistle. "Ouch." She grimaced. "That hurts!"

"Let me see your cap." She allowed him to take the cap and fiddle with it. He handed it back. "It checks out, ma'am," he said.

Penny put the cap back on while the technician climbed out of the hatch. The noise was gone but now her headset seemed unnaturally quiet. She pressed the transmission switch. "This is High Eagle. Anybody hear me?" She heard nothing, not even static. "Great," she grumped. "Doesn't anything work out on this pad?"

Penny saw out of the corner of her eye a blue-suited man crawl through the hatch. He stood up and looked at Penny. He seemed surprised to see her. "Dr. High Eagle," he said, finally. "I'm Hoppy Cassidy. I just came by to wish you luck." He laid a big grin on her. He had about a million teeth, it seemed.

Penny recognized Cassidy from the photographs along the wall at the astronaut office in Houston. He was still a good-looking guy. She would have flirted with him had she not been wrapped inside a foul-smelling rubber suit. "Where's the rest of the crew?" she asked.

Cassidy shrugged. "A glitch. I'm on a consulting team, here to keep things safe. Don't worry. I'll make sure we're ready topside." He turned to the technician. "You need to take care of the rest of the equipment, Virg," he said, and then climbed the ladder to the flight deck, cutting off further conversation.

"Well, *shit*," Penny grumbled under her breath. "What a lash-up."

After a few minutes the burly technician crawled back through the hatch, pushing several duffel bags of equipment and what appeared to be the rest of the crew parachute packs. He was below her so she couldn't see what he was doing, but it sounded like he was stowing everything. That didn't seem right. Weren't the other crew members supposed to wear their parachutes too? Penny squirmed under the tight straps, trying to see what he was doing. "I think my headset's dead," she complained. "Did you find out what happened to the rest of the crew? And why are you stowing their parachutes?"

"Just putting them up for protection until they get here," he said, coming up beside her. He was fumbling in a duffel bag for something she couldn't see. "You won't believe this, but their elevator got stuck. We're working on it now. Your headset? I wouldn't worry about it. Not much going on over the loops right now. But I'll look at it in a minute. We're having a few glitches."

The telephone in the white room rang and Virgil abruptly left her to crawl through the hatch and answer it.

A *few glitches?* Penny thought that wasn't the half of it. The air-conditioning unit on her suit was definitely broken. And she had already used her diaper for number one. If she was going into space today, she was going hot, wet, and stinky.

Flight Deck, Orbiter (OV-102) *Columbia*

Cassidy settled into the commander's seat and checked a laptop computer and a playback unit plugged into the comm system by Virgil. The playback unit had the voice of each crew member recorded during the countdown training the week before. The computer "listened" for the standard queries from the Launch Control Center and had each crew voice respond appropriately via the playback unit. The system had worked perfectly. Launch Control believed all the crew members were comfortably seated, answering calls, and ready to go. With the automatic sequence initiated he felt *Columbia* begin to wake up. She first needed her own internal power. Three hydrazine-fueled auxiliary power units (APUs) gave her the hydraulics to actuate propellant valves and move the main engines on their gimbals. Three fuel cells provided her electricity. Inside the cockpit the indicator lights blazed. Cassidy patted the panel in front of him, whispering a greeting: "G'mornin', sweetheart. Daddy's home."

Interior, Crew Elevator #1, LC 39-B

Grant assessed the situation. "This is bullshit," she summed up. She tried the telephone. Dead.

"Maybe they don't know we're stuck yet," Brown offered.

"They expected us topside ten minutes ago," Grant replied. "Somebody's pulling something." Her eyes fell on Barnes. "Janet, you're small enough to get through the access hatch. Do you think you can climb up the shaft?"

"Sure, Ollie." Barnes struggled to get out of her LES suit, peeling it back from her shoulders.

Brown and Betsy Newell lifted Barnes to the elevator roof. She pushed open the access hatch. The next level was twenty feet straight up, reachable by a ladder between the two shafts. "I can see the doors," she said. "Here I go."

"Good woman," Grant called after her.

Columbia

Penny recognized the sounds from her one session in the shuttle simulator. The shuttle stack was readying itself for launch. But that didn't make any sense. Where was Ollie Grant and her crew? She looked up at the flight deck, saw Hoppy Cassidy coming down the ladder.

"What are you doing?" she yelled at him. "Where's the crew?"

"Who was that on the phone, Virgil?" Cassidy asked, ignoring her.

"LCC. Wanted to know why there wasn't any video. I told them the camera's fried. They bought it."

Cassidy looked at Penny. "Dr. High Eagle, there's been a change in plans. You've got a new crew. Sit back, relax, and we'll haul you on into orbit safe and sound." When she started to protest, he held up his hand. "Not now. Later." He walked past her.

"If you think I'm just going to sit here . . ." Penny bristled, twisting until she saw Cassidy and "Virgil" by the hatch.

"Sorry, Hoppy," Virgil said, loud enough that Penny could hear him. "I didn't know what else to do except strap her in. She must have come up in a different elevator."

"The rest of the crew?"

"In the other elevator, I think."

"How about Jack?"

"He ain't here yet," Virgil said, peering worriedly out the hatch.

"Where is he?" Cassidy demanded.

"I don't know. *He just ain't here!*"

Penny had heard enough. She started struggling with the unfamiliar straps around her chest, but the thick gloves of the LES suit defeated her. "Help me out!" she demanded.

"*Why do you have a gun?*" she heard Cassidy say.

"Are you nuts?" Penny demanded, twisting around again to see the two men. "This bucket is about to blast off and somebody's got a gun?"

SMC, JSC

Sam Tate vultured his control room. Everyone on console had his head down, talking over the loops or scribbling notes. Sam sat down, keeping his eye on the clock, and then stood up and sat back down again. He couldn't keep still. He and his people were ready to take over the moment *Columbia* lifted a millimeter off the Cape Canaveral pad. That was the jealous responsibility of Houston. Everything seemed to be nominal, but there was something about this flight that still bothered him. He'd called the IG office but the woman who'd answered the telephone claimed she didn't know anything about an inspection team at the Cape. She was going to check on it, get back to him. That had been over an hour ago. At the Cape, *Columbia*'s automatic internal sequence had begun. Sam resisted calling Bilstein. What did he expect Bilstein to do, challenge NASA headquarters a few minutes before launch? Sam stood and started vulturing again. Glaring at his controllers made him feel better, anyway. Tate's Turds, as they called themselves, kept their heads down. A murmur filled the room behind Sam and he turned and saw Center Director Frank Bonner settle into a chair in the glassed-in VIP room. Sam had known Bonner for over twenty years. Bonner had come down as a young fireball from headquarters and was placed immediately into positions of authority. He had even been the chief of flight operations for a year. Bonner was a good manager. He knew every NASA directive by heart. But he was tricky, too, a backstabber. He would attend meetings and just sit in the back, say nothing, and then later one of the participants would be out of a job. Sam wasn't afraid of Bonner but he kept his distance from him too.

Someone tapped Sam on the shoulder. Sam recognized him as Hank Garcia, Bonner's assistant. "Frank would like to see you, Sam," Garcia said. The thin, balding man wore a sorrowful expression, as if he were summoning someone to an execution.

"I'm busy," Sam retorted, turning away and pressing his hand against his headset as if he'd just received an urgent communication.

"He really wants to see you," Garcia said, undaunted.

Sam eyed Garcia. The man looked pitiful. *Might as well get it over with.* Sam took off his headset, marched into the VIP room. "Dammit, Frank, I've got a shuttle about to launch."

Bonner smiled as Sam came in the room, reached out his hand. "Sam. Been a long time. You used to come by the office, play cards at lunch. You never do that anymore."

Sam shook Bonner's hand while straining to remember the occasion Bonner was talking about. It had to have been at least fifteen years ago. "Been busy, Frank." He shrugged. Like most engineers he wasn't comfortable with small talk.

"Sam," he said, "is your team ready?"

"I guess you know that they are. You approved our training budget. We've drilled this team with a dozen full-scale sims, thrown every mal at them known to God and man. They're a good bunch. Hell yes, we're ready."

"Good," Bonner said, and then was quiet for a moment. "It isn't my fault *Columbia*'s being retired, Sam. I fought against it. The vice president had his mind made up."

"I never said it was your fault, Frank," Sam said truthfully.

Bonner nodded. "Have a good flight, Sam."

Sam left the viewing pit, went to his console, put on his headset. "What did Bonner want, Sam?" Crowder, his assistant Flight, asked.

Sam shook his head. "Nothing. He's just the loneliest man I've ever known."

Launch Complex 39-B

With a groan the crew access arm began its automatic retraction. The ingress team, hunkered sullenly in the baskets, stood up, eyes wide. "Automatic launch sequence! We got to go!" Guardino screeched.

"Yes," Jack replied calmly. "You do."

Firing Room, Launch Control Center, KSC

Aaron Bilstein stood at his console, his plump body swaying as he looked over his team camped out in front of their blinking consoles. This countdown was as smooth as any he had ever run. The only glitch he could name offhand was that the television camera in the white room had kept frying itself until it had gone off completely. No problem. C-SPAN, the only network carrying the launch, didn't come on board until seconds before launch, anyway. It was all going like a precision watch.

"Launch control, this is security."

Bilstein squeezed the transmission button on the comm unit attached to his belt. "Go ahead, Ty." Ty Bledsoe was the chief of the security guards at the pads.

"Aaron, UAC says the ingress team never showed up at the fallback. I checked with the gate. They don't have a record of them leaving the pad."

UAC was the United Aerospace Contractors, the ingress team's employer. "You think they're still at the pad?"

"Not really. The team got permission some time ago to go over to the slide-wire landing-area blockhouse and watch the launch from there. They were only supposed to do it for one launch, but you know Shorty Guardino and his guys."

Bilstein's eye fell on the countdown clock, a huge digital timer above the launch control room. T minus one minute, twenty-four seconds. The ET was pressurized, the nozzles on the main engines were aligned. A hell of a time for a glitch like this. He was going to raise hell with UAC during the debrief. "Get some eyes on the tower, Ty," he growled. "Thanks for letting me know."

"Anytime, Aaron."

Fifth Level, FSS, LC 39-B

Barnes reached what she hoped was the crew accommodations level after climbing up the inside ladder. One of the lifts was there, blocking her. The door of the shaft of the stuck lift was closed. She hung on with one hand, stretched her body as far as it would go, and pushed her fingers inside the crack between the doors. She got a grip through the rubber bumpers and pulled with all her might. She worked out at the gym constantly. Her strength training paid off.

When she got the door pulled back a few millimeters, it automatically opened.

Slide Cage Area, LC 39-B

Jack handed Guardino an envelope. Puzzled, Guardino turned it over. "What the hell is this? What are you trying to pull?"

"Give it to NASA," he said, and slammed the release levers forward. The baskets fell until the cables took up the slack, then the overhead pulleys began to screech. Guardino opened his mouth but Jack couldn't hear what he was yelling. Then he was gone. The two baskets raced down the cables. Jack watched until they slammed into the restraint net at the bottom and then, to his relief, saw the ingress team get out and run like rabbits for the bunker. Jack moved quickly to the mini–control room behind the IG curtain and threw the switch that sent a signal to the connection terminal room located below the pad's elevated hardstand. A series of ten blasting caps on the main line were actuated, any one of them enough to blow the three-inch-diameter cable apart. The Launch Control Center no longer communicated with *Columbia*.

Firing Room, LCC, KSC

The voice level suddenly rose, calls coming over the loops. Ground Control got to Bilstein first. "Launch, we've lost service to the stack. Looks like a break in the main line."

Bilstein responded. "All positions, this is Launch. This is a hold! Stop all launch proceedings immediately!"

The GC immediately came back. Commands were not getting through to *Columbia*.

"What the hell do you mean . . . ?"

"The line's dead, Aaron."

Bilstein looked at the countdown clock. It was stopped at T minus thirty seconds. But what was going on at the pad? The answer came quickly in a call from Ty Bledsoe.

"Launch, this is Security. We got people coming down the wire. I say again, people in the cages coming down the wire!"

"What the hell, Ty . . . ?"

"I know, Aaron. I got a team going out there now to pick them up."

"No, wait!" Bilstein cried. "We don't know if *Columbia*'s on hold or not. Just wait. . . ."

"Jesus, Aaron!"

SMC

Sam couldn't believe what he was hearing, but still he resisted the urge to get on the JSC/KSC push and yell at Bilstein. He knew the man had his hands full. From the excited chatter on the KSC loops it sounded, in fact, as if a full-blown disaster was in the making. In frustration Sam pounded both his fists on the console table. Tate's Turds ducked their heads. He turned to look over his shoulder. Bonner just sat, staring, disbelief written all over his face.

FSS, LC 39-B

Jack ran into Barnes just as she emerged from the elevator shaft. He tripped over her, both of them sprawling on the deck. He stared incredulously at the tiny astronaut. She was looking back and Jack realized his blue suit made her think he was also an astronaut. He took advantage of that. "There's a fire in the shuttle," he said, helping her up. He pushed her inside the open elevator. "Go down to the ground level and stay inside and you'll be safe."

"The rest of my crew are trapped in the other elevator," Barnes said.

"I know. A glitch. But we think they're safe there."

She looked at him suspiciously. "Why don't I know you?"

Jack looked over his shoulder, anxious to be on his way. "I'm an ex-astronaut, never flew. They let me wear the blue suit anyway. I'm here with the, uh, fire team—contract outfit."

Barnes stared at him but didn't move, so he reached past her and pushed the ground-floor button. "Don't come back up," he warned as the doors closed on her.

Jack turned, saw to his astonishment that Cassidy was coming down the passageway carrying a pistol. It was a big, blunt, and ugly instrument, a .45 automatic. "What the hell, Hoppy?" Jack demanded.

"I took it off Virgil," Cassidy said, disgustedly brandishing the weapon. "I guess he was afraid we'd have to fight our way off the pad. I came out to pitch it and find you. We've got trouble. Dr. Penny High Eagle is strapped in—"

The sudden groan of the last flush of the propellants washing through the cryo pipes drowned out the rest of what Cassidy was trying to say. "Let's go!" Jack yelled. Whatever it was, they'd have to sort it out later.

The elevator door suddenly opened. Barnes was standing there. "Listen—" she started to say, then stopped, her mouth agape at the sight of the two men and the pistol.

Instinctively, Cassidy raised the .45 toward the astronaut. Barnes ducked and threw herself forward, hitting Cassidy's arm. He dropped the pistol and it hit the steel deck, punched out a round, and slid over by Jack's feet. Cassidy lurched forward and fell onto the deck, taking Barnes down with him. "Jesus." Cassidy gasped, his face contorted in pain.

Barnes quickly got to her feet while Jack snatched up the pistol. "Holy shit," she breathed when she saw him point it at her.

"The shuttle's going!" he bellowed. "Get in the elevator now!"

Barnes's eyes rolled at the grumble of the cryos, the flexing of the ET with the super-cold liquids. She didn't move. "You're sure I'll be all right in there?" she asked plaintively.

Jack kept his finger outside the trigger guard. He was taking no chances on another misfire. "Yes. We've tested it," he screamed. "Now, go! Go!"

Columbia

Penny struggled to see what was going on behind her. The roar of the propellants flushing through the external tank was like a locomotive. "For God's sake, close the hatch!" she screamed when she saw it was still open. "We're about to lift off!"

"Come on!" the big technician was yelling at the opening. "Come on!"

"Are you crazy?" Penny yelled. "Close the hatch or we're dead!"

FSS, LC 39-B

Jack tucked the pistol in his belt and made for the crew access arm, hauling Cassidy with him. He'd lost all track of time. It might already be too late. He pressed the hydraulic actuator, and stumbled down the catwalk, Cassidy leaning heavily against him. The swinging, swaying arm, 150 feet off the ground, started to move. *Columbia* came into view at the end of the arm and Jack saw the open hatch, Virgil inside urging him on.

Then something happened. Not used to being slammed wide open, the hydraulics jammed and the arm stopped, frozen in place. There was a yard of empty space between the catwalk and the hatch.

Cassidy was coughing. "Jack?" He looked up into Jack's face. "I'm sorry, Jack."

"Not your fault, Hoppy." He looked up, saw Virgil at the hatch. "Help me with him, Virgil!"

Virgil reached out, grasped Cassidy beneath his arms, and dragged the pilot aboard. Cassidy screwed up his face in pain. A little blood was staining the right thigh of his coveralls. It had to be a flesh wound, Jack thought. It was only a ricochet. There was a medical kit aboard—antibiotics, sutures, everything. He could fix his pilot, he was certain of it. He also had no choice. There was no time to get Cassidy off the pad. *Columbia* was the only refuge left.

LCC

Incredulous, still not quite grasping the enormity of what might be happening, Bilstein turned to look out the viewing windows at pad 39-B. He knew that if *Columbia* was continuing her automatic internal countdown, the solid rocket motors were already punched up, their control systems fully activated. The solids were unstoppable once lit. But the solids wouldn't go until the main engines were turned on and no matter what the shuttle's internal computers were doing, the mains could not ignite without a command from the LCC. That was Bilstein's ace in the hole. No matter what happened out there, without an order from the LCC, *Columbia* was going nowhere.

Cedar Key, Northwest Florida

No one on the little island in the Gulf of Mexico took note of the eighteen-wheeler pulling out of the otherwise empty parking lot at the MEC facility at the airport. Inside the truck packed with electronics, Sally Littleton pressed the return button on a desktop computer and the disk inside started its program. "Godspeed, you guys," she mumbled. "Amen," someone else in the trailer automatically added. A red light on the console confirmed the connection with *Columbia*. The screen blurred with a column of numbers and then stopped. GO FOR SSME START, the screen blinked. GO FOR SSME START. A wild cheer erupted inside the trailer.

Crew access arm catwalk, FSS, LC 39-B

Jack heard *Columbia*'s pumps start to whine and knew she was about to come alive. The sound of the pad's massive deluge system hit him first, a roar from the great waterfall of water sweeping beneath *Columbia*'s tail. Then the shuttle began to shake and a burst of fire and billowing exhaust suddenly erupted from her mains. *Columbia*'s engines were being fed by turbo pumps capable of emptying an Olympic-sized swimming pool in seconds, each of her SSMEs producing nearly a half-million pounds of thrust. That thrust pushed up against the shuttle stack. The external tank took the brutish strain, absorbing the energy, shooting it throughout the structure, storing it in minute twists and strains. *Columbia* had turned into a coiled, monstrous spring.

From the end of the access arm Jack reached for Virgil's hand just as the sonic blast created by the shuttle mains struck him. Knocked off balance, all he could do was jump, aiming for the hatch. He hit it, bounced off, grabbed air, and then fell away. Virgil, in a desperate lunge, caught his coveralls. Jack reached up and grabbed his savior's big arms to pull himself inside, both men falling on the curved plate of the airlock.

Virgil got to his knees to close the hatch. Just as he clamped it down, the solids let go. A combined total of five and a half million pounds of thrust kicked the *Columbia* stack off the pad. In a crashing thunder of fire and smoke it all began to rise, not slowly like the lumbering giants of the *Saturn-Apollo* era, but like a white-hot arrow unleashed from a huge bow. *Columbia* leapt for the sky, the jackrabbit of all manned spacecraft, her solid rocket boosters screaming, her main engines erupting in licking thunder. Virgil went howling onto his stomach. Jack was pressed against the middeck firewall. The massive g-forces felt like an elephant standing on his chest.

NW Florida

The MEC tractor-trailer crawled out of Cedar Key, turned left up highway 19, heading north. It would be traveling, day and night, along back roads for as long as *Columbia* was in space. Littleton, boss of the MEC ground team, scrolled down her PC screen, and clicked on an icon shaped like a computer monitor. A red light on her modem flared for five seconds and then went off. *Columbia*'s guidance parameters, the code that instructed the shuttle where to aim her nose throughout her ascent into orbit, had just been completely overwritten. She looked up at the monitor tuned to NASA Select closed-circuit television. *Columbia* was batting for the sky. "Go, sweet Jack," she whispered. "*Go!*"

Columbia

Jack knew it was critical that someone answer Houston if they called. If Mission Control believed there was no crew on board, it might recommend to Cape Safety that it blow the explosives on the solid boosters and external tank to abort the launch. And that meant death to all on board.

Virgil was wrapped around the airlock. Cassidy was on the other side, curled into a ball on the aft bulkhead. Jack fought the g-forces, felt them ease a little as the mains cut back to make the roll. The bulkhead rivets still felt like nails being driven into his back. His arm seemed to weigh a ton, but he managed to reach up and plug his headset into the jack located on the back of one of the empty crew seats. Just as he clicked it in, he heard a Houston controller's callout for the roll maneuver completion. Jack flipped the external comm switch. "Roger, Houston. Roll maneuver complete," he gasped.

Then *Columbia* lurched. Her engines boomed in Jack's ears, rattling the crew compartment. It felt as if she were coming apart.

SMC, JSC

Sam saw the capsule communicator mouthing something to her assistant. "Talk to me, CAPCOM," he boomed. "I need to know what you know!"

"Sam, I didn't recognize who called down the roll maneuver," the CAPCOM answered, chastened. "It wasn't Ollie Grant."

"Engines realigning!" the booster systems engineer yelled. "There they go! Coming back up!"

"Flight, GNC." GNC was the guidance, navigation, and control systems engineer.

"What the hell is going on, GNC?"

"Um, Flight, something caused *Columbia* to change her flight path. It doesn't match up with the predicted trajectory at all. Whatever course she's on sure as hell ain't the one we programmed. We don't know where she's going."

Sam had trained for this contingency, hoped it would never happen, but now it had. He had a bird out of control. "LCC, this is Flight. Prepare for autodestruct."

Columbia

Jack heard the solids punch off and felt the g-forces abate. He needed to get to the flight deck. He pulled himself to his feet and caught sight, for the first time, of Penny High Eagle. She was riding uphill with her eyes closed, her seat rattling with the thunder of the booming mains. She opened her eyes and saw him. "Who are you?" she asked, gasping.

Jack shook off his surprise at seeing the famous Dr. Penny High Eagle in the seat. However she had managed to get aboard, he'd deal with her later. He clawed his way past her, got a handhold on the ladder going up to the flight deck. "Are we going to die?" she asked, plaintively.

"Not if I can help it!" Jack called, and then pulled himself up, his arm muscles feeling as if they were being torn apart. He grasped the pilot's seat, got a toehold on the edge of the deck, and kicked himself up. He fell into the seat, breathing hard. He wasn't a shuttle pilot. He desperately tried to recall what Cassidy had told him needed to be done, how the switches had to be configured.

"Are we going to die?" High Eagle had asked. All of a sudden Jack wasn't certain of the answer.

SMC, JSC

Sam tried to suck the blurred video picture of the *Columbia* stack into his brain. When the solids blew off, the picture changed to a view of the big boosters coming down, swinging on their parachutes. Then the NASA Select video went back to the shuttle, three glowing circles at its base showing perfect mains. Sam had to take his frustration out in some way. He kicked his chair, sent it flying. *Dammit!* The most beautiful machine in the world and it was going to be lost on his watch! Reports were rolling in from KSC. An ingress team in the escape bunker, screaming bloody murder about hijackers. A crew apparently stuck on the elevator. Up there, high above the contrail wisps blowing away in the jet stream, were some goddamn assholes *who had stolen his spacecraft*! By damn, he'd see about that!

Sam suddenly realized Bilstein was on the KSC/JSC loop, trying to talk to him. "We've got a situation here, Sam." Bilstein was nearly sobbing. "I think it's a runaway shuttle."

"No shit, Aaron," Sam hissed. "You blew it. Where the hell was your security?" He tore off his headset, not waiting for a reply, and vultured his people. Many of his controllers seemed to be praying. Some were crying. Sam looked over his shoulder. Bonner was standing, his hands pressed against the VIP-room glass. Sam tossed a handful of antacid tablets into his mouth and stood at the rail, hands on his hips, his long face drawn down to a baleful stare, thin nose pushed ahead, his jaw crunching the tablets. He had to get control. Carefully, he fitted his headset back on. "Aaron, are you prepared for autodestruct?"

There was a pause. "Roger. Is that what you want?"

Sam chewed his lip. He looked down on his troops, took his frustration out on his chair once more, giving it another kick with his size-twelve shoe. "No, dammit! There's some-body on board. We don't know who."

Sam took a deep breath. The room was completely silent except for the intermittent chirp of a push being reset. All his troops were looking at him, waiting for his guidance. He remembered *Apollo 13*, the *Mir* fiascoes. But there had never been anything like this before in space. He took a deep breath. "Folks," he boomed, "this institution has a reputation. We've never lost a ship once it reached space and we're not going to start today." He paused as if daring anyone to contradict him. The space shuttle *Challenger* had never made it to space, barely reaching 65,000 feet before that awful conflagration.

Sam continued, low and slow. "There's only one way we're going to be able to continue that record, and that is if every one of you does your job exactly as you've been trained. That is what I have demanded of you before this . . . *thing* . . . and it is what I expect of you now. I will give you information about what we are dealing with as I learn it. You have my word on that. Now hop to it. Protect *Columbia!*"

There was a brief moment of silence but then all at once his people, first the GNC and then the other controllers, began their clamoring systems readouts and parameter checks.

"Bonner is gone, Sam," Crowder advised. Sam didn't acknowledge. He didn't care about Bonner, didn't care about anything except how to recover from what had happened. He watched and listened and was satisfied by what he heard coming over the loops. He had no doubt about the outcome as long as Shuttle Mission Control kept its head. No one could fly a shuttle without them. There were things a shuttle crew, any shuttle crew, would need. It was all a matter of time before they called and Sam was going to be right where he was supposed to be, ready to reach down their throats and tear out their stinking livers when they did.

At Base of Pad Hardstand, LCC 39-B

Bilstein saw four white-smocked men walking unsteadily from the bunker beside the pad. Guards were posted around them, their pistols drawn. Up on the pad hardstand he could see four of the five astronauts he'd sent out to fly the shuttle. They had been found in the elevators, deafened by the launch but otherwise in good shape. The tiny one— Janet Barnes, he remembered now—had been yelling about a shooting. Ty Bledsoe was there to debrief them on the bus, find out what the hell had happened.

One of the ingress team jerked his arm away from a security policeman. "I don't need your help now, you sumbitch!" he bellowed. Bilstein realized the man was nearly deaf, the result of being so close to the shuttle at liftoff. The gruff little techie saw Bilstein, stomped up to him. "Everybody be a witness!" he yelled, handing Bilstein an envelope. "I turned this over to NASA!"

Bilstein took the envelope, a standard manila mailing pouch from the look of it, and withdrew a thin pink slip of paper. With trembling fingers he unfolded it. When he saw what it was, he stared at Guardino. "This doesn't make any sense."

The team leader cupped his ear and then his face registered understanding. He'd obviously looked inside because he roared, "You got that right, buddy!"

Bilstein looked again, just to be sure he wasn't mistaken. He wasn't. The pink slip of paper was a receipt "pursuant to our agreement." There was much more, all in fine print. The letterhead on the receipt said "MEC." Bilstein had heard of the company but couldn't quite place it. Attached to the receipt with a paper clip were also two cashier's checks from the First Bank of the Cayman Islands, BWI. One made out to the Department of Transportation. The other made out to NASA.

Each for one million dollars.

3

Low Earth Orbit

Cut off from the land that bore us,
Betrayed by the land that we find,
When the brightest have gone before us,
And the dullest are most behind—
Stand, stand to your glasses, steady!
'Tis all we have left to prize:
One cup to the dead already—
Hurrah for the next that dies!

—Bartholomew Dowling, "The Revel"

Postinsertion Checklist (1)
Columbia

Jack savored the orbital maneuvering system burn, the last punch *Columbia* needed to insert herself into orbit. He rode with joy the two engines in the pods above the mains, merged with them, delighted in their sound and vibration and power. He knew every valve, line, and sensor in the OMS, could picture the monomethyl hydrazine and nitrogen tetroxide pushed by pressurized helium to mix and explode in thrusting power. *Columbia*'s reaction-control system jet-puffed hot gas at opposing sides of her nose and, snorting like a giant flying bull, she turned herself over according to her program until the cockpit was head-down toward earth. Then, with a final grunt, the OMS and RCS snuffed out and there was silence. The shuttle was in a free-flight trajectory. Physics and orbital mechanics would keep them aloft for at least a week without another burn.

Jack didn't bother to check the onboard computer. There'd be time enough to check exact positioning later. He looked instead through the cockpit window, allowing himself a moment to rise out of his seat, move in closer, press his nose almost up on the glass, and relish the view of the vast expanse of blue and brown turning beneath him. The Indian Ocean was a glittering blue lake, snowy clouds winding sinuously over it. Ahead was a gigantic black shadow, swallowing the planet. The translucent rainbow hues that defined the curved edge of the earth were crushed by the vast gloom and then *Columbia*'s nose penetrated it, disappearing into the darkness of planetary night. Jack saw a wondrous spiderweb of lights below and realized *Columbia* had taken him over a vast city. Then, as the city receded, another wonder could be seen. On the face of the Pacific Ocean there rode a molten orb, dancing on the shimmering dunes of the dark water. The moon! Transfixed, he stared at it until he was distracted by a woman's voice coming from the middeck. "Houston, we have a problem. Houston? Dammittohell! *Houston!*"

Jack pushed away from the windscreen, marveling at his ability to fly in the microgravity of space. He allowed a small moment of pleasure in it, then pulled himself quickly over the seats to the hatch to do what needed to be done.

Cedar Key (1)
Beach Road, Cedar Key, Florida

Every morning Cecil Velocci ritually took a drive along the beach. On this morning, as always, it was peaceful. Cedar Key, Florida, Cecil's hometown, had spent its history being quiet. For a brief period it had been the pencil capital of the United States but after the cedar trees were all chopped down, the pencil factories went away. About all that was left was the fishing, and it waxed and waned; nothing seemed to stay permanently on the island except the solitude, and perhaps the colorful characters who were drawn to it. Cedar Key sat off by itself, a piece of Florida that was always about to be discovered but never quite was. And for that, Cecil Velocci, the Key's only lawyer, was profoundly grateful.

At this hour very few of the permanent population were up, except for the fishermen who had gone out through the cut at sunup. All that could be heard was the lapping of the Gulf of Mexico, and the whisper of the wind in the big white oaks that grew near the shoreline, and the forlorn call of a seagull missing its flock. Three small motels and a bed and breakfast in a redecorated old general store on the narrow main street catered to what visitors there were. Richard Boone, of television Western fame, had been the B & B's

most famous guest and his picture in his all-black cowboy
suit hung in one of the tiny rooms. In a protected sound
there were real fishing families in small frame homes, their
weathered old boats tied up on rickety piers. Cecil had
come out of one of those families. His great-grandfather had
been the first of his line to come to Cedar Key. To escape
the battles raging between unions and businessmen in the
garment district of New York, Levi Feldman had chosen to
come to the strange semitropical climes of northwestern
Florida to work as a clerk for one of the pencil companies.
He eventually became the patriarch of a small but active
Jewish community on the island, and imported a young
woman from New York to be his wife. Levi had sired only
daughters. One of them had married Cecil's grandfather, an
Italian fisherman named Antonio Paggiano, and one of their
daughters had been Cecil's mother. She also married an
Italian fisherman, Bernardo Velocci. Through all those mar-
riages the women had steadfastly clung to their original
faith, and so it was that Cecil was an Italian Jew, although
hardly anyone on the island was aware of it, or cared.

Cecil had decided not to follow his father and grandfather into the fishing business. He had been the first in his
family to attend college and had gone on to law school at
the University of Florida. Because he loved the place, he
returned to Cedar Key, set up practice in an office just
beside the B & B—mostly working real estate, some criminal law on the side—married a local girl, had a son and a
daughter barely a year apart. Cecil anticipated a quiet life
working small law on a small island. That was, of course,
before MEC arrived. Since then life had been a bit more
complicated.

MEC had leased the old abandoned Harper Aviation
hangar at the airport and Cecil had drawn up the lease.
With the arrival of MEC it was as if the heart of the sleepy
island sped up a few beats. The MEC workers moved into
town and became a part of it, hanging out in the bars at

night, shepherding big trucks filled with machinery and things covered with canvas into the hangar by day. For the price of a beer they were only too happy to regale the locals with tales of the glory days of space, of the *Atlas* booster, which they called the Beast, and the *Titan*, which they called the Old Lady, those grand machines built for war but used to explore the heavens instead. And, of course, they spoke in reverent tones of the great old *Saturn*, the rocket to which some of them had given their youth, others too young to work on it but knowing its design as if it had been their own.

In the process of working the property deal Cecil had gotten to know the president of the company, Jack Medaris. When Terri, Cecil's wife, had been hired as Medaris's personal secretary, Jack gradually became a family friend. Cecil had given Jack a standing invitation to go out to fish and sail anytime he had a minute free. A couple of times Jack had taken Cecil up on his offer. During those day trips on Cecil's small sailboat he and Jack had gotten to know each other, spent hours talking about philosophy and politics. Cecil had come to admire Jack but was never certain he ever understood him, at least not until Jack finally told him about his wife and what had happened to her in Huntsville. Another time, during a visit to the plant, Jack had walked Cecil through the bustling little factory, leading him to a big rocket engine on a hardstand in the center of the hangar. "That's the nozzle and there's the combustion chamber," Jack told him, not even asking if he wanted an explanation. "Controlled explosions occur in the chamber and then hot gases flow through the throat of the nozzle and out the bell. That's the action. The reaction is motion. It's Newton's third law, Cecil. Do you understand?"

Cecil didn't, not entirely, but he claimed he did and kept listening. Cecil remembered Jack circling the engine, his hand reaching out but not quite touching it. "That's the physics involved," Jack said. And, in fact, this is an advanced hybrid engine. It combines the best features of liquid and solid propellants. "But do you know what really makes this rocket fly, Cecil?"

"No, Jack. What really make this rocket fly?"

Jack had touched the engine, *caressed it*, Cecil thought. "This rocket flies on dreams."

Cecil turned at the beach road, contemplated the lapping sea. To his delight he found Paris and Helen and their kit, Magnus, feeding in the shallows. He stopped his truck and smiled at the dolphin family. They ignored him, intent on the hunt, but Cecil didn't mind. It was enough that he could enjoy the sight of them. He watched as little Magnus darted between his doting parents. Paris was big but moved quickly past the fry, which reacted by condensing into a tight, protective ball. He circled them, building up a vortex, and then Helen clipped the ball, taking her fill. She touched Magnus with her fin and the stubby dolphin-child followed her example, gulping in two quick bites of fry-ball. Paris then went in hard, going for the center, the silvery fish scattering like a shattered mirror. Cecil felt like applauding as the dolphin family vented for air and then eased out toward deeper water. "Good luck," Cecil wished the family. He wished the same for himself.

After the MEC hangar had burned on that dark night back in February, Jack and his people had gone into a shell for a while. They'd kept to themselves, working, it seemed, night and day. Cecil could see the lights on at the old airport far into the night. Then Jack had taken a big chance, telling Cecil, an officer of the court, about what he and his people had decided to do to meet the terms of their contract with Isaac Perlman and the January Group. Jack must have known it was entirely possible that Cecil would run straight to the FBI. He hadn't, of course, but he had certainly thought about it. Never in his wildest dreams would he have thought his friend and the hardworking, good people of MEC, including his wife, might be involved in such a scheme. It had taken a lot of quiet walks along the beach road, and arguments with himself, and long discussions with Terri, before Cecil made up his mind to help. After a while he wasn't certain why he had joined the project except that Jack was his friend, and obviously determined to do the thing, no matter what it took, and also because Cecil wanted to keep the MEC people, including the mother of his children, out of prison.

From that moment Cecil had kept himself strictly above the details of what MEC was doing. He worked only on matters of law involving the legitimate contract involved. Although Cecil knew it could be argued otherwise, he had not, to his knowledge, broken any law—just followed it to its arcane letter. Cecil had once discounted classmates who argued there are times when principle and purpose must be above the law, no matter how moral the law itself. Now he finally understood why that was so.

Cecil had also arranged for Jack to sell the patent for his sling pump, saw to the division of the money to the thirty employees. Jack took nothing for himself. MEC was out of business, perhaps forever.

The strange thing was when you came right down to it, all this effort was for dirt. Cecil pondered that as he walked up the old wooden steps that led to his office. It seemed to him there was always something else Jack was after, something that he kept from everyone.

Cecil looked through the stack in his in-box and then went to his desk and had a slow cup of coffee and watched cable news. As he knew they would, the announcements concerning the shuttle finally came on. The correspondent, a frowning woman with a puffy blond hairdo blowing in the Cape Canaveral breeze, reported that *Columbia* had gotten off but there were irregularities still unknown. "If you only knew the half of it," Cecil said to the television set. He put down his coffee cup and picked up the phone. It was time to get the plan going.

He dialed the Department of Transportation number he had memorized. A woman answered, explained that the officer Cecil asked for was on vacation (as Cecil well knew), and asked if she could be of assistance. Cecil identified himself. "I called to tell you," he said, following the script he had rehearsed a dozen times, "that I have received word from my client that, pursuant to the clause in paragraph four dot five dot one of contract Alpha one dot two dot two four three five, the company known as MEC is notifying the Department of Transportation as required in said contract that it is initiating its physical study of the capabilities of the Space Transportation System in a modified mode, utilizing the orbiter *Columbia* and having provided experts in the field of pilotage, navigation, and engine design for safety purposes as according to OSHA regulation four seven nine dot two dot three dot—"

"Wait a minute," the contract officer interrupted, exasperated. "I'm not familiar with this agreement." Cecil heard the click of fingernails on a computer keyboard. "Okay, here it is. Now would you mind telling me what you just said, only in English this time, okay?"

Cecil cleared his throat. "The clause I just cited requires MEC to notify the Department of Transportation that it has invoked the clause in their contract with you that allows them to fly a space shuttle in order to conduct tests."

The DOT woman still didn't get it. "Fly a space shuttle? In a DOT contract? That doesn't sound right."

"It's in the contract," Cecil replied, trying hard to sound nonchalant. "MEC has paid the United States government in the form of two checks drawn on a bank in Grand Cayman, British West Indies, a sum of one million dollars each to DOT and NASA as specified. That seems to be about it. Are there any questions?"

There was a short silence and then the contracting officer asked, in a voice so faint, Cecil had to strain to hear,

"Would you say again about the shuttle thing, the *Columbia?*"

"Yes, of course. That, as authorized in the contract, MEC is conducting its tests in the orbiter *Columbia.*"

There was a strangled sound and then the woman, in a voice suddenly loud, demanded Cecil's name. He calmly gave it again along with his telephone number and then asked her if she wanted him to fax a copy of the contract showing where the DOT officials had signed. "Yes, right away, please," she said, her voice so tight Cecil thought it could have been plucked like a violin.

Cecil hung up the phone, asked his secretary to do the faxing, and patiently waited. An hour later he heard a polite tap at his door. His secretary escorted in the town constable, Sergeant Buckminster Taylor, Trooper Buck, as he was called. Buck hefted his bulk into the chair nearest Cecil's desk. "Damnedest thing, Cecil, got a call from the FBI just a few minutes ago. Asked if I'd mind baby-sitting you for an hour or so. There's a couple of agents on their way from Tallahassee to see you. You in any kind of trouble?"

"Let's just say I think I know why they're coming."

"Why's that?"

"I believe I'll hold fire on that for now, Buck."

Trooper Buck, who kept an eye on everyone on the Key, didn't miss a beat. "Didn't I see your missus leaving town last night with both the kids?"

"A little vacation," Cecil said.

"I almost believe you," Buck said, turning in his chair. "You expecting trouble?"

"Trouble?"

"Where's Jack Medaris these days, by the way? Went out to the plant, everything's deserted."

Cecil nodded. "Believe I'll hold fire on that one, too, Buck."

Postinsertion Checklist (2)
Columbia

"Houston, this is Penny!" she yelled into her headset. "Houston, answer, dammit!" Then she remembered she hadn't heard anything since the big technician had "fixed" her headset. "Shit!"

Penny stopped and listened. She heard nothing except the sound of her own shallow breathing. It was unnerving. "Hello? Who's here with me?" she called, but no one answered. She didn't know whether to unstrap or not, what she should do. She squinted, a habit when she was worried or scared. Was there enough air in the cabin? Did something need to be done to turn the oxygen and nitrogen banks on, to get the filters scrubbing?

"Houston, come in, Houston!" she yelled into her mike, but no one answered. She'd seen Cassidy dragged through the open hatch. What had happened to him? And where was the big technician? And the man who had somehow climbed past her to the flight deck during ascent? My God, he had to be strong to do that! Penny had been unable to even raise her arm at the time.

The middeck was dark, gloomy, a pale blue fluorescent glow from a single square ceiling panel providing the only light. She sniffed the air, wrinkled her nose. The cabin's stale, sour smell, like a mix of old athletic socks and detergent, made her wonder how many unwashed bodies had camped out inside the tiny compartment. She tried to focus on the frost-white lockers in front of her but couldn't get a fix on them. Up and down seemed to have no meaning. Her LES suit felt light, crinkly, as if it were made of paper. Then she saw a tiny silver circle, a washer, wobble past her eyes. She watched it, fascinated by its independent trajectory, wondering what bolt it was supposed to encircle and what else had been left undone on *Columbia*. It was an old bird, after all. Not *it*, she recalled from her PR briefings, *she, her*:

the shuttles were feminine, the same as ships. *Columbia*, then, was an old lady. Penny had been in middle school when the world's first shuttle had made her maiden voyage into space. That had been more than twenty years ago. God only knew what else was wrong with the damn ancient thing!

Penny snapped back to her situation. Those men—who the hell were they? Only one answer fit: She was probably on board with hijackers. And then—in a tumble of thoughts —she realized that whatever had happened, or was about to happen, it was going to make one hell of a story. The end result, if she survived, might be the attainment of all that she had ever desired: superstar status, perhaps even love. She reveled in that thought for a split second before cursing herself for having had it. What manner of insecure person was she that, in the midst of disaster, she was pondering if her public would love her for it? Still, if she lived . . . she *was* Penny High Eagle! Her public had to be served. And what a hell of a story!

Penny's internal debate was interrupted when she heard movement behind her seat and then the ingress technician's voice. "Jack?" she heard him call out. "Jack?" Then there was the unmistakable sound of vomiting. Penny wrinkled up her nose again.

Then the man who had climbed to the flight deck came floating headfirst through the hatch, pulling himself hand over hand down the ladder. He was dressed in the flight coveralls of an astronaut and Penny reflexively thought perhaps there had been some kind of mix-up at launch, that in fact she was still in the hands of NASA. Then she saw the ugly red scar that ran from the man's left jawbone around to the back of his neck and she knew he was no astronaut. "Dr. High Eagle?" He was upside down, his head above hers. "I don't know how you got aboard but just tell me this. What happened to the rest of the crew?"

Penny scrutinized the man. She had learned to memorize features to help her in recreating people for her articles. Even wearing coveralls and upside down, she could tell he was trim and athletic and probably in his early forties. He had black hair, dabbled with silver threads, and a strong chin. His clear brown eyes seemed to brim with intelligence. She thought about not talking to him but then dismissed the idea. Who else was she going to talk to? "The last time I saw them they were on the elevator," she said, pulling off her helmet. She let it go and it drifted away. She watched, mesmerized by its motion. "I came up alone in the other one."

He seemed to study her. Penny had the sense he was trying to make up his mind about something. "I'm Jack Medaris, Dr. High Eagle. I think I'm going to need your help to get this spacecraft configured."

She looked up at him, squinting. "Would you mind turning right side up? You're making me sick to my stomach."

"Do you have SAS?" It sounded like an accusation.

"S-A-S?"

"Yes," he said, his upside-down eyes looking deep into hers. "Do you have it?"

She turned away from him. The man talked in riddles, the same as every other NASA engineer she'd run into during the past six months. "Who the hell are you, Jack Medaris?" she asked.

"I know you've got questions and I'll get to them," he replied, at the same time complying with her request and rotating until he was in a heads-up position relative to her. "But right now I need your help. How about it?"

"Why should I help a hijacker?"

"I'm not a hijacker. I have a contract."

"What?"

"It's top secret. As soon as we're done, we'll land. I'll explain it all later. Got to look at my PLT and SMET. How about helping out? Start by activating the WCS."

Penny's head was spinning. "What's a P-L-T and a smet? And what's a W-C-S?"

He apparently had not heard her, or chose to ignore her. He disappeared beneath her seat. "Let's have a look, Hoppy," she heard him say.

Penny pulled off her gloves, released her belts, and disconnected her suit connections, then watched in dismay when her feet floated toward the ceiling. She awkwardly twisted around, grappled with the back of her seat, managed to pull herself into a position to look behind it, toward the aft bulkhead. Medaris was there, Cassidy beneath him, apparently unconscious. "Listen," she said. "I need some answers."

"Just a minute, Dr. High Eagle," Medaris said in a mildly irritated voice.

"Listen, you . . ." She pulled over the top of the seat, expecting to drop down beside him, but instead she banged into the aft bulkhead, bounced off it, and went flying, arms and legs flailing, until she managed to snag a cloth foot restraint strap on the deck. She fully expected to be laughed at but Medaris was busy tightening a cloth belt from his overalls above a spreading red spot on Cassidy's right thigh. A haze of red seemed to hover above it and Penny realized with a shock they were floating blood drops. "Medaris, what happened to him?" she asked, shaken.

"Remain calm," Medaris said, turning to look at her. "Moving around too much in preact isn't a good idea. It can degrade several EC parameters to off-nominal. Are you going to get the WCS activated?"

Penny stared at him. "Can you speak English?" she asked. When he didn't answer, she put her boots together and launched herself at him, intending to grab his collar, make him talk sense to her. She crashed into the airlock instead, and bounced back, flailing. Her eyes filled with tears of pain and frustration. Then she seemed to lose her ability to focus. She closed her eyes, tried to figure out which way was up or down. When she opened them again, she saw Medaris pondering her from across the deck. "Is there any particular reason why you keep doing that?" he asked.

"Screw you," she grumped.

He pulled to the bank of stacked lockers, opened one up. "The reason you can't go where you want to is because you're judging your trajectory based on one g." He slid out a drawer, pulled shaped pieces of foam from it. He plucked out a white box by its handle. A green cross was inscribed on it. "Your brain is programmed for horizontal range as computed on earth," he continued while she gaped at him. "Range on earth is the product of velocity squared divided by the gravitational acceleration constant and the cosine of twice the launch angle. Here in space the gravitational constant is essentially zero. That's why you can't hit your target."

Penny was certain she was being mocked. Nothing made her angrier. "You son of a bitch, I'm going to kick your ass."

He frowned at her, as if she was something he needed to fix. "Do you have a vocabulary other than curse words?"

"Do you have a vocabulary other than acronyms?" she replied, squinting.

He ignored her comment. "I've got a wounded PLT and—" he peered past Penny "—what appears to be a sick SMET. I need to take care of them first. Then I'll take care of you."

Penny took his words as a threat. She held her hands turned flat, moved them in a circle. "Take care of me? You come near me, you son of a bitch, I'll kill you! I have a black belt in karate."

"Dr. High Eagle," Medaris said patiently, "we have a long haul in front of us. To get through it we're going to need to be friends."

His comment was so ridiculous that Penny spontaneously burst out laughing, only to quickly strangle it. She hated her laugh. She'd been told by her last boyfriend that her laugh sounded like a braying mule. She'd kicked him out that night, sent him packing without even his toothbrush. "Friends?" she rasped, choking the laugh down her throat. "I don't need any friends, especially a damn spacejacker!"

He arched an eyebrow. "Your laugh . . . it sounds a little bit like a—"

"Screw you!" she interrupted, then squinted, jabbed her finger toward the deck. "I want to go down, now!"

"You're aiming in the wrong direction," he said, opening the box.

"What?"

He pointed at the deck. "When you point in that direction, you're not pointing at the earth. We're in an omicron plus-X center-of-earth attitude. The direction you're pointing is out along the plane of the solar system. That's a generalization, of course."

"Well, let me give you a generalization, shithead," Penny sneered. "I want the hell off this goddam shuttle."

He shrugged, took scissors from the box, began to snip away the red-soaked material on Cassidy's pants.

"All right," Penny breathed. "Let me make this a very simple question. Are we going to land? And no P-L-T or W-C-S acronyms!"

"PLT and WCS aren't acronyms," Medaris replied, folding the hole in the material back with his finger. "They're initials. PLT means pilot. WCS is the waste control system. SMET's an acronym. Shuttle main engine technician. You didn't know that?"

Penny was starting to feel homicidal. The man was a complete nerd. "I know this," she seethed. "If you don't answer my question, I'm going to use that goddamn equation of yours, gravitational whatever and twice the goddamn whatsit, and come over there and wring your stinking stupid-ass neck, even if I have to wait until you're asleep to do it. *Are you going to land this thing or not?*"

"Yes," he said as if it were the most obvious thing. She had a surge of hope until he added his final word. "Eventually."

"Bastard," she hissed.

"My mother would hate to hear that opinion of her favorite son," he said, disarmingly.

Penny refused to be disarmed by a spacejacking geek. "You and your mother can go . . ." she muttered, trailing off, because she had suddenly become aware of her bladder. It felt as if it had swollen to the size of a basketball and someone was sticking needles in it. A remnant of a class she'd had in Houston came back to her. There was something called space adaptation syndrome. SAS! So that's what this idiot was talking about! Weightlessness in space caused a shift of blood to the head, disorienting the brain. The stomachs of astronauts often paid a price for that. But blood also poured into the upper torso, causing the body to create urine in copious quantities to get rid of the excess fluid. Penny groaned when another thought struck her. Ollie Grant had insisted she drink a lot of water that morning, saying it would keep her from being dehydrated in space. She realized she'd been had. But it didn't change the fact she had to pee, seriously, *now*.

Cedar Key (2)
Office of Cecil Velocci, Attorney at Law, Cedar Key, Florida

Two FBI agents arrived three hours after Cecil had made his call to the Department of Transportation. By then Trooper Buck had received a call concerning a fender bender on Gulf Street and left. The agents pounded up the steps and strode purposefully past Cecil's secretary, who waved her arms at them futilely before they hit the door. "Cecil Velocci?"

"Attorney-at-law. Yes. FBI?"

"You got it," one of them said, displaying his shield. The other agent did the same. "What is all this? I understand you turned in a report, something having to do with the shuttle?"

Cecil showed them the Department of Transportation contract. The agents inspected the document and then one of them left to make a call from the cellular phone in their car. He returned, grim faced. "I'm going to have to ask you to come with us to Tallahassee," he said. "The boss wants to question you himself."

"Am I under arrest?"

"Arrest? Technically, no."

"Then . . . ?"

"Look, Velocci, don't ask, okay? Just move your butt."

Cecil picked up his briefcase and went through the outer office, waving good-bye to his secretary. "Hold down the fort, Mildred," he told the wide-eyed woman as he and the agents filed by.

"Cecil, what the H is goin' on?" she demanded.

"Now, don't you worry, Mildred. I'll be back in a jiff." He gave her a big grin. Despite the fact that he was terrified, Cecil was determined to display an airy confidence. He figured he might as well. *Columbia* was up there. There was no turning back now.

Puckett

Puckett Security Services, Lafayette Avenue, Washington, D.C.

Carl Puckett reveled in his plush office with its view of the United States Capitol building. He'd paid his dues, worked hard for the location, the expensive furnishings, the busty blond secretary out front. For years his little company had worked the desert fields as muscle for the oil industry. When heads needed cracking or security was a problem, Carl and his bad boys were called upon to visit the miscreants, to guard the wells, to shepherd the tanker convoys. Over the years Puckett had taught himself Arabic and Farsi, got to know nearly everyone in the desert kingdoms, even the old gnarled sheiks who owned not much more than a couple of camels up a dry wadi. In the bad old days of the first energy crisis of the 1970s, he'd personally taken one of the top oil executives in the world to a tiny country on the Red Sea that was wavering on its support of OPEC. There was mob rule at the airport and in the streets but he'd gotten the executive into the palace, helped him talk turkey to the sheik-in-charge, got him a deal. When the big boys heard about what he'd done, PSS had suddenly become the hot-ticket enforcer in the oil industry. Puckett had not stopped since, always ready for a special assignment wherever it came from, as long as they were able to pay.

Puckett was built like a fireplug, with a face to match—a nose that had been broken more than once, and a brushy mustache that covered a partial harelip. With arms thick and heavy, and legs built like tree trunks, he looked like a tough customer and he was. He'd kicked an American to death once in a bar in Beirut, had barely escaped the police on that one. The man he'd killed, a roughneck oil driller, had stood just over six feet tall. He'd called Puckett "Tiny," as in "Hey, Tiny, you lookin' for trouble?" The driller had never called anybody anything after that. Puckett had slowed down some during the last ten years, had let himself get soft, at least in the gut. He let his employees, mostly street trash he'd trained in a paramilitary camp on a farm in Virginia, do his fighting these days.

Puckett had the television on in a corner, not really listening, just background noise. But he raised his head as the first reports of the hijacking of *Columbia* started to filter through. He put his hands on his big desk, listened intently.

"Well, I'll be damned," he said. Puckett prided himself on his clairvoyance. He'd always had a sixth sense about things, who was responsible for what. This one he knew from the moment he heard the news. "I should have killed the son of a bitch," he growled. "If they'd paid me enough, I'd of done it."

This was going to be delicate. It was only a suspicion but he remembered the way Medaris had fought that night, the hate in his eyes when he'd left him standing in his own blood in that parking lot in front of the burning hangar. God, that was a good rumble, and easy money too. Puckett had put a video camera in the air vent of Medaris's clean room days before, watched everything going on. He knew when everybody had left and Jack was left behind alone. He would have waited for him to leave too, but it looked as if he was staying the night. It had been bad luck when they'd arrived the same time Jack had closed and locked the door. Things had gotten messy real fast after that. Puckett shrugged at the memory. Things tended to get messy often in Puckett's particular business.

He dialed the pager of the customer who'd paid for the MEC gig. When he got the reply, he used the code that required a physical meeting between him and the Man. He always thought of them as the "Man," no matter who they were. None of this needed to go over the phone, and they didn't need to meet in an office that might be under surveillance. They had a place. Puckett required it of each of his customers. He'd meet the "Man" at the designated place, tell him of his suspicions, see what he wanted him to do.

Puckett put down the phone receiver, laughed, and rubbed his hands. *Damn!* If he was right, this one could turn into one helluva payday!

Postinsertion Checklist (3)

Columbia

To Jack's relief Cassidy blinked back to consciousness. "It hurts, Jack," he admitted between gritted teeth.

"Stay still, Hoppy," Jack said as he snipped a final fragment of blood-soaked material away. He looked at the wound. It was a ragged cut but didn't appear to be very deep. If Jack could get the bleeding stopped—it appeared already to be slowing—then Cassidy should be fine, a little sore, perhaps, but capable of flying the shuttle.

Jack heard High Eagle grunt, trailing away to a sigh. "Medaris, I need the toilet," she admitted shamefacedly.

"Better take care of the woman, Jack," Cassidy said, trying to smile but ending up grimacing, sucking in a breath.

Jack touched his pilot on his shoulder. "Be right back." He pulled himself over to Virgil, who was stretched out on his back beside the hatch, holding his stomach. He had his eyes tightly closed. "Virgil?"

"I'm sick, sir. Sick to death." The big man wracked a sob into a plastic vomitus bag. He looked up, his eyes nearly swollen shut. "What happened to Hoppy?"

"An accident with your pistol. Damn, that was a dumb thing to do, bringing a gun on board. Why'd you do it?"

"Don't know. Thought we might need it. I'm sorry, boss."

Jack gripped the man's shoulder. "All right. Hoppy's going to be fine. Rest. I'll get back to you later." Jack tore away a cue card Velcroed to the bulkhead and used it as a guide to deploy the waste-control-system curtain and open the necessary valves. When a shadow fell on him, he saw High Eagle hovering overhead, her eyes filled with anxiety. "Will you hurry up?" she hissed.

As Jack cranked open the final valve, he pointed out the obvious. "You have to get out of your suit," he said.

"No problem." She already had most of the zippers undone and quickly peeled the orange outer shell off. She wore a white coolant suit underneath. She flew past Jack, nearly kicking him in the face, and snapped the curtain shut.

"Don't be too long," he cautioned. "Virgil needs it next."

"You and *Virgil* can go to hell" was her muttered reply.

Jack heard the sound of Velcro patches being urgently ripped away, and then her coolant suit came sailing over the curtain. He looked at the soggy garment in disbelief. She was obviously a woman used to having someone else pick up after her. He grabbed the suit and stuffed it into a plastic bag retrieved from the waste control locker. He heard the WCS curtain being drawn and looked over his shoulder. Penny came out, wearing a pair of panties and a skimpy bra. She caught him staring at her. "What the hell are you looking at?" She crossed her arms over her ample chest. "I thought I'd be with an all-female crew," she snarled, "instead of freaking spacejackers." Then, as Jack watched, her face turned a deathly shade of green and she started gulping.

He flew up beside her and handed her a vomitus bag. She buried her face in it. "Do you have anything else to wear?" he asked. The heaters were off-line and the middeck was chilly. She nodded, pointed vaguely toward the lockers. "Get into some clothes."

"Screw you," she barked, pulling her face out of the bag. Nevertheless, she drifted to the lockers, began to unlatch one Jack hoped held her personal gear. He headed back to his pilot.

Cassidy grimaced when Jack placed a gauze pad on the wound and applied pressure. "Sorry, Hoppy."

"Hurts, Jack," the pilot whispered.

Jack unlatched the medical kit. Inside it were vials of morphine and syringes. He started to prepare a morphine syringe and Cassidy, seeing it, nodded eagerly. "Yeah, I need that."

"Hold the pad," Jack said. Cassidy meekly moved both his hands to his thigh while Jack prepared the syringe.

"Jack?" Cassidy coughed. "I was a great pilot. You know that, don't you?"

"You still are, Hoppy. That's why I hired you."

Cassidy grimaced. "Will you tell my son? Tell him I was a great pilot. Don't let his mother make him hate me."

"You'll tell him yourself, you old fart," Jack said.

"Please, Jack."

"I'll tell him."

"Thanks. . . ." He coughed quietly and then was silent.

Jack pushed the syringe, saw a spurt of liquid from the needle, and turned back to Cassidy. The pilot's eyes looked like blue chips of glass. His mouth hung agape and tiny globules, like red beads that had come unstrung from a necklace, trickled from it in a thin line. "Hoppy!" Jack stuck the syringe into the padded cover on the wall and pressed Cassidy back against the airlock. "Virgil, I need your help!"

The curtain to the WCS opened and Virgil, his face shiny with sweat, pulled hand over hand to Jack.

"Hold him still."

Virgil pinned Cassidy against the bulkhead. Jack unzipped Cassidy's coveralls, unbuttoned the shirt underneath. He felt down his chest, across his stomach, and then along his right side. He pulled back his hand. It was covered with blood. "Dear God," Virgil said, seeing the blood.

Jack pulled the pilot's coveralls back. Then he saw it, a nearly circular puncture wound. Only a small amount of blood oozed from it, a thick scarlet paste. But it was deep. "Dammittohell, Hoppy," Jack muttered, finding no pulse.

Jack wedged himself between a seat and the wall to gain some stability, got his hands crossed on Cassidy's chest, pushed, once, twice. Red beads spurted from Cassidy's mouth with each push. Virgil moaned, put his head to one

side, reached with one hand for another vomitus bag stuck
in his back pocket. Jack heard High Eagle retching. He kept
compressing Cassidy's chest—ten times—then moved up to
give the pilot mouth-to-mouth. He opened the pilot's
mouth, pulled his tongue out. Droplets of Jack's sweat, sparkling from the sunlight streaming white-hot through the
hatch porthole, floated off his forehead in a spray. A big glob
of blood stuck in the open aperture of Cassidy's mouth. If
he blew in it, Jack knew he'd force the blood into his pilot's
lungs. He drew back, suddenly overwhelmed. It was a
nightmare.

"Boss," Virgil said, pushing his head in close. Jack could
smell the vomit on his engineer's breath. "Hoppy's dead. I
can feel it. He's gone. God bless him."

Jack knew Virgil was right. Another piece of shrapnel, or
perhaps the bullet itself, had probably punctured one of the
pilot's lungs. Cassidy had drowned in his own blood. Jack
pushed back to consider the situation. They had to land
eventually. When they did, *Columbia* would hit the atmosphere, slashing into the air at five miles per second. Without a pilot no one would survive the resulting fireball. There
seemed only one chance for survival: Call Houston and beg
to be brought in on autopilot.

Executive Orders
Building 1, Johnson Space Center

Bonner pushed past engineers and technicians as he came
out of the elevator. He was trying with little success to will
himself calm. A secretary carrying a cup of coffee came out
of one of the small assistant director's offices, saw him, and
ducked back inside. She barely registered on his radar
screen. His mind had already sorted through the probable
passage of events on Launch Complex 39-B, the likely circumstances aboard the shuttle, and several courses of action
to control the situation. The hardest part would be to get

through the next twenty-four hours, not because of the contingency that now existed in space but because of the response from those who were nominally over him. They'd be panicky, and confused, and angry, probably all at once. *Vanderheld.* The vice president was Bonner's real worry. He would probably try to use this situation to further his cutbacks at NASA. In the outer sanctum of his office Lily nervously handed him a fistful of yellow call notes. He rapidly sorted through them, throwing them one by one to the floor. "The vice president," he breathed. "What did he say?"

"He asked what happened, Frank. I had to tell him as best I knew. It's all over the television anyway," she said defensively.

Bonner pursed his lips, nodded. "Call him back." He opened the big oak door that barricaded his office, then walked to his desk, stared at the opposing wall covered with framed awards, medals, all attesting to his dedication to NASA and JSC. He could see them all being taken down, everything thrown away. There was no doubt that this hijacking, or whatever it was, was going to land on his back. JSC was ultimately responsible for manned spaceflight in the United States. JSC and its director were going to take the blame unless . . . unless he could come up with a plan, something so grand and glorious everyone would forget the screwup.

The telephone rang. "Yes, sir," he said, and then lapsed into nervous silence while he listened to the vice president of the United States.

It surprised Bonner that there was little urgency or anger in Vanderheld's voice as he got straight to the point. "In the absence of a NASA administrator, Frank, the President has put me in charge as the chair of the Space Council," he said. "It is not a situation I relish but I will do my best. I will, of course, need your support."

"You have it, Mr. Vice President," Bonner replied, keeping his voice level. Lily brought in a cup of coffee, black, and retreated to the outer sanctum.

"This is bad, Frank. I've worried about another *Challenger* for years."

"Mr. Vice President, this is no *Challenger*, but there are always risks in spaceflight," Bonner said, working hard to keep emotion from his voice. Everything needed to seem calm, situation under control: the NASA way. Bonner knew Vanderheld didn't care a whit about shuttle safety anyway. He was just looking for an excuse to ground them. But it was difficult to be angry with him. He was an American institution, a man who had made a career of trying to help the poor and afflicted in the country. The legislation he had sponsored had always been for that overarching goal: the care of the people who needed it the most.

Bonner leaned into the receiver. He'd heard the vice president was a little deaf, sometimes forgot his hearing aid. "We inspect every component of the shuttles before launch. I don't know how we could possibly make them any safer."

"You don't have to tell me how NASA does business," Vanderheld said lightly. "I've known every NASA administrator there's been since the very beginning, heard all their spiels. All I know is, I think the shuttle's a cranky old beast."

"Sir, we have tried-and-true methods of ensuring shuttle safety," Bonner said, determined not to get angry.

"But something certainly went wrong this morning, didn't it?"

"That was a foul-up at the Cape, sir. Houston isn't in charge of Kennedy."

"Oh, I know that, Frank." The old man chuckled. "But pointing fingers won't help us, either, will it?"

Bonner flushed at the accusation but held his tongue. He changed the subject to one he could control. "Mr. Vice President, we believe that one of the men who perpetrated this crime was wounded prior to launch. We also observed that *Columbia* was steered into a different orbit than what we had programmed. It seems these hijackers know something of the shuttle."

"An inside job?"

You'd like that, wouldn't you? Bonner thought. "There are many people across the country and the planet who know all about how our shuttles operate, sir."

"I understand," Vanderheld said, and then paused. "Frank, I believe we have a military situation on our hands. These are likely terrorists aboard. I'm going to consult with the Air Force."

Bonner almost came out of his chair. "Mr. Vice President, *Columbia* is NASA property!"

"The Air Force has many assets that might be useful in this situation," Vanderheld replied blandly.

"I'd like to go on record opposing bringing in the Air Force on this," Bonner said. His voice sounded shrill even to him, but it was all he could do. The Air Force had tried unsuccessfully for years to take over the shuttle program. They still had hope of creating their own astronaut corps, their own spacecraft. If NASA stumbled during the hijacking, this could be their foot in the door.

"Frank, you can write your protests but it won't do any good. The President is with me on this. Now I'm afraid I have to go. The President is getting ready to leave for Iraq and I want to see him off. Keep trying to determine the facts. I have called a meeting of the Space Council in the morning at Camp David to discuss this event. I want you to be prepared to brief the attendees on all you know by then."

"All right, sir," Bonner said dejectedly. "If that's what you want."

"My decision on the Air Force is nothing personal, you understand. It doesn't reflect my opinion of your capabilities."

"Yes, sir, I do understand."

After he hung up, Bonner sat quietly. He had no doubt

the media was going to make a circus of this, calling the
Columbia hijack a bloody disaster for NASA. He felt help-
less, impotent. How could he fight Vanderheld? How could
anyone expect him to? When it was learned that the Air
Force was taking charge, he was certain the agency, and
especially JSC, would become the laughingstock of the nation. Vanderheld had helped to kill *Apollo*. He'd retired
Columbia. Now he was leading the charge in a NASA disaster. God only knew what the old man might do!

He thought about the Rawhide, wondered if he could
hide out there for a while to think. Then he dismissed the
idea. That was the first place the media would look for him.
Everyone in Houston knew that he regularly held court in
the grungy old bar just outside the center's gate. JSC employees who could not see him during regular working
hours could find him there nearly every night, in the corner
he'd staked as his own, nursing his Jack D.

Oddly enough, it had been mostly astronauts who had
sought him out at the Rawhide, saw that his bright red
Porsche with its distinctive license plate—JSC-1—was outside, then sat with him amid the smell of stale beer and
crushed peanut shells, and told him, over the constant blare
of a television switched to sports, of things he knew he'd
never get to see for himself, of the awesome power of the
shuttle engines kicking them in the butts as they were
shoved into space, of the orange external tank breaking away
from the shuttle, tumbling like a gigantic dead leaf falling
from an impossibly high tree. They told him of what it was
like to float in zero gravity, what they felt when they looked
through the view ports and saw the planet, an endless blue-
and-white marble, rolling beneath them, how awestruck
they were and sometimes even frightened by its immensity.
Bonner heard them, envied them, and sometimes he rewarded them, finding them a position on a crew, or a commander's job. Other times, according to his whim, he
didn't. Sometimes, because he didn't like their looks or

they'd said something he didn't like, he made certain they never flew again. It was the chance they took when they took the Rawhide route.

A few times, when it was clear she was willing, Bonner took a woman astronaut home with him from the Rawhide, and bedded her with a minimum of conversation and foreplay, just a scrambling, grunting, violent coupling as if he were giving her some of his power quickly before he changed his mind. He never believed the women were with him for anything more than advancement of their careers. While he watched them from his bed, they usually told him what they wanted while they climbed back into their jeans to leave. The women had about the same percentage of success for their gift of sex as the men and women who told him their stories at the Rawhide.

Bonner kept pondering his situation. Let the Air Force try its hand at solving the hijacking, he decided. They'd make a mess of it, one way or the other. He'd seen their heavy-handed clumsy attempts in space fail before. Bonner crossed to the window, looked at the *Saturn*. A glimmering of a plan was forming. He knew how to get his shuttle back after the Air Force screwed up. All he'd need was a few volunteers. This could yet be NASA's finest hour.

Postinsertion Checklist (4)
Columbia

Jack had made his decision. He had no pilot but he didn't need one until landing and that was days ahead. There was time to come up with a solution. He peered through the cockpit window. *Columbia* was in a vacuum sea on a tether of gravity, her nose straight ahead, her back turned to earth, streaking through nothing at five miles a second. She was swinging into nightfall again, arcs of crimson, pink, and azure outlining the curved horizon of the bright blue planet below. Jack broke away from the view and began to hustle from panel to panel, throwing switches according to the postinsertion checklist. The first thing he needed to do was configure the software needed to activate the shuttle's life-support and power systems. If he didn't get the air circulation system going, they wouldn't last another hour.

Before he got far, Penny stopped him. "Listen to me!" she growled. "I need to know at least this: Are you going to kill me?" Her long black hair, pulled back into a ponytail, coiled behind her, forming what appeared to be a question mark.

Jack's mind had been clicking ahead, figuring out what he'd need to do to fix things, get back on track. At first her question didn't even register. Gradually, it formed in his mind but it didn't make any sense so he chose to ignore it. "Can you throw switches?" he asked her instead.

She looked at him as if he were mad. "Do you think I'm a complete idiot?"

"I need some help throwing some switches according to the postinsertion checklist," he said.

"Why should I do that?"

"Do you want to stay alive?"

"I want you to land this bucket of bolts and let me the hell off."

Jack reflected for a moment that she'd probably be sorry if he tried. He decided to suggest an alternative. "Will you clean up Hoppy's blood while I activate the shuttle systems?" Then he realized she didn't know the circumstances. "I didn't kill him. It was an accident."

"You didn't know the gun was loaded, right?" She glared at him, then seemed to relax. She had an interesting face, Jack thought; full lips, big brown eyes with long lashes, fine aquiline nose, and the most perfect skin he had ever seen. She wasn't beautiful, not by traditional standards, but her face commanded your attention, made you want to study it, an exotic and at the same time elegant face, though a bit

puffy, he noted, from the fluid shift caused by microgravity.
"Are you staring at me?" Penny asked.

"No," he lied. "I'm just waiting for you to make up your
mind. Sometime today would be nice."

"It's all right. I'm used to people staring at me."

"I wasn't staring. Are you going to help or not?"

"All right. I'll clean it up," she relented. "But only because I don't want to breathe it."

"There are some absorbent wipes in one of the lockers,"
Jack said. "Look on the labels and you'll find them. Also, get
a surgeon's mask and latex gloves out of the same drawer.
They'll protect you."

"I know what I need," High Eagle snapped. "I don't
need you to tell me everything."

"Glad to hear it. In the meantime I need to get *Columbia* activated."

"What happens then?" she asked.

"We'll have air and heat and guidance—"

She shook her head, exasperated. "God, you're so damn
literal! I mean what happens to *me*?"

Jack was confused. "In what way?"

"Forget it," she grumbled, and flew off.

Jack watched her for a moment, saw that she was opening the correct drawer for the absorbent tissue and surgeon's
mask, and then went to check Virgil. He was curled up.
"Sorry, boss. I've never been so sick in my life."

Jack patted him on the shoulder. "You'll live, Virg. A few
hours from now you'll be fine."

"Don't have a few hours," Virgil mumbled. "We got to
get *Columbia* activated. I got to do my part."

"Your part is to stay very still. High Eagle's helping me."

Virgil opened a single eye. "What did you tell her?"

"That we're running a few tests. Then we'll land."

"Boss, you better think about that. She needs to know the
truth."

"If I tell her, God only knows what she might do. I need

her hands, Virgil. They're all I've got right now." Jack opened the medical kit, selected a hypodermic needle, and filled it from one of the bottles within. He punched the needle into Virgil's arm. "Phenergan," he said. "It'll settle your stomach, but the only real cure is time. I'll start activation. You'll snap out of this quicker if you just stay quiet."

Virgil squeezed his eyes closed. "This ain't gonna work. Without Hoppy, how can we do this?"

"Nothing's changed. I can land the shuttle if I have to."

"No, boss . . ."

Jack pulled out a sleeping bag, wrapped Virgil in it, and Velcroed him to the wall. Then he gently placed Cassidy in another bag; saw to it that his face was covered. He hung him on the airlock Velcro tabs. It was all he could do for his pilot until he had some more time. He heard a thumping noise and turned to see Penny awkwardly moving around the cabin, armed with paper towels, trying to catch the blood droplets. She was kicking as if she were underwater and kept bouncing against the bulkheads. As he watched, she hit her elbow on the panel of switches in front of the food dispenser. "Ouch!" she griped, vigorously rubbing her elbow, which sent her into another awkward flight. She was muttering curses. Jack thought she had a most remarkable knowledge of them. "Make slow movements," he told her as he stabbed her with a hypo in the shoulder. "And don't kick."

"Hey!" She gasped, but he held her still by clutching her arm with a single powerful hand.

"Medicine," he said. "It'll ease your stomach."

"Jesus. You almost broke my arm," she muttered after Jack had withdrawn the needle. But she kept working, trying to catch the blood. "This damn stuff is everywhere," she complained.

"You're doing fine," Jack said. "When I get the environmental system activated, the rest of it will be absorbed into the filters."

She turned, her hand on one of the chairs. "Let me see. I'm just checking here. I did tell you to go to hell already, didn't I?"

For a reason he couldn't quite fathom, Jack liked to banter with this woman. "Yes, but I don't have the time right now."

She arched a well-plucked eyebrow. "You might as well put on your asbestos underwear because the goddamn Pentagon is probably right now trying to figure out how to blast you there."

"As long as we're on this shuttle together, where I go, you go," Jack pointed out.

"Screw you!" she snapped.

"Great comeback." He smiled despite himself.

She flushed. "You're a dead man, Medaris."

Jack heard Virgil groan. He had another plastic bag to his mouth. The sight of his pitiful SMET gave Jack an idea. "Would you mind looking after Virgil?" he asked her. "You're a doctor, right? You agreed to the Hippocratic oath and all. I believe you have to do it."

Penny crossed her arms. "I don't have to do anything. I'm not a medical doctor. As far as I'm concerned, *Virgil* can puke his guts out before I help him."

Amused, Jack watched while High Eagle began to rotate, the action of her crossing her arms causing her to involuntarily demonstrate the law of conservation of angular momentum. It was the same principle that made figure skaters spin. He started to point that out to her but thought better of it. "Then what kind of doctor are you?" he asked. "I suppose we can safely eliminate anything to do with human compassion and care for your fellowman."

She grabbed a handrail, stopping her spin. "My PhD's in biology. And what the hell are you grinning about?"

"Virgil's a good man, Dr. High Eagle. He has a wife and a little daughter. He's never hurt anyone in his life. He didn't mean for you to get caught up in this and neither did I."

Penny looked at the big technician, still softly coughing into the plastic bag. She shrugged. "Skip the sob story," she said. "I'll check on your friend."

"Thanks."

"You're not welcome."

An hour later Penny's stomach had calmed and her bladder was back to normal. She was starting to think clearer too. She decided to try to convince Medaris again to land the shuttle. She found him in the commander's seat. As soon as she got close, he turned and looked quizzically up at her. But Penny didn't look back. She was staring through the cockpit window. She pulled herself to the pilot's seat. "My God . . ." she whispered. Where there should have been only stars and the blackness of deep space, there was the enormous orange external tank, still firmly attached to *Columbia*. Even with her limited knowledge of the space shuttle, she knew this was not normal. "Why is the tank still attached?"

"We need it for what we have in mind," he said, his hands busy throwing switches.

"What do you have in mind?"

He uncovered a plastic checklist and began to throw more switches. "We're going to conduct top secret tests in the upper atmosphere. The ET has a storage volume in its base. There's some special equipment there we'll be using."

Penny's bladder chose that moment to strike again. "I don't believe you!" she declared over her shoulder as she headed back down to the WCS.

"After getting to know you, it is an opinion," he called after her, raising his voice as she receded, *"that doesn't surprise me!"*

* * *

It was probably a few minutes but it seemed like only seconds to Jack before High Eagle was back. "Why did you murder Cassidy?" she demanded.

"It was an accident," he said irritably. "High Eagle, I don't have time to talk to you right now." He was inside the difficult procedure required to open the cargo bay doors. They had to be open to release the heat generated by the fuel cells, the devices that provided the shuttle her electrical power. To leave the doors closed could cause the fuel cells to rupture, a catastrophic failure. Jack rushed through the procedure. He wanted to get into the cockpit and take a star sight so he could set the inertial module units to tell *Columbia* exactly where she was.

Penny grabbed his leg, hanging on determinedly. "Call Houston," she grunted. "Tell them to bring us in."

Jack gave up trying to reach a switch on an overhead panel, and unwound her. He watched her wrap herself in a defensive ball. Too tired to worry with her, he moved her into the center of the cabin, threw the switch he needed, and moved on to the next panel. Out of the corner of his eye he saw her unwrap and try to reach a handrail. When she couldn't, she yelled at him: "Hey, no fair, you jerk!"

Jack grabbed another procedure manual and soared past her, dodging her hands as he went by. He snagged a handrail, stopped, and considered her. "If I move you so you can hold on to a handrail, will you promise to leave me alone?"

"No way!" She pursed her lips and blew as hard as she could, her cheeks puffing out from the effort. She was trying to blow her way across the deck to where she could grab something. Jack marveled at her effort, shrugged, helped her to a handrail, and kept working.

When she finally managed to snag a handrail, Penny fled down the hatch, into the middeck. "Hey!" she yelled from there. "I'm going to throw switches and stop you!"

Jack wearily went to the hatch to see what she was doing.

She was getting tiresome. If only she'd help, just a little. "Stop me from what?" he demanded.

"Whatever it is you're doing," she said.

"Well, one of the things I'm doing is making sure the fuel cells don't blow up. You sure you want to stop that?"

"What I want is to get back on the ground. Call Houston. I'm going to throw these switches if you don't."

Jack gave up, came down into the middeck area, still carrying his loop of plastic checklist cards. He got a whiff of her and his nose involuntarily wrinkled. "You need to clean up. Just getting out of your diapers wasn't enough."

He hadn't meant to insult her, only to point out the obvious. She flushed and crossed her arms in front of her, sending her into a tumble. "Damn you!" she snapped.

"If you used up all the wet wipes, there's some liquid disinfectant soap and towels in locker twelve-E," he said, wondering what she was so mad about. Then he got back to his switches. Thirty minutes later he was ready to unlatch the doors. They turned on their gears as advertised, opening the bay to the vacuum. He could almost feel the heat from the fuel cells being dissipated. He pulled himself head-first through the hatchway. So far he hadn't felt even a twinge of SAS. He'd been a scuba diver most of his adult life, spent a lot of time on rocking dive boats, and hadn't been sick there either. He was one of the few lucky ones. In fact, weightlessness seemed to suit him. He did a neat somersault and, without even looking, hooked a footloop with his white-socked toe. He stopped long enough to check Virgil. "How about it, Virg?"

Virgil kept his eyes tightly closed. "Ain't there yet, boss." He opened one eye and saw the filled sleeping bag beside him. "Hoppy?"

"Yes."

Before Jack could get back to the flight deck, Penny took the opportunity to tackle him again. She smelled as if she had taken a bath in disinfectant. Jack calmly peeled her off and then left her again stranded in midair. He watched her huff and puff as if she were blowing out a hundred candles on a cake. Using lung power as propulsion was interesting, if mostly ineffective. Still, he had to admire her tenacity. "If you don't stop this, I'm going to tie you up," he warned.

"Are you going to tell me what this is all about?" she demanded.

"I did already. We have a contract to accomplish some top secret tests with *Columbia*."

"That's the biggest lie I've ever heard," she called after him.

Jack studied a set of plastic cue cards, selected one, and soared back to the flight deck. A few minutes later Penny came after him again. She crashed into him, sending them both into a spiraling zero g dance. She grabbed a handrail, but her feet swung up and her forehead smacked into a glass view port. *"Oww! Damnittohell!"*

Jack righted himself and took her by her arm to turn her around to face him. He inspected her. He could see a red spot on her forehead, but no real damage had been done. "You've got to move slowly—like this," he told her, demonstrating with the handrails. "Keep at least a hand on something all the time. And watch your head. It's just like scuba diving inside a shipwreck. Have you ever done that?"

She seemed to be searching his eyes, as if she was going to learn something from them. "Do you have any idea who you've kidnapped?" she finally asked.

"You didn't answer my question," he said, tiredly. "Have you ever been wreck diving?"

She bumped her head on the ceiling. "Owww! Does visiting the *Titanic* count?"

"Were you in a submarine?"

"Of course!"

"Then it doesn't count." He flew easily to a bulkhead, turned, and came back, hooking a footloop with his toe to show her how to do it. "See? It's easy."

"Skip the Peter Pan lessons, okay?" she said crossly.

Jack needed to get back to work. He was far behind the planned timeline. He ran his index finger down a card, then looked up at a panel and threw some switches. "If I give you one of these cue cards, do you think you could find the correct panel, throw the switches required?" It was worth another try.

She drew herself up, at least as much as she could considering she was hanging at an angle to the deck. "I already told you, I'm not going to help you."

"Suit yourself." Jack had pulled some half-glasses from his coveralls and looked over them at her.

"Look, I know I'm excess baggage here. You killed Cassidy. Are you going to kill me?"

Jack understood. If he'd been in the woman's situation, he might have wondered the same thing. "Hoppy was working with us. He . . . accidentally dropped a pistol. It went off and a ricochet got him."

"Liar!" she spat. "Tell me the truth."

Logical answers didn't seem to work with her. "I don't know. I might throw you out of the hatch if you don't let me work."

"Stay away from me," she commanded, flying over to another panel, "or I'll throw these switches!"

He peered at her and then the panel her hand was over. "Please don't," he said. "It would be a disaster."

She drew her hand away. "Why? What would happen?"

"Our food would be cold. Those switches control power to the galley."

She glowered. "You think you're so damn smart, don't you?"

Jack sighed, got back to work, but he did so with a lighter heart. The woman was at least amusing and so ignorant of shuttle systems, she was harmless. He didn't hear her moving below so he assumed she had gone into a pout. It was a bad assumption.

SMC, JSC

CAPCOM Kelly Niven's head snapped up. Sam waved at her. He would handle this. "Penny, this is Houston. My name's Sam Tate, the flight director. Are you all right?"

Her voice came in loud but the transmission was broken, dirty. "Yes. No. What do . . . think? I'm stuck up . . . two hijackers and a dead m . . . I'm speaking from th . . . middeck."

"Who's dead?" Sam asked.

"Hop . . . sidy. They may have . . . him. . . . says it was an accident. I don't know."

"Cassidy? He wasn't on the crew. He's not even an active astronaut."

He heard the exasperation in her voice. "Don't you think . . . that? Shut up and . . . n. The leader's name . . . medium height, salt-and-pepper hair, got what looks to be . . . crawling up his neck and jaw . . . forty to forty-five years old, not a bad-looking guy. Not as good looking as I bet he thinks he is but . . . a big, heavy guy. Could be John Goodman's twin. His . . . Virgil . . ."

Tate keyed the mike. "What are they doing now?"

". . . postinsertion activation checklists. By the way, the external tank is still attached . . . supposed to be, is it?"

Sam looked at his assistant Flight, Jim Crowder, who in turn gave him a thumbs-up. "Confirmed," he said. After main engine cutoff, MECO, *Columbia* was supposed to go into a five-mile dive, a roller coaster ride designed to push the ET to a splashdown in the Indian Ocean. According to the telemetry *Columbia* had not followed her standard internal software, instead climbing smoothly into a high 550-mile orbit with her ET still firmly attached.

"A patch?" Sam guessed.

"Yeah. Somehow, someway, somebody sent them a god-damned software patch," Crowder growled.

Sam keyed the mike. "We know about the ET, Penny. Did they say why they're aboard?"

"They haven't . . . with me . . . told me something but . . . all I can tell you now is that Jack's checking . . . know what he's doing."

Sam's brow knitted. "How is it you're allowed to talk?"

Sam strained to hear but there was only a hiss emanating from his headset. He looked down into the control room. Niven shook her head. "Penny, this is Houston," Sam tried. "Do you hear me? Are you all right?"

There was a moment more of silence and then a man's voice came down over the air-to-ground loop. "She's fine, Hou . . ." the man said, static cutting him off. Sam strained to hear the voice.

"We're all fine except for . . ." the voice continued. "He deserves a memorial service at least. He . . . great American hero. Remember . . . might hear over the next couple of days. *Columbia*, out."

"*Columbia*," Sam said. "This is Houston. *Columbia*, answer, dammit!"

"They're gone, Flight," Commtech said.

Sam lowered his head, resisted another kick to his poor battered chair. "Dammittohell in a handbasket," he muttered.

Columbia

Jack tucked the headset in his belt. "Cute," he said over his shoulder as he opened a middeck locker. "Most of what we said probably was broken up. The Ku-band antenna isn't aimed properly yet."

Penny grabbed a handrail. "I can tell you're tired, Medaris. You're not going to be able to pull this off. Give it up. Talk to Houston. They might be able to land us automatically."

Jack didn't reply but opened a locker door marked

SAREX—*Space Amateur Radio Experiment.* "While I set this up, how about stowing those seats?"

She started to argue but he held up his hand in tired supplication. "Just do it, High Eagle. The stowage procedure is in a pouch on the back of the chair." He patted the panel in front of him. "This is a shortwave set. In ten minutes, maybe less, I'll have it ready. Then, I promise, you'll get some answers."

Penny went to the seats and started unlatching them. *At least she's got some mechanical ability,* Jack thought, and then pulled the drawer out of the SAREX locker and unstowed a laptop computer from another locker. By the time she had finished strapping the seats to the wall, he was keying in a message, the words appearing in orange letters on a flat panel screen.

ON ORBIT. ACTIVATION PROCEEDING.

There was a whir of the diskette in the laptop and then the muffled sound of the dits and dots of a code. Jack looked at his watch. In a moment the screen went black and then a message appeared:

RECVD. NEWS ON TV IS SAYING AN UNUSUAL LAUNCH. NO DETAILS YET.

Jack cleared the screen.

CASSIDY WAS KILLED—AN ACCIDENT.

A moment passed, a shocked moment it seemed to Jack.

WILL YOU CONTINUE?

YES. SOMEBODY NEEDS ANSWERS HERE. WE ENDED UP WITH AN UNEXPECTED PASSENGER. TELL HER WE HAVE A CONTRACT. TELL HER ABOUT PLAN D.

Jack hoped Sally would remember what plan D was. It was a cover story.

The laptop whirred.

IDENTIFY.

PENNY HIGH EAGLE.

COOL!

"It's cool, all right," Jack grumbled, and then, seeing that she had pulled herself back to him, gestured at the keyboard. "Well? Go ahead. Ask away."

She cautiously positioned herself in front of the laptop. Her feet scuffled against the deck.

"Use those footloops," he said, pointing.

"Who's on the other end?" she demanded, working her feet into the cloth straps.

"MEC Control."

"Meck? What does that stand for?"

"It's another acronym. Medaris Engineering Company."

"Engineering? What kind of engineering?"

"Rocket engineering. Never mind. Hurry up!"

"You don't have to snap my head off!" she snapped.

Jack ached to close his eyes, just for a moment, to let blessed sleep take over. . . . He shook his head, trying desperately to clear his mind, to focus on what had to be done. "I'm sorry, Your Royal High Eagleness"—he sighed—"but I still don't have the Ku-band antenna completely configured yet, mainly because of you hanging off my leg. We'll be out of range soon. Ask your questions."

"This is stupid," she said. "The only question I have is when are we going to land?"

Sighing, he tapped in a question for her.

TELL ME WHAT IS HAPPENING.

"Now watch."
She watched.

THE SHUTTLE COLUMBIA HAS BEEN LEASED BY MEC FOR
THE PURPOSE OF TOP SECRET TESTS.

Penny frowned at the monitor. "What the hell?" Jack
had gone back to his checklist, deliberately ignoring her.
"What kind of tests?"

"Don't ask me," he said, looking up at a control panel,
desperately throwing switches while he had her distracted.
"Ask them."

WHAT KIND OF TESTS?

The laptop whirred.

THE TESTS ARE TOP SECRET. BUT THIS WILL BE YOUR
GREATEST ADVENTURE.

The message stopped. Penny's fingers flew across the keyboard.

CALL NASA FBI CIA AIR FORCE ARMY NAVY MARINES
COAST GUARD SUPERMAN BATMAN AND GET ME DOWN
NOW!!!!!!

"We've gone out of range," Jack said as he went by on his
way to another panel. "We'll catch them on the next pass."

She suddenly launched herself at him, clutching the collar of his coveralls with both hands. "Medaris, I'm telling
you, get me down, *now*!"

He extricated himself, holding her by the shoulder at
arm's length. "Now listen to me, High Eagle. You're here
with us. Neither of us wanted it that way but that's the way it

is and you might as well get used to it. Don't make me tie you up."

She squinted. "If I don't do something, I'm going to start puking again," she confessed.

"You have experiments aboard, don't you? Get busy. Activate them!"

Her eyes widened. "Dammit! I've forgotten FLEA!"

"FLEA?"

"The Feline Lateral Epistemology Attitude experiment! I'm responsible for it!"

"The feline *what?*"

SMC, JSC

Sam took the call on the land line. It had been reported as urgent. Bonner was on the other end. "What's the latest, Sam?" he asked.

Sam related in detail the call from the payload specialist, Penny High Eagle. "According to her the ET is still attached," he finished. "Why that is, I have no idea."

"Care to speculate?"

"I'm too old to speculate," Sam said.

Bonner pressed. "The external tank is empty on orbit, isn't it?"

"Might be a few gallons sloshing around," Sam relented.

"Could they use it to start up the main engines again?"

It was a good question. "I don't think so. Once the pumps are down, they stay down. There's also likely to be ice in the propellant lines."

"What's an empty ET good for, Sam?"

Sam had seen some studies. "There's folks who think you could use an ET to make a space station. Lot of empty volume. Take a hell of a lot of reconfiguring, though."

Bonner was quiet. Likely, Sam thought, he was trying to decide something, needed information, and that's why he'd called. "What are you going to do now?" Bonner asked.

"Sit right here and monitor *Columbia*."

"If you were so ordered, could you do her some damage, foul up her computers, something like that?"

The way Bonner had asked the question, the tone in his voice, Sam was immediately on his guard. "I'd have to check on that," he said, stalling for time. He'd already made up his mind that he wasn't going to be party to anything that was going to do damage to his bird.

"Do it, Sam, and get back to me."

"All right, Frank, I will." When Bonner signed off, Sam slowly lowered the receiver to the base set. "Approximately when the devil makes snowballs," he muttered.

Columbia

Penny dived for a bottom locker and slid out a tray holding a white box with a cooling fan on top. She opened the lid and a slightly dazed black-and-white cat emerged, clutching her arm.

Medaris moved in beside her. His mouth dropped open. "A cat?"

"His name is Paco. He's part of a vestibular acclimation experiment. The principal investigator believed that if a cat could acclimate to zero g, anything could. Sort of a worst case."

"What about food? Is he going to catch mice or what?"

She glared at him. "NASA put plenty of food on board for him, Medaris. You're the uninvited guest here, I believe."

He shook his head, looked her in the eye. "Are you healthy enough to take care of this animal?"

"Don't you worry about me and Paco, ace," she growled. When he rewarded her with a hefty purr, she whispered in the cat's ear, "We'll be just fine, won't we, boy?"

Paco struggled out of her arms and leapt for the hatchway. Medaris followed the cat. "Get off that panel, Paco!" she heard him call. "No, not those switches! Bad cat! Bad! Bad!"

Certain that she was going to get sick again if she didn't get busy with something, she proceeded with the activation of her cell culture experiments, which were supposed to be her reason for being in space. After she put the last sample in the incubator, she got an idea and quietly checked the medical kit. She found it clinging to a filter, the air distribution system sucking everything loose toward it. The kit had a range of drugs, both injectables and oral, some of them potentially lethal. She also found two scalpels. She considered the instruments and then put them back into their holsters. She was prepared to anesthetize the spacejackers if she had to, but she didn't think she could cut them up.

Feeling suddenly very tired, she went to the cockpit, settling into the left seat. She closed her eyes but was startled by Medaris crawling into the seat beside her. His face was drawn by fatigue. "You can sit there," he said. "Just don't touch anything. IMUs are probably already sliding toward an error mode," he muttered. "I'll need the star tracker. No, dammit, I need the COAS." He pointed toward her right knee. "Get that flat plastic plate out for me, okay? It's in that Velcroed cover."

"I refuse to help you in any way," Penny asserted.

He reached across her lap, grumpily jerked the device from its holster, and peered blearily at the cockpit computer monitor. "Strap yourself in," he ordered.

"What are you doing?" she worried, trying to see the computer screen.

"I've called up the maneuver display board for the orbital maneuvering system."

Penny leaned over and looked at his monitor. "You're changing our orbit?"

"Very good, Doctor," he said sarcastically. "Go to the head of your class." When she pushed in closer, he leaned back and looked at her. "How come you're squinting all the time? You need to borrow my glasses?"

She blinked, opened her eyes wide. It embarrassed her

when she was caught. "It's a bad habit," she confessed. "I do it when I'm confused . . . or thinking."

Jack shrugged and went back to the keyboard.

"What are you doing now?"

He let out a long, weary breath. "I'm putting in the engine selection and the trim load." He kept tapping. "Don't forget the external tank mass," he said, apparently to himself. She certainly didn't know what he was talking about. "Burn solution coming up."

Penny was nervously gripping her seat and squinting. She couldn't help it. He looked at her over his glasses. "Relax. I'm just making a little change in delta V to catch up with an old friend. On my mark, ten-nine-eight-seven . . . OMS burn now!"

Penny heard a muffled thunderclap, *Columbia* shuddering her length. The burn lasted for only a few seconds and then abruptly shut down. "IMUs are good," he muttered. "Let's see what the optical alignment sight says. I'll aim it at that little ol' star there." He held the instrument to his eye, turned knobs on its side. "On the money," he said at length. He put the instrument down, rubbed his eyes.

Penny heard a noise above her and then saw Paco on the ceiling, trotting unconcernedly across it, his claws leaving little nicks in the spongy material. Jack gave him an upside-down pat and he promptly ran down his arm into his lap.

Columbia was again moving into nightfall. "Look at that!" Jack pointed as the cat curled up in his lap.

Penny followed his gesture. There were no stars. A full moon had dazzled them away as if it demanded its own velvet backdrop. She turned and was surprised to see Jack had fallen asleep, just like that. Paco had also tucked his head in, was making contented squeezing movements with his two front paws. Except for the whirs and clicks and gurgles of *Columbia*, it was quiet on the flight deck. Outside, the dark line of night swept inexorably toward them. For the first time since the launch, which seemed a hundred years ago, Penny could go anywhere, do anything she wanted. Now was the time to get the medication. She could render both spacejackers unconscious for a very long time, get on the horn, call Houston, and get *Columbia* in on automatic. She could do it. Nothing could stop her. And she might have done it, too, if only she hadn't watched Jack and Paco sleep for just a little longer than she should have, and then fallen completely, utterly asleep herself.

MISSION ELAPSED TIME: 1 DAY
AND COUNTING . . .

The Camp David Conference
Thirty-one Thousand Feet over the Outer Banks, North Carolina

At oh-dark-thirty Ollie Grant had been in a teleconference with John Lakey, chief of the Astronaut Office, and Frank Bonner. The conference was short and to the point. Bonner led the discussion. To just sit and idly watch while hijackers operated the shuttle, he said, was a sacrilege to NASA. He outlined his plan. Lakey said little. Grant enthusiastically endorsed Bonner's bold scheme. It was settled. She was the commander of STS-128. No matter she'd been left behind, it was still her mission, her bird.

Grant screamed off the Cape runway in her T-38 and rocked into the cool dense morning air. An hour later she streaked past Kitty Hawk, throttled back over the Potomac, and landed at Andrews Air Force Base. A sedan with the NASA meatball symbol on its doors waited for her on the tarmac. Lights flashing, its driver sped her out of the airport, heading east to Camp David.

She arrived at the presidential retreat two hours later, just in time for the meeting. She entered the conference room in the Rosewood House and noticed a large picture window that presented a quiet, forested panorama. A bucolic view, she thought, for a team gathered to crisis-manage the hijacking of her space shuttle. She looked around the gathering and saw the Air Force contingent. They waved her over. "Hey, NASA," General Bud Carling called jovially, "come slum with us blue suiters." In a room full of strangers she gratefully took a seat behind him. Carling had been her F-15 wing commander in Germany before she'd received her assignment to NASA. She shook his hand, met the rest of his contingent, a group of nonpilot Space Command commandos. Technically sharp, she assumed, but none of them were up to her standards. If you weren't a pilot, you weren't worth much in her book. "Listen, Ollie," Carling said quietly, leaning in close. "Sorry about all this. No pilot likes to think about somebody else's butt being in his seat."

"Whoever it is is dead meat, Bud," Grant replied, bristling.

"Take it easy, lady," Carling advised. "This is now in the hands of the big boys."

If that was supposed to make Grant feel better, Carling had failed. *The big boys?* He might as well have slapped her in the face. She turned away from him, perused the assembly. Besides the Air Force the group included representatives of the Navy and the Central Intelligence Agency. Bonner sat at the front of the table. He kept snapping his fingers and flunkies kept conferring with him and flying off at a dead run. One of them came back with a muffin, another with a cup of coffee. Bonner was an enigma to Grant. He was a solid engineer and manager. A lot of people at JSC said there would have been no shuttle program, no International Space Station, no astronaut corps, if it weren't for his continuing struggle against NASA's foes. But he could also, on a dime it seemed, turn into a savage adversary of one of his own people. Everyone who worked for Bonner was afraid of him. It got him acquiescence to his commands but it got him little respect and very little loyalty. Then there were the stories from her fellow women astronauts. During some of the late-night bull sessions a few of the women astronauts had admitted they'd gone to the Rawhide, and then let Bonner take them home and climb on top of them. Grant had slugged one of the women who had confessed to having sex with Bonner and said it was going to get her a command position. That wasn't the astronaut corps Grant had signed up to fly with!

Grant caught Bonner's eye and he nodded to her and then crooked his finger. She reluctantly approached him. "If I call on you, go ahead and give your pitch. If I don't, we'll wait for a better time. Do you understand?"

Grant started to argue, thought better of it, and nodded. When she went back to her seat, Carling looked over his shoulder, gave her a sardonic smile. She ignored him. There was nothing funny about any of this. She should have been in space, not cooped up in a cabin on a mountaintop in Maryland.

There was a stir at the door and Grant saw a tall, thin, and nearly bald man enter the room—the veep, as he was popularly known. With a perpetually puffy, pasty face, framed by a smartly cut white beard, Vice President Vanderheld wore a brown corduroy jacket with patches on the elbows. Grant thought he looked more like a friendly old English professor at a junior college than a vice president. Grant recalled that he'd been a senator for practically forever from some western state—*North Dakota*? She wasn't sure—and had taken second place on the ticket after the President's first choice had been knocked off for some obscure campaign finance scandal. Vanderheld apparently was considered safe by the politicos because he had no presidential ambitions of his own. He was too old, for one thing. Most people in his party figured he'd leave when the President did, at the end of his almost assured second term. Still, he was a beloved old guy. Grant remembered a poll she'd seen that named him the most popular man in the government, even more so than President Edwards. A career of passing laws that gave largesse to poor people was obviously a very popular thing; trying to shut down NASA didn't hurt, either, she thought sourly. Still, like everyone, she respected Vanderheld. He seemed to have a conscience, which was more than most politicians had, she supposed.

When Vanderheld finally stopped shaking hands, he eased himself into a seat at the table and tapped the mike in front of him. The few remaining hairs on his head blew wispy and white in the light air from the air-conditioning ducts overhead. "Before we begin, I wish to make a general statement," he said in a surprisingly strong voice. "As you know, the President is preparing to fly to Iraq to broker a peace treaty between Iran and Iraq. This treaty will bring peace and stability to a region of vital strategic interest to the United States. As you may know, I, too, have a high-priority situation on my plate: the Senate vote on the World Energy Treaty next week. WET, along with the end of the war in the Middle East, is required for the continuing prosperity of this country and peace across the world. Now we have this situation, which may divert the people's attention from these two great endeavors."

Vanderheld put on his glasses, scanned the executive summary that each participant around the table had been given. He shook his head, took his glasses off, looked around the table with disgust clearly etched on his face. "President Edwards has given this council the responsibility to address the issue of the hijacked space shuttle. He hasn't asked us to find out how this hijacking happened or why. I know you'd all like to talk about that. So would I."

The assembly laughed. Vanderheld smiled, very briefly, put his glasses back on, and tapped the report. "Like you, I've wondered why in heaven's name would anybody want to hijack a shuttle? What could they possibly want with it? Blackmail, perhaps? Ransom?" He shook his head. "Nothing makes sense. In any case, the Justice Department is looking into that. Our charge is to give the President options on how to bring the space shuttle home, and in short order. So I'm going to need some suggestions." He nodded toward Bonner, who grimly nodded back. "I'd first like Frank Bonner of NASA JSC to bring us up to speed on the situation."

Bonner made his remarks sitting down, his hands flat on the table before him. The situation was unchanged, he droned, since the day before. *Columbia* was in a high orbit,

558 nautical miles, at an inclination of 28.7 degrees. An eyewitness had identified one of the men aboard *Columbia* as former astronaut Craig "Hopalong" Cassidy, who had apparently been shot by one of the hijackers. It was not known why Cassidy was on the launch tower. A garbled conversation with Dr. Penny High Eagle on downlink had established that she was on board the shuttle with probably two or more hijackers and that Cassidy was probably dead. "Mission Control in Houston continues to monitor *Columbia* downlink," Bonner said. "As far as we can determine without communication with whoever is on board, the shuttle is in good shape. We continue our analyses, sir," he said, folding his hands to indicate he was finished. "I will forward you any conclusions we reach as soon as I have them."

Vanderheld acknowledged Bonner's report, told him he'd done a good job, and expressed respect for the employees of NASA. Grant sank deeper into her chair. It was crap, eyewash. The proof of that followed with the next thing Vanderheld said. "Unless somebody can convince me otherwise, I believe this crisis requires a military response. Therefore, I've decided the Air Force should take front and center."

Grant started to rise in protest but Bonner caught her eye, gave her a short, negative cut of his head. She subsided, fuming.

General Carling looked around his assembled colonels and majors and then leaned over his mike. "Well, sir, I guess the question Air Force Space Command needs to ask is what do you want done with *Columbia*? If you want us to shoot her down, we can do that. Well, I take that back. We can blow her up but she won't come down. She'll stay up there until her orbit degrades. That might take some time."

The door opened and Grant saw a man enter. Some members of the group started to rise to greet him, but he used both of his hands to signal them back down. Whoever it was was a sharp dresser, Armani all the way. Grant thought he looked like a fox, sharp faced and cunning. He was also wearing what was clearly a very bad wig. The hair on it was so dense and solidly black that it looked like the fur of a dead animal just come out of a dye vat. "Bernard Sykes," she heard one of the Space Command weenies say. "White House chief of staff." Sykes found a chair directly behind the vice president, a toothy grin on his foxy snout.

"Perhaps you should skip to the bottom line, General," Vanderheld was saying. "What do you recommend?"

"Well, I wouldn't blow *Columbia* up, sir," Carling rasped. "It's pretty valuable American property and we have one of our own aboard."

"Dr. High Eagle," Vanderheld said. Grant seethed, her gut a knot. Neither she nor the astronauts of STS-128, the second all-female shuttle crew in history, had been officially recognized by the gathering. Now they were talking about High Eagle, a mere payload specialist, as if she were the only one of them who mattered!

Grant wanted to get up and make an announcement, get everybody in the room squared away. They just didn't understand. She had ridden her people hard, pushing them through simulation after simulation, honing them for instant response to her orders. Then, without even asking her what she thought about it, NASA headquarters had decided to put a usurper on her crew. Penny High Eagle's presence had completely offended Grant before she'd ever met the woman. As far as Grant was concerned, High Eagle had shamelessly used her ethnicity and sex to capture a string of dubious distinctions—the first Native American woman to go to the South Pole (she had posed topless for photographers at the Amundsen Station), to climb Mount Everest (dragged, Grant was certain, by about a dozen stout Sherpas), to visit the *Titanic* (she had stayed clothed for her submarine ride, at least)—the list seemed endless. Every adventure had resulted in either a book or an article. Although the Astronaut Office in Houston had fought to keep such self-promoters off the shuttle, High Eagle had taken a different approach to get into space, convincing the giant pharmaceuticals that sponsored most of her adventures to purchase her a payload-specialist seat under the flimsy pretext that she would perform a cell culture experiment.

"How about some options, General?" Vanderheld asked, snapping Grant back to the meeting.

Carling had been dithering, consulting with his other officers. "Well, sir, like I said, we can send an ALMV—that's an air-launched minivehicle—and bust the shuttle wide open," he said. "Or, my personal favorite, we can leave *Columbia* alone, wait these guys out."

Vanderheld glared at Carling. "Unfortunately, neither of your options is politically viable, General," he said, his voice dripping with sarcasm. "The press is already out there stirring everybody up. The American people will want this solved in short order without anyone getting hurt. We can't wait and we can't blow the shuttle up. I need something better." The vice president rested his head in his hand. Grant thought he looked tired or maybe he was just disgusted with having to deal with the situation. "Suppose you damage the shuttle with one of your missiles, just enough to make it come down?"

Carling conferred with the colonel behind him. "No, sir, at least not with any certainty. The shuttle and the AMLV are high-energy vehicles traveling at five miles per second. If they hit each other, it's going to be like smashing two eggs together. The crew cabin is pressurized at one atmosphere. You crack that cabin in the vacuum of space, whoever's aboard wouldn't survive. And as I said before, nothing's going to come down. It'll just be debris in orbit. Bodies floating around up there for a long time. Public relations is not my line, but somehow I suspect we would be criticized if that happened."

Vanderheld scanned the room, stopped on Bonner for a moment, and then moved on until his eyes lit on Grant.

"Colonel Grant? My condolences to you and your brave crew. As the second all-woman crew to fly into space, you would have represented this administration's continuing efforts to insure a multicultural and nonsexist society."

What a sack of politically correct shit, Grant thought. She looked at Bonner, who nodded back. This was her moment. She'd better make the best of it. She stood and cleared her throat before speaking. "Thank you, sir. My crew trained long and hard for their flight and would have performed in an outstanding manner." She left it at that. Grant was not a speechmaker. She was a pilot and an engineer. She got right to the point. "One thing you should know is that NASA has the ability to land the shuttle automatically; but the crew aboard must release manual control for the autopilot system to work."

"Is there a way to talk to Dr. High Eagle back-channel?" Dr. Bill Carmichael, the CIA rep, interrupted. He had a degree in aeronautical engineering, Grant recalled.

"High Eagle is a payload specialist—not a real astronaut. She hasn't been trained on shuttle systems, so talking to *her* wouldn't do us a lot of good. But that's not what—"

"Not an astronaut, Colonel?" Carling chuckled, looking slyly over his shoulder. "She's in space, ain't she?"

Grant refused to take Carling's bait. Carling knew that only members of the astronaut corps in Houston were allowed to have the title, a distinction NASA had made for three decades. You could spend a year in space, but if you weren't from NASA Houston, you weren't an astronaut. She took a deep breath, not wanting to get into that, and looked at Vanderheld. "Sir, I propose to take space shuttle *Endeavour*, rendezvous with *Columbia*, board her, and bring her home."

A rumble of voices rose in the room. Vanderheld leaned forward, his rumpled jacket rising off his neck. "Can you do that, Colonel?"

Grant's eyes glittered. "You bet your sweet . . . Yes sir, I can. We've got *Endeavour* on Pad 39-A almost ready to launch."

A woman stirred at the end of the table. "What about *Endeavour*'s payload?" she demanded. "It's a pretty important piece of hardware, a node for the Space Station."

The woman's nameplate identified her as Betty Velasquez, National Science Foundation. Grant had anticipated the question. "We'll put the node in orbit first, ma'am, then rendezvous with *Columbia*. All we need is to give the Cape permission to prep *Endeavour* early and get her off the pad."

Velasquez looked doubtful. "*Aurora* is in a fifty-one point six-degree inclination. *Columbia* is"—she leafed through the executive summary—"twenty-eight point seven degrees. How can you possibly drop the node off at the station and then chase *Columbia*? I doubt that you'd have adequate propellant reserves."

"Yes, ma'am, we're aware of that," Grant said. "We'll drop the node off in a parking orbit. The next shuttle up will rendezvous with it and then move it over to the Station."

"Yes," Velasquez said icily, "delaying the node's arrival by at least several months, and requiring an additional shuttle launch. Every launch of the space shuttle is very important, considering the likely possibility of their not being replaced after they wear out. I thought you of all people would know that, Colonel Grant."

The room fell silent. Grant's cheeks were burning with outrage at Velasquez's tongue-lashing. "I would suggest we start negotiations with the hijackers, Mr. Vice President," the CIA chief Carmichael said, breaking the hush. "If Cassidy was part of their team, and all indications are that he was, they probably can't proceed with their plan without him." He looked at Grant. "Colonel Grant, no one has more admiration for the astronaut corps than I, but I think what you're suggesting is too risky."

"May I suggest a demonstration?" It was the Navy Space Command representative, an admiral whose name tag said his last name was Lockhart. Grant didn't know him. "Don't hit the shuttle with the AMLV but come damn close," he advised. "Shake them up and then demand they let us automatically land the shuttle."

"Won't work," Carling said, pushing back in his chair, clasping his hands behind his head. "It's too fast. They'd never see it unless they happened to be looking out the right window at the right time. Even then it would be a blur."

Vanderheld picked up on the idea. "Could we blow up the missile nearby, General? Just frighten them with it? That might be enough to get them down."

Carling conferred with the colonel behind him again. A major leaned in, added his two cents' worth. "Possibly," Carling said after a minute, "but the energy of the particles released from a detonation would be very high. Any one of them, even one the size of a paint chip, could do fatal damage to *Columbia*."

The colonel furiously whispered into Carling's ear. He nodded. "Colonel Kistler has a suggestion, sir. About a modification we could make. Might work and might get their attention aboard with very little risk."

"All right," Vanderheld said coolly. "Let's hear it."

Grant looked at Bonner. He just sat there. Why wasn't he coming to her defense? The rest of the room was stealing her thunder, pushing NASA into the background. Didn't he care about his own turf? Frustrated, she slowly sat down.

"Some sort of water balloon, sir," Kistler was saying. "Water turns into ice crystals in space. Remember the fireflies John Glenn saw during his *Mercury* flight? Those things were water ice crystals floating alongside his capsule, reflecting in the sun."

Carling pounded the arm of his chair. "The first time he saw Niagara, the second time Viagra!" he hooted, and the Air Force contingent behind him erupted in laughter. Grant seethed. It was almost as if they were laughing at her.

"Sorry, I couldn't resist that," Carling said after the

laughter died. He paused for more whispering in his ear. "We could modify a *Pegasus* rather than an AMLV to do the job. One of those could climb into orbit with *Columbia*, not just whip past on a vertical trajectory. These 'fireflies' could be placed so they're visible, travel along for a while."

Vanderheld turned to Bonner. "Frank, what would NASA think of that idea?"

When Bonner hesitated, Grant leapt to her feet. "Sir, I think my proposal for a rendezvous is the only way to go. But if you decide to make this demo, NASA should do an engineering analysis so we know its predicted effect on the shuttle. We have no idea what ice crystals might do to the tiles, for instance."

Bonner glowered at her but the vice president smiled. "That's fair, Colonel Grant," he said. "Please, by all means, make your analyses. General Carling, unless you hear something from me to the contrary, go ahead with your plan." He turned, looked over his shoulder at Sykes. "Bernie, will the President approve my decision?"

Sykes tilted his head, his foxy eyes turning to slits. "I am certain he will, Mr. Vice President."

"One more thing," General Carling said. "I'd like permission to move a spy satellite close to *Columbia* so that we can keep a visual eye on what's going on. To do that I'll need the assistance of the Defense Intelligence Agency."

The vice president looked over his shoulder. Again, Sykes nodded. "All right, General. I'll make certain you get all the cooperation from the DIA you need."

It was all agreed and the conference was over. Sykes got up, walked over and shook Bonner's hand, leaned over and whispered something in his ear, and then he and the veep walked out together. Bonner stayed in his chair, his shoulders humped up. Grant thought she should go over to him, say something. "Sir . . ."

"You ever interrupt me in a meeting again, Olivia, I'll

have your hide," Bonner said although without any particular rancor.

Straightforward was the only way Grant could operate. "Sir, I think we ought to prep *Endeavour* for a rescue anyway. I have no confidence in this so-called demo."

Bonner watched the others filing out. "Of course we're going to prep *Endeavour*."

"But the vice president didn't give us permission, sir."

"He will, after the Air Force screws this up. Sometimes, when you see your opposition preparing to shoot themselves in the foot, Olivia, you just let them do it. I sincerely doubt the men who hijacked *Columbia* will be impressed by a mere demonstration." Bonner glanced up at her. "Tell me, Colonel Grant, what is your opinion of Penny High Eagle?"

Grant was cautious. "I don't know her very well."

"But you trained with her, didn't you?"

"A little. But mostly she did public relations stuff."

"And you resented that?"

Grant shifted her stance, easing her weight back and forth on the balls of her feet like a boxer ready to deliver a punch. She didn't like being questioned as if she were some rookie astronaut candidate. "I think anyone going into space should attend all the training. High Eagle wasn't interested."

"What would you be willing to do to get *Columbia* back?"

"Whatever it takes."

"Even if someone gets hurt?"

Grant steered around what she knew was a verbal trap, although for what purpose she had no idea. "I hope to design this mission so nobody gets hurt."

Bonner probed. "What if *Columbia* is manned by fanatics, Olivia? They won't give in without a fight."

"My tiger team's working on it now, trying to have a plan for every contingency."

"I would like to see your plan, as soon as possible."

"It'll be ready tomorrow morning. I've scheduled a briefing in your office at ten A.M."

"I want you and your team to come in and tell me what you want to do by midnight."

Grant stood her ground. "I told everybody tomorrow, and even that was pushing it. I can't change it now."

Bonner raised his eyebrows. "You will change it, Olivia, and I will see you in my office at midnight. With your team. With your plan. End of discussion."

Grant opened her mouth to argue. She was the commander of STS-128, her mission, her bird, her team. Then she closed it. She knew Frank Bonner was not above cutting her head off if it suited him. She turned on her heel and got out of the room while she could.

Bonner walked into the Camp David Administration Center to see Bernie Sykes as requested. Sykes waved him to a chair in his office. Bonner sat. "What can Johnson Space Center do for you today, Bernie?"

"Not for me, Frank," Sykes replied. "For the President of the United States. I just work for him."

Bonner was wary. "As do I."

Sykes pushed his thin hands together as if he were praying, tapped the ends of his long fingers on his chin, regarded Bonner. Sykes was known for being crafty, the man who was more than willing to say no for a President who hated to say the word to anybody. "You know I envy you, Frank. Ever since I was a kid I've imagined what it would be like to work for NASA, be part of your great enterprise. I wish I could go to work in your Mission Control today rather than worry about the President's trip to Iraq. It must be a very satisfying thing for you, being in your position."

Bonner nodded but was noncommittal. He didn't believe a word of it anyway. He was being buttered up but he wasn't certain why. "NASA has been my life," he replied blandly.

"During all my years in Washington, and especially in this administration, I've tried to be NASA's champion," Sykes said. "It hasn't been easy, considering Vanderheld's opposition." Sykes shook his head. "That old man's really an ass when it comes to the space program. He just hates it."

Bonner tried to think of what Sykes had done for either NASA or his center but couldn't come up with anything. "JSC is very appreciative of your help, Bernie," he replied.

Sykes folded his arms, leaned forward. "But this shuttle hijack comes at a very bad time. The President leaves for Iraq this afternoon. And then there's WET, the vice president's baby. Vanderheld's an ass about space but he's right about WET. The country needs it."

"I understand," Bonner said, and waited. For all he knew, Sykes was setting a bureaucratic trap for him. Bonner wasn't going to walk into anything. He'd let Sykes do the talking.

"Your astronaut's plan to rendezvous with *Columbia*. Will it work?"

Ah, that was it. Now Bonner thought he knew what Sykes was getting at, why he was there. "It will if we have time to prepare." Bonner had learned over the years never to agree to anything without adding a qualifier.

"I want you to know I personally wanted to let NASA handle this thing from the beginning."

"But you didn't oppose the Air Force in the meeting," Bonner pointed out.

Sykes raised an eyebrow at the retort. "I saw no reason to oppose the veep head-to-head," he said testily. "The President likes the old coot, and wants to give him something to do. Vanderheld *is* head of the Space Council, after all." Sykes tapped the desktop as if waiting for Bonner to respond. When he didn't, he continued. "Frank, I want you to prepare *Endeavour* to get on up there and get the shuttle back. I've already talked to the President about this. He wants to give the Air Force their shot but he wants you to be ready if they fail."

"Ollie Grant and a tiger team in Houston are mapping out the procedures for a rendezvous now," Bonner replied, trying not to sound too eager.

"I should have known you'd be ahead of me," Sykes said, smiling. No matter what facial expression Sykes took, it came out looking crafty, sneaky. Bonner recognized at that moment the sleaziness of the man, his willingness to flatter, to say anything to get what he wanted. "You know, I might have something to say on who is going to be the next NASA administrator," Sykes went on. "If you're able to pull this off, Frank, I think your name will be at the top of the short list."

Bonner sat up. This was unexpected. He was tempted to smile, but then he realized he was in the middle of a negotiation. How far could he push it? He decided to find out. "Bernie, I would love to be the NASA administrator. It's something I've wanted my entire professional career. But there's something I want even more."

"Go ahead," Sykes said cautiously.

"When I get her back, I want *Columbia* to stay on flight status. I need all my shuttles."

Sykes showed no surprise at the idea. "I'll see what I can do. You have my word on that. Vanderheld might be circumvented, especially if WET passes and he's assigned to the energy council it mandates. That would probably take up all his time and focus. A good NASA administrator might be able to wheel and deal, especially with me on his side."

Bonner stood, anxious to get going, to get the rendezvous plan moving even faster. "I'll let you know how we're doing," he said.

Sykes stood as well, reached out to shake Bonner's hand. "Remember, if there's a reward for success, there are penalties for failure."

Bonner nodded. "I fully understand."

"Frank, get the President his shuttle back," Sykes said.

"Yes, sir. I will," Bonner replied, and headed out the door.

The DODO
Defense Intelligence Agency, Fort Meade, Maryland

Dr. Clay Corbin, a dapper little man who always wore a black three-piece suit with a plaid vest—his one nod away from strict conformity—was in charge of the DIA satellite communications center and had it humming with excited activity. He was having the best time of his life. At the order of the President of the United States he was moving one of DIA's Keyhole sats to keep an eye on the hijacked shuttle *Columbia*. Corbin was justifiably proud of the Keyholes, giant spy satellites with optics that allowed them to see objects as small as a baseball from orbit. Their capabilities included the transmission back to earth of both still photographs and video. The Keyholes were also capable of quickly changing orbit and altitude with built-in maneuvering and guidance systems. Ground controllers only had to send up a command and the Keyholes would use star trackers to confirm their positions, compute the orbital delta solution, and within seconds begin their move. Since the Soviet Union had collapsed, two of the DIA's five Keyholes in orbit had been put into reserve, meaning they had essentially been powered off except for health and status communications every twenty-four hours. Corbin had chosen Keyhole 13, a reserve sat placed in orbit by the shuttle *Discovery*, to go after *Columbia*.

Corbin had established communications between Fort Meade and Eglin Air Force Base. Eglin's powerful radar systems could track anything in orbit. Since the radar was in Florida, the decision had been made to rendezvous the Keyhole with *Columbia* as the shuttle passed over Mexico. That would guarantee a clear radar view.

"We're still maneuvering," Corbin announced tersely on the secure land line to Eglin. "Keep me apprised, Colonel."

On the other end of the line was Colonel Scott Albright, the commander of Eglin radar. He tended to shout, especially when he was excited. "Roger that, Dr. Corbin!" he brayed. "How you read me?"

Corbin winced. "Loud and clear, Eglin. Mostly loud."

"We got a radar lock on the shuttle!" Albright kept yelling. "*Columbia* is coming over the horizon. She's got an almost perfect 558-mile-high circular orbit. And an operator just announced she thinks she's got the Keyhole . . . good clear transponder signal . . . we've got your Keyhole, Dr. Corbin! Wait a minute, got a report from one of my radar jocks. . . . We got a third object on the screen down here. Estimated intersection with *Columbia* in five minutes."

Corbin gritted his teeth in pain as Albright nearly burst his eardrums when he yelled at the jock. "What's the object? Get a reading on it! I'm going to bring you up on the radar push, Dr. Corbin. Stand by!"

Corbin shook his head, trying to get his ears to stop ringing. He heard a newer, thankfully quieter voice over his headset, apparently the radar operator at Eglin. "Still tracking, sir. . . . Number is . . . just a minute, sir. It's *I* for India, one four lima. Official listing says it's a commsat launched on an Indian *Shiva* rocket three months ago. According to this it never came on-line. It's a DODO, sir."

DODO. Corbin sorted through his mental list of acronyms. Dead Object Drifting in Orbit. *What the hell was Columbia doing rendezvousing with a misfired Indian communications satellite?* He switched off Eglin, went to his direct black phone link to General Carling at the Air Force Space Command in Colorado. "General Carling, sir? Clay Corbin here. Yes sir, the Keyhole's being moved. Sir, I've got some other news. Yes, sir. About a DODO . . ."

Orbital Rendezvous

Columbia

Penny's eyes fluttered open. She was still seated in the cockpit. A quick check of her watch revealed she had been in a deep sleep for just under eight hours. An unfamiliar land mass scrolled below—a white scraggly line of snowcapped peaks in an otherwise brown corrugated plain. In just moments the mountain range was gone and the land smoothed and turned green until an abrupt coastline marked the beginning of a blue sparkling sea. She guessed that she had seen some little piece of the Himalayas and then *Columbia* had crossed down over India to the Sea of Bengal. The entire world appeared to be unscrolling beneath her. It was truly difficult to comprehend. But Penny liked it. Her stomach growled, evidence that it had adapted to zero gravity. Stretching, she unstrapped and floated free. She was startled to see Paco curled asleep on the roof, his claws hooked into the material that covered it. Her movement woke the cat up and he stretched, careful to keep his claws embedded in the material. When Penny petted him, he responded with a purr.

She heard movement in the middeck. *Columbia*'s crew cabin, smaller than she had remembered from her limited training, consisted of two levels, the flight deck (where she was) and beneath it the middeck (so called because it was located in between the flight deck and an equipment bay). On the flight deck forward there were two seats for the pilots behind banks of controls and monitors and a six-paneled windshield; the aft flight deck had a set of control panels covered with switches and lights plus five view ports—two overhead and three more looking down the cargo bay.

Penny cautiously used the handrails to pull herself to each of the view ports, to see what she could see. At the cargo bay windows she was surprised to see someone in a spacesuit going down the port sill of the bay, pulling a blue-wrapped object behind. It was a sleeping bag. The suited man stopped, gathered the bag to himself. Penny was certain it held Cassidy's body. Whoever was in the suit, and Penny knew it had to be Medaris, paused as if in prayer, then gathered in a book attached to a tether at his waist. She grabbed a headset in time to hear him speak:

O Jehovah, our Lord, how glorious is thy name in all the earth! Thou hast displayed Thy majesty above the heavens.

When I observe Thy heavens, the work of Thy fingers, the moon and the stars which Thou hast established:

What is man that Thou are mindful of him, or the son of man that Thou carest for him?

Yet Thou hast made him little less than heavenly beings, and Thou dost crown him with glory and honor.

Medaris released the tethered book—Penny assumed it was a Bible—and held the foot of the sleeping bag with one hand while saluting with the other. "Into Your hands," Penny heard him say, "I commit the spirit of Colonel Craig "Hopalong" Cassidy, a father, an American, a patriot."

Moved by his words, Penny watched Medaris push Cassidy into space, tipping the bag as he did. The bag, now a burial shroud, started tumbling end over end until it had become little more than a speck against the white-and-blue planet far below. Medaris gathered up the Bible and made his way back down the sill. Penny found that her heart was pounding. As much as she hated to admit it, even to herself, she was frightened of the man in the suit coming her way. There was much she found appealing about him—he'd been gentle with her, after all, while she had tried to interfere with the systems activation, and Paco liked him, that was always a good sign when a cat took to a man—but that scar, and the way he could get so gruff with her . . . Of course, the way he and she had verbally barraged each other yesterday—that had been fun, she had to admit. Perhaps dangerous fun, she thought, turning it around. Medaris was, after all, some sort of master criminal, a shuttle spacejacker. She liked that term: *spacejacker*. It would look good in her book if she lived long enough to write it. She thought again of the Demerol and other drugs she'd hidden away. She should have used them. Maybe it wasn't too late. When the spacejacker came through the hatch of the airlock, he'd be vulnerable.

Penny, still not certain what she was going to do, descended through the open hatchway to the middeck. The middeck was essentially nothing but an aluminum box smaller than one of the walk-in closets at her leased house in Malibu. Forward was a wall of white stowage lockers. The starboard wall held sleeping bags and the minuscule galley. Aft, there was a cylindrical airlock. She remembered its purpose: to seal off an astronaut going outside, allowing the air within to be evacuated without affecting the other astronauts in the main cabin. Beside the airlock, behind a plastic curtain, was the WCS. The entrance hatch, which had a small porthole, was dogged to the port wall. Rumor had it the toilet got smelly after a day or two. Penny could only hope they wouldn't be in orbit long enough for that to happen.

Virgil was out of his sleeping bag and at the galley, his back to her. Then the airlock opened and Medaris, dressed in shorts and a rugby shirt, came through it. Behind him the suit he had doffed floated eerily, legs and arms quivering as if it were alive. He saw Penny. "Feeling better?"

Penny didn't think his query sounded sincere. She studied him for a moment. "I saw and heard what you did. It was beautifully done, I must admit."

He nodded, his face grim. "The Psalms are always appropriate."

Virgil approached her, holding a plastic bottle. Penny saw that he looked almost human again, the SAS apparently dispelled. "Mornin', ma'am," he greeted her in a voice laden with respect. "Got some coffee ready for you." He handed her the squeeze bottle. "Sorry it ain't any hotter. They got it regulated so it won't melt the plastic."

Hot or not, Penny took the coffee greedily and carried it with her even though she was headed for the toilet. When she came out, Medaris had gone up to the flight deck. Starving, she hooked a foot in a foot loop and dug into the scrambled eggs and ham slices Virgil handed to her on a cellophane-covered plastic tray. He busied himself at the galley, cleaning up. She watched his wide back as he wiped down the rehydrator with a sponge. There seemed to be no harm in the man whatever. "Virgil . . ."

He turned eagerly. "Yes, ma'am? Ma'am, I'm really sorry about all this. My little girl—well, I'm a pad rat, ma'am, or I used to be before I started to work for Jack. We all lost our jobs and Lori, that's my wife, was crazy worried about Dawn —my daughter has cystic fibrosis, ma'am—but Jack's taken care of everything for us. And then he needed me for this mission. I had to come along. Now, ma'am, I need to tell you something else. . . ."

Penny listened in astonishment at the torrent of information. "Slow down, Virgil," she said, "take a breath."

"Yes, ma'am." He hung listlessly from the galley handrail and then rubbed his haggard face. "Whew! I'm still beat!" A look came over his face and Penny realized his SAS was far from over. He grabbed a plastic bag and headed for the WCS.

She felt a rush of empathy. For a spacejacker and master criminal Virgil seemed, well, nice. After polishing off another package of eggs and ham, doing her best to ignore the gagging sounds emanating from the toilet—*there was no privacy on this grunge bucket*—Penny went to the flight deck. Medaris was at the view ports that looked down the cargo bay. She remembered enough from her training to recognize that his hand was on the joystick for the shuttle arm. She hooked a footloop beside him. He gripped the pistol joystick and ordered the arm up and out, at the same time rotating open the end effector, a cylindrical cage that could grasp a special probe by tightening a triangle of cable around it. The arm rose slowly as he tested it, bending at the elbow and then at the wrist, silhouetted against the blue earth rushing below.

"How do you know how to do that?" she asked, astonished.

"I helped design the RMS."

Penny stared at him. "Who the hell *are* you?"

"There it is!" Medaris announced suddenly. "Look at her! Perfect! One little RCS burn and I'll have us snugged up."

"RMS, RCS?" Penny questioned resignedly.

Medaris turned to a gray laptop bolted to a control panel and keyed in some numbers. "Remote manipulating system, reaction control system," he said without looking at Penny. After a few seconds she felt *Columbia* tremble, then begin to rotate.

To Penny it appeared that the earth was actually doing the rotating, an optical illusion that not only made her dizzy but had the entire planet turning away from the cargo bay, leaving her to face the deep black velvet of empty space. Except it wasn't empty. Something big floated down toward the cargo bay centerline, a giant cylinder wrapped partially in gold foil. On the side nearest *Columbia* she could see what she recognized from some NASA manual she'd read as a grapple fixture, a knobbed stalk on a circular plate. Whatever it was, it had been designed to be captured by the shuttle's arm—or RMS, she thought. *God, I'm starting to understand this stuff!*

"Come to Papa," Medaris breathed.

Penny watched as the arm moved toward the satellite's grapple. The end effector swallowed it and the RMS folded back on itself under his steady hand. After it was about ten feet over the cargo bay, he shut the arm down.

"What is that thing?" Penny asked, trying not to sound as awestruck as she felt.

Jack tidied up the RMS, locking it into place. "Two stacked rocket engines. I'm going to remove the shuttle mains and put one of those, the big one, in their place."

"Why—why would you do that?"

"Because the mains are no good to us now. And because we need the new engine for our experiments."

"You're going to get us killed, aren't you?" she said in a burst of comprehending clarity.

He didn't even bother to look at her, just kept diddling with the damn computer. "No, High Eagle, I'm going to do what my contract stipulates."

She impulsively grabbed his hand, stopped him from keying anything else into the keyboard. "I crave the moment when I am allowed to see that sacred document."

Medaris pried her hand off. "It might be on board here somewhere. I'll ask Virgil to find it for you."

Then he smiled and Penny decided it was a handsome smile, a bit too cocky, but really quite nice. She hated him for it.

SMC, JSC

Houston was still on the job, quietly monitoring *Columbia*. After the Air Force, busy with its own plans, had stopped updating the ground track on *Columbia*, Tate's Turds had reverted to their own devices, using the shuttle's S-band hemiantennas for line-of-sight location fixes. Every time *Columbia* came over the horizon near a fixed NASA ground station, they had her. That was why, when *Columbia* shifted her orbit, Sam was informed by the GUIDO controller. "Update the track," he ordered. As he watched, the big wall screen on the front left of the control room presented the new orbital graphic. "Not much of a mod," he mused.

"They activated the Ku-band radar during the last pass," the INCO controller said. INCO handled instruments and communications.

"And the RMS is powered up," EECOM chimed in. EECOM managed the electrical systems.

"How do you know?"

"Normal traffic," both controllers answered in unison.

Sam leaned back in his bent chair and absently adjusted his headset. "Normal traffic," he said to himself, though aloud.

"What do you think that means?" Crowder said from the chair beside him.

"It means either these guys don't care if we get health and status or they don't know how to turn it off. And I would bet against the latter."

"They want us to know what they're doing?"

"Maybe they want us to help them out, if it comes to that," Sam mused. "That makes sense. They can't watch everything. Maybe they're hoping we'll do our jobs just as in any flight. No skin off their tails if we do."

Crowder thought about it for a moment. "So we're helping them just by monitoring their systems?"

The anger Sam had felt the day before had dissipated. "She's our old *Columbia*. We'll watch over her." He keyed his headset mike. "How about it, INCO? What's going on with *Columbia*'s radar?"

"They swiveled the Ku-band dish a few minutes ago," she answered. "Pulse wave readings would indicate they got a positive lock on something."

"Can you tell what it is?"

"Negative, Flight."

"Keep me advised."

"Roger that."

"Flight? This is FIDO."

FIDO, flight dynamics. "Go, FIDO."

"*Columbia* just made an RCS burn."

Columbia was using her radar and now she was maneuvering. A rendezvous situation. That was a damned dangerous thing even with the assistance of Shuttle Mission Control.

"Sam," a familiar voice over his headset crackled, "this is Owen Parker. Got a minute?" Parker was one of the payload operations directors, a POD in the Payload Operations Control Center up in Huntsville.

"Go, POD."

"We show all the experiments on board with downlink still inactive except for three. We got green lights for FLEA, CELL, and SAREX."

Sam searched his memory. He rarely cared what kind of experiments were on board. They were Huntsville's problem. FLEA was an experiment that included a cat and had something to do with vestibular research—how zero g affected balance or some nonsense like that. CELL was . . . wasn't that Dr. High Eagle's experiment? SAREX was one he knew about, a shortwave radio that had flown on a lot of missions. Still, who the hell cared about any of them at a time like this? "Okay, POD," he said, mildly irritated at the interruption. "Thanks for the update."

"Something else too. I've been listening to the playback of yesterday's launch. I think I recognize the voice of one of them . . . the hijackers."

Now Sam was interested. After the POD had told him his suspicions, he cursed himself inwardly. *Hell, he knew that voice too!* "CAPCOM, this is Flight Director, my loop."

"Go, Flight." It was Jay Guidon. A rookie astronaut, known more for his computational skills than his ability to communicate.

"Jay, I'm going to play CAPCOM and see if I can raise *Columbia*," Sam said.

"Roger, Flight," Guidon replied dutifully.

"What are you doing, Sam?" Crowder asked.

"Relax, Jim, I'll take the heat," Sam said, and took a deep breath.

"*Columbia*, Houston. This is Sam Tate." He waited, hearing only a hiss of static in his earpiece. "Come on, Jack. Answer me, boy!"

The Contract
FBI Office, the Old Post Office Building, Tallahassee, Florida

Cecil stared at the hard-faced FBI agents across the table. He ran a hand through his disheveled red hair. Because of his hair and the sprinkle of freckles he still had across his nose, his grade school buddies had nicknamed him Howdy Doody. *Howdy Doody versus the FBI*, Cecil thought, nearly giddy because of his lack of sleep. He chuckled inadvertently, much to the consternation of the agents who, he was certain, saw nothing funny about his situation. Through most of the night they had harangued him, then put him up at a nearby cheap hotel only to drag him out at the crack of dawn to question him some more. He'd caught a glimpse of the morning papers in front of the hotel. SPACE SHUTTLE CO-LUMBIA HIJACKED was one of the headlines. The television news shows were all about the shuttle too, even though none of the reporters had any details to report. NASA, the Air Force, the administration, nobody in the government was talking. Cecil was certain that other FBI agents were descending on Cedar Key to search for any MEC employees still around and to rip through the plant at the airport for clues. He was also certain they would find nothing.

"You wrote this contract?" the lead agent, a gray-bearded black man, asked or, rather, accused.

"I did, Agent . . . ?"

"Fisk. Why did you do it, Velocci?"

"Why? Because it was my job."

Fisk slapped his hand on the table, causing Cecil to jump. "You think that's going to keep you from going to prison? That you wrote this—this travesty because it was your job? Was it your job to help perpetrate one of the crimes of the century?"

Cecil composed himself. "Crime? I don't know of any crime."

"Read it, Burrows."

George Burrows was the FBI attorney. He read from a sheet of paper he'd been caressing on the table. *Crossing a state line to commit a felony, kidnapping, skyjacking—*

"Skyjacking? That law applies only to aircraft," Cecil interrupted.

"The shuttle is an aircraft," Burrows replied.

"I heard it was a spaceship."

"As long as it's in the atmosphere for part of its flight, it's an aircraft," Fisk growled. "Go on, Burrows."

"Unauthorized use of government property—"

"MEC has a contract to use government property."

"You're going to piss me off, Velocci!" Fisk yelled.

"Dangerous entrapment—" Burrows struggled on.

"What?"

"The astronauts in the elevator."

"Oh. I heard it got stuck."

"Shut up, Velocci."

"Conspiracy to defraud the government—"

"What do you mean by that?"

"This damn contract! It's a fraud!" Fisk threw the contract at Cecil, its pages coming unstapled. Cecil ducked and the pages went flying, wafting to the floor one by one.

Burrows kept going. "Destruction of government property—"

"Oh, come on!" Cecil felt his confidence increase. The

agents, for all their browbeating tactics, still hadn't said anything that made him worry about the contract not holding up. "You can't prove any of those charges," he said. "So stop trying to scare me with them."

"I'm going to tell you one more time to shut up! Go on, Burrows."

"I'm finished, sir."

Fisk glared at Burrows. "He's finished, Velocci. Well, what do you have to say to that?"

Cecil sat back, folding his hands on his stomach. "Not guilty."

Fisk huffed, got up, walked around the table, and stuck his face into Velocci's. "This is no goddamned court of law. What do you mean NOT GUILTY?"

Cecil reached out, very slowly, very dramatically, and pointed at the contract pages on the floor. "MEC has a legal contract with the government."

"Let me get this straight. You think that crummy little paper makes you not guilty on which charges?"

"On all charges." Cecil got up, picked up each sheet, sat down, and restacked them. He looked around the room. "Am I under arrest?"

Fisk stalked back to his chair and sat down. "There's one charge we haven't written down, not yet. You need to know about it, think about it very carefully. Did you know Dr. High Eagle is a Native American, Mr. Velocci?"

Cecil felt the hairs on the back of his neck stand up. *Now* he was scared. "Yes, of course, but what—?"

"Your clients have detained against her will a minority citizen of these United States, Mr. Velocci. That, by definition, is a hate crime, a federal offense. Any lawyer who defends anyone accused of a hate crime becomes very unpopular, subject perhaps to being accused of committing a hate crime himself."

It took a lot to anger Cecil but Fisk was nearly there. "Are you threatening me, Agent Fisk?" he growled.

Fisk shrugged. "Yes, Mr. Velocci, I am. You need to think this through. You're out of your league."

"Are my clients officially charged with anything?" Cecil asked coldly.

"Not at this time. But I want all their names."

"I will provide you with a list of all MEC employees. Am I free to go?"

"Not at this time. You're due on a plane to Washington in one hour."

"For what purpose?"

Fisk grimaced, or it might have been a grin. It was hard for Cecil to tell. "You'll find that out when you get there, Mr. Island-in-the-sun attorney. It ain't gonna be fun, I can tell you that!"

Cecil pointed. "I'll want a copy of that," he said, indicating the list of charges. "I'll need them to start the preparation of the defense of my clients should they in fact be charged with anything."

Fisk nodded agreement and Burrows excused himself and scurried off toward the copier. Cecil sat comfortably in his chair, ignoring Fisk's sullen stare. It was dangerous but strangely exciting to tweak the nose of the federal government. Burrows returned with the copies and Cecil was escorted out. As he went, FBI staffers came into the hall to get a look at him. Cecil straightened as he walked by. He could almost feel his stature growing as he was hurried toward the waiting limousine.

Extravehicular Activity (1)
Columbia

Jack had managed six hours of desperately needed sleep in the cockpit after which his mind seemed sharper than it had ever been, as if all his synapses were suddenly open, keen in the face of danger. When he found both Penny and Virgil still sleeping, he'd taken a big risk going out into the cargo bay alone to send off Cassidy. Single EVAs were potentially dangerous things—if he'd gotten tangled in his tether out there, or the backpack had had any kind of a problem, he'd have been on his own in the harsh vacuum. Still, there was simply no way to keep Cassidy's body aboard, even in the cargo bay, considering the likely effects of vacuum and solar radiation on an exposed human cadaver, and Jack had seen no reason to delay. He had come to the conclusion that the remainder of this flight would include many such risks. All the margins he and his MEC team had carefully inserted into the mission profile were gone with the loss of Cassidy. Virgil had signed on for the worst, and would take the complications in stride, he reasoned, and as for High Eagle—well, High Eagle would just have to get used to it. Jack found, for some unfathomable reason, that he liked to tantalize her with bits and pieces of information while holding other things back. He couldn't quite put his finger on why—but decided he didn't have time to think about it, in any case.

Some numbers crunching on the computer screen caught his eye. He was looking at radar data. "That's strange," he said aloud. He called down through the hatch. "Virgil? Need you."

Virgil appeared from below. "What's going on, boss?"

"I put the system in the co-op mode so it would trigger the transponder in the engine package. Now I've got another transponder signal. If it's not our package . . ."

"Company?"

"So it would seem."

Virgil put his hand to his headset. "He's still calling. Jack, why don't you just say hello to him? What could it hurt?"

Jack sighed, nodded. "All right, all right. Let's see what the old cowboy wants."

SMC

Sam jerked upright in his chair. He'd been droning calls to *Columbia* for ten minutes. "This is *Columbia*. Make it quick." The voice was brusque but he recognized it all the same. *Jack Medaris.*

"This is Sam Tate," Sam said. "Would you go to air-to-ground three?" Air-to-ground 3 was the encrypted voice channel from the shuttle.

A moment passed while Sam held his breath. Would Medaris do it? He breathed a sigh of relief when he heard him come back on the secured push. "Go ahead, Houston."

Sam keyed his mike. "Jack, cut the crap. This is Sam. What the hell do you think you're doing?"

There was a momentary crackle of static. Then Sam heard the click of Medaris's mike. "Hello, Sam. I guess it won't hurt to be informal on the chatter channel. How's Geraldine?"

"Dammit, Jack. She's fine. She's missed you. We all have. I was glad to hear you were back in the space business with your sling pump. But, Jack, listen, this is wrong what you're doing—"

"I don't know what you mean, Sam," Jack interrupted. "I'm involved in a commercial enterprise that has been approved by the Department of Transportation. It's all in our contract. Our lawyer is probably working with authorities now to straighten things out if there's a problem."

Sam wasn't buying it. "Listen, old son, I don't know why you've done this . . . hell, boy . . . come on back. The quicker you get off the shuttle, the less trouble you're going to be in. As slick as you pulled this off, there might even be a few old boys around who'll call you a hero. What happened to Hoppy?"

A long pause and then: "An accident at launch. But he was with us, Sam. You would be, too, if you knew everything."

Sam rubbed his face, pinched his nose. "What—what have you done with him?"

"He got what he would have loved, Sam—the first burial in space. I gave him the requisite tumble so he'll reenter in a few weeks. I know Hoppy wouldn't want to pose a hazard to spacecraft. Please give my regrets to his family. Tell his son that his father was a great pilot."

On console some of the controllers crossed themselves. An American had died in space. Sam tried to contain his rising anger but he gave in to it. "Damn you, Jack! You were once part of this agency! We trusted you!"

"I have a contract," Jack replied placidly. "This is nothing against NASA."

Sam pounded his fist on his table. "Nothing against NASA? You're killing this agency single-handed! The media's dragging out every problem we've ever had. Do you think Congress is going to give a tinker's damn about us after this stunt? They'll shut us down! And you've caused Hoppy's death." He tried to haul himself back but failed. "And it's not the first death you've caused either!" He regretted his words nearly as soon as he said them.

There was a long silence. "I'm well aware of that, Sam," Jack finally replied in a subdued voice. Then, more spiritedly, he said, "They've been looking for an excuse to shut NASA down for years. I didn't cause that."

Sam gripped his console table, fought for the right words, tried to bring himself back from the edge. "Look, Jack . . . I'm sorry. I shouldn't have said that. But it's over. I don't know what you and Hoppy were trying to do but it can't be done, not now. There's a satellite with a very big eye moving into your neighborhood. Whatever you're doing, you're going to be seen. They got your number, son. Come on back and we'll sort things out."

"Is it a Keyhole or a Big Bird?"

Sam cursed his big mouth. Medaris was no rookie. He knew everything there was to know about a shuttle. He'd probably already seen a blip on his radar but hadn't known what it was. The shuttle was maneuverable. Jack could give the spy sat a merry chase if he wanted to. "Even if I knew I couldn't tell you," Sam said. "But this thing is just the start of it. They're coming after you with blood in their eyes, Jack. Let us bring you in. We'll glide you down at Edwards. Big runways there. It'll be easy."

"Sorry, Sam," Jack responded. "But thanks for your concern."

"Jack—"

"Two minutes to Tee-drus L-O-S," CAPCOM announced. LOS, loss of signal. *Columbia* in company with the Keyhole was moving into a blackout area where the TDRS tracking, data, and relay communications sats couldn't hear them.

"Jack, don't maneuver again without letting us know, okay? It's dangerous without us watching over you. How about it? We're kinda fond of that old shuttle."

"Thanks but no thanks, Sam," Jack answered amiably. "We can take care of ourselves."

"You pigheaded sumbitch!" Sam growled.

"He's signed off, Flight," Commtech advised.

Columbia

Jack had pulled the plug on Tate because an alarm had sounded. It was SAREX with word from the MEC control center now rolling across southern Mississippi.

BE ADVISED SPY SAT COMING YOUR WAY.

Jack guessed that MEC had tapped into the back rooms of Houston and Huntsville, getting their intelligence from the techie buzz over the loops. He keyed an answer.

COPY. ON TIMELINE. EVA TO UNPACK ET NEXT.

The laptop whirred.

ALL FINGERS CROSSED HERE.

"Here too," Jack muttered to himself.

SMC

Sam answered the urgent call coming over the land line push. "And what can I do for the dear old Defense Intelligence Agency?" he growled.

It was Clay Corbin. "Mr. Tate, that was very unwise. This is considered black business. Do you understand? You are not authorized to tell the people on *Columbia* anything about what we are doing. Do I have to make that an order?"

Sam smiled at his controllers, who were all looking back at him with wide eyes. "An order? I don't think I'm in your chain of command, son," he drawled, utterly delighted to have the opportunity to irritate one of the men who'd usurped control from Houston.

Corbin came back, obviously outraged. "I have my authority from the highest level. The highest level. Do you know who that means?"

Crowder tugged at Sam's sleeve. "Sam, maybe you better—"

Sam shook Crowder off. "Dr. Corbin, I am the flight director for this mission. I will do whatever I think is necessary for the safety of my spacecraft."

Corbin's voice went up an octave. "Your spacecraft? That isn't your spacecraft. You let the bad guys steal it. Remember?"

Sam snarled and punched the land line off. He vultured his people, sending their heads diving back to their monitors. Then he eyed the shuttle's track on the big video screen. "What are you doing, Jack?" he breathed. "What are you doing?"

"What's that, Sam?" Crowder asked.

Sam didn't reply. He just kept looking at the screen, trying to figure it out.

Director's Office, JSC

Frank Bonner, just arrived from Washington and back in his office, received a call from Sam Tate. He listened, then repeated the name he'd heard. "That's right, Frank," Sam said. "He used to be head of the Propulsion Lab in Huntsville."

"I know who he is," Bonner snapped, and hung up the telephone. He slumped in his chair. *How could it be?* He felt as if his mind had been torn from its hinges. Bonner sat, staring at, without seeing, his office wall blanketed with awards and autographed photos, all representing the career he'd built to replace the happiness the man had snatched from him. *Medaris!*

Everything was swept clean from Bonner's mind, his hopes to be the NASA administrator, to get *Columbia* back and operational again. Nothing made sense except for one thing: *Medaris*. Bonner would see that this time he was destroyed. Permanently.

Columbia

Penny hung from a handrail, watching Medaris inside the airlock, checking the extravehicular mobility unit (EMU) suit he had worn on the burial EVA. There were three other suits stowed there. "I heard what you told Houston," she chided. "You said your contract was for a commercial purpose. I thought it was top secret. You can't even keep your lies straight."

"There are plenty of commercial activities that are secret," Medaris answered, his voice sounding hollow from the airlock. "Company proprietary. I'm sure you've heard the phrase."

"This ain't right, boss." Virgil interrupted the argument to start one of his own. "It ain't safe for you to be outside alone."

"You're in no condition to help me," Medaris answered. "Don't worry. I can handle it."

"Isn't it against the rules for only one person to go EVA?" Penny questioned.

Medaris stuck his head out of the airlock hatch, gave her *that* look. Penny felt like slapping his face. "Don't tell me. You went to the EVA class?"

"She's right, Jack," Virgil said in a low tone.

Medaris shrugged. "You might have noticed I already did it once."

"That wasn't right neither," Virgil muttered.

Penny was starting to feel left out. "What are you going to do now?" she demanded to get back into the discussion.

"There's some gear in the base of the external tank. I'm going out there and get it. After that I'll start removing the shuttle mains."

Penny looked at Virgil. "Tell me the truth, Virgil. You two are escapees from a nut ward, right?" She looked out of the corner of her eye to see Medaris's reaction but was disappointed when he turned away to work on his suit.

Virgil looked thoughtful. "Seems like that sometimes, ma'am."

"Just in case Virg gets sick again, how about staying on comm with me?" Medaris asked Penny.

"Look, I told you. I'm not going to be a part of this."

"High Eagle"—he sighed, coming back over to the airlock hatch—"Virgil and I have a job to do, one that we're going to do. And the quicker we get it done, the quicker you get to go home. All I'm asking you to do is answer the phone. How about it?"

"If only I knew what you're really doing. . . ."

"One more time." He sighed. "We're on a top secret *and* a commercial mission. And unless you can get limo service up here, you're going to have to stick around until we're finished. You can't go home until then."

It popped out before she could stop herself. "I don't have a home."

"What do you mean?"

"I just lease a place. I'm mostly on the road."

"It's sad not having a home," Medaris said. "I guess I don't have one either."

"This is sort of our home now, ain't it?" Virgil offered.

"I guess it is," Medaris said.

Penny looked around. "I never figured my home would have the bed and toilet all in the same room."

"Consider it an efficiency," Medaris said.

"You always have to have the last word, don't you?" Penny growled.

He pulled the airlock door shut. A faint hiss signaled the beginning of his oxygen prebreathe, necessary to avoid decompression sickness in the lighter pressure of the suit. Penny slapped the view port. "He's so damned full of himself!" she griped to Virgil.

Virgil nodded agreement. "Jack's got his ways, all right."

Penny squinted at the big man. "Listen, I'm walking on the edge here. If I don't get the truth, I'm going over it and I swear I'll take you with me. I don't want to hear *nuthin'* about no damn contract, you hear? Tell me the truth. Start with him. Who is he?"

Virgil mopped his brow. "He used to be the head knocker up at the Propulsion Lab in Huntsville."

Penny could see Virgil's space sickness was coming back. Very soon, she knew, he would make use of the vomitus bag Velcroed just within reach. "What is he now?" she asked.

"President of MEC. My boss."

"And why isn't he still a wheel in Huntsville?"

Virgil swallowed a burp. "An engine he was testing went out of control on a test stand ten, eleven years ago. Killed one of his engineers. NASA blamed him for it."

"Let me guess," Penny said harshly. "Those engines hanging on the arm—they're the same kind as the one that went out of control?"

"Yes, ma'am."

Penny shook her head. She understood now. "He just had to do something to prove himself right. Even if it meant spacejacking a shuttle. Yes, I think I've got your number, Mr. Jack Medaris."

"A couple of things you ought to know before you start bad-mouthing Jack, Dr. High Eagle." Virgil's eyes were squeezed shut, sweat beading on his forehead. "The first one is that he's saved a buncha guys—rocket engineers, technicians like me—by giving us jobs when NASA didn't want us no more."

Penny shrugged. "Saved them for prison, you mean?"

Virgil was holding the plastic bag just beneath his mouth, ready to use it. "The other thing was that the engineer that got killed, it was Jack's wife, Kate. Turned out she was pregnant too. He got that burn scar on his face and neck trying to save Kate and their baby."

Cargo Bay, *Columbia*

Jack exited the airlock, tethered on to the guide wire that ran down the starboard sill of the cargo bay, and pulled hand over hand down it until he reached the vertical stabilizer. There, he set up a silvery reflector he had taken out with him. It acted the same as a convenience-store corner mirror, giving a wide view all the way down to the external tank. "Anybody see me?" he called.

"I see you, Medaris."

Jack turned to look behind him, saw a figure at the aft flight deck view port with binoculars. "High Eagle?"

"Yeah. What do you want me to do?"

"Just keep watch."

"Okay. But if you slip off, what then?"

"Well, at least you can tell everybody where you last saw me."

"Medaris, look . . . we need to talk, okay?"

Jack hooked his feet inside the propellant feed lines on the external tank and used his waist tether to clip to an attach strut. "What about?"

"Everything."

Jack eyed the curved base of the ET. There had been no way to train for this EVA and it wasn't going to be easy. "I'm kind of busy to talk about everything." He reached for the strut to stabilize himself. "By the way, you haven't killed Virgil, have you?"

"Of course not. He got sick again. He's asleep."

"Just don't lock the door on me, okay?"

"Don't put any ideas in my head."

From a T-bar attachment that held a set of special EVA tools on his chest, Jack selected a pair of thick shears and used them to wedge out a chunk of ET foam. Underneath he found the loop of wire that Estes and Tribble had embedded for him. He snagged it and pulled. The wire cut a square in the foam as it came out, revealing underneath it a hatch. The effort had taken more out of him than he'd anticipated. Working in the pressurized EMU suit was not easy. He was breathing hard.

"Medaris, are you all right?"

"I'm fine," Jack muttered, but he wasn't. Besides his fatigue he had suddenly felt a massive presence. When he looked up, he found himself turned away from earth, facing deep space. There was nothing, only emptiness. For the first time since he'd been in low earth orbit, he felt scared.

"High Eagle?" he called, almost against his will. He hoped she wouldn't notice the strain in his voice.

"I hear you."

"It's big out here. It's easy to feel . . . alone. The stars aren't much company."

"I'm watching you, Medaris." Her tone was casual.

"Thanks."

"You're not welcome."

"Hatch is off," he grunted to no reply.

The Attorney General
Department of Justice, Washington, D.C.

After an FBI jet dropped Cecil off at Ronald Reagan, an agent drove him to the Justice Department, brusquely directed him to a conference room, and left him alone. Cecil sweated out the silence for an hour and then a heavyset woman—Cecil recognized her as Attorney General Tammy Hawthorne—came in, followed by a retinue of dark suits. The AG wore a flowery print dress, big bug-eyed spectacles, and was clearly irritated. She snapped her fingers, directing the lawyers to the table and then motioning in quick choppy movements for them to sit down. Hawthorne was as formidable as he had been told.

She eyed him through her thick glasses. "My boys tell me you've been cooperative, Mr. Velocci. That is wise. I'm just a shit-tick from having you put into the dungeon we keep under the Washington Monument."

Cecil squared his shoulders. "I've tried to be helpful, Miss Attorney General."

Hawthorne harrumphed and consulted a sheet of paper one of her lawyers handed over, the list of the MEC employees Cecil had given the FBI. "Which of these bastards is on board the shuttle?"

"Jack Medaris, Virgil Judd, and Craig Cassidy," Cecil

replied, wondering why it had taken so long for anybody to ask him that question. It was a relief to get the information out. "According to the contract between the Department of Transportation and my clients, they are conducting a commercial enterprise. Admittedly, there may have been some communications problems with the ground crews at Kennedy Space Center, but if you will read the contract, you will see that DOT had the responsibility to inform NASA of our plans."

"Yeah, right," Hawthorne grumped. "I'm not buying it, Velocci. We'll be specifying the charges on your clients soon. Except for Cassidy. I don't think he's your client anymore. We hear he's dead."

This was news to Cecil but he kept his game face on. Jack had told him there would be some rough spots during the mission, no matter how well he planned it. This sounded as if it was the roughest spot of all. "You say you're specifying charges?" he asked, his voice just shaky enough to betray him. "Have you determined what those charges might be?"

Hawthorne seemed to be studying Cecil, to perhaps find the lie. "You mean other than treason?" she said. "We'll go for murder of Captain Cassidy, and skyjacking, I'm sure. And kidnapping. That would be of Dr. High Eagle."

Cecil kept his composure. "I believe I'll be able to show that Captain Cassidy was a bona fide employee of the MEC company. If he's dead, it must have been an accident. As for the skyjacking and kidnapping charges, could I ask you what evidence you have of either?"

The AG's eyes narrowed into two thick lines behind her glasses. If she had eyelashes, they were invisible. "Well, for one, NASA's missing a space shuttle, Mr. Velocci. For another, they're missing an Indian princess astronette. Your clients will be lucky if all they get is the death penalty."

Cecil was beginning to believe this attorney general

really *did* have a dungeon beneath the Washington Monument. "Ma'am, I can only restate that MEC has a legal contract with the government. And as for Dr. High Eagle—perhaps she went along to help."

Hawthorne leaned forward, shook her finger at Cecil. "Let me advise you of something, boyfriend. President Edwards and Vice President Vanderheld are a couple of swell fellows, all gooshy and kind and worried about the poor people. Me? I'm the bitch witch in this administration. I've been a prosecutor my entire professional life. You break the law, I don't care who you are, I'm gonna come after you, make you wish you never crawled out of your dung heap. You want to bandy words with me, be my guest. In the end it won't matter. I'm gonna have my size tens up your ass. Got it?"

Cecil grimly nodded. He'd gotten it, loud and clear.

Hawthorne stood up. "I just wanted to lay my eyes on you, bud. I've done that, so now you can go as long as you stay within ten miles of this building. Bill Miller"—she nodded to one of the suits at the table—"will be your contact. Now get out of my Justice Department!"

High Eagle's Decision (1)
Airlock, *Columbia*

Jack was neither awake or asleep. He was in some sort of half-world, caught in a web of space and time, adrift in a current carrying him across the sweep of the galaxy, past giant red-hot stars, immense cold planets striped by streaks of gold and silver. . . . Then he was in a control room, the night outside cold and bitter, the consoles glowing, his team hunched over them. Kate was there. "No . . ." he said but it was unstoppable when it began. It had to play itself out. They'd all had launch fever that night, even Kate. Maybe especially Kate . . .

* * *

"What are you waiting for?" she said. "Go on and do it. You know you're going to anyway."

The plan that night had only been to run software tests. But everything had gone smoothly, including the propellant loading. It would save them a week's worth of preparation if they just kept going. They were desperately short of funding. A week of work was a lot of money. Jack nodded, ordered the countdown to continue all the way through engine activation for a five-second hot fire test. With a clap and a cheer his team jumped to do his bidding.

There was still an hour to go before the hot fire when Jack heard a steady tone in a nearby monitor. An engineer ran his finger down his screen, tapping it twice. "We have an automatic hold on the TCDC," he said. "The oxy FDP is showing a vacuum." Jack puzzled over it. The FDP was the fine distribution pump. "I don't see how that can be. The FDP's wet. I can see it spiking but going negative isn't an option here."

The TCDC was the terminal countdown clock, the computerized clock and operations software that monitored and controlled the steps toward ignition. Jack knew there was trouble but he couldn't identify what exactly it was. If the TCDC sensed an anomaly, it was supposed to put itself into an automatic hold, alerting the TCDC operator. A loss of pressure was the likely reason the TCDC had shut things down. But Jack was still puzzled. The weight of the propellant alone should have resulted in at least some pressure.

Kate brushed by Jack, sitting down at her monitor, her fingers playing staccatos on her keyboard. "Sensor problem, I think," she said. "Need to replace number two dot six oh four three seven. On my way."

"Send Joel," Jack said as she stood up, pulling her headset off. "That's what he and the test stand people are paid for."

"Joel's busy on the signal generators," she replied. "No time. I gotta go. Won't take me a sec."

"Be careful."

She touched his shoulder lightly. All it took was a touch from Kate to stir his soul. She gave him a quick smile. "I will, Jack," she said quietly, and then she was off, snapping her fingers at another engineer to follow her. Jack watched her plop on a hard hat as she went out the door. "Be careful," he said again but she was gone, the door slapping shut behind her.

Jack turned to her monitor, to see what she had seen. There was an analysis of pump pressures. The points on her graph were distributed erratically. He accepted her conclusion. A bad sensor. Had to be.

"Hey, we're still counting," he heard the TCDC engineer say excitedly. "That can't be right. The TCDC shut itself down."

Jack leaned over the man's shoulder. "Show me," he said.

He called up his previous displays. "See, a hold mode right there. Now everything is active again. The code jumped over the hold. It's not supposed to do that."

Jack thought of the people out on the test stand, including Kate. "Shut it down," he ordered harshly. "*Now.*"

Penny swung open the airlock. Medaris was inside, mumbling something about a shutdown. She grabbed a leg and pulled him into the middeck. His lips were cracked and dry. She handed him a water bottle but all he did was bat at it. She held it for him, squirted water in his mouth. It bounced off his tongue, little crystal spheres. "Drink it, damn you," she ordered. "You're dehydrated."

Penny had watched the entire five-hour spacewalk. Medaris had taken six large sausage-shaped packages from the external tank and moved them to the payload bay, bungeeing them behind the tether satellite rig. She had listened to him breathing, gasping at times, the work with the uncooperative cargo apparently more difficult than he had planned. He had stopped between each of his trips down to the base of the tank to let the cooling capacity of his suit catch up but he kept sweating, he reported, his eyes stinging from it. She had watched him keep going, doggedly retracing his path back and forth to the tank and the payload bay. As soon as he got back into the airlock, she'd watched him get out of his suit, saw the color of his face, and knew he was in trouble. It occurred to Penny again that she had yet another opportunity to end the spacejacking. Virgil had taken his SAS medicine and strapped himself into his bag on the wall. Medaris was close to collapse. She could tranquilize them both, get on the horn, end this thing, and be America's hero forever. Something kept her from it. She didn't know what it was but whatever it was, it was frustrating.

Penny strapped Medaris to the floor and washed him down with damp towels. He fought her lightly and she slapped his hands away. "Stop it, Medaris! I've got to cool you down or you could die. *Stop it!*"

He subsided and Penny continued to wipe him down. She had noticed a small battery-operated fan in a locker. She got it and clamped it to an overhead panel, directing it on him. He had gone to sleep, his breathing deep and steady. She ran a wet towel over his chest, along his shoulders, then each of his arms and legs. Although it irritated her to do so, she couldn't help but notice that Medaris was a fine-looking man. His shoulders were wide, with muscles that rode along the surface, a swimmer's look to him, or maybe a climber, she decided, although his packed leg muscles indicated that he was a runner too. When she dabbed at his face, she noticed for the first time that the scar tissue along his jaw pulled down one corner of his mouth, giving

him the sardonic look she had thought was always deliberately aimed at her. She used her long, delicate fingers to
touch the scar, trace it down his neck. It ended abruptly
halfway down it as if there had been something protecting
him there. Penny thought of his wife, wished that she had
asked Virgil more about her. What kind of woman designed
rocket engines? What kind of woman had made this man
love her so much that he would enter fire to save her? There
had been a lot of men in Penny's life but not one of them,
she thought, would have been willing to so much as wave
his hand over a match for her. She doubted that she would
ever inspire such love. She found herself incomprehensibly
envying someone who had been burned alive. She felt
Medaris's scarred jaw, ran the palm of her hand along
it. . . .

The SAREX suddenly rang and Penny jerked as if she had
been shot. She felt embarrassed, *caught.* She carried Jack to
the shortwave instrument so she could tend to him while
answering. Everything was already set up. Virgil had recently
been using it, probably asking MEC about his family.

WAITING FOR A REPORT ON ET UNPACK EVA.

Penny exploded. She was angry and ashamed at the confusing emotions she was feeling. "I'll give you a report, you
bastards!"

IT'S OVER. BOTH YOUR BOYS ARE OUT OF COMMISSION.
CALL HOUSTON. BRING US IN.

Penny glared at the screen, waiting. A minute passed,
then another. Jack groaned. She used the plastic bottle to
squirt more water into his mouth. The SAREX whirred.

YOU MUST HELP.

Penny's hands leapt to the keyboard.

GIVE ME ONE GOOD REASON.

The laptop whirred.

FOR YOUR COUNTRY.

Penny studied the screen. She identified herself firmly with the Native American movement, had called for reparations and special consideration for all the tribes. She'd lobbied personally with President Edwards for an apology and she had heard it was in the works.

MY COUNTRY IS THE CHEROKEE NATION. TRY AGAIN.

The SAREX sat silently for a moment, then clicked and whirred.

BECAUSE IF YOU KNEW ME WE'D BE FRIENDS. MY NAME IS SALLY LITTLETON AND I'M FOND OF THOSE TWO BIG LUGS YOU'RE WITH. TAKE CARE OF THEM FOR ME PLEASE PENNY HIGH EAGLE.

Penny was startled by the reply. She stared at the screen for a long time. Despite her fame, friendship had always been difficult for Penny. Her father had died a drunk in a ditch before she was born, and her mother had died of tuberculosis a few years later. Her grandmother, a sour old woman who had never shown her a moment of affection, had taken her in, raised her, was forever quick to tell her how much of a burden she was, and how ugly she was. Penny had been a gawky, geeky child until she'd blossomed when she hit puberty. Then the boys were after her like bees to honey, but all they wanted was sex. Her grandmother was always quick to point that out. The other girls in her class were jealous of her, kept her at arm's length, made up spurious stories about her. Not much had changed since. The truth was, Penny High Eagle, one of the most famous women in the world, was profoundly lonely, would have done almost anything to find a friend.

The words kept hitting Penny between her eyes.

TAKE CARE OF THEM FOR ME PLEASE PENNY HIGH EAGLE.

Penny High Eagle. The truth was, there was no Penny High Eagle. She was an invention, created the day after Penelope Ingle, an insecure high school girl, had won a local 10 K road race. FIRST NATIVE AMERICAN FEMALE WINS RACE, the headlines had screamed. The importance of that headline kept growing to that girl. She desperately needed to have the attention it had brought. That was when Penelope Ingle realized there were lots of things that hadn't been done by a "Native American Female." After she'd gotten her education through a series of scholarships, she found an agent—Oscar Pennington—and convinced him that she could turn "First Native American Female" into a profession.

Penny hesitated, then typed:

YOU DON'T KNOW WHO I AM.

The laptop whirred again.

PENNY. I CAN'T BELIEVE IT. THIS IS WONDERFUL. WE'LL MAKE MILLIONS ON THE BOOK.

Penny stared at the screen, slowly pecked in her response.

OSCAR?

SOME WONDERFUL PEOPLE BROUGHT THIS DELIGHTFUL MACHINE TO MY OFFICE. THEY ARE HERE WITH ME NOW.

HOW DO I KNOW IT'S YOU?

THE FIRST THING I EVER SAID TO YOU WAS THAT YOU OUGHT TO BRAID YOUR HAIR INTO PIGTAILS, STICK A FEATHER IN YOUR HAIR LIKE PRINCESS SUMMERFALL WINTERSPRING. YOU TOLD ME TO STUFF IT. PENNY THE NEWSPAPERS AND TELEVISION ARE GOING NUTS OVER THIS THING. BUT THEY DON'T KNOW WHAT I KNOW. KEEP YOURSELF SAFE DARLING BUT GO ALONG ON THIS JOURNEY AND KEEP WRITING! IF YOU DO THIS, YOU'RE GOING TO BE THE BIGGEST SUPERSTAR ON EARTH!

"What are you going to do, Dr. High Eagle?" She turned, saw Virgil peering over her shoulder at the screen.

Penny turned back to the SAREX, her fingers poised over the keyboard. But she was at a loss what to type. It wasn't Oscar's hide hanging out in orbit with a couple of loonies. Penny moved away from the keyboard, squinted at Virgil. "Why are we here?" she demanded.

Virgil hooked his foot through a footloop and settled in beside her. "We have a contract."

Penny's eyes flashed. "I know you have a contract, you big idiot. But who with and to do what?"

"It's around here somewhere," he said. "I'll look for it."

"Do that, Virgil. And while you're at it, see if you can round me up some other fiction too. I always enjoy a good read."

An hour later, with both Virgil and Jack sleeping

soundly, Penny found Paco and took him in her arms and went to the cockpit and strapped herself in. She watched the earth turn below, the beautiful blue, implacable earth. She couldn't think clearly no matter how hard she tried to order her mind. She had never been so confused and yet so strangely excited. And as much as she hated to admit it, no small part of that excitement was caused by the strange, handsome, scarred, obviously disturbed man she had stripped, washed, and put away in a sleeping bag as if he were her child.

MET 2 DAYS AND COUNTING . . .

The Peg
OSC Manufacturing Plant, Dulles, Virginia

Joe Rodriguez was the Orbital Science Company group leader assigned the task of rapidly preparing a *Pegasus* rocket for the Air Force's "demonstration" in space. The point of the demo wasn't exactly clear to Rodriguez, but in any case it was above his pay grade to worry about. He just had the job to do. Rodriguez and his people were working on "Peg" in a clean room of the plant just twenty miles from downtown Washington, D.C. Because of its proximity to the Pentagon, it didn't take long for General Carling to dispatch a team of Air Force inspectors to Dulles to bird-dog Rodriguez and his troops. Rodriguez was not surprised. He was used to having government inspectors looking over everything he and his team did, often as they were doing it. Rodriguez was just sealing a Peg electronics test and checkout panel when he heard a whoosh of air and saw six Air Force officers, all dressed in "bunny suits"—clean-room uniforms—enter the room. Rodriguez and his team were dressed the same, white full-legged smocks, legs tucked into white shoes, arms with elastic bands at the wrist, collars buttoned up to the neck, a white surgeon's mask, and translucent latex gloves. A clear plastic cap pulled down to the ears completed the outfit. Only the eyes of the engineers were left uncovered. Moisture and dust, including dandruff, hair, and flakes off human skin, were all potentially cloggers of the delicate internal Peg mechanisms.

OSC had chosen a *Pegasus*-E (*E* for "enhanced") launcher. The trim little rocket with wings sat on its trunnion support. Rodriguez directed his techs to keep working and walked over to meet the Air Force cohort. After introductions all around, the leader of the inspectors, a Colonel Ted Wingate, wanted to see the payload. Rodriguez led him to one of the tables that had been set up around the Peg. He gestured toward a thick aluminum cylindrical canister, covered with a dozen intricate devices that looked a bit like claws, each of which had a bundle of cable leading to it. "This is our small assembly deployment device. We've had SADD under development for some time. It's never been used in space but it's passed all its design reviews."

"What does it do, Joe?" Wingate asked, assuming the easy informality of the aerospace community.

"It's designed to carry a number of small satellites aboard a single launcher," Rodriguez explained. Seeing the quizzical look on the blue-suiters, he explained further. "A lot of small companies or universities can't afford to pay for their own launcher. The idea is that they can save money by combining their payload with a bunch of others, everybody riding on the same rocket."

"You're going to put the water bags aboard this SADD, then?"

"Yes. The water bags will be attached in bundles to each of these clamps. The wires have squibs attached that will automatically deploy the clusters. A timer will blow other squibs within the bundle. The trick to this will be deploying all the water bags in the proper pattern. We think we've solved that too. Of course we'd like to run a test—"

"There's no time for that," Wingate said, eyeing the SADD appreciatively. "Beautiful design. I hope it works."

Rodriguez shrugged. "You fly without testing, you never know."

Wingate didn't respond to the comment. What was there to say? Rodriguez led the blue-suiters to another table to show them the water bags. "What do you call them besides water bags?" Wingate asked.

Rodriguez grinned. "The boys came up with the Space Punitive Reaction Against Hijacking. Pronounced 'spray.'"

"Spray, huh?" Wingate laughed. "If you want to be politically correct, better change the *P* to stand for 'Protective.' The President doesn't believe in punishing people."

Rodriguez nodded, remembering President Edwards's opposition to capital punishment. Wingate studied the bags, each a black polypropylene packet about six inches square. Rodriguez handed one of them to the colonel. "The plan is for the *Pegasus* to rendezvous with the shuttle and deploy SPRAH in a circular pattern with a slight retrograde motion. Timers will rupture the bags. Should be quite a show when all that water crystallizes."

Wingate moved the bag back and forth in his hands, the water inside making a sloshing sound. "Can the Peg get close enough to *Columbia* for the spacejackers to see it coming at them?"

"We think so."

Wingate grinned. "That ought to scare the shit out of those bastards!"

Rodriguez shrugged. He wasn't so certain. "We'll use a minisensor to home in on the shuttle. The boys in the back room just assembled it."

"And what's that package called?"

Rodriguez could not help but look embarrassed. "The guys call it the Nakey."

"Nakey?"

"From the group leader's comment when he was told to build it in twenty-four hours. Not a chance in hell. N-A-C-I-H. Nakey."

Wingate put the bag back on the table. "You've done a fantastic job, Joe. Box your Peg up as soon as you can. Orbital insertion in twelve hours."

An Air Force major spoke up. "Joe, are you sure this won't damage *Columbia*? Looks like there could be a lot of debris flying around up there."

Rodriguez frowned at the major. *I sure hope not* was what he wanted to say. "It's not supposed to" was the best he could muster.

The Researcher

Shirley Grafton was still officially listed as a researcher on the vice president's staff, but over the last two years she had become more of a confidante, attuned to her boss's restless mind. She had come to Washington from her native South Carolina with a degree in journalism from East Carolina State to work as an intern with *The Washington Post*. There she found herself just one of two dozen young women graduates, all trying desperately to get a byline. By chance she'd heard the veep needed someone who loved to spend time in front of a computer, or in a library, and began the long interview process. When Vanderheld met Shirley for the final once-over, their minds had clicked. Both of them knew it. There was nothing romantic, of course—Vanderheld was a widower with a passel of kids, two of whom were older than Shirley—but their brains, both curious for knowledge, seemed to work in tandem from the first day they were together. After a while Shirley felt as if she was an extension of the vice president, his mobile self able to travel to do research while he was stuck in the tedium of the political jungle of Washington. She was always ready and eager for any quest for information he gave her. Vanderheld's interests were kaleidoscopic—everything from the melting of the glaciers in Antarctica to the poverty in the new dust belt down in Oklahoma. Always, it seemed to Shirley, Vanderheld sought knowledge to better people's lives. Shirley was proud to tell acquaintances and family that she worked for a man who would go down in history as doing more for the poor and the unrepresented than any politician since Franklin Roosevelt.

Shirley attended the vice president's FBI briefing on the second day of *Columbia*'s hijack. The President would be getting the same briefing, the man said, in Iraq. The latest information was that the attorney general had some Florida lawyer tucked away who claimed to represent the hijackers. The lawyer had said their leader was a man named Jack Medaris. He had also confirmed that Craig "Hopalong" Cassidy had been part of the plot. The third hijacker was a man named Virgil Judd. Not much was known about him. Medaris, however, was well known to the FBI. He had brilliantly headed up the group that fixed the shuttle's solid rocket boosters after the *Challenger* disaster. And then he had been involved in a test stand accident that had killed his pregnant wife, an engineer on the team, and put him in the hospital for months. When the government brought charges of dereliction and manslaughter against him, he'd resigned and the charges were dropped. Although apparently he'd had some success with a start-up called MEC in Cedar Key, Florida, he had recently been dealt another blow when a fire had destroyed part of his factory. Arson had been suspected. Although the FBI had not done a psychological profile on Medaris, it was believed that he had snapped, hijacking the shuttle perhaps as an act of revenge against NASA or the government.

The FBI agent said the attorney general had ordered all news of the lawyer and the hijackers to be kept from the press for the time being. Media speculation was rampant, most of it suggesting that homegrown terrorists were responsible. An Internet reporter had come up with the story on the DOT and NASA million-dollar checks but no one could figure that one out. The media was broadcasting the public's calls for action but it wasn't clear what could be done.

The vice president thanked the briefing agent, emphasized the report's confidentiality to his staff, and dismissed them. As the group of technocrats filed out, Vanderheld stopped Shirley. "Wait with me a bit," he requested, remaining silent until everyone else had gone, the door to his office closing behind them. "Listen, Shirley—do something for me," he said. "The FBI's report is pretty shallow. We need more information. Dig into that accident that killed Medaris's wife."

Shirley wrote down the note and then just seemed to catch what the vice president was thinking out of the air. "You think this Medaris is dangerous to the country, don't you, sir?"

Vanderheld slouched in his chair. "Isn't that clear by his actions?" The old man cocked his head. "We may need to prepare the public for a stronger response."

"Stronger response, sir?"

Vanderheld held her eyes. "Desperate people do desperate things, Shirley. I don't know what Medaris has in mind but I guess we're not going to like it when we find out. We may need to destroy *Columbia* before this is all done. If we do, we'll have to justify our actions to the American people. If Medaris is a madman or a terrorist, we need to know that."

Shirley made the note. "Sir, I've looked back at your record and your general opposition to the space program—"

"I'm not opposed to the space program." The veep smiled, opening his hands in that way he had, as if he were embracing his subject. "I am opposed to government waste. It just happened to fall on my plate to question the huge outlays of cash for dubious programs starting with *Apollo* and continuing through *Aurora*."

Shirley's pen was still poised over the pad. She thought it best not to write what the veep had just said, but to carefully probe. A researcher had to know the best approach to her questions, even when interrogating her boss. She needed to know what he really thought. It always helped her research if she did. "Could you tell me why?" she asked.

"It's all in my Senate speeches," Vanderheld said, a little

irritably. He looked tired, worn-out, she suddenly thought. "Let me just put it in a nutshell for you, Shirley," he said, sighing. "There are too many starving children who need to be fed, too many endangered species that need protecting, too much hate and mean-spiritedness that needs to be stopped, too many wrongs to be righted, for the government's money to be spent on something that just gives us pretty pictures of planets or makes us feel good about ourselves. The truth is—and I don't like this any better than anybody else—space is not somewhere we're ever going to go, nor is it a place where we're going to get any kind of a dividend, certainly not equal to the investment it takes to do anything up there. It's just a circus, entertainment for the masses, and that's not the job of government."

Shirley was intrigued at how passionate the veep was on the subject. It was one thing to hear a speech read, another to get an extemporaneous response. "Yet there are millions who believe in it," she said, her statement meant to elicit more information.

Vanderheld waved his hand in a dismissive gesture. "They've bought into the science fiction of it. I'll go along with anything NASA wants to do up there that gives us a return down here. But in all my years in the Senate and the last two years in the Space Council, I've seen nothing that warrants spending a dime in space."

To her discomfiture Shirley found herself disagreeing with her boss, an unusual situation. Still, the veep had given her a quest. She'd do her research for him to the best of her ability, no matter how it might be used. "I'll start my investigation right away, sir," she said, and headed for the door.

"Shirley?"

She stopped. "Yes, sir?"

"Bring everything you find to me first. Don't discuss it with anybody, even in the office."

"Of course, sir." Shirley went back to her cubicle, sat down at her computer and stacks of books and memos and

articles. Vanderheld had never given her such an admonition before. Surely he knew that she could be trusted.
Didn't he? Her hands, hovering over the computer keyboard, were trembling. She thought she knew what she was
looking for. But for the first time since she'd been employed
by the veep, she wasn't exactly sure why.

Sam and the Astronauts
SMC, JSC

Sam brooded over his controllers as they pondered their
consoles. They were watching the blinking numbers that
defined what was going on aboard *Columbia*, looking for
anything that seemed to be ticking in the wrong direction,
varying from nominal. *Nominal*, Sam thought bitterly. That
was one thing this mission could never be.

He had first worked in this same room as a controller for
the old *Apollo* missions and if he wasn't careful it could
flood him with memories. There were a lot of buildings
around the center like that, reminders of the time when the
country had gone to the moon. Those were exhilarating
days and he'd loved working for NASA. But by the time the
space shuttles began to fly in 1981, NASA had changed.
Sam thought the NASA administrators he had seen come
and go had done the best they could, but he also had the
nagging feeling that all but one or two of them had betrayed
the dream instead of nurturing it. After the demise of
Apollo, the wind had just seemed to go out of the dream of
space that NASA was supposed to cultivate. Now with the
shuttle hijacking, he wondered if the agency would even
survive another year.

Sam was watching the shift change when someone
tapped him on the shoulder—John Lakey, the chief of the
Astronaut Office. He was a nervous character for a flyboy.
The way he bobbed his head always reminded Sam of a

turkey. Lakey said something and Sam turned to him, incredulous. "Two shuttles in orbit at the same time? I don't have enough people or instrumentation for that."

"Orders, Sam."

Deborah Kimbrough, another astronaut, handed Sam a copy of a letter. "It's signed by Bonner, authorizing us to prepare for *Endeavour*'s launch." She took a step back. "It's a contingency, Sam. We haven't gotten the final go."

Sam read the order, crumpled it, and threw it on the floor. "If you do this, you could put both shuttles in jeopardy."

Lakey bobbed his head. "That's one of our own up there, Sam," he said. "Dr. High Eagle. The Astronaut Office feels we have to think about stepping up to the plate, be ready to take a swing at this thing."

Sam sneered. "That's the first time I've heard you astronauts claim a payload specialist as your own. Usually you're busting your ass to keep them and anybody but yourselves off the shuttle."

Kimbrough put her hands on her hips. "Don't get in our way, Sam."

"You're crazy if you do this," he said. "You'll end up killing somebody."

"As long as it's one of the hijackers," Lakey said, "so what?"

"*So what?* I know that man up there. Jack Medaris was a good man. Maybe, for all I know, he still is—"

"If you don't want to be Flight on this mission," Kimbrough said, "you can always quit."

"That's right," Lakey added. "Bonner can and will replace you." His eyes cut toward Jim Crowder, who'd been watching. Crowder ducked his head, went back to his paperwork.

Sam looked down on his troops. There was some whispering going on between a few of them nearby. They had heard the argument. Morale was already rock bottom at

Shuttle Mission Control and this wasn't going to help it. "Get out of my control room, both of you," he hissed at the astronauts. "Get out or I'll throw you out."

"We're going, Sam," Kimbrough said over her shoulder as Lakey meekly followed. "But if the Air Force demo doesn't work, we'll be back."

Prepping *Endeavour*
LSS, Pad 39-A, KSC

Colonel Olivia Grant pushed her way out of the elevator at the level-three platform on the fixed tower of the pad, a retinue of contractors and Kennedy Space Center managers in her wake. She barged into the center of a group of white-suited pad rats and snatched a logbook from one of them. "Tell me what you're doing," she barked.

"Closeouts. External tank subsystems," one of them answered, gulping. "Everything checked and double-checked."

Grant waved the logbook at the managers. "This is what I mean, people. Stop checking what's already been checked." She put the book down with disdain and kept moving, pointing to other workers. The Cape managers stumbled along behind, trying to keep up. "There's too many people here. If they aren't doing anything constructive, get them off this pad!" Grant yelled, loud enough so that everybody on the tower could hear her.

She grabbed a Cape manager by the arm and pulled her alongside *Endeavour*'s cockpit. Her grip was powerful. "See there?" Grant pointed. "That's a flight-ready bird."

The woman peered closer at the tiles beneath the cockpit. They were cracked, chipped, and glued. "To tell you the truth, Colonel, if I were an inspector, I would have trouble passing these tiles."

Grant laughed. "You're a paper-pusher. Tiles get dinged

all the time. Just glue 'em in place and we go. People like
you think these shuttles are fragile birds. Truth is we don't
know how much abuse they can take. I'd fly one as soon as
it landed if I had to. Just prop it up, juice the ET, and go."

Grant caught other pad rats staring at her. She put her
hands on her hips and gave them the evil eye. "I want
Endeavour prepped so if we get the word, we can start fuel-
ing no later than 0500 hours the day after tomorrow!" she
bellowed. They scattered.

The tower lead, a woman in a short white lab coat, spoke
up. "We'll need longer than that, Colonel. This bird's just
starting its prep. We can't—"

Grant turned on her. "I don't want to hear excuses.
You're professionals. Figure out what you need to do and
then *do it!*"

Grant kept moving, kicking butt all over the launch
tower and taking names. "Penny High Eagle, I'm comin'
after you, babe," she muttered as pad rats scattered before
her.

The Flight of the Peg
OSC L-1011 Tristar Launch Platform (the Cow),
Patrick Air Force Base, Florida

Pilot Jim Durrance wound up the Cow's engines, powered
her off the runway with full flaps, and then steered her into
a series of rising spirals while copilot Bill Parise kept his eye
on the readouts coming from the Peg. Durrance settled
back, happy in his work. The Cow was the best aircraft he'd
ever flown and he'd flown a lot of them. The Lockheed
L-1011 Tristar airliner had been modified by OSC to
launch the *Pegasus-E.* She was a sweet flier, smooth to the
touch, exquisite even in the roughest air. Today the winds
were negligible, visibility unlimited.

To synchronize with *Columbia*'s orbit, Durrance and the

Cow had been shifted to Patrick Air Force Base in Florida, just south of Kennedy Space Center. Despite her dance with the Indian DODO, *Columbia* had kept her essential ground track and orbital inclination. If she didn't maneuver further, it had been calculated that her orbit would carry her over the point of her ground launch at near five A.M., eastern daylight time. The Cow would fly to 38,000 feet, loiter until *Columbia* came over the horizon, and then launch her rocket.

"Thirty second countdown," Durrance announced. "At your go, Cape."

The Cape range safety officer came back immediately. "You're go for launch, OSC."

"Copy that."

"All nominal," Parise droned. "Gyro set, power go. Nominal, nominal."

Durrance had a perfect mental image of the checks the Peg was putting herself through, because OSC required that the pilots know the launch vehicle as well as her designers. Fifty feet long, 4.5 feet in diameter, weighing 48,000 pounds without a payload, the bird was a three-stage solid-propellant rocket that could carry three quarters of a ton into low earth orbit. The orbit reached on this mission would be higher than usual but the payload was lighter, so that posed no problem. Guidance was inertial and internalized. Once dropped from the Cow, the rocket would climb into orbit on its own.

Durrance lined up on the assigned course and drove the Cow like some gigantic eighteen-wheeler down an air-slab highway in the sky. The monitor bank on the cockpit console did the counting with no voice output, the numbers filling the screen, going from red to orange and then green. Far below, a gigantic cloud formation swarmed toward the coast, the Atlantic glittering through a tear in the bank. Durrance, with the L-1011 on autopilot, gloried in the view.

God bless OSC for letting him drive the Cow. God bless the Peg, and Godspeed.

The winged rocket dropped away cleanly. Durrance powered the Cow over, diving away. Five seconds later the stage 1 motor ignited and the *Pegasus-E* pulled out of her fall and dug into the air, the Hercules engine pushing her to an altitude of 38 miles, wings and fins mounted on the first stage providing pitch, yaw, and roll control during the initial powered flight and the coasting period after burnout. The second stage ignited four seconds later, driving the Peg up to 105 miles. Five minutes and forty-six seconds later the third stage turned itself on, pushing the rocket all the way to an altitude of 558 miles and into orbit at the same inclination as *Columbia*. From there tiny sensors searched the cold vacuum, sensed *Columbia* two miles off and slightly behind. It had been a perfect launch. The Peg used her cold gas reaction system to nudge herself toward *Columbia*, a lateral shift. In slightly less than thirty minutes she was in position. The Air Force called Houston and took Mission Control off-line. This operation would be handled entirely by the Air Force from Eglin and the DIA in Maryland.

Columbia

The galley aboard *Columbia* consisted of an oven, a rehydration station, and a hot water tank. Food trays were warmed in the oven, and dehydrated food was moistened via a needle injector in the rehydrator. The pantry was well stocked, including almost every kind of spice that the astronauts could tolerate—needed because the aroma of food did not drift into the sinuses or caress the palate in a microgravity environment. Sweets were also much appreciated in space. Jack, waking alone in the middeck and starving, had finished a spaghetti meal and was on his third brownie square when the message on the SAREX came through.

DUCK. SHOT ACROSS THE BOW ON THE WAY.

He stared at the screen. *What the hell?*

"This is Colonel Bud Ragusa," a voice crackled over his headset moments later. "United States Air Force Space Command. And this is . . . ?"

Jack, still disoriented after the EVA, remembered nothing except . . . He shook his head. He had this odd memory of High Eagle undressing him. He'd heard astronauts often had strange dreams when they were in space. This was one of the strangest.

"Jack Medaris, Colonel," he replied cautiously. "What can I do for you?"

"Can it, Medaris, and listen up. We've let you have your little ride into orbit but it's time to come down."

Jack finished the brownie and went for a wet wipe. "Colonel, I don't know where you're going with this, but be advised we have a legal contract that allows us to be aboard *Columbia*."

"You don't have a contract to murder and kidnap astronauts, Medaris."

"We didn't murder or kidnap anyone," Jack replied curtly. "Listen, our lawyer—"

Ragusa interrupted him. "That dog won't hunt, boy." His voice softened a little. "All of us down here have read your 201 file. You were once a good man for NASA. Then you kind of went overboard. Looks to me that's what you've done again. Jack, I want you to think about what you're doing and to help you think, me and the boys down here are going to give you a little demo. You may think you're safe up there, outside our reach, but it just ain't so. We can splash you, Jack, any old time we want to."

Ah, a shot across the bow. Got it. "Let's don't do anything foolish, Colonel. Wait until our lawyer gets our case out."

"No can do," Ragusa answered. "I'm assuming you're in the standard plus-X attitude, cargo bay down. Check your cockpit windscreen. Demo of our splash capability coming up in two minutes."

Penny flew down through the hatch from the flight deck. "I need to tell you something," she said, rotating so she was in the same foot-down position as Jack. Jack noted it was slickly done. She had completely adjusted to weightlessness. "No time right now, High Eagle," he answered her brusquely. "The Air Force is up to something."

"Nothing you can't handle all by yourself, I'm sure," Penny replied, rolling her big browns.

"I guess I can," he replied. He left her in the middeck and headed upstairs.

Virgil was strapped in the pilot's seat. "What do you think they're gonna do, boss?"

"Just scare tactics, Virg. They haven't had time to get anything organized. You're doing better, I see."

"Some. As long as I don't move around much."

Jack floated over and examined him. "Your skin's still clammy. Better stay strapped in. Thanks for getting me cleaned up after the EVA, by the way. That couldn't have been easy for you. Guess I was bushed."

"I don't even remember the EVA," Virgil said. "How'd it go?"

"It went fine," Penny said, following from below. "Except our leader here managed to go into heat exhaustion. I had to take care of him."

Jack peered at her. "You took care of me?"

"Well, somebody had to."

He looked down, remembering he had woken up in nothing but his shorts.

"Yeah, that's right," she sang.

The speaker crackled. "Not much time left, Medaris. One minute, thirty seconds."

Jack stopped staring at Penny and keyed his headset. "Listen, Ragusa. Mr. Cecil Velocci of Cedar Key, Florida, will verify our contract."

"One minute."

Penny was hanging in front of Jack, a smirk on her face. It angered him far more than it should have. "You talk to them, High Eagle," he spat. "Your butt will be in the same sling as Virg and me if they damage *Columbia*."

She shrugged. "What can I say? They know I'm here. Apparently they don't care."

"Thirty seconds."

"Dammit!" Jack hit the mike again. "This isn't right, Ragusa!"

"Zero, *Columbia*!"

Low Earth Orbit

The Peg was in perfect position, aimed directly at *Columbia*'s nose from a distance of one thousand yards. At the ground sequence command the SADD deployed its SPRAH payload, five hundred bags of water propelled by a spring ejector. The bags immediately began to spread apart, unfolding like black orchid petals. At a distance of two hundred feet from *Columbia* the bag cluster had expanded to a diameter of one hundred yards and still growing. At that moment the timed squibs inside each bag split the thin plastic, releasing the water, which instantly became a spray of icy needles. The Air Force had done its calculations perfectly, the sun at its best possible angle for the effect. To the trio on *Columbia* it looked as if a gigantic firework had erupted directly in front of them leaving a hoop of rainbow fire. *Columbia* pierced the hoop, the droplets turning into fireflies, darting and turning. . . .

Columbia

It was beautiful. The droplets spread and then formed a doughnut of shimmering particles. Jack watched the display coming at them and then moved aft to watch it pass behind.

"Ragusa," Jack called, "it's incredible! Glorious! Thanks for the great light show!"

Jack's mood changed in an instant from wonder to concern when Virgil pointed at the starboard cockpit windscreen. In the center a white smudge had suddenly appeared. Jack inspected it, squirming to get his eye as close to it as possible. "Something hit us," he concluded. "Probably from the container that held the water."

"Will it be okay?" Penny worried behind him.

"Probably, but we'd better do a high-tech NASA repair job on it just in case."

Virgil perked up. "You mean . . ."

Jack smiled and watched for Penny's reaction out of the corner of his eye. "That's right, Virg," he said, winking at his partner. "Where's the duct tape?"

The Test Stand
Marshall Space Flight Center, Huntsville, Alabama

Marshall Space Flight Center in Huntsville, Alabama, had been expressly built for the purpose of designing and building rocket engines. Big high-bays, utilitarian and factorylike and reflecting their Army heritage, squatted within a web of blacktop roads and railroad tracks built to hold the gigantic boosters constructed by the von Braun team for the *Apollo* program. Frank Bonner drove through the center, scarcely looking at it. The JSC director had an executive jet at his disposal and he'd used it that morning, clipping in to land at the Redstone field, where a rental car awaited him. Ordinarily, it would have been impolite for him to come to the center without letting the Marshall director know he was there. But this was a personal quest. He had awakened with a need to see the place where she had last lived, where Medaris had killed her, his Kate, his life. He'd given the astronaut chief, John Lakey, blanket authority to run JSC for the day. Then he'd taken off. He had to come to this place.

The old test stand had been originally constructed to test

the huge F-1 engines that boosted the *Saturn V*. Bonner remembered how Medaris had begged for funding to refurbish it for a series of engine firings. He'd received nothing. Naturally, he'd done it anyway, shifted accounts, broken NASA directives, and juggled budgets to get what he wanted.

Shimmers of heat rose from the packed earth that surrounded the stand. It stood tall and gray, its center still showing evidence that something had once gone terribly wrong there, a scorched shadow and melted framework about halfway up. Signs warned of danger but Bonner ignored them. The gate was unlocked. Some of the surrounding buildings were still being used for storage. Bonner walked up the steel griddled steps, each footstep ringing hollowly. The only evidence of life on the stand was the cooing of unseen doves, and the flutter of wings high above, deep in the dark vastness of the structure.

Bonner reached the level where the nozzle bell of Kate's engine had been held in place. It had long since been removed, of course, needed for the investigation and evidence for the hearing that followed. The media had followed the tragedy briefly, then dropped it. Only one person had been killed. Only one. In a world where thousands died daily from war and tragedy, what did it matter if only one person died?

Bonner stood at the edge of the scorched platform. His head seemed as if it were going to explode. She was here. He could feel her. She seemed to be reaching out to him as she had once done so willingly, so long ago . . . *before Medaris.* "It's too late," he moaned so loudly that he heard the scratching of something in the bridgework, behind the steel panels, some startled animal scrambling to get away.

Save me.

It was her voice. He looked around. "How, Kate? How?"

Bonner squatted and looked out over the peaceful landscape, a forest of trees, the line of mountains that cut off the Cumberland Plateau. When Kate had died, it had been a cold winter night. The trees had been ugly, leafless skeletons, and the mountains lost in the frigid night. He let himself cry. Tears ran down both his cheeks. This was where she wanted to be, he thought. This was what she loved. But Medaris should have known that, should have held her back. Bonner suddenly realized had he stayed with them, he would been there that night and the accident wouldn't have happened. He was too much the stickler for rules and regulations. He would have stopped them.

Bonner took off his jacket, threw it over his shoulder, thought about his life, how it might have been, how it instead had gone. He was ashamed. He could feel the dream of the people who'd built the test stand, the dream Kate shared of a better way to get into space. Bonner had all but forgotten that there was a dream, a purpose, for all that NASA did.

It was too late now. Bonner had gone too far in the other direction. He had to stay focused on Medaris. Bonner climbed to his feet, walked back to his car. On the flight back to Houston he remembered Bernie Sykes's promise. He could be the administrator of NASA. Then, perhaps, he'd have the power to make Kate's dreams come true. To do that for Kate, Bonner thought, required the one thing he should have done from the day he knew the man existed: stop Jack Medaris.

High Eagle's Decision (2)
Columbia

Penny watched Virgil finish taping the cracked windscreen. Then Jack inspected it and clapped him on the shoulder. "Perfect," he pronounced.

He was too happy by far to suit Penny. "Is that *it?*" she

questioned incredulously. "You're going to trust our lives to duct tape?"

"Give it a rest, High Eagle," Jack said. "NASA's been flying spacecraft held together by duct tape for years."

If that was supposed to make Penny feel better, it didn't work. "You give it a rest, smart guy," she snapped. "We got hit by something the size of a gnat and look what it did. What if they hit us with something *really* big?"

"Relax. They've shot their wad."

"What makes you so sure? I think we'd better start thinking about what else they might try against us."

"We? Us? When did we get to be we and us?"

"Sounds like the good doctor's become a fellow hijacker, boss." Virgil grinned.

"Spacejacker," Penny corrected him.

Jack swung from an overhead handrail, approached Penny. She stood her ground. "Is that right, Dr. High Eagle? Are you part of my team?"

Penny barked a laugh, cut short. "Don't hold your breath for that to happen, Medaris. I only work for myself." She plowed on. "This is a commercial enterprise, correct?" she asked.

"We have a contract," Jack replied cautiously.

"I pray for the day I get to see that most magnificent document," she said.

"I saw it about an hour ago," Virgil said, looking around him.

"Shut up, Virgil. You're not funny."

Virgil put on a hangdog expression. "Yes, ma'am."

"Medaris, here's the way it's going to be. If you want me to help you, I'll need a contract as well."

Jack looked at her suspiciously. "What kind of contract?"

"A contract for my services. I know this may be a little too complex for you, Medaris, but it's like we sign a paper and then you pay me x number of dollars and I do y."

"Define the x in your equation."

"One million dollars."

"That's very funny. . . ."

"All right. Two million dollars," Penny said stubbornly, letting go of the handrail and putting her hands on her hips. She started to rotate. "Care to keep negotiating?" she demanded, grabbing the handrail to stop her spin.

"I wish you'd stop spinning around. And are we negotiating? I didn't know we were negotiating. In that case, forget it."

"You're rejecting me?" she chided.

"That's one way to put it." He turned his back on her. "Virgil, I need one good EVA out of you. Are you up to it?"

Virgil touched his stomach tentatively. "I'll try."

Penny couldn't stand that Jack had turned away. She pulled him around to face her. "You'll do no such thing, Virgil," she declared over his shoulder. "If you throw up in your spacesuit, you could choke to death."

Jack smiled mockingly. "Spacesuit? It's called an extravehicular mobility unit, High Eagle."

Penny felt as if steam were going to come out of her ears. "Really? Well, this is called the finger, Medaris."

"Children, children . . ." Virgil admonished them.

Jack pushed away. "Come on, Virg, let's suit up."

The SAREX tone sounded. Jack headed down into the middeck to see what the message was, Penny following closely behind.

ENDEAVOUR BEING READIED. YOU ARE TARGET. LAUNCH TOMORROW 8:32 A.M. EDT.

"I never thought they'd try this hard to get at us," Jack marveled.

"There's a lot of things you haven't thought about, Medaris," Penny griped, shoving her way to the keyboard.

NAME CREW.

"What difference does that make?" Jack demanded.
"Maybe a lot," Penny muttered.
The laptop whirred.

CMDR OLIVIA GRANT PLT TANYA BROWN MS1 betsy
newell ms2 janet barnes.

Penny stared at the message. "I knew it! Grant, Newell,
Brown, and Barnes—the witches of NASA. And I have a
hunch they're in a take-no-prisoners mood."
Penny tapped on the keyboard.

WARN US AT LAUNCH IF POSSIBLE.

The answer came back quickly.

COUNT ON IT.

Penny worried over the monitor, thinking about what she
was signing herself up to do. "Medaris, I help you do your
stupid tests and then it's over?" she asked. "We land, right?"
"That's the plan."
Penny pushed away from the SAREX and made a figure
four with her legs, her right foot pointed toward the floor,
hooking a footloop with a toe. "Answer my question straight.
No funny stuff. You call Houston and they get us down,
right? Everybody safe and sound?"
"Sure. No problem."
"I hate to be cruel, Medaris, but these engines in the
cargo bay aren't going to blow up, are they?"
He frowned. "They'll work."
Penny pressed. "How did they get into orbit?"
"After I left NASA, I went over to India and helped them
work on some of their boosters. Made a lot of contacts."

"India put them up for you?"

"They were well paid."

Penny pulled hand over hand to the flight deck, her dark ponytail floating behind her like a black flag. She positioned herself at the aft viewing ports and looked at the locked-down shuttle arm holding the engines. Jack came up beside her. "The big one is going to push us around in orbit," he said.

"What about the little one?"

"Another test. It's going to fly around on its own."

"What's in the sausages?"

"Inflatable modules. We're going to test them, see if they work in space. We'll inflate them and I'll climb inside."

"You're going to get in a bag in space?"

"Not a bag, a module made out of a material similar to the EMU suit—spacesuit to you, excuse me—but much lighter."

Penny ignored his gibe. "Oh, I see. You're going to float around in space in a balloon. You can't be serious!"

"I am very serious."

"I don't believe a word of any of this."

"What are you worried about, High Eagle? You're innocent of everything. You just got taken along for the ride. But there's nothing to worry about. I've planned for every possible contingency."

Penny sneered. "Every contingency? Are you an idiot, Medaris, or what?"

"Is there some point you're trying to make?"

Penny had been on a lot of adventures, seen more than a few go wrong, knew that it was the leaders and their egos that usually made the problems, caused the accidents, sent the expedition into danger. That's when people got killed. "From my observation, Medaris," she said, "you won't admit problems. I've seen it before. It's what I call persistent wrongheadedness."

"I suppose you're now going to give me some advice."

"You could begin by simply admitting when you're wrong. And also admitting when you need help."

Paco, awakened by the rising voices, hopped off his perch on the top of the pilot's seat, and ran along the cabin roof. Penny heard him coming, his claws making ticking noises in the soft material. The cat stopped over Medaris, started purring. "Yeah, well, of course I didn't plan on losing Hoppy and maybe I didn't plan on Virgil getting sick." Medaris reached up and scratched the black-and-white cat's neck at his insistent purr.

"I can't believe my ears," Penny said. "You're admitting a miscalculation? Maybe there's some hope for you after all."

At that moment the CAPCOM came on-line over the flight deck speaker. "*Columbia*, Houston."

Jack answered. "Houston, *Columbia*. Go ahead."

"The demo was just a warning," CAPCOM said gravely. "I've been directed to tell you to come down or you're going to get knocked down. Copy?"

Penny keyed her headset. "We copy, Houston. Could I talk to Sam Tate?"

"Sam's on break," came CAPCOM's curt reply.

"Then hear this, Houston. We're up here trying to do science under a legitimate commercial contract and you're not helping a bit with all these threats. I'm talking big-time lawsuit when I get back if this doesn't stop. Now, knock it off! Do you copy?"

"Copy," CAPCOM replied sullenly.

Penny smiled at Medaris. She'd had enough talking. She was in her expedition mode now. "I think we'd better get this show on the road."

Medaris frowned. "What do you mean?"

"I mean let's you and me go out and cram that big rocket up the tail of this shuttle, do this thing, and land."

"You and me?"

"I can do anything you can do." She held out her hand,

palm up. "But I'll be writing out my contract and I want my two million dollars."

"Why don't you make it a hundred million?"

"Keep arguing and I might."

"Let's wait and see how well you do the EVA."

Penny squinted, caught herself at it, and opened her eyes wide. "Another thing, Medaris. How do you plan on landing this crate when you finish your tests? Seems you're missing a pilot."

"I'll land her. I'm a pilot too."

"Is there anything you can't do?" Penny said in a more doubtful than laudatory tone.

"I can't whistle between my teeth," he said after a moment of thought.

Penny put two fingers to her mouth and blew with such volume that Paco leapt off the roof and dived for the deck hatch, meowing a complaint. "You mean like that?" She grinned.

"That would do it," Jack marveled. He looked her over, as if for the first time. "Guess we might make a good pair. I'll do the thinking, you do the whistling."

Penny reacted. "You've got a lot to learn, boy, if you think all I can do is whistle."

"Ready to prove it?" he challenged.

Penny grinned as brightly as ever she could. "Sweetheart, I was born ready!"

First Report
The Vice President's Residence

Shirley found the vice president putting in overtime in his office at his home at the old Naval Observatory. He used a big wooden desk that allowed him to spread out the books and charts of his latest interests. A line of old gray and green government steel files held research on everything from manatees to the mathematics of overpopulation. "Sir, if

you've got a minute? I've made a little progress on Medaris."
She was hugging a folder to her chest. "I'll leave this with
you if you're busy."

Vanderheld directed her to a chair. "Not at all, Shirley.
What've you got?"

Shirley sat, primly. She opened the folder, touched a
finger to her tongue, and turned several pages. "Mrs.
Medaris's maiden name was Katrina Suttner, people who
knew her well called her Kate. Her father was Gerhard
Suttner, an assistant to Dr. Wernher von Braun."

"I knew von Braun," Vanderheld interrupted. "I had him
before my committee several times. He was quite smooth,
I'll give him that. But a zealot too. All that man wanted to
do was to explore space. Everything else was secondary. I
couldn't shake him on that determination no matter how
hard I tried!"

"Gerhard Suttner died just a few months after von
Braun."

Vanderheld nodded. "It was sad how von Braun died so
quickly. I recommended to President Ford that he be given
the Medal of Freedom before he went. I was in his hospital
room when he received it. I'm sorry, Shirley, you were
saying?"

Shirley was always content to let her boss ramble. The
most interesting historical tidbits often fell out when he did.
She continued: "Ursula Suttner, Katrina's mother, died a
year after her husband from complications related to her
chronic diabetes. The only relative left is an uncle in Huntsville, a Dr. Ernst Suttner. I gave him a call. He was quite
nice. He said that he had guessed it was Jack Medaris
aboard *Columbia*. He said Medaris had a special passion for
the moon."

The vice president leaned forward, his eyebrows raised
quizzically. "The moon?"

"It's puzzling. I think as soon as he said it, he regretted it, as if it were something personal. If it is to come out, let Jack bring it out, was what he said."

Vanderbelt sat back. "Puzzling indeed."

"Sir, if you'll approve it, I'd like to fly to Huntsville. I'm not certain, but I believe Dr. Suttner would open up to me face-to-face."

Vanderheld pondered, then shook his head. "I don't think so, Shirley. I think we'll have this hijacking matter cleared up soon. I just approved NASA going up to retrieve *Columbia*. Besides, I need you to do some other work for me concerning WET. You haven't talked to anybody else about what this Dr. Suttner told you, have you?"

"No, sir," said Shirley, standing.

"Good. Let's keep it between us for now."

When Shirley just stood there, Vanderheld looked up from his books. "Yes?"

"You said you had another assignment for me, sir? On WET?"

Vanderheld regarded her pensively. "I want to give it some more thought. I'll be calling you, Shirley."

Shirley closed the door on the old mansion, walked slowly down the brick steps to her car out in the main parking lot. She had just had the rug pulled out from under her and she didn't know why. She didn't think the vice president had leveled with her. Something she'd said had upset him. Shirley was a tenacious researcher. It went against her grain to stop. There was nothing pending on her schedule. She had a little personal leave coming. Shirley had made up her mind by the time she'd wheeled out of the parking lot. She was going to Huntsville, Alabama. Rocket City, USA.

EVA (2)

Columbia

"Do you understand what we're going to do, High Eagle?" Jack asked her as he prepared the airlock.

Penny was pulling on a white spandex mesh undergarment. Translucent and orange tubes were woven into the mesh. "I look like I'm dressed for some bad Hollywood movie," she griped. "What are all these tubes for?"

"They're liquid cooling and ventilation tubes," he told her for at least the third time. Jack knew Penny was nervous or she wouldn't have kept asking. She wasn't the only one nervous. He was beginning to wonder if she was going to be more of a hindrance than a help. "I asked you if you understood our task," he reiterated.

Penny grunted as she pushed her arms into the clinging garment. "We're going to remove the three main engines to make room for the big engine you've got attached to the arm. That about it?"

"You got it." Jack kept working, preparing both his and Penny's EMU suits. He wished it were going to be as easy as she made it sound but he knew it was going to be hot, busy work, and perhaps impossible without Virgil at his side. But with Virgil still sick with SAS, he and Penny were going to have to do this thing or it wasn't going to get done. Jack tried to arrange the two suits, to make it easier for Penny to get dressed inside the airlock. He didn't want to have her worn out before they got going. The suits were bulky and complicated, consisting of a hard upper torso and backpack, and pants with built-in boots. Then there were the gloves, a data-monitoring unit worn as a chest pack, and a bubble helmet with a cover. It took careful choreography to get dressed in the airlock, which was nothing more than a small steel cylinder. To get a little ahead before Penny came in, Jack climbed into the hard torso, his head popping through the top, his arms sliding through the side ports into the arms. He checked the wrist darns installed in the suit arms. These had been installed in the EMU suit after the glove leak that had nearly killed an astronaut during construction of the Space Station. They were designed to keep pressure in the suit even if a glove failed. They were a good idea but damned uncomfortable. He would put the gloves on last. The pants were next. He deftly stepped into them and latched them to the torso. Then Penny came in, closed the hatch behind her, and Jack pressurized the airlock. As he feared, she was still clumsy in zero g and flailed about as she tried to get into her suit. "Dammit, Medaris, you're on my side," she griped, one leg in her pants, the other out.

"You're on both sides," he pointed out.

"Well, I started on my side but you pushed me out of it."

"Children," Virgil soothed over the comm loop, "if you help each other, I think you'll find things will go a lot easier."

Penny made a face at Virgil through the hatch porthole and then laughed. "All right, all right," she said to Jack. "Just help me get into my pants, okay?"

"Whew, I'm not touching that line." Virgil chuckled.

Cooperation worked, and a half hour later Jack finished latching Penny inside her suit. He saw Virgil's face at the porthole and gave him a thumbs-up. Penny looked ready, as much as she was ever likely to be. "Let's go."

Penny fumbled with her chest pack, trying to see the numbers on the digital readouts. "What about the checklist?"

Jack glanced at her gauges. They were all pointing in the right direction. "We don't need a checklist. You're all right. Let's go."

She balked. "I attended this class. We're not supposed to go outside without going through the checklist."

"Look, High Eagle, we don't have time for this."

"You look, Medaris," she said, turning to reach for the plastic card Velcroed to the airlock wall. "You should never be in such a hurry you don't have time to be safe. No checklist, no EVA. Got it?"

Jack ducked her swinging backpack. "Is it too much to ask that you not kill me while you're being safe?"

High Eagle settled down in front of him and started calling out each item on the cue card. Jack rolled his eyes but complied, affirming each of her calls after he checked them. After she had gone down the list, she pointed at the airlock depressurization switch. "Twist that, Medaris, and we'll be ready for egress."

"Egress?"

"That's NASA-speak for going outside."

Jack grinned, despite himself, twisted the valve, waited a minute for the air to leak through it, and then pulled the lever to open the outer hatch. "I'm going to e-gress now, Dr. High Eagle," he said, stretching out the word. He went down on his knees and stuck his helmet outside. There was a handrail bolted next to the hatch. He grabbed it and used it to pull himself the rest of the way out. All of his years of training astronauts in the huge Neutral Buoyancy Simulator in Huntsville made working in space second nature to Jack. He used other handrails to get to the port sill of the bay and then clipped his tether on the guy wire that ran down its length. He headed aft toward the bungeed "sausages." There he unwrapped a set of tools, each secured in its own pouch, pulled out the big battery-powered wrench he'd need to pull the mains. Penny came up behind him. Pleased to see she had managed to get to him on her own, he handed the wrench to her and then released a small tether attached to her wrist. He looped one end of the tether through an eye on the power tool. Tethering everything was essential. A "dropped" tool in space was lost forever.

Penny began to flail around, fighting for stability. "Make every move slow and calculated, High Eagle," he instructed. "Stop kicking. This isn't a swimming pool."

Her breathing was harsh. "This is like being wrapped up in a tent. I can't tell where my feet are."

"Relax and let your body settle into a neutral position and whenever you can, restrain your feet. Hook them on to something."

"I told you I don't know where my feet are," Penny retorted, exasperation in her voice.

"It'll come."

Jack retrieved a bag out of the sausage that was filled with a variety of smaller tools—wire cutters, pliers, screwdrivers, and Allen wrenches—then withdrew another tool, a socket wrench with a mushroom-shaped device on its head. The wrench—called an Essex wrench—allowed an astronaut to turn it with one hand, an energy-saving idea. Jack unclipped the power wrench from Penny and attached it to his waist tether along with the rest of the tools. He peered through the curved surface of her bubble helmet to see her face. "Ready?"

She was squinting. "I told you I was born ready!"

Jack laughed. He couldn't help it. She looked anything but ready to him.

"What are you laughing at?"

He thought to put her at ease by lightly flirting. "I just kind of think you're cute when you try to be macho."

"You trying to put the move on me?"

"No, just being friendly."

"Yeah, right. Let's go, Medaris."

Jack could see he was going to get nowhere with Penny by trying to be nice. Why he had even tried was beyond him. *Back to work.* He had four long tethers on his waist clip. He unclipped one and attached it to Penny's waist so she could use it to stabilize herself when they got to the work site. He started up, hand over hand, climbing *Columbia*'s vertical stabilizer, her huge swept-back tail. Tools were swinging from him like pots and pans on a tinker's cart. "Don't let go whatever you do, High Eagle," he called as he moved. "If you did, Virgil could move the shuttle after you but it'd be a damn hard maneuver and he's never tried it."

He turned to see if she was following. She was, but slowly. Above them was an immense blue-and-white dome —the Pacific Ocean. Jack watched Penny look up at it, then put her head down quickly. He guessed that she had been struck by vertigo, as often happened to spacewalking shuttle astronauts.

Jack came down the vertical stabilizer and gripped the huge bell of the outboard main engine exhaust nozzle. He turned again to check out Penny. She arrived, still kicking her legs futilely. "The first thing we've got to do is remove the panel that covers the engine compartment. Stop kicking, High Eagle!"

Penny immediately stopped kicking but her boots swung over her head. Jack steadied her, holding her backpack.

"I don't have anything to hang on to." She gasped, apparently drained from the exertion of climbing over the stabilizer.

Jack placed her so she could reach the rim of the nozzle. "Hold the bell with one hand to steady yourself. Then swing your boots over to the nozzle below and pinch your feet around its edge."

She tried it. "Okay. But I don't feel very secure."

Jack made the remaining three waist tethers into one long line, clipped it to Penny, then worked his way down to the external tank attach struts and attached the other end there. "You're tethered to the ET. If you let go, I'll be able to pull you back in. You're perfectly safe."

Central America rolled by overhead, then a boil of huge white clouds swirling over the Caribbean. Jack saw Penny look up again and just as quickly back down. "This is hard," she admitted. "I feel like I'm going to fall."

"It's supposed to be hard," he said curtly, more so than he meant. He softened his tone. "You're not going to fall. Sir Isaac Newton wouldn't allow it. Do you think you can hold on and let me tether to you while I work around the nozzles?"

He heard her take a ragged breath. "I can try," she squeaked.

"Grab hold of my feet," he said, swinging his boots up to her free arm.

For the next thirty minutes Jack worked steadily, using the power wrench on the bolts holding the engine shroud, a flat plate that protected the guts of the engines with cutouts for the big nozzles. Penny kept her boots clamped on the lower starboard nozzle and one hand on the top nozzle. Twice, Jack had no hand- or foothold and swung against the tether. Penny had to hold him or he would have slipped off into space. She was a lot stronger than she looked, Jack thought. When the last bolt came out, he thumped the shroud with his fist, popping the edges loose. Then he peeled it away and set it adrift, exposing the workings of the monster engines.

"Look at *that!*" Penny blurted. *That* was the incredible complex of pumps, tubing, pipes, cables, and wire bundles that had been exposed.

"Six tons of useless mass that we've got to move," Jack muttered. "The Big Dog's going in there."

"Why do you call it Big Dog?"

"When you hear it fired, you'll understand. It sounds just like a pit bull."

"Cute." He heard her breathing easier. She was becoming acclimated. "I love the way you men make pets out of your machines," she added.

He smiled, actually pleased that she was doing so well on her first EVA. The standard-issue astronaut would have gotten at least a hundred hours of training in the Neutral Buoyancy Lab before Houston would have even considered letting him do an EVA. Jack kept the banter going. "Well, I'm glad we're at least a source of amusement for you, High Eagle."

"This is going to be a lot of work, isn't it?" she asked suddenly.

"The record for changing out a shuttle main is eight hours. We have about the same amount of time to remove all three if we want to get back on our timeline. Fortunately, we don't have to follow ground procedures."

"We're just going to rip the engines out?"

"We're going to *carefully* rip them out."

Jack adjusted the camera attached to his helmet and flicked it on. If it worked, Virgil should be able to see what Jack was doing. "Do you see us, Virg?" Jack called.

Virgil's comeback was instantaneous. "Yep. I see the shroud's gone and you're at the coolant control valve of the number three engine."

Jack was thankful he was going to have Virgil giving him advice as he proceeded. There were few at the Cape who had changed out more shuttle mains than Virgil Judd. Jack untethered and turned to face Penny. He pointed into the dark recesses of the engines. "If I get stuck in there, I might need you to come help me out."

Penny peered into the tangle. "Don't get stuck, okay?"

"I'll do my best." Jack began to worm his way into the wires and tubing, moving slowly, gauging each move, trying not to get his backpack snagged. When he got deeper, he switched on his helmet lights. "What do you see, Virg?"

"Good picture, Jack. You're at the engine interface panel."

A cavity allowed Jack to straighten up and turn around. He swept his light back along his path, tubing and cables still vibrating from his passing. He faced the bulkhead and directed his lights at the big bolts that ran along the edge. When he saw that each bolt had a recess, he got worried. "What are the holes for, Virg? Not for squibs, I hope."

"Negative. There are no pyrotechnics in the engine compartment. Those are for the transducers used to measure torque."

"How much torque?"

"Only about twenty foot-pounds. You should be able to manhandle them with the Essex wrench if the power tool can't do it."

Jack set about his task. He clipped the safety wires and then put the power tool on the first of the bolts. "It's turning!" he cheered.

"Great. Okay, don't do any more on the bolts," Virgil advised. "Cut all the propellant lines and electronics first. Let me see everything you cut before you do it and I'll give you the go-ahead."

Jack needed more hands. "High Eagle, could use some help in here. You'll need to untether."

He heard her sigh but then she said, "Coming in." The girl had guts, he had to give her that.

When Penny came up beside him, he handed her a pair of heavy wire cutters. "Here's the drill, High Eagle. I'll point, Virgil will say if it's okay, and then we'll take turns cutting. It'll be slow going and hard on our hands. When I need to rest, you'll cut. Then vice versa. Got it?"

She was squinting again. "Got it."

Jack knew that getting Virgil's permission before any tube or wire was cut was critical. There was little danger if the main engine propellant lines were cut because they contained only water and ice, but the OMS and RCS lines that ran along the aft bulkhead were extremely hazardous. If they were accidentally cut, the resulting high-pressure spray of nitrogen tetroxide or monomethyl hydrazine could deteriorate the EMU suit fabric rapidly. And if both got loose and mixed, the engine compartment would become a giant bomb.

After cutting out two engines Jack called for a stop when he heard Penny groan. "It feels like my fingernails have been pried back to the quick," she complained. "These damn gloves!"

"I know it's hard, High Eagle," Jack said quietly, his voice thick with fatigue. "But you're doing a damn good job."

There was a vibration in the engine compartment. Jack put his glove against the bulkhead. "Did you feel that?"

"Did something hit us?" Penny worried.

His glove picked up another vibration. "There it is again. I wonder—"

Before Jack could finish his thought, the engine compartment exploded in furious movement, wires and cables and cut tubing flying around like maddened snakes. A thick cable whipped Jack, sending him smashing into an RCS line. The line flexed and then broke, flooding the compartment with toxic monomethyl hydrazine.

SMC

"Flight, PROP."

Sam keyed his mike. *What the hell did the propulsion controller want?* "Go ahead, PROP."

"Flight, there was indication of ice in the port aft RCS line. I just popped it out of there. Then I compensated with a burst from starboard. Looks like I might have started an inadvertent tumble."

Sam felt his stomach bottom out. "You didn't tell *Columbia* what you were going to do?"

There was an "uh-oh" pause from the woman. "Negative. It's normally routine. We do it all the time."

Sam stood up, found the woman on the PROP console, and glared at her. She raised her head, looked embarrassed. "Propulsion, this flight is never going to be routine." She nodded her head, ducked it back behind her monitor. Sam punched up the comm loop. "CAPCOM?"

"CAPCOM. Go."

"Tell *Columbia* what we did and that we meant no harm."

"Roger that."

Columbia

Virgil looked up from a drawing. *Columbia* shuddered, then there was a big thump, like a distant bass drum. Virgil looked out a window, saw the shuttle was starting to tumble slowly on her Z-axis, tail over nose. Then there was a long, staccato series of muffled drumbeats. Virgil pawed the transmitter of his headset. "Houston, *Columbia*. Are you firing the RCS?"

"Sorry about that, *Columbia*," the CAPCOM replied. "We were clearing your port aft RCS of ice. Can you stabilize?"

Virgil fought his way to the pilot's seat, found the OMS/RCS power switches, and safed them, but still an engine burned. *Columbia* tumbled ever faster, like a boulder rolling down an eternal black slope. Virgil kept working, desperately going after all power distribution switches. When he finally gave up trying to isolate the problem, he slapped off the main computer power bus and the muffled roar abruptly stopped. Turning off the computer had caused valves upstream to slam shut, not a good thing to do to sensitive hardware.

Virgil held his hand up to shade his eyes. The sun was flashing through the flight deck windows like a doppler spotlight. *Columbia* was in a head-over-heels somersault. Virgil braced himself against the artificial minigravity caused by the centrifugal force of the tumble. Drops of sweat were flying off his face. He clawed his way back to the view ports. Every ten seconds *Columbia* completed a rotation. The earth and stars seemed to be playing leapfrog. Virgil felt his stomach start to complain. Just as he reached for a barf bag, something white flashed past the aft view ports. An EMU suit glove. Someone had died out there. He pressed the bag to his mouth, his body racking spasmodically.

SMC

"Sam, it's Bonner."

Sam turned in his chair, saw Bonner coming out of the VIP room. He was weaving. "Shit. He's drunk!"

Bonner plowed up to Sam's console, looked at the

graphic of the tumbling shuttle on the CRT. "You've got him! Good work, Sam!"

Sam saw Lakey standing over the CAPCOM. He was putting down the long line phone. His mouth was open in astonishment at Bonner's appearance. He'd probably called the director, tracked him down at the Rawhide from the look of him, told him that *Columbia* was in a tumble because something the SMC had done. "Frank, you're in no shape to be here," Sam said, waving all his controllers' eyes away from the scene.

Bonner leaned on the console. "Keep pumping the RCS jets," he said, summoning up the precise words with obvious difficulty. "Do it, Sam."

"It was a mistake, Frank. We're correcting it now."

"No. Keep pumping or you're relieved."

"You can't relieve me while you're drunk. Go home. Sober up and then come back and do it if that's what you want."

Bonner lurched to the edge of the platform. He looked down at the youthful controllers, who were all staring back, eyes wide. "I am ordering you to . . . to . . ." He seemed to catch himself. He turned back to Sam. "That bastard is a murderer."

"That isn't true, Frank," Sam replied softly, understanding a little what was upsetting Bonner. "Medaris made a bad mistake but that's all it was. He paid the price. And it was a long time ago."

Bonner leaned against the console, "He took everything away from me."

"What's he talking about, Sam?" Crowder whispered nervously.

Sam saw Hank Garcia watching from the VIP-room door. "Get over here!" Sam mouthed.

Garcia ran over, took Bonner by his elbow. Bonner straightened, as if remembering his dignity. He looked at

Sam. "Sam, stop Medaris. I'll give you anything you want to do it."

"You don't have the power to give me anything," Sam muttered. "Get him out of here, Hank," he ordered Garcia.

"You're relieved, Tate!" Bonner yelled over his shoulder as he was half pushed, half carried, from the SMC. "Relieved!"

Sam went after Lakey. "I told you not to interfere with my control room."

Lakey took a step back. "Sam, listen to me. I didn't realize Bonner was drunk. But he doesn't matter. Think about it. If we put them in a perpetual tumble by firing up the RCS, we'll get them so sick all they'll be able to do is puke. Then we can bring them in and end this thing."

Sam pushed his long, bony finger into the astronaut's chest. "You listen to me. This control room was built to protect spacecraft, not to harm them. And as long as I'm in charge, that's the way it's going to be. I don't want to see you in here again."

"You can't banish me from the control room, Sam. I'm the chief of astronauts."

Sam grabbed him by his collar, spun him around, and pushed him in the direction of the security guard at the door. "Take him out of here and flush his clearance," he ordered the guard. Then he went back to his console, knowing his hours in Shuttle Mission Control were numbered. He punched up all the loops. "SMC, this is Flight. Forget what you just saw. The director is having a bad day. If I hear a word of this on television or read anything about it in the newspapers, I'll find out who did it and have their hide. Understand?" When no reply came, Sam gave the room a good vulture and then as good a smile as he could summon up. "CAPCOM, get *Columbia* back. Let's see if we can help them for a change."

Columbia

Jack was knocked against the propellant line. It broke, a blast of bluish spray erupted, just missing him. Penny lunged for the line, grabbed it, twisted it away from both of them toward the aft bulkhead. It stopped spraying, a valve upstream snapping into place. But her suit felt strange. She looked down at her right glove, saw the reason. The fuel had eaten away some of the material from the tip of the index finger. Reflexively, she pressed the finger to her suit. *Wrong move.* More of the material sloughed off. She gasped for air, a fog of moisture beginning to condense on her faceplate. . . .

Jack gripped a dangling bundle of cables and pulled toward Penny, arriving just as she started to subside into unconsciousness, her arms waving in front of her. He pinched the affected glove but the material was too degraded to seal. Even in zero g the suit seemed to sag on her, the awesome vacuum pulling the life out of her. The internal wrist seal wasn't working. There was only one thing he could do. He had heard it discussed as a contingency among the astronauts, always dismissed as impossible. He squeezed the latches on her glove and pulled it off, pushing her hand back inside the arm and then swinging the aluminum wrist joint against the folds of his outer suit, creating a temporary seal. He was rewarded with the sight of her suit filling, the emergency 6,000 psi oxygen tank inside automatically venting. Behind the fog of her faceplate he saw her eyes flutter and then open. "Relax, High Eagle, I've got you."

"Medaris, I don't feel so good."

He looked at her DCS readout. The pressure was still down. He braced his feet and dug into the bag at his waist for a roll of duct tape. He couldn't think about it. He had to do it.

He unlatched the wrist of his left-hand glove, stripped it off. His hand emerged momentarily into the icy chill of space before he plunged it inside the open arm of her suit. A hot fire shot up his hand to the wrist seal, the capillaries of his exposed skin bursting. He clamped the two rings of the space-suit arms together and wrapped the gray tape around them, once, twice, three times. The blinking numbers on her chest pack told the story. Pressure dropping, shutdown imminent . . . He started another wrap of tape.

Virgil ran his hands over his face again and again, trying to get control of himself. He stared back into the payload bay. He would have to go out and get them. Not that it would matter. He was as dead as they. He couldn't land a shuttle, not with it tumbling like it was, and he didn't know how to stop it.

He heard Sam's voice. "*Columbia*, Houston. Fire up your computers. We'll get you out of your tumble. It must've been the ice. All the valves stuck open. We'll get 'em closed."

Virgil did as he was told without comment. Within a minute the RCS thrusters started to pump forward and aft. *Columbia* settled down. That was when a movement in the cargo bay caught his attention. "Hey!" he screamed at the universe. "Hey! Would you look at that!"

Before his disbelieving eyes Jack Medaris and Penny High Eagle were coming down the sill toward the safety of the airlock hatch. The real miracle was they appeared to be holding hands!

The Veep's Party
The Vice President's Residence

The vice president's official residence was on the corner of Thirty-fourth Street and Massachusetts Avenue, a rambling brick house on a broad green lawn. It looked more like a museum than a place to live but Vanderheld had put his stamp on it, turning it into a stately mansion filled with artwork and the veep's eclectic collections of butterflies and books. To help along the World Energy Treaty, he had decided to hold a party for the Senate. Vanderheld would remind them of the President's journey to Baghdad. The treaty Edwards had gone to broker was tied, he'd explain, to WET. With WET's restrictions on dangerous alternative energy schemes, oil was all the more important to the United States. The Middle East needed to be a stable region. Iraq and Iran were the keys to that. Vanderheld was known as a great storyteller. He was wowing a group of half-drunk senators with his story about the time, as a very young man, he'd climbed the Matterhorn. "I looked around for my guide and saw him sitting down on this ledge," he said to their grins. " 'What's wrong, Günter?' I asked. He threw up his hands. 'I came to climb, not run, up this mountain, Herr Vanderheld!' "

While the appreciative audience chuckled, Vanderheld spotted the attorney general and FBI Director Mark Hennessey coming in an hour late for the party. Hennessey saw him at the same time, said something to Hawthorne, and came up to the veep. "Sir, the attorney general and I need to talk to you."

Vanderheld raised his eyebrows. "Is it that important I should leave my guests?"

"Yes, sir."

Vanderheld shrugged, led the way into his study. The AG was wearing a gown that hung off her big shoulders like a black tent. She shook the veep's hand, patted him on the shoulder, but that was as far as she went. She never gave out hugs. "I thought you needed to hear this right away, sir. The committee of federal judges I appointed to study the contract that damned southern lawyer has been waving around has come in with an opinion. They tell me it's likely to hold up in court. In other words, it's a legal contract between this MEC outfit and the government, signed and sealed by that idiot the President has for a secretary of the Department of Transportation."

Vanderheld absorbed her rapid-fire delivery. "Why does DOT have anything to do with the shuttle?"

Hawthorne snorted. "The space business, especially the launching of commercial payloads, is so full of overlapping agencies and congressional mandates, it's a fool's paradise. DOT has a piece of it and so does the Department of Commerce, and they're always wrangling for a bigger share. The contract specialists at DOT liked the idea that the MEC contract would establish DOT as a player in lining up shuttle payloads." Hawthorne sighed, shook her head. "The devil is always in the details. There's one paragraph in there that can be interpreted to mean if MEC pays a million to DOT and a million to NASA, it gets exclusive use of the shuttle, period. It doesn't say that they have to do anything other than pay the money. And it doesn't say that they have to adhere to any schedule other than their own."

"Tammy, let me get this straight," Vanderheld said. "You're telling me that the *Columbia* hijack is legal?"

"I'm telling you exactly that, sir. Oh, we can get them for little technicalities on safety and so on, might even get them for endangering the astronauts in the elevator, but their presence aboard the shuttle is covered by their contract."

Vanderheld walked to the window, looked out into the darkness. "*Endeavour* has launched," he said stiffly. "It was against my better judgment, frankly. I told the President that. Bernie Sykes convinced him otherwise. I fear someone will be hurt up there."

"Well, maybe you should call it off," Hawthorne said. "Especially since it looks like those old boys are up there more or less quasilegal."

"I don't think the President will agree, Tammy," Vanderheld said sadly. "He just wants this over. It looks bad for him while he's trying to negotiate a peace treaty in Iraq."

"Well, God bless America," Hawthorne said sarcastically. "This is going to be a bloody mess when it hits the courts."

Vanderheld turned, his face a mask of concern. "The courts will figure something out, find a compromise, if it ever gets that far. *I* worry about the children of this country. What will they think when they see on television that their space shuttle has been attacked by another one?"

Hawthorne snorted. "I think the little rug rats will get over it."

Vanderheld shook his head. "No, Tammy, you're wrong." He sighed, put his hand on his ceiling-high bookcase, dragged his fingers across a row of books as if they might impart some wisdom to him when he needed it the most. "It is a traumatic thing we're doing to them this day, I fear. Perhaps to the nation at large."

MET 3 DAYS AND COUNTING . . .

Raid of the *Endeavour*

Endeavour

Endeavour's pursuit of *Columbia* began at MECO, main engine cutoff, and lasted twelve hours. With Ollie Grant at her side, Pilot Tanya Brown made a long OMS burn that took the shuttle up to a 558-mile-high orbit. With one eye on the computer that gave her a constant update of the target, she used two coelliptic burns to shift to *Columbia*'s track. "On the money, Tanya," Grant said, clapping her crewmate on the shoulder. "Now let's catch those bastards."

Grant took off her launch helmet, shaking out her short hair. "I'm going to go doff my LES and check the airlock," Grant called over her shoulder, heading below.

Brown nodded and gripped the control stick. Rendezvous between two shuttles, each going five miles per second, required complete concentration to avoid disaster. The rendezvous was also complicated by the need for *Endeavour* to approach *Columbia* without being seen. Brown would have to work to keep the RCS jets aimed away from the target. For that she would use what was called a low-Z axis approach, a maneuver requiring the cant of the aft firing thrusters and the scarf of the forward firing thrusters to produce the needed accelerations. That would minimize plume impingement—meaning no one on board *Columbia* would see the burst of flames produced by *Endeavour*'s thrusters—but it also meant burning a prodigious amount of propellant.

Six hours later *Endeavour* was starting to edge into range of *Columbia*. "There she is," Brown said.

Grant, back in the commander's seat, saw *Columbia* with

her external tank still attached. It looked like a big orange blimp floating in space. "Give me the stick, Tanya," she said. For the final maneuver Grant intended to "eyeball" it, using the seat of her pants to put *Endeavour* into position. She was the best pilot in the astronaut corps. She didn't need a computer to tell her how to fly *Endeavour*. With a light touch on the stick she eased the shuttle closer, steadying three hundred yards beneath *Columbia*.

A glint of sun reflecting off something large behind *Columbia* attracted Grant's attention. Puzzled, she investigated with binoculars, recognizing the distinctive conical shape of rocket nozzles. She swept back to *Columbia*. *What the hell?* The shuttle mains were gone and there appeared to be something else—another engine?—bolted in the shuttle's tail. Why would the hijackers tear their shuttle apart? Grant slowly lowered the binoculars. Something didn't add up. "What do you think?"

"Beats me, Ollie," Brown answered, using the zoom on a small video camera for a better view. "Unless they need that new engine to go to a higher orbit. Could they be after a comm satellite in geo?"

Brown meant a communications satellite in geosynchronous orbit, 25,000 miles above the earth. Shuttles weren't able to go that high. Communications satellites were worth a lot of money, but Grant supposed there were better ways to make a buck than stealing a shuttle and rebuilding it in orbit just to steal a satellite. And who would you sell it to, anyway? "The only way to find out," she said, "is to get *Columbia* back. Let's do it." She unbuckled her straps and climbed out of her seat, heading for the middeck to prepare for her EVA.

Columbia

Jack, bone tired, opened the airlock hatch and pulled himself through it into the middeck. Even being weightless couldn't soothe muscles that felt as if they had been pulled into strings. He and Virgil had spent six hours pulling the remaining two engines out and replacing them with the Big Dog engine. Thank God, he reflected, that Virgil's SAS symptoms had diminished, at least enough to let him go outside and provide the brains and brawn needed to get the huge engines moved. Essentially, he and Jack had kicked the engines into space, wedging themselves between the aft bulkhead and the unbolted engines and using leg power to send them down their guide rails. There had been nothing elegant about the operation, just unbolting the engines and cutting their power and propellant lines. The original plan had envisioned a more careful approach so that someone might recover the engines, return them to earth to be used again. But the massive power-plants Jack and Virgil had sent tumbling away were just so much scrap metal now. Jack regretted that, but not enough to keep him from doing the damage. *Endeavour* was probably on her way already. They needed to get going and soon.

He looked up at the flight deck, listening. There was no sound of any movement there, just the faint clicking of sole-noid valves as the air delivery system worked to stabilize pressure and keep the oxygen levels adequate. He floated silently onto the flight deck. He was in his underwear but guessed Penny was asleep. She was, strapped into the pilot's seat. Jack quietly checked her color. It looked good. He couldn't help but marvel once again at her face, the un-blemished skin, high cheekbones, large eyes, and hawklike nose that gave her an exotic elegance. As he looked at her, her eyes blinked open and she stared at him sleepily. "Medaris, what are you looking at?" She yawned, a hand moving up to the back of her neck, underneath her hair.

Penny had been close to decompression sickness after her suit had lost pressure. Two hours of oxygen therapy in the airlock had, Jack hoped, kept her from coming down with a full-blown case. "How do you feel?" he asked.

"Tired," she replied. She was dressed in shorts and a

rugby shirt. She looked down at herself, as if realizing for the first time what she was wearing. "I don't remember much. . . ." She looked back at Jack, her eyes widening. "My suit . . . my glove . . ."

"I got to you in time," he said simply. He probed her for information to see if there had been any onset of the bends. "Do your joints ache? Any tingling in your hands or feet? Any numbness?"

She sat quietly, her eyes closed, as if searching through her body for answers. She looked at her hand. It was red. "My hand feels sunburned and I'm tired," she said, looking up at him as if for guidance.

Jack nodded. Decompression sickness sometimes caused the fatigue, but if that's all she had . . . "You're going to be all right, High Eagle," he pronounced with mental fingers crossed. "The sunburn is the capillaries in your skin. They burst when you were exposed to the vacuum. It'll clear up in a few days."

She looked again at her rugby shirt. "How did I get into these clothes?" She stared at him. "You *didn't*!"

He shrugged. "Virgil helped me. We had to get you out of that suit and into something dry and warm." To her shocked expression he continued, "You did the same for me once."

Her face clouded. "Not the same, Medaris." She shook her head, then looked around. "What's happening?"

"Virgil and I got the other engines out, put the Big Dog in their place. He's still out in the cargo bay, tidying up."

"You left him out there alone?"

"He'll be all right. He's a big boy."

She looked again at her left hand. The red color extended just past her wrist. Jack showed her his right hand and arm. They looked the same. "I got the same treatment. We were lucky we didn't get a bubble in an artery."

"I remember now," she said quietly, staring at the rash. "You saved my life," she said as if it had just dawned on her.

"I couldn't let anything happen to my EVA buddy, could I?"

"So now we test and then we land, right?" she asked.

He nodded. "Sure."

"We need to land, Medaris," Penny said. "It's what you promised. They're not going to give up. They're going to kill us if they can."

Jack's grim eyes belied his smile. "They'll have to catch us first."

Cargo Bay, *Endeavour*

As soon as the airlock was opened into *Endeavour*'s cargo bay, Grant pulled herself down the port sill guide wire to the manned maneuvering unit attached there. The MMU looked like a big white metal chair with armrests but no seat. On the arms were joysticks for controlling the built-in jets for maneuvering. Janet Barnes, following Grant, inspected the MMU and then helped to attach it to her commander's backpack. She made a quick check of connections and then gave Grant a salute. Grant put her gloved hand on Barnes's helmet. It looked like a blessing. Then, her heart in her throat, she pushed off across the bottomless void toward *Columbia*. "She's on her way," Barnes announced on the encrypted suit channel.

"You go, girl," Brown said to Grant.

It was a wild ride. Above Grant was a vast brown and green continent—Africa. Below her was deep space, the stars shining like white-hot holes punched into a deep black fabric of nothingness. Ahead was the underbelly of *Columbia*, her glittering heat shield tiles reflecting in the brilliant golden sunlight. The MMU's jets were enough to get Grant up to a speed of nearly fifty miles an hour, but she didn't need that much velocity for the short hop across the vacuum to the hijacked shuttle. She throttled back after her initial spurt and soared up and over the shuttle's port wing. Just as she went over the wing, she saw the boot of Italy and the sparkling Mediterranean passing overhead. Then the field of view narrowed to the bright white cargo bay. Working the joysticks, Grant slowed and settled feetfirst just behind the ATESS tether spool. She grabbed the handrail on its cover and doffed the MMU, tethering it to another handrail. She made a quick inspection of the cargo bay. The ATESS was still buttoned up inside its boxy cover. On the port sill the RMS arm was stowed, clamped down in place. Aft was the extended mission power pallet with its extra fuel cells and instruments covered in white multilayered material. There were, however, some alien packages in the bay. Two big rolls of tentlike material were tied up like sausages in front of the power pallet. And strapped to the aft starboard sill was a short, stout cylindrical device that appeared to be a rocket engine of a type Grant couldn't identify. She had no time to speculate on its purpose. She had to work fast, before she was spotted. She made her way to the airlock hatch. A glance at the empty flight deck view ports convinced her she hadn't been seen. She stopped at the hatch and opened the pouch connected to her waist loop. It contained a small tank of compressed chemical agent designed to render the hijackers unconscious. Bonner had flown it down to the Cape, personally handed it to her, showed her how it worked. To neutralize the hijackers, she was to climb inside the airlock, open up all the air valves to get positive pressure, kick open the inner hatch, and pitch the canister inside. She would be protected by her suit from the released gas. Once the pin was pulled, nothing the hijackers could do besides explosive decompression could clear the air. And explosive decompression would kill them unless they were in EMU suits.

Grant eased open *Columbia*'s exterior airlock hatch. It swung on its hinges, nothing pushing it. That meant there was no pressure in the airlock. That wasn't right. There should have been a rush of air. Unless someone had used the airlock to go outside and was still outside . . . She

pulled the pin on the canister, started to clamber through the hatch. She had to move quickly before—*Too late!* She felt something hinder her and then she was being jerked backward and twisted around. An ugly face in a bubble helmet appeared. She fought him but he was far too strong for her. He tore the canister out of her hand and flung it away. Grant watched it tumbling, its burnished aluminum surface flashing in the sun as it pitched end over end. She touched helmets so that her voice would carry through the plastic. "This is an order from the President of the United States!" she yelled. "You are to turn this shuttle over to me. *Now!*" Then, to her horror, she saw a spout of fire overhead and realized she hadn't been carrying a gas canister at all. She had carried a bomb. An aluminum sliver flew like a jagged dart to imbed itself into the MLI blanket not six inches from her helmet.

The man looked at the shrapnel, pulled it loose. He touched his helmet to hers. "You were going to kill us!"

"I didn't know," she gasped.

He looked at the aluminum shard, tossed it away. "It would have killed you too," he said.

Grant cringed as the sun, reflecting off the Indian Ocean, flashed white hot in her eyes. She turned away in shame and confusion. The man was right. Frank Bonner had tried to kill everyone aboard *Columbia*. Grant would have died too. He'd sent her on a suicide mission.

Endeavour

Barnes maintained a lonely vigil at the airlock hatch. There had been a brief snatch of comm from Grant, enough to know she was in trouble, and then a gout of fire over *Columbia*. Brown had gotten on the horn to talk to Houston, to get advice on what to do. John Lakey was the new flight director. Sam Tate was gone, relieved of duty by Bonner. Lakey was still mulling the situation over when Barnes saw the MMU appear over the edge of the cargo bay. It wasn't

Grant. Whoever it was was carrying a ball that Barnes recognized as a PRB, a personal rescue ball.

The PRB was a thirty-inch-diameter sphere made out of spacesuit materials. Every shuttle carried at least three of them. The person in the MMU flew down to Barnes, gave her a salute, and then tossed the ball to her. Then he soared away, crossing the gap between the shuttles. When the ball was unzipped inside the airlock, Grant emerged, stripping the oxygen mask from her face. She ignored all questions and went to the flight deck, got in the commander's chair, and stayed there, her face an impervious mask. Brown consulted the flight surgeons, who advised a mild dose of Valium. Brown took them to her. Grant furiously flung them in her face.

Monte Sano
Monte Sano Boulevard, Huntsville, Alabama

Shirley had never been to the Rocket City, but the directions given her at the Huntsville-Decatur International Airport proved easy to follow. She zipped down the eight-laned interstate spur into the city, past the Space and Rocket Center and its famed Space Camp, to the exit ramp onto Governor's Drive, which led through the medical district and then took a steep turn up a mountain. It was Monte Sano, which meant, in Italian, the "mountain of health." During the early 1950s the von Braun rocket team, finding it similar to their homeland, had bought property on the mountain and built their homes there. Many of them were still there, including Dr. Ernst Suttner, Katrina Medaris's uncle.

Shirley turned the rental car onto Monte Sano Boulevard and climbed a narrow, twisting road through a dense forest. To her left sprawled Huntsville, the town von Braun and his team had built. Redstone Arsenal's vast green acreage could be seen beyond the city and pushing into the sky the massive stands used by Marshall Space Flight Center to test

rocket engines. Near the top of the mountain she stopped for a moment and simply admired the view. As she did, the thunder of an engine being test-fired on one of the stands rolled over the valley and into the foothills. Shirley wondered if Jack Medaris's Kate had died on that stand.

The homes on the mountain, small and solidly middle class, surprised Shirley until she remembered her research. The German team could have made a fortune had they chosen to sell their knowledge to industry but instead had stuck with von Braun to work tirelessly as low-paid civil servants, dedicated to bringing the moon to the nation that had adopted them. And good citizens they had become too. Huntsville had an engineering university, a modern civic center, a new library, an observatory, a top-flight symphony, and a solid high-tech industrial base primarily because of the influence and dedication of the team of German rocket scientists and engineers who had come to live in what had been a tiny cotton-mill town.

Shirley found Suttner's house, a single-story brick dwelling, on the bluffs of Panorama Drive. She walked up the driveway and rang the bell. A cheerful woman with a mop of white hair answered. Shirley told the woman who she was. The woman smiled at her. "*Ja, ja.* I am Elsa Suttner. Ernst is in his study. Come."

Ernst Suttner was a thin, wiry man with bright blue eyes that sparkled with wit and intelligence. He greeted his guest. "Please, Miss Grafton. Sit down. Elsa will bring us tea and cookies and we will talk. It is a pleasure to meet a member of the vice president's staff. I was impressed by the speech he gave recently on the danger of global warming. It was excellent, although I do have a problem with the studies he referenced that predict the deterioration of the ozone layer. I'm afraid they rely more on emotion than good science."

"You have me there, Dr. Suttner," Shirley apologized. "I'm no scientist. Political science, though. George Washington University, 1995."

Suttner wagged his finger at her. "Ah, is there any science really more complex than politics?" He laughed heartily. "Your vice president knows that very well. But sit, have some tea. We will talk."

Shirley sat, accepted the tea and cookies, and then began her questions to the old rocket scientist. He answered all her questions on Medaris and his wife, how Katrina had grown up in the small scientific community, how she and Medaris had met, how she had died. But, frustratingly, Suttner refused to answer any questions about Medaris and what he might be doing aboard *Columbia*. "You mentioned something about the moon when I first talked to you, Dr. Suttner," Shirley probed, trying to tease it out of him, whatever it was. "What did you mean by that?"

Suttner sipped his tea, shrugged. "Jack always thought the United States should go back to the moon, consolidate our gains after *Apollo*. He isn't alone in that, Miss Grafton. There are many of us in the space community who believe that is the case. The problem is, of course, convincing our politicians! Vice President Vanderheld has been one of our major opponents all along. I should like to talk to him someday, convince him otherwise."

Although Suttner was willing to discuss the space program all day, he would say no more about Medaris and his possible motives. Frustrated, Shirley thanked him and gave up. She slowly drove toward the crest of the mountain. Before she reached it, a blue sport utility vehicle pulled out in front of her from a side road. It flashed its lights. Shirley stopped. The driver of the SUV was Elsa Suttner.

Later, as she drove down the mountain, Shirley, who was proud of her toughness, found to her surprise that she was crying. She pulled over at a scenic observation point to look out over the beautiful valley. There was another rumble, another rocket engine being tested, and she thought of what

Elsa Suttner had told her about her niece and how Jack Medaris had staggered into the hot belching exhaust of a rocket engine out of control, screaming not from the physical pain of the burning of his flesh but from the anguish of losing his very reason for living. Elsa had told her more, speculation really, on why she thought Medaris had taken an enormous gamble, just to reach back, to be with Kate again in the only way he could. *"I love thee with the breath, smiles, tears, of all my life,"* Shirley quoted softly to herself as the plumes of smoke drifted from the engine into the sky. *"And, if God choose, I shall but love thee better after death."*

She used a tissue to dab her tears away, and hurried down the mountain. She was on her way to Houston, where Elsa said there were more answers.

Ignition of the Big Dog
Columbia

Jack watched Penny, made certain she was properly strapped into the pilot's seat. She gave him a smile, then a thumbs-up. "I'm okay," she said. "Let's do your tests and end this. And, Jack?"

Jack looked over his shoulder, raised his eyebrows. "Um?"

"I'm going to testify for you down there. I'm going to do everything I can to keep you and Virgil out of prison."

"Thanks, High Eagle. Nice of you. Virgil, did you check her straps?"

Virgil was strapped in a resurrected mission specialist seat. Paco had been put back in his padded locker. "She's good to go, boss," Virgil said.

Columbia rode high and alone. Jack had her in a plus-Z attitude, her orange tank and black bottom facing earth, her nose in line with the direction of her orbit. The great mass of her main engines had drifted far behind, beginning their slow spiral into the gravity well. *Endeavour* had also drifted off. Jack could see her below, orbital mechanics dictating that because she was lower and going at the same velocity, she was gradually speeding ahead.

Jack had plotted the course and keyed it into the laptop that controlled the Big Dog engine as well as the shuttle computers, which had been cautiously brought up. He had deactivated the Ku-band antenna, cutting off the possibility of ground interference. A series of numbers marched toward zero on the laptop. Jack watched them and then reached down between the seats and pulled a handle. *Columbia* shuddered as if in regret as the ET separated. "So long, old horse," he said. "And thanks for the supplies."

Penny watched, transfixed, as the tank drifted away. "How long will it stay in orbit?" she wondered.

"We're in a high-energy situation," Jack said. "I'd say it's good for a year without a reboost. Maybe somebody will be smart enough to make use of it. Pretty cheap base for a space station. All that's required is the will to get up here, clean it out, and use it."

The numbers ticked on. Jack watched the edge of the earth. The sun was just starting to peek around it. The mantle of air surrounding the planet looked as thin as an onion's skin. "I wonder if you can see a green flash from up here," he said as much to himself as anyone.

"What's a green flash?" Penny asked.

"Sometimes," he said, "especially on tropical islands, when the sun goes down into the sea, just as it sinks out of sight, its rays penetrate the clear water. If you're lucky, you'll see it—a green flash. One of the most beautiful things there is to see on the good earth. Of course, they say you have to be in love to see it."

Penny pushed against her straps for a better view, then sat back. "I didn't see a flash," she said, sounding disappointed.

Jack shrugged. He hadn't either. He'd seen it only once, with Kate on a scuba trip to Guanaja, in the Republic of

Honduras. He never expected to see it again. He kept his eyes on the numbers flashing on the monitor screen. *Columbia* was turning slowly. The earth slid away and Jack peered into vast darkness. Astronauts had often spoken of the sense they had of the fragility of the earth. Now he sensed the same thing. *So little earth and air, so much . . . nothing.*

Jack pulled his pocket calculator from a tab on the console. He made some inputs, looked back at the screen, and then smiled when his numbers matched. *Columbia* was nearly ready. For the first time in decades a manned spacecraft was about to go *somewhere*, not just count laps in the sky. He briefly considered telling Penny where they were heading then decided against it. She'd know soon enough.

Endeavour

Brown slid back into her seat after checking Grant again. Her commander had sullenly gone to her sleeping bag, a night mask strapped over her eyes. Brown ordered Barnes to watch over Grant, hoping the sleeping pill she'd taken had started to work. Then she called Newell to come up and man the second seat in *Endeavour*'s cockpit. Per their last order from Houston they were supposed to keep an eye on *Columbia*. Dropping off the Space Station node was out of the question. Too much RCS propellant had been used to sneak up on *Columbia* and their orbit was deteriorating too rapidly. The node would drop into the atmosphere before another shuttle could come up and get it. The decision had been made to bring the node back.

Endeavour's rescue mission had cost about a half-billion dollars and nothing good was going to come out of it. Some careers were going to suffer and Brown suspected hers was going to be included in the body count. As she watched, and worried about what awaited her on earth, the external tank dropped slowly away from *Columbia*. Then the country's oldest shuttle began to assume an odd nose-up attitude.

Brown pushed against her seat straps, trying to see better. She fired up air-to-ground. "ET sep!" she announced.

"Say again?" CAPCOM queried.

"*Columbia*'s external tank has separated," Brown reiterated. "And she's in a roll maneuver. She's in a plus-X, omicron 180 attitude."

"Understand, bay back, nose up," Kelly Niven, the CAPCOM, replied, putting the pilot's words in English.

"Roger that."

Newell was using the binoculars. "The bay doors are closing. They must be getting ready for reentry."

"In *that* attitude?" Brown questioned. "I don't think so."

"What's going on, guys?" CAPCOM asked.

Brown stared at *Columbia*. It was a good question but she couldn't think of a single answer.

Columbia

Penny searched the darkness. Her eyes were beginning to adjust. There wasn't just emptiness facing *Columbia*'s nose. There were millions of white and pink and yellow and blue sparkles of light strewn across the sky like diamonds on black velvet. *Stars*, a horde of them. *Columbia* kept turning. It was as if she was looking for a special star. "Why are we pointed in that direction?" Penny asked.

Neither Jack or Virgil said anything, just sat there staring into the vast reaches of outer space. Penny felt a chill that started at her neck and went all the way down her spine. "Medaris, *damn you!*"

SMC

Ordered out of the SMC, Sam had sneaked into an auxiliary control room to listen and watch the proceedings on a closed-circuit monitor. "What are you doing, Jack?" he muttered.

"Keep us apprised," he heard Niven, the CAPCOM, beg *Endeavour*.

Brown came up after a momentary hiss of dead air. "Nothing new," she said. "*Columbia's* still here with her bay doors closed. The ET has dropped down, gone ahead of us."

Sam kept trying to make sense of it all. Medaris had torn the shuttle apart, ripped out the mains and put in their place another engine. Why would he do that? "Wait a minute," Sam said aloud to the room, empty except for a commtech who was eating his lunch. "They've lowered their mass by six tons." He swore and got on the phone. He needed to talk to the Air Force. When he got them, he said, "Eglin, what can you see?"

The Air Force liaison officer on the other end fortunately recognized him. "Keyhole's still got it, sir. We see the same thing as *Endeavour* reported. We're about to go over the horizon in a few minutes. We'll lose Keyhole then so if anything's gonna happen, hope it happens soon."

Sam sat down. Jack had lowered the mass of *Columbia*, shoved a big rocket engine up her tail, and then aimed her toward space. "*Shit!*" He went to the flight director push. John Lakey answered. "John, *Columbia's* going for escape velocity!"

Lakey's reply reflected his confusion. "What did you say, Sam? Who's escaping? Where are you?"

"You idiot!" Sam raged. "They're leaving earth orbit! They're headed out—" Sam stopped, stabbed off the push. *But where are they going?* he said to himself. *Hell, where else?* Sam sat back in his chair, rocking it spasmodically as he tried to make himself believe it. Then he stopped and allowed a huge grin to slide across his face. He had never thought he'd be alive to see it happen again. "Jack Medaris, you crafty *son of a bitch!*"

Columbia

Columbia had her star and reported it. Jack stabilized the ship with three quick RCS burns. "Nominal, nominal," he whispered. The numbers on the monitor had stopped except for a sequence in the upper right-hand corner. A countdown clock.

SMC

Sam came back inside Shuttle Mission Control. Lakey watched him in confused silence and then stood aside without resistance as Sam took back his position at the flight director's console. He called for a video patch from Eglin so he could see the shuttle through the Keyhole. "Who's on the other end, Eglin?" Sam demanded.

"This is Captain Terry Callisto, sir."

"Keep feeding us, Callisto."

"Yes, sir. As you can see, she's still just sitting there."

Sam heard noise in the background and then a man shouting, "It's blown up, sir!"

Callisto called, "Houston, I'm getting a report that *Columbia*'s blown up!"

Columbia

The violence of the engine shocked Penny. From below and behind came a sound like nothing she had ever heard, a deep rumbling howl like a crazed dog from hell. She was slammed back into her seat, the g-force a steady, heavy hand on her chest. "Medaris?" she called, close to panic. "Jack? Dear God! What's happening?"

"Let's go!" whooped Virgil.

The engine drove on. Then as abruptly as it had started, it stopped. Penny was slung against her belts. Then, as zero g crept over her again, she craned her neck to look up through the ceiling view ports. White swirls of giant cloud patterns over a blue sparkling ocean slid rapidly by and then the edge of the earth, and then nothing. She heard Jack type rapidly into the keyboard of his laptop. She looked to see. Numbers sped across his monitor. "Dammit!" he snapped. "Engine shutdown six point two seconds premature."

SMC

Sam rubbed his face, stared at the huge monitor on the wall, puzzling over the bright spot where *Columbia* had been just moments before. Then he understood. "She didn't blow up, Captain. *Columbia* has fired her engine."

"Houston!" Callisto was yelling, "She's . . . God, she's . . ."

"Like a bat out of hell!" Sam heard Brown yell down from *Endeavour*. "She was here and then she was—poof!— *gone like a bat out of hell*!"

Columbia

Jack didn't want to answer Penny's questions, not yet, not until he figured out what had gone wrong. His fingers flew across the keyboard. Everything had seemed so right. What the hell had happened? A 6.2-second premature shutdown would put them into a trajectory like an artillery shell, have them coming back into the atmosphere at God knew what angle. By the time *Columbia* got ten miles inside the air envelope, every living thing inside her would be nothing but a blackened cinder.

The laptop kept going through its reporting mode and then cycled into trajectory analyses, the numbers coming up based on a postulated delta V. Jack stared at it, pushed the return button, and more numbers began to march. He scratched his head and got out his calculator. He punched in the numbers.

"Medaris, tell me what's happened!" Penny demanded again.

Jack shook his head. "Virgil, we were way off on our calculations about ol' Big Dog." He turned, reached across the back of his chair to shake Virgil's giant, callused hand. "The dog's one hell of a lot more powerful than we thought. That's why it shut down early."

Virgil laughed, unstrapped himself, and leaned over to

clap Jack and Penny on their shoulders. It jarred Jack even in zero g. "It means we're on our way, don't it, boss?"

"Look out, moon!" Jack said, grinning at Penny. Then he lost his grin. "Sorry, High Eagle," he said, trying to appear sheepish.

Penny unstrapped herself, and went for Jack's throat. He dodged her, and Virgil held her back. She swung futilely until she'd worn herself out. Her arms drooped. "Let me go, Virgil," she said tiredly. She hung from a handrail after he'd released her. "Medaris, do you think you could answer one question without lying?"

Jack nodded.

"Why"—she licked her lips, tried to hold her anger in check—"Why are we going to the moon?"

"Because there's something there that . . . I need."

Penny shook her head, pushed away, and disappeared into the middeck. Jack felt the urge to go after her, to explain everything, but he couldn't. She was not part of the equation, never had been. This was something he had to do; he had always known it would come to this. He turned back to the cockpit windows, looked out. *Columbia*'s nose lay precisely on her star. And the world receded behind.

Montana (1)
The Perlman Plant Site, Missile Complex 22 (deactivated), United States Air Force 305th Strategic Wing (decommissioned), Montana

Deep below the Montana central prairie Perlman wandered the silent halls and laboratories of his magnificent accomplishment. His walking was hindered by his need for a cane, the result of an artificial hip implanted two years before when he had fallen from a scaffold working on the project. Perlman had a tiny efficiency built for himself just off from his lab so he didn't have to travel far. After his morning coffee and a light breakfast of a toasted bagel, he left it to see his plant once more, to remind himself that it still existed, that it might yet come alive.

Missile Complex 22 had been the old official designation of the installation: a *Minuteman III* intercontinental ballistic missile site that had once held three nuclear-tipped rockets capable of reaching out to a range of 6,000 miles. With the stand-down after the end of the Cold War, this site and the others of the ICBM Wing that controlled it had been emptied of its missiles, the holes left in the ground offered up as surplus. The Montana state government had purchased this one and Perlman had leased it for his effort.

Perlman used a key card to enter a blast door. Stepping through, he entered a short tunnel, low enough that he had to lean against his cane, one step at a time, careful not to bump his head. On the other side a steel gangplank led to an oval-shaped cavern that had once housed the *Minuteman III* launch control center. The Egg, as its crew had called it, had been empty for over a decade. Another key card was required for the next blast door and he used it, the massive structure swinging easily on its well-oiled hinges to reveal a huge room. In it was Perlman's baby, the world's first working fusion reactor, capable alone of providing all the power needed by Montana, Idaho, and Utah. But there was an If. A big If. If it had the fuel it needed.

Most Americans had never heard of fusion energy. But it was, Perlman believed, actually their only hope for the future. Hydrocarbon fuel was going to be exhausted within a few decades. Geothermal, solar, and wind energy would never be able to take up the slack. Nuclear energy was too difficult to keep safe. Chernobyl, Three Mile Island, and Sorkiyov had proved that. The world, in fact, was heading toward slow-motion disaster. Perlman believed that the governments of the world, especially the United States government, had known about the impending crisis for some decades but had suppressed it politically for short-term political gain. Why distress the people when everything seemed to be going so well? Why not let the next administration worry about it? And then the next?

The World Energy Treaty had been the answer everyone around the world seemed to grab as the solution. The treaty couldn't put a drop of oil back in the ground, nor provide a kilowatt of energy, yet it was supposed to solve the world's energy problems. All it was going to do was set up a bureaucracy that would ration energy as it started to become more scarce. WET was a coming disaster.

Perlman shook his shaggy head in exasperation as he limped down the hall. Here was the solution. Physics and chemistry, that's all it was. Quite simple, really. Fusion was the energy released when hydrogen atoms—or some isotope of this simplest of all elements—combined to form helium. More energy is required to hold two hydrogen atoms together than one helium atom. Push the two hydrogen atoms together, create helium, and energy is released. Simple. But sometimes, simplicity was difficult to create.

For decades scientists the world over had tried to make fusion work. It was the heavier isotopes of hydrogen that had shown the most promise for controlled fusion reactions. All that was required was to heat them up to approximately three times the temperature of the core of the sun—about a hundred million degrees—contain them in a plasma state, and extract all the resulting energy. But a workable plant always seemed another decade away. It was as if all of the scientists in the fusion community were like Prometheus trying and failing to steal fire from the gods. Perlman looked around his creation with much satisfaction. Here, they had done it, he and his scientists and engineers had stolen the fire.

A big cylinder on one side of the room necked down to a cone in its center and then expanded back to a larger cylinder that curved down into a square hole in the concrete floor. Farther on there was a huge turbine that spun an electric generator. A hundred feet above, a vent, hidden behind a small hillock, released the only residue of the reaction, pure water in the form of steam. There was no residual radioactivity. The only things produced were energy and water. It was the perfect power plant, the solution to cheap, safe energy.

For years Perlman had tried to gain financial support for his radical idea to make fusion work. Finally, miraculously, he'd received support from an organization called the January Group. He'd brought twenty unemployed fusion scientists out of Russia and the United States and France and Italy to the desolate Montana prairie and, within three years, was prepared for a full-scale test. Perlman's approach required a powerful laser and a particular fuel, an isotope known as helium-3. But with helium-3 there was bad news and good news. The bad news was that the isotope was rare, at least on earth. The good news was that it was abundant almost everywhere else in the solar system. In fact, Perlman had used the small amount of helium-3 that he'd gathered from *Apollo* moon rocks to test the concept. In the lab, at least, it had worked.

Encouraged, the January Group gave him more money. Perlman built a full-scale fusion plant, used the isotope left from *Apollo* to test it. The plant worked—perfectly. To go into production all Perlman needed was more helium-3. The best place to get it was where he'd gotten his sample: the moon. But when he'd asked NASA for help, the space agency had, in effect, laughed at him. The Washington space weenie who'd answered his letters had said, in effect, that NASA was no longer in the business of going to the moon. "For we are but of yesterday, and know nothing, because our days upon earth are a shadow," Perlman muttered, quoting Job, his favorite biblical prophet.

He'd heard about Jack Medaris through a friend in the aerospace industry. Medaris was a man who loved a challenge, could be audacious. Now, it had come to all this. WET was going to be approved in a few days. After that,

Perlman would have to scrap his plant. The only hope was Medaris and Perlman had no idea what was happening. There had been almost a complete press blackout on the events in space.

Charlie Bowman, a mechanic, was the only other worker with Perlman at the site. He'd volunteered to keep Perlman company and pull maintenance on the plant. "Dr. Perlman," Bowman greeted him warmly. "I replaced the thermocouples on the heat exchangers this morning on boiler number two. Probably didn't need it but I didn't trust them after they got so hot during the test. Just routine. Everything else is up to snuff."

"Thank you, Charlie. You all right?"

Bowman, a big, friendly man with close-set eyes perched above a bulbous nose, put his thumbs under the straps of his big overalls and pulled on them. He grinned. "You know me, Doc. As long as I've got some machinery to tinker with, I'm happy as a bug in a rug."

"How happy would that be?" Perlman asked, amused.

Charlie scratched his head, taking Perlman's question seriously. "Well, I reckon a bug'd be warm inside a carpet, get plenty to eat, have things to do. Just like me. Not much left to want out of life."

Perlman smiled and nodded, pleased that he'd picked Charlie to stay with him. All the others, the physicists, chemists, machinists, and engineers, had long since gone home, disappointed, convinced that their work was not going to ever be properly appreciated. "I'm glad you're with me, Charlie."

Charlie shrugged and went off, pulling a rag out of his hip pocket and disappearing into a maze of steam pipes. Perlman chuckled and then crossed the floor to a curtained cubicle. Inside, on a table, was a glass tube of what appeared to be an orange powder. He held it up to the light, admiring the translucent, glowing material within. It looked magical and it was. The powder—actually microscopic-sized glass spheres—had been brought back by the *Apollo 17* crew, inside it was a host of volatiles, including a pure elixir of helium-3.

The huge picture of the moon on the wall of Perlman's office reminded him of when he'd shown Jack Medaris where the *Apollo 17* crew had found the powder. Perlman had been surprised at Medaris's reaction. The engineer, until then unsure about taking on Perlman's quest, had suddenly gone pale. "Do you believe in fate, Dr. Perlman?" he asked. "Do you believe we all have a destiny? Until this moment I doubted mine."

In all the time he'd known him, Perlman had not asked Medaris what he'd meant by that. He wished now that he had.

A telephone buzzed in the clean room but Perlman let it ring. The recorder would pick it up, pass the message along that the silo was locked up tight. As far as the outside world was concerned, nobody was home. Then the phone stopped abruptly in midring. Perlman picked up the phone. There was no dial tone. A movement on a television monitor beside the table startled Perlman. It was connected to a camera topside, beside the main entrance. Perlman saw two men dressed in what appeared to be black fatigues. They were investigating the entranceway at the primary elevator. They walked, out of sight of the camera, and then returned to the door. Perlman used the monitor's joystick to direct the camera to zoom in on a shoulder patch on one of the men. It said PUCKETT SECURITY SERVICES. He remembered Jack's warning the day before the launch, to look out for men wearing this patch. The camera continued to track them as they trudged off across the parking lot. They had come in a big jeeplike vehicle, a Humvee, Perlman thought it was called. The men drove the Humvee down the road, through the open gate of the silo perimeter fence.

Perlman's breath caught in his throat. He hadn't counted on this. Perlman heard metal on metal somewhere deep in the maze of steam pipes. "Charlie?" he called. "Would you mind coming here? I think we may have a situation."

Houston, You *Are* the Problem

Bonner couldn't go home. The media had staked out his house. He couldn't even go to the Rawhide, try to numb with Jack D his disappointment in *Endeavour*'s failure. He was camping out in his office with firm orders to Public Affairs to say nothing, zero, *nada*. He had to think about what to do next. It was no mystery to him what had happened. Jack Medaris was heading for the moon. He didn't have to wait for the tranjectory analysis to be done. "Medaris, you bastard," Bonner seethed. There had to be a way to stop him.

The phone rang. Bonner had expected a call from the vice president but was surprised that it was from Bernie Sykes. "Hold, please," the White House operator said, "for your call from Baghdad."

Sykes came on-line. He was obviously agitated. "What a damn screwup, Frank! The president of Iraq tried to be nice about it but I could tell he was amused. 'Perhaps my scientists can be of service?' he asked the President. Can you imagine how that made us feel? I told the President I had the greatest confidence in you and now he's getting laughed at by Third World dictators!"

Bonner was out of his chair, pacing. "Bernie, Grant did her best." He stopped. "I gave her the gas canister that came from the contractor you recommended. The word I got was that it exploded."

"Had to be a defect, Frank," Sykes replied, softening his tone a bit. "You think I would want some kind of bloody disaster up there? Look, you got anything else up your sleeve?"

Bonner hated to confess the truth. "*Columbia* went for

escape velocity, Frank. They're out of my reach until they come back."

"Escape . . . what do you mean?"

"I mean they're on their way to the moon."

The line was silent for a moment. "Listen, Frank, you need help. I'm going to get you some. I'm going to send you a consultant. A man who is used to playing big games in the shadows, if you know what I mean."

Bonner frowned, started his pacing again. "Are you talking about some kind of secret agent, Bernie? I don't think I need that. I'm going to call a meeting, talk to my managers. We can still handle this. Wherever *Columbia*'s going, the one certain thing is she's going to come back. We just have to figure out where and grab her as she flies in."

"No. This has gotten too big now," Sykes said grimly. "Cooperate with my consultant, okay? His name's Puckett, Carl Puckett. One hell of a guy and knows a lot of things you don't. Got it?"

Bonner got it, all right. There'd been no more mention of the NASA administrator's job, nothing but implicit criticism. Now he was going to get help from some kind of outside contractor! *This is all Medaris's fault. Every bit of it!* The bastard always seemed to beat him.

The phone rang again. When he answered, a gruff voice responded. "I'm Carl Puckett, Dr. Bonner. I'll be at your office in an hour. You get me on the center?"

Bonner thought about keeping the man off-site. He could do it, at least for a while. Then, suddenly, he felt completely drained, defeated. It was all over, he realized that now. His career was gone, NASA was in the toilet permanently. "Stop at the gate, get a pass, Mr. Puckett. Your name will be on the approved list."

"Thanks," the man said, and hung up without another word.

Bonner shook his head and then went to his wall of awards and trophies. There was a small framed photograph, almost lost among them: Kate and Bonner together. She was looking at him, smiling. He was grinning, on top of the world. He suddenly felt ashamed. He had lost Kate's love and, over the years, he had lost or forgotten her dreams as well. He took the photograph off the wall and placed it facedown on his desk. Displaying it now seemed a betrayal of all that was, or could have been.

The Horse That Can't Be Rode
SMC

Sam was at his console at the SMC. Lakey and the astronauts had left and Bonner hadn't sent anybody to chase him out, so he decided to stay where he was. All was quiet, his controllers sitting in an exhausted trance in front of their consoles. Four hours into his twelve-hour shift he sat half-dozing in his chair, until the EECOM roused him from his stupor. "Sam, they're doing something. Just got a spike here."

Sam blinked awake. "What's happening?" He yawned.

"I'm not certain. It was just a spike. All the systems numbers came up. I think it was *Columbia*."

"I can confirm that, EECOM," a voice in their headsets intoned. It was one of the faceless technicians in the back room who kept watch on shuttle subsystems around the clock. "It wasn't *Endeavour*. She's in LOS. Had to be *Columbia*."

The EECOM shrugged. "Just a blip, I guess."

"Naw, that ain't it," the voice said, revealing all of its Texas flatland twang. "I think they came up just long enough to plug in a GSC."

Sam rubbed his face. "A what?"

"A general support computer. Probably a laptop. They plugged in their own little operating system is my guess. Took us plumb off-line, probably for good. Us ol' boys might as well lock up and go home after *Endeavour* gets in. *Columbia*'s software looks to me like it's bulletproof."

Sam understood. Medaris had cut *Columbia* off from any possible interference from Houston by putting a monitoring computer in place with all the bells and whistles of an internal Mission Control. Houston was no longer in *Columbia*'s loop, could neither monitor her systems nor control them in any way. *Guess I don't blame him,* Sam thought. All of a sudden retirement had never looked so good. There was a spacecraft on the way to the moon and its crew so distrusted Houston, it had deliberately cut them off. Sam shook his head. His controllers were all looking at him. They knew the score. He reluctantly keyed his transmitter. "When *Endeavour* lands," he announced, "we'll go to a skeleton staff here. I'll be distributing a list of who stays and who goes. Ladies and gentlemen, you've performed magnificently, but sometimes you get on a horse that can't be rode. Looks like we've found ours."

Cecil Remembers
The Marymount Hotel, Washington, D.C.

Cecil sprawled on the bed passing the time studying federal statutes and thinking about the strange circumstances that had brought him to this moment. He also thought about the man who had orchestrated it. On a clear evening with stars and planets abundant in the sky, Cecil had walked with Jack along the beach at Cedar Key. Cecil remembered Jack pointing at the brightest sparkler and saying, "The whole solar system's been a disappointment, Cecil. It started with that one, Venus."

"That's like saying the ocean is a disappointment, Jack," Cecil replied. "It is what it is, nothing more, and nothing less either."

Jack kept studying the sky as if he expected to see some

kind of sign, something that would change what he believed. "Maybe we should have never looked it over," he said quietly. "In a way it destroyed our dreams. When I was a boy all the books I read said that Venus might have rain forests and seas underneath all those clouds. I could imagine dinosaurs down there and fish-men and fish-women. What did it turn out to be, this sister of earth? We sent probes to Venus and found a planet with a surface hot enough to melt lead and sulfuric acid for rain. That acid ate up the dreams of a generation of kids, Cecil."

"There's Mars, Jack. We'll go there someday."

Jack stopped, pointed at a dim pink star. "There it is. Pretty, huh? But Mars is even worse. I remember being excited because the astronomers said that Mars had shadows that changed with the seasons. That just had to mean there was vegetation. And then there were the canals that the astronomers said they could see too. That meant maybe a great civilization. Then the space program showed us what was actually there. The vegetation proved to be dust storms, the canals just our imagination. Microbial life? Maybe, but otherwise not so much as a Mars mouse. You want to go out farther? Jupiter, Saturn—pretty but just big gas balls."

"Didn't I hear that there might be life on Europa or Titan?" Cecil asked of the moons of Jupiter and Saturn.

That night Jack would not be denied his skepticism. "Doubtful. No wonder we stopped trying to go out, just stuck ourselves into low earth orbit."

"You skipped the moon, Jack." Cecil had laughed, trying to cajole the man into some good humor. "Want to say something nasty about the moon while you're at it?"

He wouldn't be baited. "The moon," he said, "is different. It's more than what anybody thought it was. According to the *Apollo* astronauts, Cecil, it's a beautiful place. Stark, perhaps, but a beauty much like the high deserts here on earth. And it's covered with a magic dust."

It was the first time Jack had explained to Cecil about

helium-3, the isotope that could burn in fusion reactors to keep earth humming for centuries. It might be useful for rocket engines, too, he'd said. But then Jack had said something else, something Cecil often thought about. "The moon has something of mine, Cecil, something I need."

"What, Jack?"

Jack hadn't replied, just kept looking up.

Cecil rose from the bed and swept the curtain back from the window. Clouds covered the night sky. "I hope the moon doesn't disappoint you, Jack," he whispered, looking up into the darkness.

There was a pounding on his door. Cecil answered and saw two dark suits from the FBI. "The AG wants to see you," they growled, nearly in unison.

Fifteen minutes later Cecil sat sweating in the AG's office while she frowned at him from her desk. She had several sheets of paper and an envelope in front of her. She slid it across the desk. "Read it and weep, counselor."

Cecil read. It was a letter to the AG from the ex-wife of Colonel Craig "Hopalong" Cassidy. She had enclosed a letter from Cassidy to his son. In it he had written that he was going back into space and that "many people will think I'm wrong for doing it." It also included much expression of Cassidy's love and devotion for his son and his country. The envelope was marked *To be opened only in case of my death.* Cecil tried to keep a neutral look as he read but his mind was racing ahead. After he finished, he sat back. "Colonel Cassidy is clearly a great patriot."

The AG narrowed her eyes. "Maybe so, Cecil, but he's also just jerked the rug out from under your clients."

Cecil cocked his head. "I beg your pardon?"

"This letter clearly shows that Cassidy had the intent to commit a crime. He also mentions that others are in it with him. That would be your clients. Isn't it obvious?"

"No, ma'am. They are simply fulfilling the terms of their contract with DOT. As for this letter, Captain Cassidy just says that *some* people might think he's wrong. It doesn't say he plans on committing a crime."

The AG rubbed her face, tugged at her chin. "Cecil, maybe you're right, maybe you're wrong, and maybe it doesn't matter." She drew back Cassidy's letter, looked at it, tapped it with her finger, clasped her hands together, leaned forward. "But I can tell you this. No way is President Edwards going to allow this to continue. For one thing, all those talking heads on TV have got the American people stirred up. They want blood and they want the President to get it for them. Your clients are dead meat if they don't turn around and soon. If you have any way of communicating with them, let me strongly recommend you do so."

Cecil thought about continuing his argument but caught the determination in the AG's eye. This was not the time for a debate. "Yes, ma'am," he said although he knew there was nothing he could do, that Jack Medaris would never stop until he found whatever it was he was really looking for on the good, golden moon.

4

Outbound

Up goes my boat among the stars
Through many a breathless field of light,
Through many a long blue field of ether,
Leaving ten thousand stars beneath her;
Up goes my little boat so bright!

—William Wordsworth, "Among the Stars"

MET 4 DAYS AND COUNTING . . .

Victory Roll
Columbia

Jack had set *Columbia* free. He used a short puff of RCS to put her into a slow roll. He had studied the *Apollo* missions, knew the mission controllers called the maneuver the "barbecue mode," because it was used to even out the heat of the sun. Jack preferred to think of it as a victory roll for *Columbia* all the way to the moon. He went to the aft flight deck to watch earth recede. Only a few hours out, the full disk of humanity's planet had already shrunk to the size of one view port. His crewmates joined him.

"It's the most beautiful sight I've ever seen," Penny said grudgingly. She had tried sleeping but had given up, the view too irresistible.

"We're going to be the first people to see the earth get smaller as we fly away," Jack said, offering some history. Paco hung off his shoulder, a paw out toward the earth-ball. "The *Apollo* crews had just a little window and were facing the wrong way most of the time." He looked over at Penny. "I'm sorry I had to lie to you. I didn't think you'd understand."

"Shut up, Medaris," Penny said. "I'll never believe anything you say ever again, so don't waste your breath."

Virgil cupped the receding planet with his hands. "Everybody I've ever known, all on that little blue and white and brown ball." He mused over the world. "I wonder what they think about all this back at the Cape and Houston?"

"Houston!" Jack had forgotten about Shuttle Mission Control. He put Paco on the ceiling, pulled his feet out of the loops, and went down to the middeck, coming back with a laptop. "I should have set this up from the beginning," he said, "but I got overconfident. I didn't think Houston would try to do anything to us without letting us know." He typed in some commands and the computer whirred softly. "Okay, it's done. New software is in. We'll run *Columbia* through this machine from here on. There's no way the ground can break into it."

Jack looked up to find Penny staring at him, incredulity written on her face. "You've disconnected us from Houston? Why? We might need them!"

"Because I don't trust them, High Eagle. Isn't that obvious? In case you haven't noticed, so far they've let a rocket detonate close enough to ping one of our windows, they fired the RCS jets while we were in the engine bay, and they sent *Endeavour* up to attack us with a bomb."

"But who's going to watch all the systems while we're asleep?"

Jack patted the laptop. "This little baby could put a hundred mission controllers out of work. It'll look after us just fine."

Penny squinted. "I hope to hell you know what you're doing, Medaris."

"I do, High Eagle. Not to worry."

"When you tell me not to worry is when I start," Penny retorted. Then she took on an air of resignation. "Are the middeck lockers getting power?"

"Of course." Except for Paco, Jack had all but forgotten there was anything else aboard *Columbia* besides the hardware needed for the moon mission. Jack shared the belief with most NASA engineers that the vast majority of experiments carried into space weren't good for much except as excuses for professors to write learned papers. He couldn't help but ask Penny, in a doubtful tone, "Any of those experiments worth anything?"

She had caught his tone. "My cell culture experiments

will demonstrate the growth patterns in microgravity of a variety of dendritic cells."

Jack knew he should just shut up, let the woman do whatever she wanted to do. They were on a long journey. Everyone would need something to pass the time on the way. And he really shouldn't needle her, he thought, but it seemed as if he couldn't help himself. "I'm sure the world will be waiting impatiently to hear the results of that," he said. "Why, I was just saying the other day, wasn't I, Virgil, that it sure would be nice to know the growth patterns in microgravity of a variety of dendritic cells."

"Hey, don't get me into this," Virgil said, hands in the air. Jack had to admire his wisdom.

Penny pulled out of her footloops and made her way down the ceiling handrails. "Medaris, I don't know why you seem to glory in being ignorant." She wriggled down through the hatch to the middeck.

Virgil came up next to Jack. "You really like that woman, don't you, boss?"

"Like her? Virg, I can't stand the sight of her."

Virgil slowly nodded his head up and down. "Uh-huh. *Right.*"

Penny heard Medaris and Virgil talking but their conversation was muffled. *Got to remember to just ignore that man,* she thought. She opened her cell culture experiment and set up the microscope encased in foam in one of the middeck lockers. *The very idea. Are these experiments worth anything? Well, they were, weren't they?*

Penny checked the thermoelectric incubator. It had run on battery power while *Columbia* was shut down. She saw no error messages and an initial observation showed all of the sample trays with cell growth. She began a more careful examination of each tray, photographing the cells and making notes. The last sample she inspected was one she had

ruined during her hurried first setup. Still ill with SAS, she
had accidentally mixed a lamb nerve cell culture with frog
DNA. She had started to pitch the contaminated sample but
then decided to include it with the other samples in the
incubator. It might start stinking in the waste bag, otherwise.

Curious as to how the cells in her accidental mixture
were growing, she clicked the sample tray in place on the
microscope holder, adjusted the eyepiece, and added a little
extra light. She found, as she had feared, the cells a mixed
mess, lamb and frog cellular material overlapping one another, hopelessly contaminated. In one place, near the center, there seemed to be some sort of coil growing, white
wisps like fine white hairs running down its length. *Some
sort of an impurity*, she guessed, *perhaps not even biological*.
Still, it was interesting and perhaps worth watching. She
photographed the coil, made a note of it, and then put all
the samples away.

She had done her science. She hoped Medaris would be
up in the cockpit doing something, anything, so she
wouldn't have to talk to him. But when she came up
through the hatch and saw that he was indeed busy, she felt
oddly disappointed.

The Lunar Curatorial Laboratory
Johnson Space Center

Shirley Grafton hustled up the steps of the low gray building
on the Johnson Space Center campus. She was there on a
hunch. She had arrived in Houston on the first flight out of
Washington but by the time she got her rental car and drove
to JSC, it was already approaching noon. Her vice presidential ID card had gotten her on the center. Her stomach
growled to remind her she hadn't had any lunch, but she
was too excited by what she was about to see to pay it any
heed. The *Apollo* astronauts had carried back 838 pounds of
rock and dirt and dust from the moon, most of it stored at

the building she was approaching, the Lunar Curatorial Laboratory. Even more than thirty years after the last moon mission, less than fifty pounds of lunar material had left the lab. Anyone wishing to study the larger rocks or sample tubes went to Houston.

The laboratory's director, Professor Claude Koszelak, met Shirley at the door. Koszelak was thin and lanky, the kind of man that seemed to be everywhere in this corner of Texas, looking as dried out as a desert arroyo. Shirley would have bet good money that out in the parking lot, Koszelak had a truck with a cowboy hat on the seat and a rifle rack in the rear window. Those good old boys were invariably friendly cusses and Koszelak proved to be no exception. He gave her a grin, offered her all the hospitality he could deliver, and led her into the rows of stainless steel and glass sample cabinets. Black rubber gloves hung from unattended cabinets while others had bunny-suited lab workers seated in front of them, working with pieces of the moon.

As Koszelak explained what they saw, his intellect became clear despite his homespun appearance. Selected samples from the lunar breccia, he explained, were being sawn into different sizes, described, and placed in context as to where they were found. After that was done, each piece had to be photographed and tagged before it was sent out. "It's time-consuming, very exacting work. And of course we don't send out samples to just anyone. We exhaustively review all requests. We are very careful with our rocks."

Shirley peered at the moon samples. "Do you get back the results?"

"Yes, ma'am, we sure do. That's part of our agreement with anyone who receives samples."

Shirley watched a technician as he handled a gray corrugated piece of the moon, weighing it before chiseling it into smaller, more manageable pieces. "I'm interested to see if any of the scientists were investigating Shorty Crater," she said.

Koszelak raised his eyebrows. "Shorty Crater? Okay, let's check." Koszelak led the way into his office. It was no surprise that he had the horns of a longhorn steer mounted on the wall over his computer. He saw where she was looking and smiled proudly. "One of my own steers loaned his horns to me," he said. "I run a little spread down near Tyler." He sat and entered commands on a desktop computer and a list filled the monitor screen. "Here you go. There've been two hundred and forty-three requests for samples from researchers in the last ten years that have to do with material taken from *Apollo 17*'s second excursion, which included Shorty. S'pose you could narrow your interest down a tad?"

"How many requests were approved?"

Koszelak tapped. "Seventy-three. The largest number of requests approved were for a Dr. Perlman, a researcher for an outfit called the January Group."

Shirley looked over the list, recognizing none of the names. Very little of the esoteric scientific jargon in the description of their projects made much sense either. "What are they studying, Professor?" Shirley asked.

Koszelak scooted closer, studying the list. "Most of them are looking at Shorty's fire fountain debris."

"Come again?"

Koszelak rotated in his chair. "A fire fountain is lava that contains dissolved volcanic gases. When it reaches the surface, the gas comes out of solution and sends out a spray—sort of like shaking up a bottle of soda and then poppin' the cap off it. The resulting spray—very hot and molten—is thrown up into the vacuum and as it falls, it forms into tiny glass beads. Harrison Schmitt found a mother lode of these beads on the rim of Shorty Crater."

Shirley sat down in an offered chair and leaned forward with interest. "This Dr. Perlman. Does he say why he wants these beads?"

Koszelak studied the material. "Well, looks like to me

Dr. Perlman's interest is mostly in the gases contained in the beads."

"You mean the beads are hollow?"

"Not exactly hollow, just filled with bubbles. When the glassy material was sprayed above the lunar surface, gas got trapped inside the spheres that formed." Koszelak opened a desk drawer and dragged out a logbook. "Not everything is automated," he apologized as he traced his finger down the lines in the book. "Yes, ma'am, I thought so. Six years ago it was. A colleague of Dr. Perlman's spent some time with us studying the chemical composition of fire fountain products."

Koszelak looked thoughtful. "You know, I was in the geologists' back room when Shorty Crater was visited by Schmitt. The first thing he said was that Shorty was an impact crater. Then, when he found that orange soil, he thought maybe Shorty was a volcanic crater. It was a mystery. But after the pictures and samples got a closer look here in the lab, it turned out ol' Shorty was indeed an impact crater—a meteor had formed it—and the orange soil was fire fountain beads that had been uncovered by the meteor. You know, everything isn't cut and dried, even on the old moon."

Shirley steered Koszelak back to the subject. "And it is the gas inside the beads Dr. Perlman was interested in?"

"Yes. Especially one gas. Helium-3. Have you heard of this isotope?" One quick look at Shirley gave him his answer. "Well, let's see. How to explain it. Helium-3 comes from the sun, part of the solar wind. It sticks to anything in the solar system that it touches. The earth's magnetic field and atmosphere keep most of it off the earth but the moon is like a big catcher's mitt for the stuff. Pretty well covered up with it. But it's not like you can go up there and scoop up a bucket of helium-3. It's usually mixed in the soil and you need to heat it up to get it out. Unless, of course, it's already in its gaseous state inside fire fountain beads." Koszelak frowned over his log, turned back to his computer, and worked the keyboard. "Here it is. Dr. Isaac Perlman, Professor Emeritus . . . blah, blah, blah . . . Uh-huh, thought so! Researcher in fusion energy! Yep, makes sense. I betcha that explains Dr. Perlman's interest in where the isotope can be found in concentrated form." He peered at Shirley. "You do know what fusion energy is, don't you, ma'am?"

"Tell me, Professor. I'm all ears."

He did and one thing more. He looked Perlman up on the Internet. The Web site, one created for fusion researchers by the Virginia Polytechnic Institute, hadn't been updated in a year. "This is interesting," he said. "Says here Perlman has contracted with a private contractor to go to the moon and pick up soil samples that might contain helium-3."

"Does it say which private contractor?"

Koszelak scrolled down the screen. "Here it is. MEC of Cedar Key, Florida."

"Is there anywhere I could view films of the *Apollo 17* expedition, Professor?"

"Sure," Koszelak said. "Right here on my computer."

Koszelak called it up. "Anything in particular?"

"When they were at Shorty Crater. Look for anything peculiar, different. I'm not sure exactly what."

Shirley watched Schmitt struggling with the sample tube, saw Cernan come back with a capped pipelike thing in his hands. He used it to drive the tube.

"That's odd, never noticed that," Koszelak said. "He's not using a hammer."

Cernan dropped the pipe. "Wait, can you back that up?" Shirley asked, excited. "And can you zoom in with your software?"

"Sure can." Koszelak backed the video up, zoomed in on

the pipe, which, on closer inspection, seemed to be a kind of canister with screwed-on caps on both ends.

"Even closer," Shirley breathed. *"There!"*

She could see clearly the initials "K.S." on the canister. *Katrina Suttner.*

"I don't recognize it and I thought I knew every tool they carried up there. What is it, Miss Grafton?"

Shirley was digging into her purse, going after her tissues. She was crying again. At this rate she was going to have to carry a box of tissues with her everywhere she went. "It's a time machine, Professor." She sniffed. "A very bright little girl built a time machine for the man she knew someday she'd love."

Shirley thanked Koszelak profusely and left the center. She knew everything now or thought she did. She was heading back to Washington. Her boss, the vice president of the United States, needed to know everything too.

JSC-1
Fannin, Texas

Texas State highway 59 was a straight shot from Houston to Laredo on the Mexican border. It was a four-lane until it hit the little town of Fannin where it turned into a narrow two-lane. It was the perfect spot for a speed trap. A County Mountie clocked the red Porsche at over one hundred miles per hour, set his blue and reds flashing, and gave chase. The patrolman got close enough to read the Porsche's license tag. JSC-1. He called it in, kept following. The high-performance car went even faster, the driver obviously not drunk. His turns around the curves just outside the state park were taken too smoothly for that. He was just in one big hurry. No matter how hard the patrolman tried, he couldn't keep up. The Porsche finally went completely out of sight. The County Mountie grimly followed, then saw the skid marks going off the road, the crushed grass and splintered small trees. In a river upside down, wheels still spinning, was the Porsche. "Holy . . ." The patrolman gasped. The Porsche was on fire, even half submerged. It suddenly exploded, a big gout of orange gasoline-fed flame causing a mushroom like a small atomic bomb. He didn't realize he was screaming into his mike until the lady on the other end asked him to please "tone it down, boy."

The trooper hurried down the bank. The Porsche had settled onto the shallow bottom. He sat down on a rock, put his hands to his face, tried to tell himself it hadn't been his fault. Then, hearing sirens in the distance, he gathered up his courage, waded into the water. A briefcase, charred but otherwise in good shape, floated out of the broken window of the smashed little car. He picked it up, held it while he looked inside the Porsche for the remains of the driver. He kept looking. There was no sign of him. He waded back to shore, opened the briefcase. It was filled with papers, official-looking documents. He heard people coming. He snapped the case shut. Somebody else could look into the damned thing.

Something white caught his eye in the gathering darkness. He waded over to it, sucked in a breath. There, lying facedown along the creek bank, was the body of the driver. JSC-1, whoever he was. "You dumb son of a bitch," the trooper said.

Cecil Does the Media
Marymount Hotel, Washington, D.C.

Cecil picked up both *The Washington Post* and the *Washington Times* on the morning of the fourth day of *Columbia*'s flight and found himself splashed all over the front pages of both. Someone, "a well-placed source in the Justice Department," had leaked both his name and information about MEC's contract. Whoever had done it had also told the newspapers where the department had stashed him. His telephone started to ring and it rang all day. Most of the reporters were hostile, asserting in their questions that Jack Medaris was a man bitter about his treatment by NASA, and that his taking of *Columbia* and the kidnapping of Penny High Eagle was a clear act of revenge and terrorism. Cecil tried to explain, didn't feel as if he was getting anywhere, and decided he needed to go on television and tell the world the truth. *The truth will set you free*, he remembered one of his law professors saying. *Yeah, or twenty to life*, a smart-aleck law student beside him had whispered. It didn't matter. Cecil didn't figure he had much to lose by going public, and trying to build some sympathy for Jack before the government spun him into a traitor. When they called, he accepted an interview with Larry King. Then he started shaking in fear. *Please don't let me make a mess of it*, he prayed.

That night Cecil was still nervous as he sat down at the famous but simple set. Then the interviewer appeared, shaking Cecil's hand, telling him what was about to happen was going to be great fun, and to relax.

When the show started, Cecil heard the announcements over the tiny speaker in his right ear and then King spoke, introducing him as "the lawyer for the individuals who have stolen our shuttle—Mr. Cecil Velocci." And then, "Mr. Velocci is from the small town of Cedar Key, Florida, and was first retained by a group of men and women he knew as MEC. How did this all come about, Mr. Velocci?"

Cecil told his story, of the team that had come to make themselves part of Cedar Key. Since Jack had not left instructions otherwise, he even told of the rocket engine that ran on "dreams." As he talked, he felt himself begin to relax. It was a good story he was telling and it needed to be told.

"What charges have been filed against your clients?" King demanded.

"Well, the list I've heard is a long one," Cecil answered, facing the camera with the red light with no coaxing, "but as of tonight, no charges have been officially made and I frankly don't believe any will be forthcoming." Cecil tapped the contract he had laid on the table. "This is another case of one hand of the government not knowing what the other hand is doing. The Department of Transportation entered into a legal contract with MEC and the company is simply doing its job."

"Stealing the shuttle was its job?" King growled.

"*Columbia* was not stolen. My clients are simply utilizing it for a commercial enterprise per the contract."

"What about Captain Cassidy's death?" King slashed. "That was murder!"

"Captain Cassidy was part of the MEC team. There was an accident at launch. He should be considered a hero by this country."

"All right. How about Dr. High Eagle?" King snapped. "She was kidnapped, right?"

"Larry, that's a misrepresentation. Dr. High Eagle is part of the crew."

King frowned. "The reports I heard said the other astronauts were in the elevator when *Columbia* was launched. They thought they were going to be aboard. How do you explain that?"

Cecil took on a quizzical look, as if the question's implication was beyond his imagination. "Well, it was my understanding that the launch was a little . . . busy. I suppose, in regards to the other crew members in the elevator, some sort of mistake must have been made."

"Some mistake," King replied dourly. "Now, what I want to know—"

"I do have one announcement to make tonight, Larry," Cecil interrupted politely. He had received a phone call earlier in the day from Sally Littleton, still rolling along in the MEC eighteen-wheeler undetected in the Midwest. "*Columbia* has left low earth orbit."

"You mean she's come down?" King asked, his voice dropping to a growl. "Where?"

"The MEC team is now entering into the second phase of its contract with the Department of Transportation. It will be conducting tests in the vicinity of the moon."

King gripped the set table as if about to fall off his chair. "They're taking the shuttle to the moon? Can they do that?"

"They're on their way, Larry."

"Whew!" King gasped and then, despite himself, he grinned. "You heard it here first, ladies and gentlemen! Now, that's an announcement! We'll take a break and be right back!"

What King had said at the beginning proved to be absolutely correct. The interview was fun. It was entirely Cecil's show. He repeated all the accolades Medaris had told him about the bountiful moon, including the presence of helium-3 and its potential as an energy source that would last for centuries. He didn't say that was the purpose of the flight, to pick some of the stuff up. He thought it best to hold that card close to his chest. Afterward King told him that his staff had never seen the telephones light up so quick. Space fans from all over the world tried desperately to get through. A caller from Brazil summed it up.

"Mistair Velocci, it is so good . . . I don't know how to tell you . . . it is so good. We need this world to go into space. It is back to the moon! Thank you! Thank you and your brave team!"

After the show the excitement wasn't over. Cecil had to slip into the back of the hotel to escape the reporters and TV cameras. Once in his room, he found a message from Trooper Buck of Cedar Key to call him. Buck answered. "Saw you on Larry King. Gone Hollywood, Cecil. I'm impressed."

"How are things on the island, Buck? I'm homesick."

"Pretty damn quiet with you and Jack out of my hair. Say, Cecil, do me a favor. Go find yourself a phone booth — not in the hotel, someplace about a mile away at random, call me at Fred's house, okay?"

Fred was actually Buck's girlfriend, Felicia Wales. Cecil did as he was told. "I'm here. What's up?"

"Old son," Buck drawled, "got a little surprise for you. Jack told me to wait a few days and then tell you. It seems he pulled the patch off one of the perps that burned his place. It was an outfit named Puckett Security Services. He asked me to look it up. I did, tracked it down to Washington, D.C. Turns out it's run by a real heavy, Carl Puckett, who does nasty little chores for a lot of powerful outfits. For instance, an odd little bunch of players who call themselves the January Group. I told Jack, he said to hand it over to the FBI. And you know what? I did, to Mr. Mark Hennessey, the FBI Director, himself. Mark and I were in the same class at the academy."

Cecil was confused. "Why didn't Jack tell me this?"

"Aw, you know Jack. He likes to keep the whole story to himself, just hands out whatever part to the rest of us country boys he thinks we need. I didn't know anything about this moon business, for instance. And God almighty, hijacking a shuttle to do it. I hope you can keep the boy out of prison."

Cecil had been thinking while Buck had been rambling. "If you told Hennessey, then . . . *Hawthorne!*"

"Oh, yeah. The attorney general knows too. And you can bet she's been working overtime trying to figure out the connection between Puckett, Jack, the January Group, and God knows who else. She's been playing you like a fiddle, old son, trying to figure out what's really going down."

"I guess that's why she didn't put me under the Washington Monument," Cecil said, abashedly.

"What was that?" Buck laughed. "Didn't quite get that one."

"Nothing, Buck. I was just thinking out loud."

"You gonna be home soon?"

"We can only hope," Cecil said, shaking his head. "We can only hope."

MET 5 DAYS AND COUNTING . . .

The Russian Gambit

Runway 92, Edwards Air Force Base

Carl Puckett watched *Endeavour* make a night landing on the runway on the dry lake bed at Edwards Air Force Base, California. The low propellant readouts on the shuttle had caused SMC to decide to bring Grant and her crew in at Edwards rather than the Cape. It would cost NASA over a million dollars to remove the undeployed Space Station node and then carry *Endeavour* to the Cape perched atop a special Boeing 747, but the weather at the Cape was too dicey for a shuttle with just enough RCS to do anything but come straight in.

The NASA technicians of the Dryden Flight Research Facility working around the shuttle seemed to be moving in slow motion. Puckett, festooned with clearance badges, chafed at the delay. As soon as the shuttle had cooled and the ground crews had finished safing the vehicle, he headed out across the runway. He was surprised at the size of *Endeavour*. She was a big mother! He had to stop and just admire the spacecraft for a moment. Then he got going. Speed was all important. He climbed up the steps and scrambled through the hatch and into the cabin. There, he found Tanya Brown climbing down from the flight deck. He recognized her from a photograph that had been supplied to him. "Where's Colonel Grant?" he demanded.

Brown tilted her head. Puckett could tell she wanted to ask who the hell he was but she didn't. "Behind me."

Grant came slowly down the rungs like an old woman.

"Colonel Grant, I'm Carl Puckett," he said. "Puckett Security Systems. I've been hired to look after you." He flashed his badges.

"You're too late," she said, her voice shaky. "You should have been up there when they tried to kill me in space."

"I heard that was your opinion. Frank Bonner told me a tiger team is looking into it. Their first response is that it looks like a failure of the canister in a vacuum."

"Yeah," Grant said, clinging to the ladder. "Tell me another one, Carl. Then how come it didn't blow up when I took it outside into the cargo bay?"

"I don't know, Colonel. That's just what I heard." Puckett took Grant's gloved hand. "Your country still needs you."

"I gave it my best shot," Grant said. "I can't do anything more."

"Yes, you can."

Puckett helped Grant to a waiting limo. Behind them the crew of *Endeavour* started to make the traditional walkaround but then said to hell with it and got into their air-conditioned van and slumped into their seats.

Grant let her head loll on the headrest, listening with her eyes closed as Puckett told her about the new plan. She finally opened one eye. "I thought you were my security, not my boss."

"I'm not your boss, just a conveyor of a message. This comes straight from the top. The very top."

Grant shook her head. She didn't have the strength to probe further. "This scheme is nuts. It'll never work."

"The President of the United States wants it," Puckett said. It never hurt to drop a big name. Actually, he had no idea what the President might want about anything at the moment and didn't care.

"Why?" Grant sighed.

"While you were in space we found out what the hijackers are up to."

"Let's hear it."

"They have nuclear weapons on board. They're going to swing around the moon, then make a suicide run on Washington." It was the best Puckett could come up with.

Grant opened one eye. "Do they have a cause?" she asked dubiously.

"Radical right-wing religious nuts."

Grant laughed. "That's horseshit."

"It's what I was told but I could have heard it wrong. Maybe it was left-wing atheists. What difference does it make? They've got a nuke and plan on using it."

"How'd they get a nuclear weapon on board, Carl? The lightest one I heard of weighs at least a half ton."

"Ground crew put it there. They were part of the plot."

"Radical right-wing atheist pad rats?" Grant laughed, shaking her head. "That I would like to see." She subsided and became thoughtful. "Have you talked to the Russians?"

"They're waiting for you with open arms. You're money in the bank to them."

"How do I get there?"

"Private jet all the way. Everything you need is aboard—clothes, toiletries, money, everything."

"Whose jet?" Grant asked suspiciously.

"Charter outfit. They're expensive but they know the way."

"You're certain this comes straight from the President?"

"He told me to tell you that if you pull this off, NASA is going right to the top of his priority list in the budget next year."

The limousine braked. Spotlights lit up a huge Boeing 747. Grant gaped at it. "Jesus Christ! How many people are going with me?"

"Just you," Puckett said. "As soon as you're aboard, you're off."

"But this airplane can hold three hundred passengers!"

"We didn't have time to shop around. It's a little roomy, but you can stretch out anywhere you like and rest."

Grant shook her head and tiredly dragged one foot after the other up the waiting steps. Puckett waited until the jet had roared off the runway, disappearing into the night. Then he called for his leased helicopter. He'd been told there was a man who knew how to kill anybody in space, even as far away as the moon.

On the Way to the Moon
Columbia

For the first time since they had gone into space, the crew of *Columbia* relaxed. While some men slept, Penny sat in the cockpit, strapped into the commander's seat, one leg tucked under the other, and worked on her log:

> *What choice do I have but accept this journey? Medaris has lied to me every step of the way, and probably will continue. I don't blame Virgil. He has his reason, his little girl. He explained to me how Jack had covered all her medical expenses and the bonus of a million dollars stashed in a Grand Cayman bank would see them through all the doctors that followed. . . .*
>
> *That explains Virgil. But I keep wondering about Jack. Virgil told me all about this helium-3 business. I don't believe this is all there is to it. I know something about Medaris after all we've been through together. There's always something going on with that man, something he never says. What could it be? I'm determined to find out.*

Jack used the time to study the stars with his binoculars and to simply contemplate all that had happened.

"Medaris?"

"What, High Eagle?" Jack asked harshly, pulled from his dreams of space.

"What are you doing?"

"Thinking."

"About what?"

He considered telling her the truth, but for some reason he just couldn't. "Right now I'm looking at the sensor reports. With Houston off-line, somebody has to do it."

She hung from an overhead handrail, looking doubtful. "You know, sometimes it would be nice if you just came around and talked a little to me. Virgil and I have run out of things to talk about."

"Is that so? What would you and I talk about?"

"I don't know. You always lie to me, so it's hard to tell."

"Did you interrupt me just to pick a fight?"

"No. I'm trying to talk to you. You've kidnapped me and forced me to go to the moon, so the least you could do is try to be halfway nice."

"I am being nice. I'm just trying to work right now."

"I think you just don't want to talk."

Jack shrugged. "Okay, High Eagle." He opened his arms. "Talk."

"You first," she said. Then, at Jack's expression of disbelief, "What?"

"You said you wanted to talk, I said okay, then you said me first. That doesn't make sense."

"That's it, Medaris," Penny said. "I'm never talking to you again." She headed for the hatch.

"Fine," he said. He put his binoculars to his eyes. "Works for me."

The End of a Dream
SMC

Sam was called out of Shuttle Mission Control by John Lakey. There were three men with him. They were dressed in black fatigues with PUCKETT SECURITY SERVICES shoulder patches. "What now, John? I'm a little busy."

"These are our contractor guards, Sam. They're new and so are my orders. Your team is disbanded. You are to leave the center until further notice."

Sam flicked an eye on the guards. They were big and burly, pro linebacker quality. "John, the last time I heard, you weren't center director. Where is Bonner, anyway?"

Lakey acted as if he hadn't heard him. "The first thing we must do, Sam, is to make a transition in Shuttle Mission Control. I've called in more controllers."

"John, anybody you call hasn't been properly trained. We know *Columbia*. She's our shuttle."

"No, it ain't," one of the guards growled. "It belongs to the hijackers."

Sam ignored the guard, kept speaking directly to Lakey. "*Columbia* is still an American spacecraft, John. You're an astronaut, you know that. We have to be ready to assist her."

Lakey looked distressed, bobbed his head. "I'm sorry, Sam. You're not getting any downlink anyway."

"Get off this center, Mr. Tate," one of the guards said, "and take your people with you, or we'll throw you off. That's our orders. Don't make us do something all of us might regret."

Sam turned away. "I'm going to give Bonner a call."

"Bonner's dead!" Lakey blurted, his voice cracking. "I just got a call from headquarters. Car wreck. Just outside Farley. Something else, too, Sam. They found papers on him. He's been draining JSC director contingency accounts for years, shipping it down to a bank in Central America. Looks like he was sending a ton of money to Russia, too, probably getting a big kickback. He must have been heading for Mexico. It's a mess, Sam. Congressional investigators are going to be in here like bees to honey."

Sam frowned at Lakey's nervous deluge of information. "It don't change the fact we got a spacecraft up there, John. Somebody has to be here in case they call."

One of the guards took a menacing step forward. "Time to go, Mr. Tate," he said, his big lip curling down.

"For Christ's sake, Sam, do what the man says."

Sam considered running to the SMC door and locking it behind him, but then he relented. He went back inside and looked over his brood. He felt a million years old. "Folks, I have an announcement. . . ."

Tate's Turds looked up at their leader, their fresh young faces open and curious. For the first time in his life he was at a loss for words. He struggled for something to say that would make a difference but he couldn't do it. He had to say aloud what in his heart he believed. "It's over for us," he said. "It's all over." And he wasn't just talking about the SMC. It was America's future in space. Sam Tate, the best Flight director the agency ever had, was certain NASA was dead as a hammer.

Starbuck

Carl Puckett directed his limo driver to park in front of the Jetfire Arcade in San Jose, California, just off El Camino Real, the main drag. The store manager mulled over Puckett's request and then jerked a thumb over his shoulder. "Over there," he said, chomping on an unlit cigar. "White coveralls."

Puckett made his way through the din and turmoil of a hundred teens and preteens sitting at computer-driven games, thoroughly engrossed, their hands tight around joysticks or splaying reflexively at guide balls. A plump Oriental in a white jumpsuit sat at the controls of a large blue gamebox. Puckett looked over his shoulder. On the monitor was a starship weaving through a belt of careening asteroids and alien warships. The man, an unjolly, intense Buddha, gripped two joysticks, occasionally jumping down to a guide ball in the center. The starship turned and rolled, darting this way and that as lasers slashed at it and massive plane-toids crashed across the screen. A trio of preteens were watching admiringly to one side.

"Why doesn't he fire his lasers?" Puckett asked one of them.

"Man, Starbuck's way past that," the girl said with disdain. "Anybody can blast rocks. He's fighting the machine, man."

"But the object of the game is to shoot up things, isn't it? Don't you get points for that?" Puckett pointed at the score shown at the lower right of the screen. It said 0.00.

"If you're up to master and that's it, sure," the girl said, her arms crossed and her eyes never leaving the screen. "Starbuck's a universal deity class. They play the game different."

"Yes," Puckett said dryly. "I suppose a universal deity might." He was in a hurry, deity or no. He tapped the man on his shoulder. "Excuse me, Mr. Starbuck? I need to talk to you."

Starbuck ignored him and kept his hands flying from joystick to guide ball and back again. Finally, the screen pulsed into a rainbow of colors and then a hot white light descended abruptly to black. YOU . . . the screen said, ARE . . . GOD. The scene changed, the alien warships lined up in honor, a trackless road opening up that seemed to lead to the stars. There was a tinny trumpet fanfare. ALL HAIL.

Starbuck turned in his seat, squinting up through thick wire-rimmed eyeglasses. "Whatcha want?" he demanded.

"Norio Starbuck?"

"Depends. Who're you?"

"I'm Carl Puckett. I'd like to give you a job."

Starbuck peered around the cluttered room, finally settling on the manager, who was watching him. "I have a job and it was damned hard to come by."

Puckett laughed. "Custodian at a video game parlor?

Scraping chewing gum off plastic seats? I believe I can give you a better job than that."

"Yeah?"

"Yeah. The perfect job for a deity of the universe."

Starbuck heaved his bulk out of the bucket seat. "Tell me about it."

"Can we go somewhere I don't have to yell?"

Starbuck led the way to a cashier's booth where it was marginally quieter. "Okay. What's up?"

"What do you remember," Puckett asked furtively, "about Project Farside?"

Starbuck studied him. "Everything. But who's asking?"

Puckett produced his fake White House and NASA identification cards. It showed him to be a "special consultant."
"Good enough for you?"

Starbuck studied the cards. "You're one of the bastards who shut us down."

Puckett shrugged and then said, "What would it take to activate Farside again?"

"That depends. What for?" Starbuck asked suspiciously.

"Farside is needed for service to this country," he said gravely.

Starbuck cocked his head, a gesture of suspicion. "With all due respect, Mr. Puckett, you'll have to be more specific than that," he said. "Activating an old piece of hardware and software would be extremely difficult, take a lot of my time. I'm not sure it could be done, tell you the truth."

"Too bad. You'd have made a lot of money," Puckett said.

Starbuck grinned. "You got a car?" he asked eagerly.

Bingo. "I have, Mr. Starbuck, a limousine."

"Beats the bus." Starbuck whistled between his teeth. "Hey, boss? Go screw yourself. I'm outtahere."

The manager shook his head. "You'll be back." He turned his attention to a balky game.

Starbuck slid inside the limo, kneaded the black leather

seats, and hummed appreciatively. "Nice," he said. At Starbuck's direction the limousine worked its way out of San Jose and onto the freeway to Sunnyvale.

Puckett sat in the seat opposite Starbuck and used a switch on the door to roll up the window between the passenger compartment and the front, sealing off their conversation from the driver. He leaned forward, his elbows on his knees, ready to tell the lie as he had been instructed. "We found out about Farside from one of your former managers. He's retired now and shall remain nameless. He called my employer for patriotic reasons, said Farside might come in handy considering the present situation with the shuttle. I was dispatched to look you up."

Starbuck nodded. "Figured as much. I caught Larry King last night. You're messing around with a black project here, Mr. Puckett, but I guess you know that." He cocked his head, as if wondering if Puckett had understood him. "A lot of the old Strategic Defense Initiative budget was hidden in black projects, ones that were kept from even the most exalted government bean-counters. But Project Farside was black for more than the budget busters. It was also, by international treaty, illegal. When SDI was canceled, we who were working Farside had already deployed hardware for testing." Starbuck shrugged. "Since we were told to shut down immediately, we had no choice but abandon the test articles in place."

Puckett smiled. "And that place I understand, Mr. Starbuck, was very far from earth."

"Yes."

There was one thing about Starbuck that bothered Puckett. "Why did you change your name?" he asked.

"Kamigaichi was too hard to say at the plant. Starbuck had a ring to it, you know? Star Wars, Starbuck. I just liked it. Mom still hasn't forgiven me. Dad understood, though."

At Sunnyvale, Puckett cracked the window enough for Starbuck to direct the driver to turn toward the mountains.

Across the river and into the first patch of forest was a house built of pine logs, a big rambling design with an attached garage. Starbuck directed the driver into the driveway. "My dad built it. He was first generation. He thought if he lived in a log cabin it would make him feel more American. He died three years ago. Mom's visiting relatives. I take care of the place. My stuff's in the basement."

Starbuck led the way to his "stuff." The basement proved to be a large carpeted room, apparently meant to be a game room or a den. Instead, metal cabinets, computer disk drives, monitors, and consoles were jammed inside.

"Farside," Starbuck explained sadly, "or what's left of it. I bought all the equipment when they had the surplus sale. Cost me about ten thousand dollars. Cost the government maybe fifty million, just for the hardware. The software? Shit, who knows? I'm guessing a billion, easy. I kept a copy of it too."

"Why?"

Starbuck shrugged. "I felt like it. Me and the guys invested five years of our lives in Farside and then we got orders to close down, and I mean *down*, in one day. That hit kinda hard. I didn't want to let go, I guess."

"Can you get Farside going again, Mr. Starbuck?"

Starbuck surveyed the jumbled stacks of equipment. "I'd need about ten of my guys and full access to all five active NASA data and relay satellites. And," he concluded, "the usual supplies."

"Ten people to help you set up the equipment?"

"No. I could do that with two. But I need software geeks —good, fast ones. Ten's the minimum I can get by with. Farside's a test project. The software aboard is for specific objectives. We'll need to change that. What will be our new objective, by the way?"

"Stop *Columbia*, of course."

"Piece of cake. Destroy or disable?"

Puckett hesitated. "That far out," he said, "what would be the difference?"

"Good point. All right. One million dollars per man. And I'll need discs, tapes, upgrades all around. The technology has already changed enough in two years to make all the difference. That'll be another couple million or so. Just give me a government purchase order authorization and I'll go out and get what I need. Lucky this is Silicon Valley or it would take weeks to pull it all together. As it is, I know just where to go. There's a ton of old SDI stuff sitting around, plus compatible upgrades."

"Forget the purchase orders. We'll deal in cash. You got a bank account?"

"No, but I can open one."

"Okay. Give me your account number and bank as soon as you know it. Here's my card. Just use the pager and I'll get right back to you." Puckett stopped and considered for a moment. "A million dollars per person?"

"Five million for me. One for the rest. Take it or leave it. The guys all have jobs they'll have to quit."

"You mean high-paying jobs like the one at the arcade, Mr. Starbuck?"

"Take it or leave it, Carl."

"Three for you, and five hundred K each for the rest," Puckett said, parrying. He'd been given a budget, and got to keep what was left over.

"Three mil and five hundred K? Okay, that's a deal." Starbuck shoved a console into a corner and perused the other equipment, trying to figure out where everything would go.

Puckett ran his hand over his bald head, his walrus mustache twitching. He was calculating his profit. It ran to millions. He stifled a grin. "All right. But forget the NASA comm satellites. I've been told to tell you we can't use anything NASA or any other federal agency would know about. Do you get my drift?"

Starbuck peered through his thick glasses, speculatively. "You're not asking me to do anything illegal, are you, Mr. Puckett?"

"Don't worry about it."

Starbuck shrugged. "I wasn't worried. Just wondering. All right. We'll use commercial commsats. Bounce around between them to throw off what we're doing. It'll cost you, though."

"Okay. Let me know how much," Puckett said.

"That's the spirit," Starbuck said cheerfully. "I guess you want me up and running in two days?"

"One," Puckett said. "Intercept them before they get to the moon."

"Can't do it that fast. I've got some checkouts to do first. Give me two days and I'll still be able catch them before they complete their first lunar orbit. But go get the money, Carl, or I won't make even that."

Starbuck heard the faint sounds of Puckett's limo leaving. He took off the white coverall. He was wearing shorts and a *Star Wars* T-shirt underneath. In one corner of the den was a console he'd set up with a partial software load. He had long since figured out how to break into NASA's TDRS satellites when there wasn't a shuttle in orbit. With *Endeavour* down, and *Columbia* not likely to be using it, he called up his program. It spun through its numbers and then advised that TDRS number three, southwest quadrant, was open for business. Starbuck sent a password through the small parabolic dish on his garage roof and then followed up with another command. The TDRS received it and flashed the coded signal in the general direction of the moon.

In two and a half seconds he received a double-lined stripe across the screen and an icon of a sword and shield. Farside was awake.

Starbuck's fingers flew across his computer keyboard while he visualized the devices he was sending greetings to. Five Farside canisters sat behind the moon. Starbuck remembered seeing them before they were shipped to the Cape for launch. Only one meter long and a half meter wide, they looked like tiny plastic jet skis but they were each a sophisticated marvel. Inside each was an array of miniaturized infrared and heat sensors, a compact hypergolic propellant rocket engine, hydrazine vernier and cold nitrogen steering jets, a box of solid state artificial intelligence including an attached logical computer that allowed autonomous operations, and a nose cone consisting of two video cameras behind aluminized semitransparent covers that looked like eyes. The canisters had been dubbed "BEMs" early on in their design—bug-eyed monsters.

The first complement of BEMs had been blasted into space aboard a *Titan IV* booster that had also carried a Lacrosse imaging radar satellite. Starbuck had heard that intelligence communities around the world had noted the launch, suspecting either a Lacrosse or a Keyhole as the payload. As expected, their radars concentrated on the bulk of the payload, the Lacrosse, and took little note of the scattering debris usually associated with a deploying satellite. Part of the debris, however, had been the BEMs, each deliberately sent outward by tiny puffs of their maneuvering systems into higher and higher orbits until gravity breakaway could be made. Starbuck chuckled at the deception as his fingers continued to peck away at the keyboard.

The deception had continued. A direct Hohmann transfer was not attempted, since the flotilla might be spotted along the traditional route. Instead, the BEMs were sent to the earth-sun-moon gravity boundary a million miles out and then eased back until captured by lunar gravity. It was a trajectory mathematically postulated but never previously attempted, the three-body, or "fuzzy-boundary," path to the moon. It took six months for the canisters to reach their destination but the theory worked perfectly, and as far as Starbuck was aware, no prying intelligence agencies ever had a clue.

Starbuck succeeded in activating the visual software, brought up representations of the BEMs and their location around the moon. He'd need the help of the others to make the graphics better, but this would do for now. He peered at the monitor, saw that, as suspected, most of the BEMs were positioned about ten thousand miles out from the lunar far side, the moon always between them and earth.

Starbuck had directed the games the BEMs had played with one another, some zipping out and slamming back to offer themselves as targets, some acting as hunter-stalkers. Others simply detonated themselves in acts of selfless self-destruction to allow their makers understanding of how debris distributed itself in space. To avoid detection the signals Starbuck had sent to the BEMs were embedded in data streams shunted back and forth between a half-dozen communications satellites in high geosynchronous orbit. Data streams coming back from the little monsters were sent out in nanosecond bursts on varying frequencies to a tiny commsat in orbit around the moon, which retransmitted in equally brief bursts to sensitive receivers positioned at White Sands Missile Range in New Mexico.

Another *Titan IV*, with only a mockup of a Keyhole aboard, sent out a second flotilla. For nearly a year Starbuck and his software people in Silicon Valley had played their computer games, and their advancements had been astonishing. The BEMs had proved to be more than brilliant. They were nasty little geniuses. If deployed, Starbuck believed they might have provided a missile-free safety zone over any area of the earth desired. With Farside so successful other SDI weapons followed the BEMs to the moon, all using the fuzzy-boundary route. In their turn the weapons were tested and the software honed.

Then, when the Cold War ended, everything was

abruptly shut down, all Farside workers on the streets. Starbuck remembered that day, still felt the anger and frustration that had welled up inside of him. Now, finally, he was going to be able to bring Farside alive again, prove what it could do.

Starbuck peered at the representations of the BEM canisters and picked one out, number XJ-249, commanded it to transfer to a ten-degree lunar equatorial orbit, one hundred miles above the surface.

Starbuck imagined what happened next. The white canister would split and XJ-249 would emerge like a butterfly from its pupae, sensors switching themselves on and taking note of the environment. Its artificial intelligence would probably be puzzled. It had been commanded to search but it would find nothing of interest nearby. Its logic would work through the probabilities, adding and subtracting the odds, but would come up with no satisfactory answer. The flood of data streaming back to Starbuck told him XJ-249 was immediately fooled by the earth coming over the lunar horizon, and briefly considered firing at the planet, thinking it a large blue warhead. But when it received no return from its short-range radar, it thought again and then looked away after registering the object in its memory.

Starbuck wasn't concerned. XJ-249 did not have free will, so its logic exercise was just that—an exercise. The Farside software grunts had placed a manual override on everything the BEMs did. It could not attack anything unless that override was removed. Starbuck sat back in his chair, imagining XJ-249 soaring easily over the tortured lunar surface, an impulsive hornet easily angered, itching to get out from under its override.

Starbuck watched the numbers on his screen. "Hi, baby," he whispered. "It's God."

The Armstrong Sea
Columbia

"Where are we, Medaris?" Penny asked, coming up beside him in the cockpit. She poised her pen over a notebook.

Jack put aside the procedures manual for the moon landing module and regarded her. "I didn't think you were talking to me."

"I'm not. I'm asking you a question. Where are we?"

"Why do you want to know?"

"I'm keeping a log."

Jack looked around, shrugged. "Cislunar space."

"I knew you'd have some bland engineering term for it."

Jack frowned at her. "That's what it's called."

Penny finished her jotting and gave Jack a smug smile, then pushed off, sailing back to the middeck. Jack turned to watch her feet disappear down the hatch. "That's what it's called!" he said defensively.

Jack went after some coffee. Penny was working on her cell culture samples. "Armstrong Sea," she said to him as he mixed up a bag of coffee at the rehydration station.

"What?"

"We should call where we are the Armstrong Sea instead of cislunar space. After the first man who walked on the moon."

Jack snorted. "High Eagle, cislunar space is a precise term. Why do you want to call it some name?"

"So it makes sense."

"It makes perfect sense already."

"For you"—Penny smiled—"which does not surprise me in the least. Is that coffee? Can I have it?" She took it from him while he stared at her. She inserted a straw. "This is awful stuff."

"Sometimes," Jack said, "you really irritate me."

"I do? Could you let me know when that happens?"

"Why?"

"So I know when I'm doing it right!"

"What's gotten into you?" he asked suspiciously.

She smirked above the cup. "I'm just trying to enjoy myself on this voyage of folly."

"It isn't folly. We're going to get Dr. Perlman his helium-3. It's important to the future of the world. I thought Virgil explained all that to you."

"Oh, he did. It's a good story too. But what I'd like to hear, Mr. Jack Medaris," she said seriously, "is the rest of the story. Want to tell it to me?"

He answered sourly. "You've been told all you need to hear."

"I don't think so." She sent the bag of coffee floating across to him, watched as he caught it with one hand. "You need to tell me. Maybe it would help you if you got it off your conscience. You've fooled all of these people for all these months. Now you've by God hijacked a space shuttle, done it so it might even be legal. Now you're on your way to the moon, might even be able to land on it, although I can't imagine how your plan's going to work. Still, it's something to be proud of, Jack. But not if you do it as a lie. I've gotten to know you over the last few days. You're not such a bad guy. You're just driven by something you keep inside. Tell me. I want to hear it."

Jack gazed at the beautiful and irritating woman. His face betrayed his need to tell, to hear it told, especially to her, and he knew she could see it. He flew away from her, up through the hatch to the cockpit where he might be alone with his computers and his sensors, free of this woman and her questions. He felt relief when she didn't follow him. Then he felt lonely because she didn't.

On the Road to Baikonour
Allah Akba Airport, Alma-Ata, the Sovereign State Republic of Kazakhstan

Olivia Grant gripped the armrests of her seat as the TU-144 transport dropped sickeningly out of the turbulent sky and slammed into the rough, cracked runway of Alma-Ata, the capital city of Kazakhstan. She had landed in Moscow and into trouble, since she didn't have the necessary visa for entrance to either Russia or Kazakhstan. After a lot of arm waving and the arrival of a contingent of grim-faced men from the Russian Space Agency, it was decided Grant, as a NASA astronaut, fell under the general visa issued for the corps when they'd flown to the *Mir*. After that Grant had been stuffed into an airplane for a six-hour flight in a seat with a backrest that wouldn't stay up and in a cabin so filled with acrid cigarette smoke that the far bulkhead had been nearly invisible. As soon as the aircraft quit taxiing, Grant pushed down the aisle through the crowd of heavyset women in kerchiefs and men in dark, smelly woolen suits and stumbled gratefully into the cool, crisp air of a high desert. She had a splitting headache.

At Kazakh customs what appeared to be a Russian officer needing a shave held up a sign with her name misspelled on it. OLAF GRAANT. She went to him and identified herself. His eyes widened and he threw down the sign and grabbed her in a drunken bear-hug, then spirited her to a dirty black car. The driver, a man with a soft army cap pulled low over his eyes, was smoking. She rolled down the window, gasping for breath. The boozy officer climbed in beside her, said something, and the car was off. Grant was pummeled by the officer, slapping her on the shoulder.

"As-tro-naut!" the officer shouted, a big grin on his round face. He touched her hair. "Lady!"

Grant recoiled. The car sped past truck after truck loaded

with what appeared to be cabbages. She pointed ahead.
"Baikonour?"

"*Da, da.* Baikonour!"

The old Soviet Union had built its major launch center
at Baikonour for a simple reason: it was far enough south
that spent stages of the rockets launched from there fell on
Siberia rather than China. After the breakup of the Soviet
Union it was left stranded in the independent state of Kazakhstan, a country that, in 1991, declared the cosmodrome
to be Kazakh property. Since then the Russian Space
Agency had been charged a high tariff for every launch.

"How long?" Grant asked, pointing at her watch.

The officer grinned and pointed at his own watch. He
held up eight fingers. Eight hours. Grant groaned. The officer dug a bottle out from under the front seat—no label
but Grant knew a bottle of vodka when she saw one. He
poured a plastic cup full and handed it over. Grant took it
greedily.

"Cos-mo-naut!" the officer grinned, pounding his chest.
"Cos-mo-naut Nazarbeyev!"

Grant frowned at the bleary-eyed man. *This was a cosmonaut?* She had spent her entire life preparing to be an astronaut. She had two doctorates, one in physics and one in
mathematics. She was a graduate of the Air Force Test Pilot
School at Edwards Air Force Base, California, and had more
than five thousand hours in forty different high-performance
aircraft, not to mention her flights into space aboard the shuttle. And this *thing* in front of her was supposed to be her
equal? "God help me." She groaned. *What had she gotten
herself into?* She thought of Carl Puckett, the obvious lies
he'd told. What game was the American government playing
with her life? Maybe she should stop now, get back to the
United States somehow, be done with it. But all her life
Grant had met every challenge that came to her. Even
though she was caught up in what seemed madness, she had
to do her best to see it through.

Ten hours later, after a jolting journey across two mountain ranges on roads that barely deserved the name, plus two flat tires, waiting once for what appeared to be ten thousand sheep to cross the road, and stopping at a baked mud hut for the worst meal in her life—something greasy swimming in something greasier—Grant beheld the Baikonour Cosmodrome, the pride of the dead Soviet Union.

As she walked through the filthy glass doors into the dank hall of the main administrative building, she saw dust balls blowing across the floor, a hot, stale wind whistling through a broken window. Down the hall a knot of men dressed in heavy, ill-fitting suits surged toward her. One of them, a tall, thin man with a cigarette stuck in the corner of his mouth, hugged her before she could push him away.

"Come, come," he shouted at Grant. "I am Dubrinski. We speak English, yes?"

She followed him past a mural of Yuri Gagarin in his spacesuit, looking nobly up at something in the corner with other cosmonauts below him following his gaze. Grant couldn't see what they were supposed to be observing. A Kazakh flag had been nailed over that corner of the mural.

They went into a meeting room furnished with an assortment of wooden chairs and flimsy card tables. "These Kazakh dogs stole all the furniture and just about everything else in the building," Dubrinski said. When he said *Kazakh*, it sounded as if he were spitting.

A thick coffee was served and the men chattered along to Grant's increasing discomfort and rising anger. Finally, she grabbed Dubrinski by the shoulder. "What the hell are we doing?"

"These are Kazakhs, Colonel," Dubrinski said mildly. "They have nothing to say, really, but they have insisted that you spend at least one hour with them before we Russians can have you. It is their way of showing that the launch center belongs to them. They were also very interested in seeing the American woman who claims to be an astronaut. It is actually their considered opinion that you are some kind of rock star. In a way, they wanted to see if you were Madonna."

"This is bullshit," Grant muttered harshly, and stood up abruptly. The Kazakhs, drinking coffee and smoking, stopped their buzz of conversation and looked at Grant curiously. "I want to see the equipment we'll be using. There's no time to spare!"

"Sit down, Colonel," Dubrinski said firmly, "or much more time will pass before they allow you out of this room. Sit down and smile and drink coffee with them. It is the quickest way for us to begin our tasks."

Grant sat down but she wouldn't drink coffee with the swarthy men. The stink of their cigarettes and body odor was making her sick. Glumly, she answered in monosyllables all questions put to her. Dubrinski apparently elaborated on everything in the translation as the Kazakhs all nodded appreciatively as he spoke. Finally, one of the men clapped his hands, they all stood up, and Grant and Dubrinski were released. He led her out of the administrative building to the same dirty black sedan, bored driver, and stinking-drunk cosmonaut. They drove down a pothole-filled road to a huge hangar. Gigantic doors were rolled back and Dubrinski led Grant through, stepping across rusting railroad tracks. Pigeon droppings pelted them from the rafters.

Two huge rockets lay on their sides in the rear of the building, three-stage vehicles, each stage on its own railroad car. Canvas awnings drooped over the stages. "That is the one you will ride, Colonel." Dubrinski pointed and led the way, carefully skirting several piles of broken lumber and bent aluminum tubing. As Grant neared the giant rocket, she saw the skylight over it had collapsed and what appeared to be electrical cables snarled out of a conduit nearby. Another pile of cables had been thrown in a corner in a tangled wad. Cigarette-smoking workers, dressed in ragged gray coveralls, picked nonchalantly around the rocket.

Grant ducked under one corner of the protective tarpaulin and walked toward the rocket. She stopped at the booster stage and ran her eyes over it, spotting chipped paint and signs of corrosion on the propellant feed tubing. As she watched, a mangy brown dog ambled up next to it and urinated on the railroad wheels of the booster carrier. "My God, is there no quality control here?"

Dubrinski stepped up beside her. He yelled at the workers, who slouched off after giving him derisive hand signals. The drunken cosmonaut staggered after them, yelling a stream of what sounded like Arabic obscenities. "Do not be deceived, Colonel," Dubrinski said. "The facilities are old, and our workers have not been paid for many months. But this is a *Proton*, the most reliable space booster the world has ever known. It will take you and your pilot wherever you ask it. Let me show you something."

Dubrinski led Grant up the length of the booster. He pointed at a cylinder capped with a cone at the end of the rocket. "Your spacecraft. It is all under this shroud. Two stages and a *Soyuz-Y*."

"Where is the simulator for the *Soyuz*?" Grant asked anxiously. "I'll need some training."

Dubrinski lit a cigarette. "Our simulator is in Star City, near Moscow," he said. "You will be trained on-orbit by your pilot."

Her "host" on the drive from hell to Baikonour was coming back toward them, wiping his forehead on his sleeve. "That moron is going to be my pilot?"

"Him?" Dubrinski cocked an eyebrow, and then laughed. "No, Colonel. He is a Kazakh we flew to the *Mir* space station just to make his government happy. Every time he tried to touch something, we slapped his hands away. I will be your pilot."

Grant looked at the thin Russian carefully. "Do you have experience?"

"A little," he said. "Enough, I think. I am a colonel in the cosmonaut corps."

Grant eyed the man. "How much did NASA pay you to do this?"

Dubrinski shrugged. "Me? Nothing. I am a salary man. The Russian Space Agency? A hundred million dollars, so the rumor goes. Cash. Up front. Some RSA officials are very pleased, I would imagine. Most of the money will go into their pockets."

Grant looked around at the dingy hangar and the rusty rocket. "Can we get inside the *Soyuz*? I'd like to familiarize myself with the controls."

"Certainly. We can do that tomorrow when they raise the rocket on its pad and begin the necessary checkouts."

"What do we have to do to get clearance?"

"Clearance? Nothing. I will just open the hatch and we'll climb inside, fiddle with the controls until you understand everything."

"There's no procedures involved? It would take a stack of paperwork as high as this hangar for me to do something like that at the Cape."

Dubrinski laughed heartily. "You Americans make everything too difficult, Colonel. Relax, enjoy the Russian way. Tomorrow I'll train you on the *Soyuz*. Tonight, get drunk with me!"

Grant pulled her coat tight around her neck as a bitter wind whistled through the open hangar. She considered the invitation. She hadn't gotten where she was by being the tentative sort. She could use a little fun. "You're on, Colonel."

"For tonight?"

"Yes, by damn! And tomorrow you will teach me to fly the *Soyuz*."

Dubrinski clapped her on her back. "We will rescue the people on board the shuttle as they return from the moon."

"Sure, Yuri," Grant said, pleased that he believed the lie about their mission. That would make it easier, at least until they got into space. She'd take it from there. She grinned up into his handsome Cossack face. "You bet your sweet butt."

MET 6 DAYS AND COUNTING . . .

Montana (2)
The Perlman Plant Site

"Listen!" Charlie Bowman said, cupping his ear with his hand and cocking his head toward the ceiling.

Perlman listened but could hear nothing but the faint whir of the air handling units spaced along the massive concrete corridor. He looked up to where Charlie was pointing, at the big circular hatch painted a bright red on the roof of the corridor just outside the old Egg missile launch control room. Charlie had come after him, finding him in his quarters, and brought him out to stand in the concrete causeway that led from the elevator blast doors. Perlman buttoned up his lab coat to ward off the chill of the unheated causeway and listened, but then shook his head. "I'm sorry, Charlie. I can't hear anything."

Charlie reached up and put his hand on the hatch. He nodded as if it confirmed his suspicions. "Put your hand here, Doc. You can feel it too."

Perlman didn't share Charlie's concern, whatever it was. They were deep in the silo, behind two huge reinforced concrete blast doors that were locked up tight. But he gave in to Charlie's insistence, and placed his hand on the red hatch, feeling the pebbly roughness of its cast surface. He also felt an intermittent vibration, a distant scratching. He stood on his tiptoes, cocking his ear to the hatch. "Digging?" he guessed.

Charlie nodded. "Sounds like they've got a troop with a shovel and a bucket. They've found our one vulnerable spot, Doc."

Perlman studied the red cover. "What's this thing for?"

"Escape hatch. It goes from here up to ground level. The tunnel is filled with sand. The idea was that if the crew was ever trapped in here, they could open this hatch up, let the sand empty out, and crawl up to the surface. The exit up there was camouflaged but I guess whoever is after us found it."

Perlman felt a chill that had nothing to do with the temperature. "How long will it take them to get to us?" he asked the machinist.

Charlie shrugged. "My hunch is they'll dig for a while and then they'll get tired of that and start blasting. It'll take a lot of dynamite but they'll manage to get at us. I'd say we have maybe twenty-four hours before they punch through."

"Anything we can do to stop them?"

Charlie looked around, at the Egg, the cavern roof, and the blast door that led to the fusion plant. "I been thinking about that, Doc, but I ain't come up with nothing yet."

Perlman frowned and rubbed his eyes. "There has to be a way out of this. What do we have going for us?" He walked around in a tight little circle, snapping his fingers, mumbling to himself. "We have plenty of generators and lots of fuel. Can we use them for some defensive mechanism?"

Charlie also paced. Then he stopped and looked at the hatch. "Say, Doc, we got a lot of water down here, don't we?"

Perlman shrugged. "You know we do. We need it to cool the fusion plant and also for the steam generator that turns the turbines. We don't have to worry about dying of thirst, Charlie. We're more likely to drown if any of those bastards up there start blasting and crack the reservoir open."

"Pumps are in good shape," Charlie mused.

Perlman looked at the machinist. "What are you thinking, Charlie?"

Charlie's white-bearded face took on a diabolical grin. "Water, pumps, and generators. Doc, that's all we need!"

He looked up at the hatch. "Keep diggin', boys. All you're gonna find is a whole lot of trouble!"

Penny's Log (1)
Columbia

The flight deck is warm and the middeck cool. When I go below, I have a sweater there that I put on. I checked my experiment and the cells were doing well. I looked at what I think of as my "ruined" sample and am surprised to see that the coil in the center has grown even more and has started to take on what appears to be mitosis. It is the sheep nerve cells that have divided, and they are assuming a definite pattern. I am interested in the white strands that seem to be interweaving them. Virgil watched me with interest while I went through my routine. While I worked, he and I talked about his family.

Virgil's daughter is undergoing expensive procedures at the Mayo Clinic this week involving genetic splicing. I have read about it, and can give him a hopeful report that it has had some success in lung diseases, including cystic fibrosis. But I still wonder how a man can choose to leave his family, probably forever, on a dicey mission such as this. He is a fanatic, I suppose, made so by his belief in spaceflight and his loyalty to Jack.

Jack, Jack. Our mystery man, Jack. What is he doing here?

When I ran out of anything else to do today, I watched the earth. The best place for that is the aft flight deck. The earth at this altitude assumes a three-dimensional aspect that is not evident on orbit. My home planet sits, a giant blue sphere wreathed in white cloud streaks and whorls and eddies, on a cushion of deep velvety blackness, her thin atmosphere a shimmering corona. There is no fuzziness to her, as she is seen in the photographs by the Apollo astronauts. Her edges, her landscape, even her clouds, are starkly defined.

The earth is also getting smaller—orange-sized now—but

I find to my surprise I feel no sadness, or longing. I am strangely excited by what lies ahead, not nervous or afraid at all. Only rarely do I catch a glimpse of the moon, usually from the cockpit windows. She must be behind the earth or maybe just on the other side of Columbia, but I don't bother Medaris to ask about her. It's interesting that I think of the earth and the moon and our Columbia as females. Two of them are nurturers, earth and spacecraft. The moon, however, is to me like an aunt who travels and never marries, who brings her nieces and nephews strange, incomprehensible gifts that we treasure but never love. The moon has a streak of independence that causes us to admire her, but she has a callousness, too, that makes her unloved. But maybe, I think, that is because we do not know her. Soon, we shall.

Medaris has been instructing me and Virgil on a lot of things we may need to know when he's on the surface. Shuttle systems, how to operate the RMS, things like that. These were the things Cassidy would have done but now it's up to Virgil and me. I would avoid it if I could, but it makes sense to learn as much as I can if Jack is really going to try to land on the moon. The truth is he might not come back. I might as well accept the reality of it. To have any chance of ever getting home, I have to learn all I can, work with Virgil and Medaris, no matter how hateful he is. It is just us out here.

Us.

I like the sound of that.

Cecil's Compromise
Attorney General's Office, Justice Department

Cecil was led once again into the office of the attorney general and told to wait. He passed the time looking at the AG's family photos, a grim lot of farmers in coveralls and chintz. No awards or diplomas decorated the wall. She favored agrarian scenes. Then she was there, pointing at a chair. She looked tired, heavy bags under her hazel eyes. "Sit," she ordered.

He sat while she hunkered down behind a big oak desk. "Well, Velocci. None of my boys and girls can figure out how to break your contract. It's legal. And our interrogation of astronaut Janet Barnes has shown that Cassidy's death was an accident, so it's unlikely a murder rap would stick to your clients either."

"Yes, ma'am."

"However," she continued, "assuming they survive this idiocy, which I think is doubtful, they're still going to jail. MEC deliberately endangered astronauts in the launch tower elevator. Tacked on to that is the destruction of considerable government property." She consulted a file. "A data line at Kennedy Space Center plus three shuttle main engines and other unauthorized alterations to the shuttle *Columbia*. Estimated damages are in the neighborhood of five billion dollars. Since it is clear now that they are headed to the moon, unspecified in your contract, it appears they may also be in violation of the 1967 Outer Space Treaty, which stipulates no operation may occur on or near the lunar surface without consultation with the international community."

Cecil scratched his head. "Excuse me, ma'am, but I believe the treaty does not make such consultation an absolute requirement. It is caveated, as I understand it, to say that it should be done 'to the greatest extent feasible and practicable.' My announcement on an international television show accomplished that."

"Don't con me, Velocci," Hawthorne retorted. "Going on *Larry King Live* was hardly in the spirit of the treaty."

"That may be, ma'am, but with all due respect I don't believe my clients have broken any international laws." Cecil dug a document out of his crammed briefcase. "I think you should be aware of this: it is a copy of the incorporating papers for the Medaris Engineering Company in

Grand Cayman, British West Indies. MEC is not an American company but Caymanian. And Grand Cayman is not a signatory to the Outer Space Treaty."

"You really think this kind of crap would hold up in court?"

"I think it would hold up for many, many years of appeals."

To Cecil's amazement Hawthorne allowed a toothy grin to slide across her plain face. "By God, if I ever get into trouble, I want you to be my attorney, Mr. Velocci!"

Cecil blushed and looked down at his lap. "Thank you, ma'am."

When he looked up, she was no longer grinning. "All right, Velocci, let's get down to cases. All smoke and mirrors aside, we'll find something on your clients that's going to stick. Considering what they've done, how's it going to look if we don't?"

It was Cecil's turn to surprise the AG. "I understand you've been looking into the Puckett Security Services. Find anything useful yet?"

Hawthorne grunted. "That's not anything I can talk about, Velocci. But we're interested in PSS, yeah."

"They tried to burn Jack out. Must be pretty bad hombres."

"The baddest," Hawthorne said, and then was silent.

Cecil brightened, as if an idea had just popped into his mind. "May I make a suggestion for a compromise—off the record, of course?"

Hawthorne shrugged. "Fire away."

"I fully understand that you can't just let my clients go— a bad precedent and all that—but what if we were willing to stipulate that there were certain . . . irregularities in the manner in which a portion of the contract was performed? I'm speaking specifically of the 'modification' of the data lines at the Cape Canaveral launch complex."

"You mean cop a plea?"

"I think a fine equal to the amount of repairs would be appropriate."

"What about the damage to the shuttle?"

"We believe there's been no damage done to the shuttle. The modifications undertaken by MEC have in fact improved her. She was a vehicle capable of only low earth orbit, but now she's one that can travel to the moon."

Hawthorne pursed her thin lips. "Interesting logic. I'll need some time to think about what you've said." She waved her hand in dismissal.

"May I go home? The wife and kids have been staying in a motel all this time for safety. We've all had it. We just want to go back to our island."

She leaned her head on her hand, tapped her temple. "Yes, but don't go anywhere where I can't find you."

"No problem." He headed for the door, trying to imagine where on the planet he could go that this woman couldn't track him down.

"Velocci?"

Cecil stopped at the door. Almost made it! "Ma'am?"

"What's your plans—after all this?"

"I'm never going to leave Cedar Key again."

"Sounds like a wise move. Any beachfront property down there available for an old warhorse like me?"

Cecil raised his eyebrows and dug into his briefcase. This MEC gig was just a one-shot affair. *A man still has to make a living.* . . . "Now that you mention it, I just happened to have these brochures. . . ."

The Exalted Leader
Farside Control

Starbuck assembled his troops before the refurbished Farside Control Center. On the front wall hung two big virtual panels to give a visual representation of both the Farside controlled vehicles and the target, i.e., *Columbia*. A tier of six control consoles stood in a line in front of the panels. Behind them, on a pedestal, sat a bank of three consoles canted so that the person in the single chair behind them could swivel easily to see what each screenload held. The nameplate on the chair read EXALTED LEADER.

Starbuck, in a King Arthur costume, his favorite, reviewed his troops, ten programmers plus one guard, all members of the local Society for Creative Anachronism, each in the costume of his or her choice. The guard had stretched the concept way past medieval times, appearing in the full-dress regalia of a Klingon warrior from the *Star Trek* series.

"To victory!" a knight cried, raising his wooden sword.

"And may might make right!"

"And to our blessed king," another knight exhorted while the ladies curtsied.

Starbuck, choking with pride, looked over his people. "God bless California!" was all his emotions would allow him to say.

High Eagle's Discovery
Columbia

Columbia was one hundred thousand miles out from earth when Penny decided to check her cell culture experiment again. She examined each one, photographing as she went, carefully marking each sample, and taking notes. Finally she clicked the last sample, the contaminated one, into the microscope tray and took a look, not expecting much. What she saw amazed her. "Medaris, get down here!" she yelled.

He poked his head through the hatch. "What?"

"Look!" She pointed at her microscope.

Jack came headfirst through the hatch, did an easy somersault, and settled in behind the microscope. He put his eye to it, fiddling with its adjustment knobs. "So?" he said after lifting his eye away.

"Medaris," Penny said, her eyes wide, "I think it's a neural pathway fragment!"

He looked into the eyepiece again. "You're growing a spinal cord?"

Penny nodded vigorously. "Yes! How can you be so blasé about it? I've got to let researchers back on earth know about this!"

Jack shook his head. "I don't think that's a good idea, High Eagle. I don't want to rattle any cages back there."

"Look, Medaris, what I have here could be more important than anything else on this mission!"

He shook his head. "Think about it, High Eagle. What good would it do to tell the ground? You can't send them any photographs. The SAREX has no way of sending pictures even if you had a way of developing them, which you don't. And let me ask you something. With all the accelerations this culture has had on it, how could you ever hope to duplicate it?"

She glared at him. "You just don't get it, do you? It's very clear what's happened. A lucky accident! The combination of sheep nerve cells and frog growth DNA in an incubator in a microgravity environment has produced something remarkable. Space just might be the place to grow nerve tissue for paralysis victims, Medaris! This could be a suicide mission—*don't argue with me!* It could be! We need to get this news back to earth while we're still in shape to do it!"

Medaris looked at her, then sighed as if she were the source for every problem known to all mankind. But he opened up the SAREX. "All right, High Eagle. You win." He keyed a greeting and waited. Nothing happened. "There's no response. Go look at the earth."

"Why?"

"Just do it, High Eagle. Tell me what you see."

Penny relented, went to the flight deck, looked, and returned. "It's still there," she said.

"What hemisphere did you see?"

"I saw Africa."

"That's what I thought. SAREX requires a straight line of sight. We'll have to wait until the planet rotates."

"When will that be?"

"About ten hours." He put his thumbs in his ears, wiggled his fingers, and stuck his tongue out at her. "We should still be around as long as your spinal cord doesn't grow scales and start chasing us around the shuttle."

Penny made a face back at him. "Very funny, Medaris."

He shrugged. "We do the best we can with the material we've got."

Ten hours later, as promised, Jack tried the SAREX again, Penny hovering over his shoulder. A message came back. MEC was there. "It's all yours," he said, moving aside.

She entered her message, requesting retransmittal to her sponsoring pharmaceutical lab. MEC answered immediately.

WILL FORWARD. EXCITING STUFF.

The next message that came was not for her but for Medaris.

HOUSTON HAS GONE SILENT. NO NEWS FROM PERLMAN.
CECIL CHECKED IN. SAID NOT TO WORRY.

Jack replied.

TOO LATE TO WORRY. ALL WELL HERE AND ON TIME-
LINE. MOON IS GROWING LARGER BY THE MINUTE. WISH
YOU COULD SEE IT.

BRING A PIECE OF IT BACK FOR US.

YOU GOT IT.

Shirley's Report
Catoctin Mountains, Maryland

It had been the devil's worst time trying to track him down, but Shirley finally found the vice president. Vanderheld had gone off on a field trip into the mountains of Maryland, looking for some kind of rare bird. She found him in a pretty green meadow scalloped between two forested hills. Breathlessly, she told him all she'd learned at the Lunar Curatorial Lab.

"I believe I told you it wasn't necessary to continue your research on Medaris," the Veep said, grimacing. He had his hand in the small of his back. He'd hurt it tripping over a log, he'd said.

"I went on my own time using my own money, sir," Shirley said.

"And so you discovered Medaris is going after helium-3," Vanderheld said. "I've heard that already. Interesting information but it doesn't change much. He still hijacked a shuttle."

Shirley took a deep breath, knowing, no matter what their relationship might be, she was about to overstep her bounds. "Sir, I think you must help the people aboard *Columbia* and help this Dr. Perlman, wherever he is. I believe he and Jack Medaris are trying to do something wonderful for this country."

Vanderheld limped over to a rock outcropping and took a load off. He lifted the straps of both of the heavy cameras over his head, set them gently beside him. "All right, Shirley," he said. "Let's hear your reasoning."

Shirley explained all that Koszelak had said at the Lunar Curatorial Lab, how the fire beads of *Apollo 17* held helium-3, how it could be used in a fusion reactor. Then she told him about her research on Perlman, how he had published the results of his last test with the helium-3 he'd managed to get off the old *Apollo* rocks. "Fusion energy is so clean, that's the wonderful part," she said with the breathless energy of a convert. "Fossil fuel will become obsolete, all those dirty oil fields and coal mines. And fusion energy can be made to be cheap. Just think of it, sir, the advantages will accrue to poor people with access to cheap energy. Sir, fusion is going to provide for nearly everything you've fought for all your life!"

Vanderheld listened, his eyes closed against the bright afternoon sun. When she'd finished, he kept his eyes closed for a minute, his brow furrowed in thought. "It saddens me," he said, finally, "that you seem to have forgotten the World Energy Treaty, Shirley. WET will do all that you give fusion credit for. There will be a board and I will be on it, and I will make certain that no decision is made on energy that does not take into account the poor and the downtrodden. I am going to make certain that the provision of energy everywhere across the planet is fair and equitable. This I will do without introducing a dangerous new energy form into the world."

"But, sir, fusion is nonpolluting. It's—"

Vanderheld held up his hand. "That's what they said about fission energy too. Just a few by-products. It turned out it was plutonium. A trace of plutonium can kill millions. I fear you've fallen prey to the fusion propaganda machine."

"No, sir, I studied a hundred different independent sources," she said, hoping she sounded braver than she felt. "Sir, I know you worked hard on WET but I think this could be even better. The way I see it is that we may be about to embark on a new age of peace and prosperity. No more wars for oil, no more pollution, energy for all, even the poorest of nations. I think that's wonderful. I was certain you'd think it was wonderful too!"

Vanderheld slowly shook his head back and forth. "No. You're wrong. Fusion using helium-3 from the moon will introduce an age of nations vying against nations for this new gold in this new world. There may very well be war in space."

"You expect there to be a war for the moon?" Shirley asked, shaken. "Who will be the combatants?"

Vanderheld looked up into the sky, squinting. "To start, Russia, China, Europe, Japan, India, Great Britain, the United States, all the spacefaring nations. Great Britain, I expect, would throw in with us. How the other countries would divide themselves up I'm not certain. Japan would be inclined toward us, maybe. We've treated them pretty shabbily the last few years. China and Russia would be tempted to work together, but, based on their traditional animosity toward one another, that might prove to be a difficult alliance, might even spark a war between them. Europe would probably try to go it alone but eventually they'd have to choose between us or the Russians, neither choice particularly palatable to them. France, for one, has spent trillions on thermonuclear energy. Fusion energy would destroy that investment overnight. The world structure would be knocked into a cocked hat. The results would probably be quite bloody."

"Sir, I think you're wrong," Shirley said. "I see competition, sure. Mankind is at its best when it's moving out, striving to gain advantage. But war? Space is too big a place for war. I think we'll stop looking inward, recognize that all our worries about Social Security and people wearing helmets on ski slopes and all this internal bickering would be a thing of the past. Great strides would be taken that wouldn't be abided during normal times, strides that would advance all areas of technology and science."

Vanderheld's eyes turned sorrowful. "You are indeed a dreamer, Shirley," he said softly, kindly. He waved his hand, sighed. "What is it you want me to do?"

"I got a call from Professor Koszelak. Shuttle Mission Control is closed down. The shuttle is at the moon. Let me go to Houston, get Mission Control fired back up. Let's not let Americans get killed up there. Let's help them bring us this new gold."

Vanderheld nodded, started to get up, then slumped back down. Shirley went to help him. "No, I'm fine," he said. He struggled to his feet. "I just get stiff. Go on with you, Shirley. Go help your gold hunters. I think you got smitten with this Jack Medaris while you were out there. Am I off the mark?"

Shirley hadn't thought of it that way. As she had so often learned, the vice president could see right through her. It made her happy. They were back in synch. "You could be right, sir. Could you sign this?" She produced a document from her briefcase. "It authorizes me to reopen the SMC."

Vanderheld laughed, stretched out his hand for the piece of paper, searched his shirt pocket for a pen. "You are something, Shirley Grafton," he said. "A cheerleader for a new paradigm in a new world."

Penny's Log (2)
Columbia

We are more than 100,000 miles out as I write this. We are slowing now, only going a little less than 4,000 miles per hour. Two days ago, when the Big Dog engine pushed us out of earth orbit, we were going 25,000 miles per hour. We are in the influence of three magnets, Medaris says, the sun, the earth, and the moon. It is earth that is slowing us, the weaker pull of the moon only just now being felt. It will cause us to speed up again later today.

Medaris called Virgil and me to the cockpit after lunch. We would need a slight midcourse correction, he said. Virgil put Paco in his box and then came back up and lay down on the deck and grabbed foot-loops. I strapped myself in beside Medaris, in the pilot's seat. When Big Dog fired, there was just a bump and it was over. Medaris pulled out all his nav

stuff again, putting the laptop through its paces, and check-
ing the star trackers. Finally, he announced that we were
back into the hands of Isaac Newton and precisely on course.

We still can't see the moon. Yesterday, I was starting to
feel an affection for it. I dread it now as we begin to fall into
its sterile embrace. I look back at the warm earth and find no
solace there either. It seems I am happy only on my Arm-
strong Sea.

Penny climbed over the pilot's seat, settled down into it.
She had left Paco's hairbrush attached to the forward panel.
Jack was in the commander's seat, reading a book and keeping one eye on the computer display. He sniffed the air as
she turned to fly back out of the cockpit. "You smell good,"
he said.

He'd said it as if it was a surprise. Penny remembered the
time when they'd first been in orbit and she was still in
stinky diapers. Perhaps that was why he'd said it. It was
another slam in her direction. "Go to hell, Medaris," she
snarled.

He frowned. "What for?"

"I smell good. Thanks," she said sardonically.

"No, really," he said sincerely. "You do. Sort of like"—
he cocked his head, sniffed—"like sage, I think."

"Sage? You're saying I smell like a tumbleweed?" Penny
considered slapping him. This was going too far.

"No, sage is sort of like fresh grass, I think. With a tang.
All women seem to have a distinctive odor. . . . Are you
wearing something?"

"No." She eyed Jack critically. "Do you go around smell-
ing women? Is that how you get your kicks? And women
have an odor? An *odor*? God, what a geek you are!"

Jack shrugged. "Sorry."

"You're a jerk, Medaris."

He went back to his book. "Remind me not to ever try to compliment you again about anything."

"I will," she said, pulling over the seat and soaring off. She couldn't resist having the last word. "And if you ever need to know how to give a compliment, Medaris, ask me. I will try to teach you."

"I'd like to teach you. . . ." Jack grumbled, trailing off.

"What was that?"

"Nothing, dear."

MET 7 DAYS AND COUNTING . . .

The Doomsday Command
Farside Control

Starbuck proudly watched his Farside software engineers
working, diligently calling up each weapon, interrogating it,
studying its health and status. Besides the BEMs a weapon
known as the Homing Overlay Experiment (HOE), a fifteen-
foot-diameter umbrellalike web of metal strips, a powerful
radar, and a battering-ram attitude, was stationed at the fuzzy
boundary behind the moon. HOE had proved difficult to
bring up. Starbuck's suspicion was that a transistor located in
its communications transceiver was operating intermittently,
probably due to the intense heat and cold inflicted on all the
devices in the Farside orbit. HOE had worked over Kwajalein Island in the Pacific several times in the 1980s against
Minuteman intercontinental ballistic missiles fired from California. If it had worked then, Starbuck was certain it could
work again. He had his engineers assigned to it search the
drawings and tinker with the software to look for alternate
routes for the current.

The BEMs had proved almost savage in their demeanor.
"Have a look," the BEM lead invited Starbuck. "I asked
them for health and status. They transmitted routine parameters and then I got this."

The screen read:

```
LETMEGO  LETMEGO  LETMEGO  LETMEGO  LETMEGO
LETMEGO  LETMEGO  LETMEGO  LETMEGO  LETMEGO
LETMEGO  LETMEGO  LETMEGO  LETMEGO  LETMEGO
LETMEGO  LETMEGO  LETMEGO  LETMEGO  LETMEGO
```

LETMEGO LETMEGO LETMEGO LETMEGO LETMEGO
LETMEGO LETMEGO LETMEGO LETMEGO LETMEGO
LETMEGO LETMEGO LETMEGO LETMEGO LETMEGO
LETMEGO LETMEGO LETMEGO LETMEGO LETMEGO
LETMEGO LETMEGO LETMEGO LETMEGO LETMEGO

LOVER

Starbuck peered at the screen through his half glasses. "What do you make of it?"

"It wants to be let loose to find something and then kill it. BEMs are like tigers. They've got this killing instinct."

"Does it repeat itself indefinitely?"

"No. It stops there at *LOVER* for an hour at a time and then starts up again. I went back and looked at the code and there's nothing there that would cause this. This is a load that went up without documentation."

Starbuck frowned. "Documentation's not worth a shit on most of this stuff. SDI was pushing us so hard, I had to let everybody get on with it, figuring we'd go back and do the paperwork later. God only knows what's missing. The guy who did this last piece of code managed to kill himself in a hang glider. He was a crazy sonuvabitch. You got any idea what's going on during that hour of *LOVER*?"

"Yeah." The lead wore jeans and a T-shirt, the standard uniform of the Silicon Valley warrior. He keyed in a command, bringing up a string of code. "Take a look. I had a hunch and dropped down in the comm mode and found this."

Starbuck studied the symbols. "It's interrogating us," he said, softly whistling. "What does it want?"

"It wants to know if we're still alive. Remember, these things are built to fight during a nuclear war. If it's on manual, and the Air Force base controlling it gets blasted, it wants to know that."

Starbuck whistled again. "It can take itself off manual override?"

"I think so. If we lost power I think one of these things might just cook itself off."

"Break contact and attack on its own?"

"Yep. I think your crazy man embedded a doomsday command. If we're not responding, the BEMs are going to assume we're nuked and take off to destroy anything they find."

Starbuck pondered the information. "We'd better fix it if we can. Can you figure it out, maybe backtrack into the code? If it's interrogating us and we're responding, there has to be a hook and a scar in that code."

BEM Lead nodded but looked dubious. "I've tried but so far no go. If there's a scar, it's embedded." He brightened. "I did figure something out while I was digging into the documentation. There's a microchip in the nav hardware that's capable of making tones. You want to make the BEMs talk?"

Starbuck's eyebrows lifted. "In what way?"

"I can give you a voice-emulating transducer, no sweat."

Starbuck grinned. "Hell, yes! How about comm otherwise?"

"Give me a freq and you got it."

Starbuck went back to his Exalted Leader pedestal. This was going to be even more fun than he'd thought. It appeared that he would be able to talk to his target before destroying it.

Starbuck eagerly rubbed his hands and looked down at the backs of his engineers, the lines of code streaming across their consoles as they joyfully hacked. On the port virtual panel screen the BEM XJ-249 was shown. Its two bright aluminized visual acquisition ports seemed to be inspecting Starbuck, contemplating him. He checked the BEM screen-load. It said:

LOVER

Starbuck shuddered involuntarily. The BEM was interrogating him, hoping he was dead. He looked up and the antennas on XJ-249 were twitching. It seemed to Starbuck that it was an angry gesture.

5

Low Lunar Orbit

But if in vain, down on the stubborn floor
Of Earth, and up to Heav'n's Unopening Door,
You gaze To-day, while You are You—how then
To-morrow, when You shall be You no more?

—*Edward Fitzgerald*, The Rubáiyát of Omar Khayyám

Arrival
Columbia

The moon was huge, completely filling *Columbia*'s cockpit windscreen. Awestruck, Jack observed its approach. It seemed to be bulging toward him, so close he felt as if he could reach out and touch its plasterlike surface. Penny joined him to gape at the formidable sphere. "We *are* going to miss it, aren't we?"

He turned from the moon to look into her eyes. They were as wide and deep as space itself. He liked that, liked everything about the way she looked, one toe hooked in a footloop, relaxed, that fabulous body floating in zero g, her breasts restrained only by the spandex top she favored. Zero g did wonders for any woman's figure but for High Eagle . . . Jack fought against the stirrings of lust. He reminded himself of Penny's argumentative nature, her arrogance, her . . . but, God, she did look fine, didn't she?

"Medaris? Are you listening to me?"

He snapped out of his musings. "Will we miss the moon? Yes, High Eagle, we will. Unless the laws of physics take a holiday."

Penny was quiet for a moment. "Tell me about her, Jack. Kate."

Jack was ambushed by her question and it made him feel ashamed of the desire he'd just felt. Kate was so near now. How could he have feelings for someone else? He lurched around for an appropriate response. "I can tell you this much," he said, finally. "Kate would have *loved* this."

"Is it true she designed the Big Dog engine?" Penny probed.

"She did the preliminary work," Jack acknowledged. "Everything MEC has done was based on her work."

"That must make you proud, that you were able to complete what she started."

Jack nodded and pulled away from Penny, using the handrails to go back to the cockpit. She followed him, settling into the seat beside him. "Does it make you uncomfortable to talk about her?"

"To you, yes," Jack said honestly.

She blinked her big browns. They were filled with innocence. "Why?"

Jack ignored her, opened up a monitor, began to tap in instructions. "Got to get Big Dog configured to circularize our orbit."

"You don't want to talk about her."

Jack closed his eyes, took a deep breath. "Yes, High Eagle. You're right. I don't want to talk about her."

"What is it, Jack? Is she the reason you're here?"

"Not now, High Eagle." Sweat had broken out on Jack's forehead.

"What could possibly be on the moon that has anything to do with Kate?"

"I said not now!" He kept working. "Later, maybe," he relented when she kept staring at him. "But not now."

"Later, never, you mean," Penny huffed.

Jack kept working. *Columbia* was coming in over the lunar surface at an altitude of fifty miles. Gravity would swing her around the far side, but to stay in lunar orbit Big Dog would have to be fired to slow *Columbia* down.

"Am I right, Medaris?" Penny demanded. "Never rather than later?"

Jack gritted his teeth. "Yes, you're right. Happy now? Strap yourself in, High Eagle. This will be a big kick in the pants."

Virgil came up from the middeck at Jack's call, strapped himself into the seat behind the cockpit. Paco was already stowed in his carrier. Penny stayed where she was, strapped in beside Jack, looking him over as if at any moment he was going to suddenly break down and confess why he was really at the moon. Jack kept his head down, immersed in his work. At the appropriate moment he gave the GSC computer the go-ahead and *Columbia* rotated around, tail-first to its direction, and Big Dog made its guttural roar for three-plus minutes, pressing them back into their seats.

Jack called up the data on the GSC to check the orbit. "All balls," he announced, meaning only zeros had come up in the computer's discrepancy analyses. "We won't need an OMS burn. Only a little tweak to the RCS to bring *Columbia* into a nose-first, cargo-bay-down attitude."

Columbia soared from behind the moon and began her first lunar orbit. Jack pointed at the earth as the great globe edged over the horizon. "This was always a happy time for the *Apollo* boys," he said. "They'd call Houston and tell them to celebrate, they were in lunar orbit."

"Shall we do the same on the SAREX?" Penny asked him.

"Why not?"

High Eagle pushed out of her seat and went down to the middeck. Jack followed her.

LUNAR ORBIT ACHIEVED.

The SAREX whirred. Almost instantly a message came back.

BEST NEWS EVER. BE CAREFUL. WE LOVE YOU.

Penny poised her hands over the keyboard.

WE LOVE YOU TOO AND ALL THOSE WHO ARE THERE.

The SAREX whirred, transmitted, and received.

SAY HELLO TO THE MAN IN THE MOON.

Battle in Space (1)
Farside Control

When Starbuck gave the command, the Farside commsat locked on *Columbia* and relayed her position to the designated BEM. The BEM instantly fired its engine and soared toward an intersection with the target. A virtual panel at Farside Control tracked the converging orbits. "Whoa, put on the brakes!" Starbuck ordered.

BEM Lead moved his mouse, and dragged the acceleration parameter toward zero. On the panel the BEM bullet slowed. "Rendezvous in six minutes," Lead called, his voice tight.

"Copy," Starbuck replied calmly, working hard to maintain an attitude of nonchalance. He knew pressure should never be applied by the director of a control room. He'd learned that the hard way from SDI generals who'd screwed up a couple of the tests at Kwajalein Island, getting everybody uptight by bellowing orders.

On the virtual panel Starbuck watched the BEM come in behind *Columbia* and hover over her tail. Its data stream showed XJ-249 begging for permission to attack. Starbuck sent back a negative code and then put the BEM under manual joystick guidance control. He'd take it from there.

Columbia

Jack tenderly watched Virgil dozing in the pilot's seat, as if he were looking at a child. The big guy deserved the rest, he thought. He wasn't liable to get much over the next day or two. Jack was checking the software code on the lander when he heard a scraping sound. He turned around just as Virgil jumped out of his seat, cracking his head against the rows of deactivated switches on the ceiling console. Jack pulled up beside Virgil and found himself looking into the silvery eyes of a monster. Virgil was trying to form words but all that came out were little gasps. When his voice finally came, it was a bellow: *"My God, what is that?"*

Jack knew exactly what it was. "I'll be damned," he said, marveling at the thing bumping and scratching at the cockpit windscreen.

Penny arrived. She screamed when she saw the thing and clutched Jack's arm. He pried her loose. She had squeezed him so hard, it still hurt after she let go. "SDI," he told her. "Strategic Defense Initiative. Star Wars stuff, High Eagle. This device is called a BEM, a bug-eyed monster. It's a killer satellite."

"You think it followed us here, Jack?" Virgil asked, obviously still shaken.

"Most likely been here the whole time, Virg. What a great place to go about your business undetected!"

Jack leaned forward, inspecting the "bug." It backed off and then steadied itself with little puffs of gas. It was apparently inspecting him as well. He waved in what he hoped would be interpreted as a friendly gesture and then waited to see what it did next.

Farside Control

Carl Puckett was in a side room watching the activities on two monitors. One monitor observed the control room. On the other, in crystal-clear color, was a view as seen by the BEM. A man in *Columbia*'s cockpit was waving. Puckett put on a headset. "Are you just going to look at them, Starbuck? Ram them!"

Starbuck came back, his voice nonchalant. "The BEM contains no warhead, Carl. I'm not sure of the results of a bows-on strike. The life-support system pallet would be the best target or maybe the OMS. But I want to talk turkey with them first."

"Listen, you nerd," Puckett brayed. "I'm paying about a million dollars an hour for this rig. Ram them, I said, and get it over with!"

Starbuck didn't respond. Puckett stood up and tried the door. It was locked.

Starbuck switched Puckett's comm off. "BEM Lead, can you give me the voice transducer?"

"Ready, Exalted Leader."

"Go for contact. You have the con. Easy now."

BEM Lead eased the joystick forward. Starbuck watched the data, the BEM fussing a bit, asking for permission to ram. The transducer would allow voice communications through vibrations. It was crude but if the crew aboard *Columbia* put their ear to the windscreen, they might be able to understand him. This was going to be fun! He was going to talk to the hijackers!

Columbia

Jack put his hand on the windscreen. He could feel the vibration as a staccato of gas from the bug's control nozzles hit *Columbia*. Then the eye cover of the BEM touched the glass. He put his ear closer. "High Eagle, get me a stethoscope out of the medical pack."

"On my way," Penny said compliantly. She headed below, was back within a minute with the instrument.

Jack used the stethoscope on the windscreen. "Greetings, earth people," he said, interpreting the tinny voice coming through the stethoscope. "Go to UHF two five nine point seven for voice." He took off the instrument and handed it to Penny. "I think we'd better do as it says." He settled into the commander's seat, called up *Columbia*'s central processor and activated the UHF power amplifier circuit, selected the 259.7-MHz UHF simplex, and then activated the audio distribution system. He put on a headset. "This is *Columbia*," he said. "Are you receiving me, Mr. SDI bug-eyed monster?"

"You know what I am?" The voice sounded surprised.

"I've studied SDI a little," Jack allowed, and then probed, trying to engage in conversation with whoever was electronically connected with the little killer bug. Any information he could get would be helpful to figure out its intentions. "Isn't it illegal for you to be in lunar orbit?" he asked. "The Outer Space Treaty prohibits any weapon of a strategic nature to be in the vicinity of the moon."

"Maybe you shouldn't aggravate the little sucker, sir," Virgil worried.

Jack peered at the BEM, watched its twitching antennae. "Looks pretty pissed already to me, Virg."

Farside Control

Starbuck let XJ-249 flit in, coming, he calculated, within two milli-micro-nano seconds of attacking before its software hauled it back from the brink. Starbuck thought it amusing the spacejackers had no idea how near they were to destruction. "All right, you pukes," he rasped. "You're mine anytime I want you."

Columbia

The BEM disappeared from Jack's view. "Hey, Mr. BEM, where'd you go? We're friendly, just out here on a peaceful commercial enterprise."

"Why don't you tell him you have a contract?" Penny said acidly, apparently recovered from her initial fright.

The BEM scuttled down *Columbia*'s cargo bay, viewing the tethered satellite system, the shuttle arm, the "sausages," and the Little Dog engine tied down with heavy rubber straps just behind the long-duration power pallet. "I see it, Jack!" Virgil called from the aft flight deck view ports. "It looks like a bloodhound sniffing all around."

The BEM needed to go away, however interesting it was to Jack from an engineering point of view. He had an inspiration on how to take care of it. "BEM, we're in trouble," he said. "Can you help us?"

"What are you doing, Medaris?" Penny demanded.

"I have a plan."

"Medaris . . ."

"What's your problem?" the man speaking through the BEM responded.

"Don't get cute," Penny advised. "Talk to them first."

"Look, I can take care of this!"

Penny shook her finger at him. "Medaris, this is a killer weapon! That's what *you* said. Stop playing games with it!"

"I said it was a killer," Jack said. "I didn't say it was smart. Watch and learn, High Eagle." He keyed the transmitter. "Mr. BEM, could you go aft and check our propulsion? We may be stranded. Data indicates that we might have cracked an engine nozzle on our last firing. I can't tell which one. If I knew, I could safe it or go out and remove it. Would you look for us?"

Jack turned to High Eagle, to see her reaction. She stared at him, slowly shaking her head. Then she looked up at the ceiling as if to pray. "Oh, ye of little faith," Jack said.

The voice from the ground came back. "Look at your engine?" it said. "Why not?"

Jack worked the Big Dog laptop, flashing through the pages, enabling as he went.

Dismayed, Penny watched him. "You're enjoying this, aren't you?"

"It's dropped down behind us, Jack," Virgil called.

"What do you see, BEM?" Jack asked innocently.

"No sign of damage, *Columbia*," the voice said. "What kind of engine is this, anyway? Where are the shuttle mains?"

Jack grinned. "It's a special kind of engine, BEM. By the way, do you have a name?"

"Starbuck," Starbuck said.

"I'm Jack Medaris. Listen, Starbuck, give it a good once-over, won't you? Can you see the nozzles clearly?"

"We're using the zoom lens."

"Could you come in just a little closer?" Jack asked. "Take a good look?"

Penny plugged into a comm jack. "Mr. Starbuck, this is Penny High Eagle. We're on a peaceful mission here. I assure you that's all it is."

Farside Control

Starbuck frowned. Puckett had told him the spacejackers had murdered the Indian princess.

"Want me to go in, Exalted Leader?" BEM Lead asked.

"Just check the nozzles for us, please," he heard "Jack" call down. Starbuck nodded. BEM Lead eased the joystick forward. The BEM fussed, darted, and then slowed, grumbling.

```
LETMEGO  LETMEGO  LETMEGO  LETMEGO  LETMEGO
LETMEGO  LETMEGO  LETMEGO  LETMEGO  LETMEGO
LETMEGO  LETMEGO  LETMEGO  LETMEGO  LETMEGO
LETMEGO  LETMEGO  LETMEGO  LETMEGO  LETMEGO
LETMEGO  LETMEGO  LETMEGO  LETMEGO  LETMEGO
LETMEGO  LETMEGO  LETMEGO  LETMEGO  LETMEGO
LETMEGO  LETMEGO  LETMEGO  LETMEGO  LETMEGO
LETMEGO  LETMEGO  LETMEGO  LETMEGO  LETMEGO
LETMEGO  LETMEGO  LETMEGO  LETMEGO  LETMEGO
```

Starbuck studied the screen. "We've got our nose in your crack, *Columbia*, and all looks A-OK. Now, listen up, here's what I want you to do. . . ."

Columbia

Jack stabbed Big Dog's execution button. "Go, baby!"

Big Dog awoke, pulsing for a half second. In the mid-deck Paco was jarred awake and found himself catapulted into midair. His banshee moan came from below.

Farside Control

Starbuck whipped off his headset and stood. Where a second before there had been a view of the inside of one of the exhaust nozzles, there was now nothing but snow on the panel. For a microsecond he thought there had been a flash of yellow-white light. . . .

He sat down. "We've been had," he said grimly. He studied the blank screen. He wasn't angry. He was impressed. "This guy is good, very, very good," he mused, rubbing his jaw. "How long to bring in another BEM?"

"We can catch them in one hour, thirty-two minutes, six seconds, O Exalted Leader."

"Make it so," Starbuck said resolutely. He switched on Puckett's comm, listened to his ranting for a moment, and then replied, "No, Mr. Puckett. We didn't get them. But we will. This battle's just started."

Battle in Space (2)

Columbia

Virgil was happy to put on an EMU suit and get away from the bickering couple inside *Columbia.* "They ought to be married," he grumbled to himself. "They sure fight enough to qualify."

Virgil's EVA was to prepare the landing craft (LC or "Elsie" as the MEC engineers had dubbed it). Jack stopped arguing with Penny long enough to maneuver the shuttle arm and its Little Dog payload until it was positioned over a circular aluminum base plate with a thick sheath of cabling and interface plugs. Working quickly and following the color coding, Virgil attached them to the matching plate on Little Dog and tested them, then pushed the plates together, carefully stuffing the cables into precut recesses. Spring tabs tightly clamped the two plates together.

The next step was to inflate the dome. Two compressed air tanks, each about the size of a standard eighty-cubic-foot scuba tank, were sufficient for that. Virgil attached one to an exterior pressure port and the white dome began to fill until it was about twelve feet in diameter, its exterior dotted with flaps, black lettering underneath indicating their function. S-band and VHF antennas were attached to the exterior at the indicated ports.

An airlock protruded from the base of Elsie. Virgil unzipped its inner and outer flap, and entered with an armful of plastic tubing to form an interior geodesic-shaped lattice. A simple rendezvous radar, a console with a radar altimeter and communications rig, and a set of locked-down nickel-hydrogen batteries went in next, followed by packages of food and water, three big bottles of emergency oxygen, and a set of battery spares. A small emergency solar panel was also Velcroed to the interior in case all the batteries failed.

The next setup included an optical rendezvous sight, a joystick rig for attitude control, and an air-conditioning unit that was not much more than a fan to stir the air around. The last thing in was a console for controlling the throttle on Little Dog. View ports were located below, in front, and above the console to give the pilot a view of the lunar surface.

Virgil finished by attaching attitude control jets to interfaces on the dome. He was just starting to come in, pleased with his work and the condition of Elsie, when two BEMs came rushing over *Columbia*'s tail like maddened hornets. Virgil saw them and was afraid.

Farside Control

"Give me a wide turn on two-four-six!" Starbuck ordered. From his Exalted Leader pedestal he peered at the split-screen panel, which gave him a view from the noses of the two BEMs, XJ-246 and XJ-247. The port panel showed a representation of *Columbia* and the two attacking devices.

The BEMs were looking at *Columbia*'s cargo bay. Starbuck could see a big dome hanging off the port sill. *What the hell was that?* There was also someone in a spacesuit frantically going hand over hand along a wire tether that ran the length of the bay.

"Want me to let two-four-six go?" BEM Leader called. "It's locked on the power pallet."

"Negative, drop down in front of the suited subject. Keep him away from the airlock."

"Roger that!"

BEM Lead pushed the joystick ahead and then down, BEM XJ-246 grumbling in its software all the way. It had a positive lock on something. It was supposed to kill that, not go dawdling off.

Starbuck sent XJ-247 flying out for a long-range view. He called up the UHF frequency. "*Columbia*, any last words?"

Columbia

Jack heard Virgil yelling. The BEM was right in front of him, looking itchy.

Jack pulled on his EMU suit. "Hang on, Virgil, I'm on my way!"

"Medaris, you haven't prebreathed!" Penny protested at the airlock porthole.

"No time!" Jack mouthed as he climbed into the hard upper torso.

Penny snatched a headset. "Bug-eyed monster, this is Dr. High Eagle. We're on a peaceful mission!"

"Tell me another one, Pocahontas," Starbuck's voice crackled.

Jack came out of the airlock behind the new BEM. Apparently it didn't sense him, since it kept its eyes on Virgil. "Get some cover, Virgil," he ordered. He ripped away the insulating material from the forward bulkhead and rammed his left arm underneath to give him some stability. He raised Virgil's .45 pistol, took aim, and fired. The BEM jerked spasmodically from the impact of the big slug. Then, another of the bullets apparently hit its cold nitrogen propellant tank. With a gush of high pressure gas the BEM started spinning like a maddened pinwheel.

Farside Control

"Dammit!" Starbuck saw XJ-246's crazy dance. He decided to send XJ-247 plowing into the dome thing. If there was a nuke on board, that was probably it. He rotated the stick but overmaneuvered, the BEM sweeping past the dome to the vertical stabilizer. He adjusted, the dome coming back into view.

"I can release it!" BEM Lead called, meaning the software hold on XJ-247.

"Negative! He's all mine!" Starbuck jammed the joystick forward, the dome right in his crosshairs.

Columbia

Jack saw the other BEM turn toward Elsie. He raised the pistol and fired.

Farside Control

"Damn!" BEM Lead yelled. "Two-four-seven just dropped off-line!"

"No!" Starbuck screamed, disbelieving. "I had the nuke!"

Columbia

"Holy mother of—" Virgil clutched his tether. A BEM had slammed into the cargo bay sill and catapulted out into space. He looked up and saw the other BEM suddenly change direction, narrowly missing Elsie and speeding down the cargo bay past Jack. Jack kept pumping lead until it zipped out of sight.

Space

BEM XJ-247 stood off *Columbia* as if trying to catch its breath. It had not been hit. It had broken off the attack because of a power loss in a microcircuit, weakened over months of alternately freezing and frying in space. Sensing the spike, its software pointer had directed it to get away from all harm and then reboot. The reboot took thirty seconds. When it was finally ready, it was no longer under manual control, a glitch in its software dropping it into automatic mode. It began to scan its surroundings. When a movement caught its visual sensor, it went after it.

Columbia

Jack braced himself, the BEM coming at him as if it were sliding down a guy wire attached to his chest. One of his rounds hit one of its silvery eyes, another caroming off its snout. The BEM suddenly turned away, shot straight up, and then stopped. Jack had no way of knowing it, but its heat sensor had latched on to the power pallet. The BEM started a kamikaze run. When it struck, a silent geyser of fluid and debris erupted. Jack saw Elsie shake from hits. Behind him, on board *Columbia*, the lights flickered, then died.

Jack went after Virgil. He looked into his helmet. The big man was shaken, his eyes popping. Sweat bubbled off his forehead, clouding his faceplate. Jack could only hope his cooling system could keep up. "Take it easy, Virg," he said. "We're all right now."

"Sir, we got to give in. They're going to kill us!"

"I told you we're okay. We beat them this time and if they try again, we'll beat them again. Now get hold of yourself."

Virgil blinked, nodded, and Jack released him and headed aft, working his way past the tethered satellite payload and Elsie. He inspected the power pallet. A fuel cell had been cracked wide open by the BEM. There was nothing he could do about that, so he pulled himself back to the dome. To his relief, it didn't look as if there had been any penetration, just three small tears in the fabric. They wouldn't need to inflate the spare dome just yet. He inspected Little Dog, and found only a nick on the aluminum collar that circled the baseplate.

He thought again of Virgil, looked down the cargo bay, but couldn't see him. "High Eagle, is Virgil in yet?"

There was no reply. He worked his way forward, noting that the aft flight deck view ports were dark. Power was off. As he came down off the ATESS, he saw the lights come back on. "High Eagle, you there?"

"Here, Jack." He felt a twinge of surprise. It was the first time she had ever called him by his first name. "I turned off all the heaters on the pallet and then turned the cells off too."

Jack marveled at how quickly she'd learned. He had only spent a few minutes with her on the pallet controls. "Well done. Is Virgil in?"

"He's in the airlock. I brought up fuel cell number two to take up the slack and that seems to be enough. I had a main bus undervolt light but it's out now. Almost every circuit breaker got tripped. I reset them, one at a time just like you showed me."

Jack was astonished at how much she had absorbed during his lessons. "You did good, Penny." He had returned her favor, using her first name too. He turned around and saw that the mist from the pallet was diminishing. "Looks like the cell that got hit is running out of fuel. Any cautions on the pressure control system?"

"Negative. Air pressure is good, oxygen and nitrogen partial pressures on the money." She paused. "Jack, you were right to try to destroy them. What did they do to us?"

"We were in fat city with three weeks of power, air, and water consumables. That just got cut at least in half. We should still have plenty if we can get back to earth in five days. No sweat, that's well within the timeline."

Jack paused at the door, making certain no more BEMs were in sight, and then entered the airlock and closed the hatch behind him. He hit the pressurization switch and slowly the airlock filled with air, air that now needed watching very closely. One more damn thing he had to do. . . .

Farside Control

Starbuck pored over the logic tree. "Damn, it's a mess," he groaned.

BEM Lead stabbed a routine on the screen. "Your boy really loaded his program up with glitches before he got himself killed."

"He was in a hurry," Starbuck said defensively. "We were all in a hurry. For a test vehicle it's not doing too bad, but for a war machine it ain't ready."

He sighed, turned on Puckett's audio. Puckett came on immediately. "Did you get it, Starbuck? Tell me you did."

"Maybe," Starbuck answered indifferently. He leaned over, patted BEM Lead on his shoulder. "Bring in our last two monsters."

"What do you mean by maybe?" Puckett asked.

Starbuck sighed. "We hit it, yeah."

"Well?"

Starbuck had not liked Puckett from the moment he had met him and that distaste had been cranked up several notches since. Still, he was paying the bills. "I don't know, Carl," he said politely. "The BEMs don't have warheads. I think we struck the power pallet in the aft cargo bay. That could have caused anything, including a rather large explosion. But I just don't know."

"You only hit it with one BEM?" Puckett snarled.

Starbuck smiled grimly. "You won't believe this, Carl, but one of your terrorists climbed out into the bay and started blasting at us with a pistol." He shook his head. "Those boys got grit, I'll tell you that. Dr. High Eagle asked us not to attack, by the way."

"I told you Dr. High Eagle is dead," Puckett said.

"It sure sounded like her. I called a disc jock friend of mine at the local rock station and asked him to play a recording of her during a news conference. It was a damn right-on impersonation, I can tell you that."

"Well, don't worry about it," Puckett grumbled. "If she's not dead, she's joined them. In any case, just get it done. And, by the way, what the hell's the idea of lock—"

Starbuck grinned at his troops. He had pulled the audio plug on Puckett again. "I love doing that," he said.

Columbia

"Jack, they've got us!" Virgil yelled, panic-stricken, grabbing him as soon as Jack climbed out of the airlock. "We've got to get the hell out of here!"

Jack pushed him away. "Remain calm, Virg. They don't have us by a long shot." Jack looked at Penny with admiration. "You did great."

Virgil turned to her. "Penny, don't listen to him. He's crazy, don't you see that?"

"Virgil, it's going to be okay," she soothed.

"You're as crazy as he is!" Virgil cried. He clambered through the deck hatch. "We're going home—right now!"

Jack soared after him, catching him as he reached the Big Dog laptop. Virgil tore loose, sending Jack flying. Penny came up from behind and plunged a morphine sulfate syringe into Virgil's hip. Virgil looked at Penny and then at Jack. "Damn, that hurt!" The morphine had not had time to work but the pain of the needle seemed to have brought him back to rationality. "Hey, guys. I'm sorry. I didn't mean to go crazy like that."

"I'm sorry, too, Virgil," Penny said, patting his face.

Virgil's eyes fluttered. "Jack, I'm okay now. I'm just so tired. . . ." His eyes closed and he drifted, his arms dangling loosely in front of him.

Jack cautiously raised one of Virgil's eyelids. "How long will he be out?"

"Eight, ten hours," Penny guessed.

"Eight hours! Dammit! I'll need him before that!"

"Well, I'm here. What do you want me to do?"

Jack shook his head. "You don't understand, High Eagle, I need somebody with some mechanical ability."

Penny squinted. "Medaris, for your information, I changed out the transmission on my BMW."

"Another talent emerges," Jack said, sarcastically, "High Eagle the master mechanic!"

"That's right, Medaris!" Penny shot back. "I thought maybe you noticed I know my way around this shuttle pretty well. And did I mention that I've drifted across the Andes in a balloon? And been to the South Pole? Did you think I was just the token female on those expeditions? I ran them, Medaris, fixed things when things got busted."

Jack raised his hand. Another plan was forming and he needed to get on with it. "Fine, High Eagle. You win. But would you mind collecting up all the used lithium hydroxide canisters?"

"What do you want them for?"

"High Eagle. Please. Just do it, okay?"

"Why? And tell me what's down on the moon you have to go after?"

"It's none of your business, High Eagle."

"You're a geek and a goon, Medaris."
They were solidly back to last names.

Battle in Space (3)
Farside Control

Farside Control was quiet except for a continuous buzz of conversation from the HOE console. Still wrestling with the defective bus, looking for a way to bring up the propulsion unit, the HOE team worked with the software code, trying this and then that. Starbuck watched them benevolently. Soon, he thought, it wouldn't matter. *Columbia*, if not already dead, was shortly going to be history, an artifact circling the moon, an advertisement for SDI for a very long time.

His eyes narrowed as he watched the port virtual panel describe the orbital progression of BEMs XJ-250 and XJ-251. He had ordered BEM Lead to rocket them out to an orbit a mile above the moon, where they could gain an assist from the moon's gravity to whip them in behind *Columbia*. The BEMs were to stop only long enough to take one quick look and then plow into the aft portion of the payload bay, to take out what remained of the power pallet, probably destroy the nukes, and maybe even crack open the OMS. That would be the end of *Columbia*.

BEM Lead switched in the video feed and a view of the distant point of light that was the shuttle came up on both halves of the screen. The BEMs were flying in formation, not more than fifty feet apart. The white point gave way to a fuzzy smear. BEM Lead tried to adjust the focus but that wasn't the problem. They were approaching a debris field. "Starbuck?"

"I see it. Slow down."

"Roger."

"All stop," Starbuck commanded, and the two BEMs fired their retros and coasted with just intermittent puffs of cold nitrogen until they reached the same velocity as the debris field. From that perspective it appeared they'd stopped, even though the moon kept turning below. It was all relative.

Starbuck watched the BEMs, on automatic, nervously turn this way and then that. The field was apparently confusing them, both by the nature of its spread and also because there were hundreds of relative velocities within it. A quick check of the data stream showed that their sensors were sensing neither heat nor vapor, only minute unidentified velocities that changed by the microsecond. The BEMs couldn't focus properly. Starbuck pressed his fingers to his temple, rubbing, trying to imagine what exactly his little monsters had encountered.

Columbia

Penny used binoculars to help her see the BEMs. They had stopped, seemed to be sniffing around the debris field.

"They've taken the bait," Medaris said beside her. In the lull between battles he had suited up and gone into the cargo bay and torn apart a dozen used lithium hydroxide air scrubbers and pushed them ahead of *Columbia*. He had sent along flares and a "space mine." As he'd explained it to Penny, "First we're going to bait 'em, then we're going to kill 'em."

She had to admire his initiative, especially the construction of the mine. She had held a portable lamp for him while he removed the cover of the T-handle box located forward of the side hatch. Inside were actually two T-handles, one to jettison the side hatch, the other, called a pyro vent valve, to blow a hole into the cargo bay that would depressurize the cabin in case of a shuttle abort during launch or reentry. Jack disassembled the vent valve explosives, recovering a length of what looked like plastic-covered clothesline—primer cord. Jack's "mine" consisted of the primer cord, a flare from the emergency landing kit, and two electrical squibs taken from the pyro vent valve. He added to that an electrical remote circuit made from one of the radio headsets and two nine-volt batteries to boost the spark. For shrapnel he used an aluminum sample container from the acoustic levitating furnace experiment in the middeck. Inside it he packed in pins and badges from the souvenir kits. Even if the mine did no damage, Jack told her, it would at least create another debris field. Then he taped the flare to the outside of the ALF container and on top of it another wrap of duct tape attaching an aluminized space blanket. It was decoy and destroyer all wrapped up in one, Jack said.

"If it works," Penny had replied nervously.

"Oh, it'll work," Jack assured her, preparing to touch a bare wire to the battery. "As soon as they're close enough . . . here they come. Watch this!"

Penny watched as Jack touched the wire to the battery. Then she saw a distant flash of light. One of the BEMs was close enough that apparently it caught a snoutful of STS-98 souvenir pins. It started tumbling. She saw its thrusters fire but the tumble continued.

"I think we hit its nav platform." Jack laughed. "Gimbals are probably in permanent lock. Look at it. It's wandering off, shaking its head. One BEM down, one to go."

Farside Control

Starbuck got a readout. XJ-250 was screaming for help but there was nothing that could be done. It was out of control. XJ-251 reported that it was still healthy, having escaped damage from whatever had caused the blast of light and heat nearby. Starbuck switched to manual mode, to see if he could snake it through the debris. He'd turned Puckett back on too. "You got only one chance now, Starbuck. Ram that son of a bitch!"

That's what Starbuck meant to do, except he was distracted by the tall boom protruding out of *Columbia*'s cargo bay and the white mass attached to the tether coming out of it. He joysticked it past the mass, swooping in close. *Might as well have a video record of everything,* Starbuck reasoned. Then the view changed. No matter what direction he pointed the joystick, his BEM rotated. It was caught on something. A silky something draped over the eyes of the BEM. Starbuck moved the BEM, the white cloth sliding off the eyes. He recognized the material, figured out the trap. The BEM was tangled in a parachute.

Columbia

Jack gave Penny an admiring glance. It had been her idea to attach a parachute shroud to the ATESS boom as a decoy. She thought it might fool the BEM, make it want to attack the ATESS and not the Elsie. It was just plain luck that it had instead managed to snag the BEM as it passed. "Come into my parlor, said the spider to the fly," High Eagle said with a laugh.

Farside Control

Starbuck kept trying but the last BEM seemed to be stuck. Medaris called down. "Starbuck, how do you read?"

Starbuck answered, his voice glum. "Lima Charlie. Loud and clear. What now, Medaris? Time for your terrorist demands?"

"We're not terrorists." It was the woman who claimed to be High Eagle.

"We have a contract," Medaris added. "Hasn't there been anything in the papers about it?"

"The papers have been full of you hijacking the shuttle," Starbuck said. "Your lawyer got on television and told us about you going to the moon. Some people think you're a bunch of heroes. I know better."

"Damn you, Starbuck," Puckett said. "Stop talking to those bastards. Get another one of your sci-fi weapons going, and blast them!"

Starbuck looked at the HOE console. The HOE controllers looked back and shrugged. Still no joy. And Starbuck's last BEM was ensnared. He pondered the situation. There was always something that could be done. He just needed to think it through.

Columbia

Jack studied the BEM through his binoculars. "Reel it in slowly, High Eagle," he said. "Its movement is causing *Columbia* to wobble. It needs stabilizing against the boom."

"Roger that," she replied crisply. As the tether came in, the BEM slowly rotated. When it was pulled against the boom, its video eyes were looking forward in the bay. She brought the boom down until the BEM was looking directly at them.

Farside Control

Starbuck watched the screen on the wall, saw where the BEM was looking. He peered into the view ports and saw the faces of the people he had been attacking. He assumed the man was Jack Medaris but the other person was definitely Dr. Penny High Eagle. "You join the terrorists, Doc?" he asked.

"Blow them up, Starbuck," Puckett demanded.

"We're here on a peaceful mission," High Eagle said.

"And we have a contract," Medaris added.

"Hey, cut the crap," Starbuck said. "I've been in the aerospace industry all my life. I know static when I hear it. Now, what the hell's going on? First of all, do you have a nuke on board?"

"He'll lie to you," Puckett said.

"Of course not," Medaris said. "How could we have carried nuclear weapons on board? You say you've been in the industry. Then you know nukes are a little too heavy to just backpack in."

"Maybe they were already on board," Starbuck answered.

"Why would we come all the way to the moon to launch nuclear weapons at earth?" Medaris asked. "That would give you three days to figure out how to stop them. We could have launched them from low earth orbit a lot easier."

Starbuck rocked on his pedestal. Scenarios rolled through his head, stopped, started up again. Puckett kept mumbling. "Just blow them up, just blow them up."

Starbuck leaned forward. "The word we got was that you were a bunch of loonies who were going to blow up the *Apollo* sites and then take out some earth targets. Or maybe you wanted to be a long way away from defenses before you started making your demands."

"What demands?" Medaris questioned, his voice rising. "Have you heard any demands? Until you started attacking us, we had turned off all comm. It doesn't make sense!"

"All right," Starbuck said. "What *does* make sense? You guys took the shuttle, that's clear. Yeah, I read about your contract in the paper. That's just a smoke screen for all those ninny liberals who are scared of anything that looks like an official document that might stand up in court. Now, if you're not up to no good, what the hell are you doing at the moon?"

Jack told him the essential facts about the fusion reactor, helium-3, how the country needed it, if not now, then soon. Starbuck then heard that Puckett had battered down the door and had left the house. To Starbuck that pretty well confirmed he was hearing the truth.

"But why all the secrecy—stealing the shuttle and all that?" Starbuck asked.

"Think about it, Starbuck," Medaris said. "All the energy the world will ever need, cheap and clean. Now, who do you think might be against that?"

"Yeah." Starbuck whistled. "It don't take much imagination. Wait one." He signaled for someone to take his place. He handed the woman his headset and then went after

Puckett. As Starbuck came outside, Puckett's limo was taking off in a scatter of gravel.

Starbuck returned to his pedestal and keyed his headset. "Cut my BEM loose and I'll fly shotgun for you as long as my fuel reserves hold out. Sorry about the misunderstanding."

Columbia

Jack hugged Penny spontaneously. She hugged him back, giving him a surprise kiss on the lips. He held on to her, slowly, deliberately pulled her into an embrace. Their eyes locked and then they kissed again, this time slowly, passionately. She melted into him, clung to him as if without him, she would die. Their kisses were long, passionate, their hands seeking each other, unbuttoning, heedless to where their clothes floated. He marveled once more at her skin. It was like silk. He kissed her neck, worked his way down, lingered there for a moment, her beauty a feast for his eyes. Her breasts floated free, unbound by either clothing or gravity. He kissed them, savored them. It had been so long. . . . "I think I hear my heart ringing," he said breathlessly.

Penny clung to Jack but looked over his shoulder at the controls. "It's a caution and warning buzzer on fuel cell number two," she said, nuzzling his cheek. "A main bus undervolt."

Jack had no choice but to leave Penny to turn off the alarm and the fuel cell. He did it and then considered the situation. If fuel cell number two couldn't be restarted, *Columbia* would have only one fuel cell left. And if that one failed, they were all dead. Reluctantly, he pulled out the troubleshooting checklist, to search for a fix if there was one.

Then Paco came out, meowing like he was hungry. Penny went to check on his food delivery system. She gave Jack a sad smile and a pat on his shoulder as she passed. Their moment was over nearly as soon as it began.

Clear Lake

Clear Lake, a suburb of Houston, Texas

It was one of those Houston days the natives called "close," moisture clinging to the skin and the sun beating down so hard, it actually seemed to have weight. Geraldine Tate led Shirley Grafton into the backyard where Clear Lake lapped against the shore. Sweat streamed down Shirley's face. She was hot, but she was also nervous. She was taking a lot on herself, even with the vice president's approval. She considered turning around and running for home.

Tate eyed Shirley with amusement. "Honey, you look like you could use something cool. I got some lemonade in the fridge."

"No, thanks. Got to get moving." She wiped her forehead with a tissue. Soaked, it fell apart. Shirley stared at it. "I don't think there'd be any Houston if air-conditioning hadn't been invented," she marveled.

"Aw, we'd manage, one way or the other. Texans don't give up easy." She pointed to a distant dot on the lake. "That's Sam. If you want him, you'll have to go out and get him."

Shirley shaded her eyes with her hand. She could barely see the bobbing boat. "How do I do that?"

Tate pointed to a boat tied off on the neighboring dock. "Take that one. The Comptons are out of town. We're watching it for them. They won't mind. Here, take my gardening hat. Keep the sun out of your eyes."

Shirley, not much of a sailor, edged cautiously out onto the lake and then set off for the distant speck that she hoped was Sam Tate. As she neared, she cut her engine too early but at least she drifted to within hailing distance. "Sam? Sam Tate? Is that you?"

* * *

Sam didn't hear her. Lost in his thoughts, he hadn't even bothered to bait his hook. He was just sitting there, remembering the glory days, from *Thor* to *Saturn*. Shoved aside now, probably forever, he couldn't help but think of the tough old guys of *Apollo-Saturn*. He'd heard from some of them over the years, some still nursing the bitterness of working their youth away on a magnificent achievement that had been treated like a dead end by the country, shoved into the history books almost from the moment Neil Armstrong had placed his boot on the regolith of the moon.

Still, he thought, sighing, even though it was true that his newbies were more likely to celebrate a successful mission with sparkling water than cigars (which had been banned, in any case, from Mission Control in 1990), he had gotten to like those kids, like them in his way, that is, which meant snarling and growling at them most of the time while they grinned and ducked their heads over their consoles. But he wondered what the old guys would have done if a pissant like John Lakey had tried to kick them off their consoles. The thought made him smile, despite his doldrums. "God, I miss the old days," he moaned to himself.

"Sam?"

Sam looked up and was shocked to see a woman wearing what appeared to be his wife's straw gardening hat struggling with a bass boat that looked suspiciously like his neighbor's rig. She had gotten a paddle out and was trying to manhandle the boat closer. "Stay there," Sam said. "I think I'd better come to you."

Sam fired up the outboard, eased over, and tied off. He climbed into the bass boat. "Yes, ma'am, what can I do for you? Is that Geraldine's hat?"

The woman doffed the hat. "Geraldine was kind," she said, and then introduced herself. "Sam, I work for the vice president of the United States. He wants you to reopen Mission Control."

"Why?"

"Because there's an American spacecraft in orbit around the moon and very soon there's going to be a landing." She handed him a manila envelope. "I think they're going to need help from Houston. If you'll look at the letter in this envelope, you'll see that the vice president has authorized you to go back into business."

Sam looked at Shirley, saw that she was serious, and sat down, his long legs astraddle. He opened the envelope, read over the letter Shirley had prepared and the veep had signed. She had also provided a summary of everything she knew that Medaris was doing and why. After he'd finished, he slowly raised his long face, looked off into the distance, back toward Johnson Space Center. *"Gawdalmighty!"* he said. It sounded to Shirley like a cheer.

MET 8 DAYS AND COUNTING . . .

Penny's Confession
Columbia

In the cockpit, before the vast moonscape, Jack tried to relax by watching the craters and rilles scroll beneath him. Before long he didn't even notice them. He was thinking of Penny, how it had been so easy to take her into his arms, how good and right it felt. But it couldn't be right. Kate was so close now, after all these years and miles. He forced himself to think of Huntsville. He needed to remember the test stand on that cold night, how it was, what he was thinking, Kate. . . .

Inside the control room the panic had just begun. . . .

The engineer nervously tapped at his keyboard, and then touched the screen, pulling up a schematic of the countdown network. "TCDC's still counting. My override won't work."

Jack moved urgently to his master console. He initiated his own hold but the power to the pumps kept going. He looked at the numbers counting down. Shaking his head, he reluctantly went to his big gun, the icon marked TEAC. TEAC meant terminal deactivation. Clicking on TEAC was the same as jerking the power plug out of the wall. It was a hard shutdown of the TCDC and all the controller software. Not only would it shut everything down, but reconfiguring would take hours.

It went against his grain, but Jack had no choice. A gremlin was playing games with the TCDC software and would need ferreting out. All the dog engine software had been written quickly, a lot of it patched in from older programs. It had been tested in stages but never all at once. Jack cursed under his breath. He should have had an end-to-end software test run before he'd hooked up the hardware.

He bowed to the inevitable, moved the cursor over the TEAC icon, a clock face. Better fix it, no matter how much it hurt. He'd be talking to some software engineers this night, and not kindly either! The clock icon disappeared when he clicked on it. That wasn't right. Then it winked back on. In the upper right-hand corner of the screen the TCDC showed one minute, zero seconds until activation. It kept counting down. Frantically, Jack went active on his headset, lighting up every push. "Clear the test stand—now!" he ordered. "This is Jack. All personnel, clear the test stand now!"

"Jack," Paul Dalton, his assistant, said over his push, "what's wrong?"

"Kate doesn't have a headset," Jack said in sudden realization. "The TCDC jumped ahead, Paul, and I can't kill it. We've got less than a minute. Get everybody off the stand. *Now!*"

Other engineers were picking up on what he'd seen. Their fingers were punching up the test-stand loops, ordering everybody who could hear them to get away.

Jack threw down his headset and headed out the door, yelling at Paul to keep trying the TEAC. The test stand stood like a giant praying mantis above him as he came through the blast door. It rattled metallically as team members hurried down its steel steps. On the first level he stopped one of them. "Have you seen Kate?" The woman shook her head. Jack looked up into the shadowy maze of tubing and support beams and then saw a row of fire-retardant suits. He grabbed a jacket and gloves, pulling them on while he charged up the steps, two at a time.

He was almost knocked off his feet by a running technician. The man grabbed him. "Jack! We've been ordered off the stand!"

He shrugged him off. "Keep going! Go!" he yelled, and then flew up the steps, heading for level six, where the exhaust nozzle of the dog engine hung like a church bell, an impossibly complex maze of tubing and ducting running to it, preparing to nurture it into white-hot fury.

Then he saw Kate! She was at the bell, a clipboard in her gloved hands, scrutinizing the fine distribution pump. She was wearing sound-suppression earmuffs, to protect her ears from the high-pitched whine of the pumps. The engineer with her, also wearing the muffs, turned toward him, perhaps hearing the vibration of the steel platform as Jack raced toward them. He looked with openmouthed curiosity as Jack yelled and waved for them to get away. Jack heard the groan of the pumps coming up to speed, smelled the strangely sweet fumes of the oxidizer flushing through the pipes. He screamed another warning. Kate turned, saw him.

The engineer accompanying Kate was running. Jack passed him, reached for Kate when the nozzle bell suddenly became rigid with pressure, a shower of yellow sparks turning into a blue-white gush of fire. A gigantic shock-wave blew Kate toward him. For a moment he had hope she was going to escape. He reached for her as she opened her arms for him to embrace her.

And then, before his horrified eyes, a luminescent halo enveloped her, defining her shape, and then began to devour her. Her hand stretched out to him. An insane thought reached him: If he could just reach her, he could pull her out of the halo, protect her with his body.

Then he had her! Tendrils of fire ran over his gloves, up the arms of his coat, to his unprotected neck and face. He felt his flesh burning, the skin on his neck crackling like bacon. He ignored the pain, bringing her into his protective embrace. He reached for her waist, to pull her all the way to him. She felt sticky, soft, like hot dough. And then she fell backward. She was a shadow, black as the farthest reaches of space.

The great nozzle bell fell silent, as if its fury had been sucked up inside it. And then the luminance around Kate faded, leaving behind a dark shape that broke into two pieces and fell away. Jack's glove was covered with a charred, dripping material. Something black and horrible seemed to writhe beneath him. When he started to scream, he thought he'd never stop. . . .

Jack started awake. He had fallen asleep but his mind had kept going, reliving the old nightmare. Virgil was patting his face. "Jack, time to get with it, son."

It took Jack a moment to remember where he was. Then all the rest came cascading back. He heard a noise, looked around, saw Penny floating past. If he expected at least a warm smile from her, he was disappointed. He looked after her, confused.

"I safed number two fuel cell," Virgil said, coming up beside him. "I'll troubleshoot while you eat breakfast. Number one is working just fine. If we can't get number two up, we'd better head for home, at least by all the rules."

"I guess we're not much for rules on this mission," Jack said, still watching Penny. She was gazing at the moon, her back turned.

"Sorry about yesterday, partner. I guess it got to me," Virgil said.

He looked at the big man's wide, expressive face. "You just had to let off some steam, Virg. No problem."

Virgil nodded toward Penny. "I told her everything, Jack.

About Kate and what's down there. I'm sorry. I got tired of lying to her."

Now Jack understood. "That's okay, too, Virg. I don't blame you."

Virgil got busy elsewhere. Penny pulled herself away from the view ports and came determinedly hand over hand across the ceiling. She settled down in the pilot's seat beside Jack. She stared straight ahead. "I want you to know I understand there's no place for me in your heart, Jack—"

"Penny—"

"No. Let me have my say," she said angrily, her eyes wetting. "You're not going to find Kate down there. You already have her"—she turned to him, reached across the console, and touched his chest—"right there in your heart."

He opened his mouth but no words came out.

"It must be wonderful to have someone love you so much that they would risk everything in life for you even after you're dead. I've never known a love like that. I'm sure I never will."

"Penny, will you just listen to me?"

"I am so envious of her. It's insane but I am."

He took her hand. "Don't you understand that everything's different now"—the words just leapt from his mouth, surprising him—"that I love you?"

She looked at him long and searchingly, then pulled her hand away. "Well, I don't love you."

Jack's heart felt as if it were being squeezed.

"I can't fault you, Jack," Penny said sadly. "I have my own reason for being here too." She peered ahead, watched the moon unscrolling below, craters piled on craters, sinuous rilles, soft-contoured mountains. "This is what I've always wanted, I think. What could be better than running all the way to the moon?"

She turned to face him. "I'm going to tell you something about myself. It's important to me that you know." She smiled ruefully. "There was this boy in high school. He

. . . I got pregnant. My grandmother insisted I have an abortion, said there were enough half-breeds. They told me at the free clinic it would be so easy. I've hated myself for it ever since." She bit at her lower lip, the tears floating from her eyes. "Everybody said I was doing the right thing, that a baby would ruin my life, keep me from getting an education. I'm sure it was a little boy, Jack. I just can't get him out of my mind. I keep trying but I just can't. All my adventures have been just me running away from him." She looked at her lap. "You can't love me, Jack. Because I don't know how to love you back. I have to keep running."

Jack touched her shoulder, tried to find the words. He couldn't. "I'm sorry" was the best he could do.

She raised her head, looked him in the eye. "Listen, Jack. Don't go down there, okay? Let's just go home."

"No, we have to finish this."

She squinted at him, then, in a spasm of despair, reached out and slapped him hard across his face. "*You* finish it," she hissed while he held his cheek and stared at her. "You and your damn Kate!"

Back On-Line
JSC

At the entrance to Johnson Space Center Sam confronted a guard wearing the PSS patch. Shirley scrunched down in the passenger seat of his pickup, trying to get as small as possible. Behind Sam's truck was a traffic jam. Two more PSS guards came out of the guard shack, holding up their hands. "The base is closed!" they yelled. Shirley saw another PSS guard settle in behind a small sandbag barricade just behind the shack. He had a rifle. The line of pickups, the universal transportation choice of Houston mission controllers, idled furiously. "I have a right to be here," he yelled at the guards. "You don't. Who the hell hired you, anyway?"

"I'm warning you, mister," the guard who had stopped

him said, and then pulled a pistol from the holster strapped to his waist. Then the guard with the rifle cut loose with a round, hitting Sam's windshield. Shirley screamed and scrambled to the floor, her hands over her head. The doors of the pickups behind suddenly were thrown open, Tate's Turds all armed with pistols and rifles leveled at the guards. "Fire!" somebody yelled, and the PSS guards ducked for cover while a rain of lead shredded the shack and the barricade. Sam helped Shirley back into her seat. "Guess this outfit don't know we got a law here in Texas, says we can carry concealed weapons in our vehicles." The PSS guards had run for their lives.

Sam raised his hand, waved the convoy on.

"You're not authorized to enter," the PSS guard at Shuttle Mission Control growled. Sam walked past him. The guard went for his pistol and then stopped when the dozen mission controllers came trundling in behind their leader. They were all carrying guns. The guard meekly put his pistol back into its holster and found an exit door.

Sam burst into the empty SMC. "Baby, I'm back!"

Tate's Turds followed, went to their consoles, fired them up, tucking their guns away. Sam stood proudly above them, vulturing grimly until he could no longer restrain himself. To the astonishment of his people he suddenly did a little jig and clapped his hands. "C'mon, folks! Let's go back to the moon!"

Battle in Space (4)
Columbia

In the glare of the cargo bay spotlights Jack went hand over hand down the guide wire of *Columbia*'s starboard sill. Below, in shadow, was the far side of the moon. In preparation for the descent he had lowered the shuttle's orbit to nine miles mean altitude and then rolled her over, bay down, tail forward. Getting that close to the surface made the timeline very tight but also allowed a quicker descent. Little Dog didn't have the fuel reserves to allow a leisurely landing.

Jack could still feel the sting of Penny's slap. He told himself to ignore it, put it aside, that it didn't matter, never had. There never had been a chance for them. He had momentarily been fooled that she could be a part of his life, but the truth was Jack knew that he had no life; only this mission to the moon. He had to keep his focus. This was all that mattered. It was all that had ever mattered since the day he had caused Kate and their child to die. Jack went grimly ahead, one hand over the other. There was nothing aboard *Columbia* for him, nothing back on earth. Everything that meant anything was below, on the moon. He had to concentrate on only that.

He went past the ATESS tether boom, back in its locked position. Virgil had gone out, climbed the boom, and disentangled the BEM to let it go. Starbuck had signed off, anxious not to interfere with communications, critical in the next hour of operations. He had boosted the BEM's orbit and reported he was following, keeping an eye on *Columbia's* wake. It was clean. Jack heard him report as he did on the hour. "BEM on patrol, *Columbia*. Everything's clear."

Jack inspected the Elsie dome, especially the ragged places left by the first BEM attack. The damage wasn't critical. There were a dozen layers of material and only the first few seemed to have been breached. He moved down and inspected Little Dog. The compact rocket engine looked solid and powerful. It had better be, he thought.

Jack remembered the debate that had raged on Cedar Key as to the design of the landing system. One faction had demanded that there be two dog engines on the landing craft performing the same role as the two engines that had been aboard the *Apollo* Lem. The argument had to do with weight versus redundancy. Two engines would give Jack a chance to abort. One engine meant less weight. Jack had settled the argument. Only one engine would be used, and to lighten the load further, there would be no heavy landing gear. Instead, three inflatable spheres attached to the Elsie/Dog interface collar would be used. The spheres were made of the same tough material as the Elsie. There was also an extra ablative covering capable of withstanding the Little Dog's fiery exhaust plume.

Jack inspected the landing spheres. Made out of the same material used by the Mars *Pathfinder* mission to land its payload, the spheres were designed to take the impact of the Elsie landing on the moon. A collapsible steel rod protruded from the collar to a tip ten feet beneath the spheres. When the rod touched the lunar surface, Little Dog would shut down automatically. It was a piece of KISS hardware that Jack always strived toward—*Keep It Simple, Stupid.*

A nylon Jacob's ladder was rolled up at the hatch. Jack had never tested it but wasn't too concerned. He wouldn't be as far off the ground as the *Apollo* astronauts had been. If necessary Jack planned to simply sit down on the landing spheres and slide off. To get back on he would do what was needed, either taking advantage of the low gravity to jump back to the hatch, or, using the tethers around the collar, pull himself back up. He'd figure it out when he got there.

Jack climbed inside and inspected Virgil's setup. Sunlight streamed through the double-pane portholes. *Columbia* was in the light zone, coming around over the *Apollo 17* track. A laptop counted down. It was time for Jack to take his position in the footloops. He pushed the comm button. "Ready when you are, Virg."

Virgil was at the controls of the RMS. "Roger that, Jack."

Jack steadied himself as Virgil picked up the Elsie, rotated the arm over the bay. He watched the sill of the bay slip past and then he was looking at the moon below.

"Ready for release, Jack?"

It had been a long time since Jack had prayed. He did so now, a long stream of incomplete thoughts that included a jumble of hopes, dreams, requests. . . . "Kate . . ." he whispered.

"Say again, Jack?" Virgil called.

Jack gripped the Elsie's hand controller. *Time to get this done.* "I'm ready for release, Virg," he said.

Farside Control

Starbuck kept his eye on the virtual video screen. His BEM was still trailing *Columbia*. A glint of sun caught the shuttle just before it went into shadow. The BEM followed dutifully behind. All seemed serene.

"Starbuck," BEM Lead called. "Got something curious going on here. Memory's being used in prodigious chunks by the HOE team."

"How could that be?" Starbuck had told the HOE team to go home, the game over.

"Somebody is running the HOE full-up. They must have solved their circuit problem. But I can't figure out how they're getting in on our mainframe."

Starbuck knew. They were doing it the same way he would have done it. They were hacking him, breaking in and using his mainframe from a remote terminal. An easy job: they knew all the passwords. He thought of Carl Puckett. Puckett had gotten to the HOE team, bought their expertise. They were somewhere out there, hacking in on him. They had finally fixed HOE. It was a dangerous weapon that could tear *Columbia* to pieces.

Starbuck considered the situation. He could break off the modems but he was using them for at least one critical comm channel. He could simply shut down the computer. That would do it. *Or would it?* Starbuck would be off-line but the HOE team might have been copying the software to their own machines and could keep going. There was only one thing for him to do: go surfing.

The Elsie

Jack punched in the go-ahead and the Elsie's verniers puffed briefly, rotating him into a head-down position. Little Dog fired for thirty seconds and then the Elsie's laptop commanded verniers to pitch them back upright. Jack saw all the landmarks he'd memorized: the Lincoln Scarp came into view first, a long sinuous valley that snaked down to the Taurus-Littrow range, then the North Massif of the Sculptured Hills. It was an awesome sight, glorious. Jack's heart raced. He was going to land on the moon. The Elsie gave him a tone, offering manual control. He took it.

Farside Control

Starbuck was surfing the code. He called up the HOE program and was not surprised to find himself locked out. He tried some obvious passwords, failed, and then dropped down into the initiation phase of the disk operating system. He'd written it himself and had left a back door so wide, a tractor trailer could drive through it. He called up the DOS and simply wiped out every password there and put in new ones. Maybe he couldn't knock the HOE team off but if they dropped out for a nanosecond they'd have the devil to pay to get back in. He kept surfing, taking a curl through the disk directory, deleting anything that looked like HOE memory. He got a lot of it, but it was minor stuff and he knew it. The main HOE system was in use and the central processor wasn't going to let him delete, change, or move any part of it until it stopped being used. By then, Starbuck figured, it wouldn't matter.

He brought HOE up on the virtual panel. It was ahead of the BEM, and much lower. It was tracking something. It wasn't the shuttle.

"Dammit," Starbuck swore. "They're going after the lander!"

"Give me a position!" BEM Lead called.

"No," Starbuck said. "HOE has a built-in signal generator. Feed in that frequency to the BEM as priority tracking and let it go. It's all we can do. Things are happening too fast for us now."

BEM Leader signaled the BEM its new instructions.

LETMEGO LETMEGO LETMEGO LETMEGO LETMEGO
LETMEGO LETMEGO LETMEGO LETMEGO LETMEGO

"You got it, Lover!' BEM Lead cried, sending the release command.

The Elsie

Jack wiggled the hand controller. He had come in a bit too far north and needed manual control to find the landing site. Elsie stopped and hovered, waiting for his command. Jack pushed the stick forward. Little Dog swiveled on its gimbals and the Elsie moved laterally across the North Massif. The large crater named Shakespeare scrolled past and then a flat plain, covered with craters. The photographs Jack had studied of the landing site had shown only a few craters of only medium size but he saw hundreds, and it was difficult to judge how big they were. He checked the Little Dog. There was plenty of propellant left.

A large crater passed below with a smaller one bisecting it. He knew it because he had named it himself during his study of the *Apollo 17* photographs. "I've got Onizuka," he announced, the first words he had spoken since he started his descent. Ellison Onizuka had been one of Jack's friends at NASA. El had died aboard *Challenger*.

The reply from Virgil was filled with crackles and pops. *Columbia* was about to go over the lunar horizon. "We copy, Jack."

Jack switched back to automatic pilot to allow the Elsie to stabilize herself while he made a quick survey. He was in the triangle of Camelot, Steno, and Sherlock craters. A little nudge north and he should be at Shorty. He used the hand controller to pitch the Elsie down so he could look things over. The site below was as smooth as a baby's butt. He took a deep breath and gave the Elsie the go-ahead to land. He felt like cheering.

Space

BEM XJ-251, released from Farside Control, made a quick scan and picked up HOE's scent, then cut in its thrusters, dropping low and accelerating. It came out of the shadow of the moon in a rage.

The HOE, also on automatic, took no note of the BEM. It worked to get an exact fix on the lander. At a distance of five kilometers its nose cone blew off and a fifteen-foot web of metal strips spun up to buzz-saw velocity.

XJ-251 sensed that its propellant would be depleted in twelve seconds. It accounted for the lunar gravity, its own acceleration, and the velocity of its target, predicting a new intersection. It screamed ahead. With one second of propellant remaining it cut itself off to ensure a smooth transition to unpowered flight. Silently, the BEM coasted, its silvery eyes staring seriously ahead.

HOE closed in on Elsie, aiming for the center of its radar return, but jumping to its heat sensors every nanosecond in case the radar failed. When it was still one hundred meters away from the lander, the BEM struck it. HOE, made of composite material, broke up on impact. Pieces of it and the BEM flew in an embrace, crashing into the lunar surface.

The HOE web, broken loose from the main body, kept spinning chaotically, answering only the call of the tumbling gyroscope that it had become. Along the way it caught the base of the Elsie. It did not puncture the spheres—they were too tough for that. It tore two of them away from the collar, knocking Elsie awry, sending her wandering.

The Elsie

Jack felt a thump, checked the laptop, but no caution and warning messages were showing. He pushed his feet into the footloops and clutched the hand tethers. Little Dog kept firing but Elsie seemed to be drifting. The guidance package seemed confused. Little Dog's gimbals shuddered as if trying to throw off its worry and then Jack saw the light that indicated the contact sensor rod had struck the regolith. Little Dog shut down and Elsie fell to the moon.

He felt more than heard the crash. There was the grinding of metal on metal of the contact, and then the Elsie took a sickening lurch. Jack, his feet ripped from the footloops, fell, his hands losing their grip.

A dust cloud rose up around the Elsie as she hit and then, very slowly, fell back, a gray rain around the ruined lander.

Mankind had returned to the moon.

Farside Control

Starbuck, shaken to his core, looked at the blank panels and his equally empty console screen. "I only hope to Christ we were in time."

The phone was ringing. It was the leader of the HOE team. "Sorry, Starbuck," she said.

There was no use getting angry. They were all outlaw hackers here. "What did you see before the BEM got you?"

"Looked to be some kind of landing craft."

Starbuck swallowed. "Did you hit it?"

"I'm not sure. I don't think so, not directly anyway. There was a lot of shrapnel near it, I would imagine."

Starbuck asked the question but he knew the answer. "Why did you do it?"

"Puckett promised us a million dollars if we tried."

"Did you get the money?"

"Already cashed."

Starbuck hung up. BEM Lead was standing, stretching. With a sigh Starbuck ordered the Farside computer to shut itself down. Star Wars, Ronald Reagan's Strategic Defense Initiative dream, after one hundred billion dollars, had fought its first, last, and only real battle.

HOE Facility, San Jose

Puckett stared at the screen. "You did it," he exulted.

"We did it, all right. The question is *why* did we do it?"

Puckett grinned triumphantly. "You got well paid. What the hell do you care?"

HOE Lead stood up, rolled up her sleeves. "I want you to leave, Mr. Puckett."

Puckett shrugged. "Sure." He started toward the door, then turned. His .38 Police Special was more pistol than he needed to do the job but it was all he'd brought. Four well-placed shots to their big heads before the damned nerds could even move was all it took. He inspected each of the bodies with a professional interest, giving himself the benefit of the doubt considering that they'd all been moving targets. He was satisfied, acceptable wounds within a small circle of where he'd been aiming. It looked, though, as if he was pulling slightly to the right when he pulled the trigger. He made a mental note of it, to correct it on the practice range. Then he saw his shoe was in a spreading pool of blood from the HOE lead's head and stepped back daintily. He wiped his shoe on the carpet, went out the door, whistling. *Mission accomplished.*

6

Frau Mauro

Though earth and moon were gone,
And suns and universes ceased to be,
And thou wert left alone,
Every existence would exist in thee.
There is not room for Death,
Nor atom that his might could render void:
Thou—Thou art Being and Breath,
And what Thou art may never be destroyed.

—Emily Brontë, "Last Lines"

On the Moon

Columbia

Virgil had heard Starbuck's explanations and apology, passed it all along to Penny. She sat in the pilot's seat, her face a mask of loss and pain. Virgil knew Jack better than she did. He hadn't lost hope, not by a long shot. Jack was one tough country boy. If anybody could survive even this catastrophe, it would be him. "Talk to Jack, Penny," Virgil urged. "Maybe he can hear but can't answer. Maybe he needs to hear a friendly voice. Talk to him!"

Penny made no reply, just kept staring at the implacable moon. It had been an hour since they had last heard from Jack, just before his landing attempt. Virgil watched earth, shrunk to the size of a blue-and-white marble, slowly rise over the edge of the moon as *Columbia* came around the far side. When Taurus-Littrow came into view, he climbed into the commander's seat, used the binoculars Jack had left there, to study the terrain, looking for evidence of a crash landing. He could see nothing but craters and rilles and mountains, the silent, everlasting, harsh moon hanging suspended in vast and hostile space.

Penny suddenly moved, fitted her headset on, squinted at Virgil. She'd come out of her shock. "What do you want me to say?" she demanded.

Virgil gave her a big grin. "Attagirl. Just anything. Let him know you're here."

She took a deep breath, keyed the transmitter. "Jack, this is Penny. Dammit, Jack. Answer!"

There was no answer, just a faint whisper of static. Virgil kept looking through the binoculars and Penny kept calling.

When Virgil next looked at her, he saw zero g tears flying from Penny's eyes like pearls from a broken necklace.

Taurus-Littrow

On his back, looking up at the bent lattice still supporting the fabric of the Elsie, Jack moved his arms and legs and flexed his fingers. No bones seemed to be broken and his backpack was delivering air. *At least that.* He started to speculate on what had happened, then dismissed it. He needed to get out first. He turned over, easy in the light gravity of the moon, and crawled to the hatch. If he was going to die, he wanted it to be outside, not in the crushed egg the Elsie had become.

We choose to go to the moon and the other things, President Kennedy had said, *not because they are easy but because they are hard.*

Jack unzipped the hatch and poked his helmet through the opening. The ground below was a gray, puttylike dust. He grasped the edge of the entrance, turned around, and dropped feetfirst. He landed off-balance and fell hard on his back. "You were right, JFK." He sighed. "This ain't easy."

He turned over and climbed to his feet, then crunched over the regolith to look at the Elsie's base, to see if he could figure out what had happened to cause his crash. There was, inexplicably, only one landing sphere attached to the landing craft, abraded material the only thing left of the attachment points of the other two. Little Dog was a ruin.

Jack checked his suit. Pressure and power were normal and the communications mode selector switch was on, although he heard nothing in his earpiece. He clumped around and looked at the UHF antenna and saw the reason. It was torn from the strap that held it, dangling down the side of the smashed dome. He'd have to reaim it to communicate with *Columbia.*

Jack found it easy to move on the moon, even in the EMU suit, which was not designed for lunar EVA. MEC had designed a coverall to keep moondust out of the EMU joints, and added booties with soles made from old tire treads for traction. More KISS, and it worked perfectly.

Jack turned around, trying to get a fix on his location, spotted the cliffs of the North Massif, the South Massif, and the smaller Family Mountain. They looked like huge sand dunes that a giant had sprinkled with boulders. As he turned, he saw a flash of color out of the corner of his eye. He trotted in its direction, raised the sunshield visor on his helmet, tried to get a fix on whatever it was.

Then he saw it, and gasped with recognition.

The crash had almost dumped him on top of the *Apollo 17* landing site.

The old *Apollo 17* Lem, named *Challenger*, sat on a rolling plain, looking like a spraddled four-legged milk stool. The top part of it was gone, used by Schmitt and Cernan to fly up to the *Apollo* capsule. Jack looked closer and saw the Lunar Rover parked nearby. It had been the Rover's golden parabolic antenna that had attracted his attention, catching the sun in a spray of rainbow light.

Jack's joy at seeing the *Apollo 17* landing site was tempered by the realization that he was miles away from Shorty Crater. He checked his oxygen pack again and considered his overall air situation. His mind jumped ahead, to imagine how it would be when it inevitably ran out. When the last of the oxygen seeped out of the cylinder on his back, he would only have what was left in his helmet to breathe. Carbon dioxide would quickly build up until Jack would begin a reflexive gasping. Then a pounding headache would follow, one that would feel as if a spike were being driven into his forehead. It would probably drive him to his knees, where he would begin to strangle and choke, his lungs burning as if corrosive acid had been poured into them. He would pant, froth pouring from his mouth, his eyes rolling back into their sockets. He would begin to hallucinate. It would not be an easy death.

Jack contemplated puncturing his suit when the time came. That wouldn't be easy, the material tough and multi-layered, but he could do it, perhaps with the screwdriver in the toolbox aboard the Elsie. He would die quickly but it wouldn't be painless. He remembered his brief exposure to the vacuum when Penny's suit had failed. To open his suit on the moon would make his skin feel as if it were being torn in strips from his body. Massive embolisms would course through his blood, lodging painfully in his heart, his lungs, his brain stem. He remembered reading of rescuers finding trapped cave divers who had spit out their regulators while there was still air in their tanks, breathed in the water, drowned rather than face their last gasp of air. Others had breathed their tanks down to nothing, never giving up hope. Jack had always admired the latter. They had not given up, lived until the last possible moment. That's what Jack decided to do, to face the agony of suffocation squarely. Only one other decision remained: whether to strike out for Shorty, probably die on the way in total isolation; or poke around the old site, gasp his final breath among the oddly familiar relics of the last *Apollo* mission.

He lowered his sun visor and trundled ahead, stopped briefly at the Rover. The unimpeded sun had faded and cracked the nylon seat covers but otherwise it looked as if the *Apollo* astronauts had just parked it and might be back at any moment. Dust from their boots still lay like beach sand on the floorboard. Had the evolution of spaceflight gone as many in the nation had hoped, this would have been hallowed ground, a place for visitors to see and contemplate. Instead, Jack decided it would be where he was going to die, a lone American, starved for air, wearing tire-tread boots. The irony did not escape him, though he had little time to waste on its contemplation.

Jack took long strides toward the *Challenger*. He had already perfected the gait required to move in a two-hundred-pound suit that now weighed just thirty-four pounds in the reduced lunar gravity. Although he could move along at a quick pace, he had to gauge his center of gravity and plan several steps ahead. There was really nothing to it and he would've been having fun except it was difficult to forget that he was on an oxygen countdown that was going to leave him dead. He bounded over a thin red wire running along the ground from one of the *Apollo* experiments, the surface electronic properties (SEP) dipole antenna, then began a stutter of small steps to stop in front of the lander. The plaque on the landing leg—*Here man completed his first exploration of the moon, December 1972 A.D.*—and the ladder identified it as the front of the spacecraft. Just before entering the Lem, Eugene Cernan had made a little speech that Jack had memorized:

This is our commemoration that will be here until someone like us, until some of you who are out there, who are the promise of the future, come back to read it again and to further the exploration and the meaning of Apollo.

"Gene, somehow I don't think I'm what you had in mind," Jack muttered. He loped around the lander until he came upon a pile of discards—cameras, unused sample tubes, sundry wires and cables. Numerous boot prints were tramped into the dust all around the Lem, but farther out there were distinct paths to the *Apollo* Lunar surface experiment package (ALSEP), an experiment that measured the violence of moonquakes, and the LACE experiment that studied the tenuous moon atmosphere. Jack went all the way around the Lem, completing his exploration, then checked his oxygen again. He estimated he had a little over three hours left before he would need to recharge his backpack. He trudged to the front of the Lem, looked at the Rover, then walked over to it.

The Rover's power switch was still turned on, left that

way by Cernan and Schmitt to provide power to the television camera and communications package. All the gauges were pegged at zero, the batteries long dead. Jack sat down in the starboard seat and took hold of the hand controller, toggling the switch. Nothing happened, the Rover as dead as he was about to be. He got out, looked back toward the Elsie's dome protruding above a low dune. An idea was forming. He saw no way to save himself but there might be a way to get to Shorty Crater before he died. *Kate.* He could die with her.

Columbia

Virgil watched Penny, still desperately trying to raise Jack. *Columbia* was coming around the far rim of the moon and lifting above the bright gray surface. "Jack, this is Penny," she called. "Answer me, Jack!"

There was no reply. Virgil heard the SAREX tone and went down to retrieve the message. He read the report, replied, and came back up. "MEC reports Houston is still trying to contact us," he told her. "I'm thinking maybe we should respond. What could it hurt? Presuming they're friendly, they might be able to help us make contact with Jack."

Penny nodded agreement. "Can you configure the comm channel?"

"Yeah. No sweat." Virgil settled into the pilot's seat and brought the shuttle computers back on-line. When he enabled the comm page, he immediately heard a droning voice come through the speakers. "*Columbia*, this is Houston. We want to help you. Please answer us. *Columbia*, this is Houston—"

"We got you, Houston!" Virgil exclaimed. "Go ahead!"

A reedy Texas drawl filled his ears. "*Columbia*, this is Sam Tate. How do you read?"

"Loud and clear, Mr. Tate! How me?"

"Call me Sam. Yes, we hear you loud and clear. Can we be of any assistance?"

"You're damn right you can!" Virgil yelled back.

"We're ready to copy, *Columbia*. Who am I talking to?"

"This is Virgil Judd. Call my family. They're at the Mayo Clinic. Tell them I'm okay. Find out how they are. Got that?"

"Consider it done, Mr. Judd."

"Virgil. Now, here's the situation. . . ."

San Jose Airport

Puckett called the Man at the appointed time and reported his success. "What about *Columbia*?" the Man asked.

"What does it matter? They're going to get nothing off the moon. And Medaris is as good as dead."

"Because you used Farside, we've got another problem. The people aboard *Columbia* know about it. The United States broke international law having it up there. There must be no witnesses. Do you understand?"

"Yes. How about Starbuck and his people? I left them alive." He snapped his fingers, remembering the HOE team. "Well, most of them, anyway."

"You can take care of them later. Starbuck won't talk right away. He's kept it secret all these years, we think he'll keep it secret for a little longer."

Puckett hung up, went out on the tarmac, waved to his pilots to follow him. This time he'd chartered a DC-10, empty except for him as its only passenger. He was headed to Russia, to make sure Ollie Grant was sticking with the program. Although they would not be coming back to earth with fusion energy fuel, the people aboard *Columbia* were witnesses. They still needed killing. "Let's go!" he called to the pilots, who gave him the high sign, moved forward into their seats, started to wind up the engines. Puckett collapsed into a first-class passenger seat, cinched his seat belt. "Russia!" He grinned. "Where the vodka is cheap, the girls are blond, and the men in charge know how to deal!" His kind of place.

Taurus-Littrow

Jack finished hauling everything he needed out of the Elsie. The MEC team had devised a way to pump oxygen into his backpack through a port on its service and cooling umbilical. Their commandment always KISS, they had also built external scrubbers and batteries for the backpack. He topped his tanks off with the oxygen reserves from the Elsie, snapped fresh scrubbers and batteries into place, was ready to go. A full oxygen pack gave him six hours. The Elsie's reserves, if he used them all, would give him two days to explore and then to die, probably out at Shorty.

The next step was to restore communications, to let Virgil and Penny know that at least he had lived long enough to walk on the moon. That was selfish on his part and he knew it. Perhaps if that had been the only reason, he wouldn't have done it, but he also wanted to hear Penny's voice. He wanted one last contact with her. That was selfish, too, he realized, but he kept working, unable to be completely and utterly noble in the face of oblivion.

Jack detached the UHF antenna and taped it to the side of the dome so that it aimed skyward. Still hearing nothing, he went inside to check the Elsie's comm panel. The circuit breakers had all been thrown, probably on impact. He reset them, one by one. As soon as he threw the last one, he heard a crackling in the helmet comm set. When he stuck his head out of the hatch, he heard Penny and her pleas for contact. He switched to the VOX mode, so that all he had to do was speak to automatically transmit. "I'm here, Penny. How do you read?"

Her voice, worried but steady, came back. "Jack! Thank God! Are you all right?"

"I'm fine," he responded, "but I've had a little problem. Is Virgil listening?"

"No. We have Houston back with us, Jack. Sam Tate is talking to Virgil. He says they want to help."

Jack inwardly shrugged. He could see no way out of his dilemma but recognized it was still a good thing to have Mission Control on the side of Penny and Virgil. Houston could help *Columbia* get home. After all, they'd done it for *Apollo 13*. "Tate's a good man," Jack allowed. "But listen to me, High Eagle. I've got something to tell you—the Elsie crashed. I think it got hit by something, I don't know. Anyway, I lost two of my landing spheres and the Elsie is lying on its side and Little Dog is a mess. I'm only about two hundred yards from the *Apollo 17* landing site. I'm okay for now." He paused, trying to decide how much more to tell her, then decided to tell her the whole truth. "I've decided to go on out to Shorty. . . ."

He stood on a mound of moondust, listening, hearing only the sound of his own breathing. The next voice he heard was Virgil's. "Hey, partner, how we doing?"

"I'm fine. How's Penny?"

"She's a little upset but she'll be okay. What can we do about you?"

"Me? Nothing, Virg. How's the fuel cell situation?"

"Number two is still chugging along. Should last for another day, at least. Number one still looks good."

"You'd better go. You can't depend on one fuel cell."

"Let me talk it over with our lady here."

"Virgil, would you also check on the voltage the Rover used?"

"Wait one."

Several volumes of pertinent *Apollo 17* data had been brought along on disk. "It had two thirty-six-volt batteries, Jack," Virgil came back.

"I thought so. Elsie runs on 36 volts, too, and I've got spare batteries for her that I won't need now. I'm going to see if I can jury-rig some power for the Rover, get on out to

Shorty. I can at least report on the helium-3 fire beads out there, give the next guy an idea of how to pick it up."

"You think that thing will run after sitting on the moon for three decades?"

"I'm going to give it a shot."

"Jack." It was Penny. "Stay where you are. Save your oxygen. Let us work on it. You don't need to go to Shorty. I know you're not going because of the helium-3. Kate's not there, Jack. Kate is dead. You can't bring her back."

Jack felt spiritual, disembodied, caught up in the machinery of fate. He knew what he must do, that all that had occurred was part of some foreshadowed accumulation of events, some sort of fateful curve for which there had to be purposeful result. He had to complete what the gods demanded. "Penny, listen to me. Fire up Big Dog and get out of there."

"I'm not going to leave you, Jack," Penny said resolutely. "I love you, you moron!"

Jack wasn't listening, not really, as he looked into the sky, hoping to catch a glimpse of *Columbia*, to see the manmade star streak past. "I've got two days' worth of air," he said as much to himself as to Penny. "I can't sit here and watch the earth and the stars go round and round. I have something I have to do, something I was meant to do."

"Jack Medaris, this is Houston," Sam broke in. "How do you read?"

Jack looked up, spotted earth. "Loud and clear, Houston. Is that you, Sam?"

"It's me, Jack. Just wanted to let you know we're on the job. We're going to get you home, son. You just hang in there."

"Oh, sure, Sam." That was Houston, all right. If there had been a Mission Control for the *Titanic*, they would have been devising work-arounds from the moment the great liner struck the iceberg. That thought amused Jack as he imagined it:

"Ah, Houston, this is the Titanic, we've got a problem. Looks like a twenty-meter tear at the bow by an iceberg spur."

"Roger, Titanic. We see that. We're already working on it. A lifeboat count follows and recommended sequential manning. The guys down in the trenches have come up with this plan in the interim. Recommend you have duct tape available. . . ."

Jack carried the Elsie's oxygen tanks to the Rover and then went inside the dome, brought out the spare battery pack and a toolkit. He followed his tracks back toward *Challenger*, his mind filled with the final plans for his life.

On the Job in Houston
SMC

Shirley called the vice president and apprised him of what she had done. "Houston's abuzz, sir. That's the only word to describe it. All three shifts have come in and nobody's going home until the mission is over. Some of the off-shift controllers are sleeping on the floor underneath their consoles, others have moved into the back rooms and are curled up on top of desks. It's amazing. I think some of them aren't sleeping at all."

The veep was silent for a long time. Then, in a shaky, tired voice, he asked, "What are they doing to help *Columbia*?"

Shirley looked around. "I don't know, sir. I'm not an engineer. Writing code and debugging software, I heard somebody say. They're doing whatever it takes, I guess."

"What about the press down there?"

Shirley looked at the glassed-in press room. It was packed with reporters and cameras. "They're everywhere!" she exclaimed. "Their vans are surrounding us like tanks lining up to attack. Here's something else, sir. Did you know SDI had assets around the moon? Well, a man named Starbuck does. I just heard a minute ago he hacked his way in here. Sam

Tate—he's the flight director—talked to him and told me he was for real. He's been invited to join the effort. Sam told me it was an old project known as Farside and that there's a communications satellite around the moon. It's providing us the orbit of *Columbia*. You won't believe this, sir, but it's also transmitting a visual of the lunar surface and *Columbia*'s position over it."

"I see." Vanderheld's voice sounded neither surprised or excited, merely sorrowful.

Shirley sought to cheer him up. "Sir, calls are coming in here from around the world. The Japanese, Chinese, Indian, and European space agencies have all volunteered to help us in any way they can."

"The dream of space is alive, Shirley," Vanderheld said, finally. "Is that what you're telling me?"

"Yes, sir. That's good, isn't it, sir?"

"I don't know, Shirley. I used to think I did but now I don't know."

"I'm sorry this stresses you so much, sir."

"Shirley," Vanderheld said, "let me talk to the flight director."

Sam took the phone. "It's been the most amazing day, Mr. Vice President," he said.

"Well, clearly, you're doing a wonderful job down there, Sam," Vanderheld said. "What do you think the chances are for *Columbia* and her crew?"

"That's hard to say, sir, but we've got tiger teams on it around the clock. If there's anybody can pull this off, it's Tate's Turds—pardon the expression, sir."

Sam heard the veep's well-known rich, melodious chuckle. "Shirley told me that international space agencies have volunteered their help. Please allow them to do so. I think it would be splendid if all this was seen as an international effort."

Sam shrugged. "Sure. No problem."

"I've heard on this end from the Russian ambassador.

The Russian Space Agency would like to launch a manned spacecraft and rendezvous with *Columbia* as she comes in, to be there to assist if such is required."

"I haven't heard anything from them, sir, but if I do, I'll see that they get what they need from us. Not that *Columbia*'ll need it. If we can get them out of lunar orbit, we'll have it made, I think."

"You seem to be quite happy about this, Sam," the veep said. "Aren't you still angry over what Medaris did?"

Sam guffawed. "Aw, that ol' boy ain't got the sense God gave ducks, Mr. Vice President. But I think I'll forgive him. *Columbia* is bringing home the energy source of the future. I figure that's a pretty damn good thing to do."

"But at what price, Sam? There will be wars over this."

"Hell, sir, there's been wars since the beginning of time. If we start squabbling over the energy on the moon, that's not a bad reason to start a fight. Let's go for it, I say."

Shirley came back on. "We're going to do this thing, sir. I wish you were here. You'd love it."

"You're a brave woman, Shirley," Vanderheld said. "The bravest I've ever known, I think."

"Thank you, sir. The admiration is mutual, I assure you."

Montana (3)
The Perlman Plant

Perlman and Charlie pushed the last pipe into the gasket fitted into the big red hatch that covered the sand tube. Perlman thanked God that a fusion reactor test project required a completely fitted-out machine shop and a vast plumbing inventory and Charlie knew what to do with them. Overnight he had fabricated his design, adding in Perlman's own expertise of pumps, hydraulics, and fluid mechanics. The resulting pipe stretched from the reservoir to the hatch. In-line pumps, capable of building thousands of pounds of water pressure in seconds, were in place, and the hatch had been braced with a bridgework of steel beams to take the added pressure.

Perlman inspected some of the attachments and worried over the gaskets. "We're on the edge of their specs, Charlie. All we can do is hope they hold."

"If they leak a little, we can live with that, Doc."

It was at that moment a thunder from above shook the Egg and the cavern. They were starting to blast. It was only a matter of time, hours probably, before they blasted down to the hatch. Perlman looked at Charlie. "Well, Charlie, old boy, I guess it's time we fought back."

"I'm on it, Doc." Charlie grinned. He opened the first valve while Perlman got the pumps going. Then they stood back, listening to the thousands of gallons of water flushing out of the big reservoir and into the pipe. Some of the gaskets leaked but most held, including the one they had worried about most, the one at the hatch. There was a gurgling sound, as if someone had stuck a hose down a gopher hole. In this case it was water going up the hole, into the sand, blasting it from a solid into a slurry with the consistency of quicksand.

"You're a genius, Charlie," Perlman said.

"So are you, Doc," Charlie replied.

Perlman shrugged. He guessed he was. He had, after all, solved the most difficult energy problem known to mankind. "So here we are," he said, smiling, "just two geniuses standing a hundred feet beneath the Montana prairie waiting for a man on the moon to come to our rescue."

"That pretty much sums it up, Doc," Charlie said. "And you know what? If he's still alive after all these days, I think he'll make it the rest of the way."

If he was still alive. Now, there was the question. Perlman looked up toward the gurgling lake forming above him. That was indeed the question. Otherwise, everything else was academic.

The Rover

Taurus-Littrow

After attaching the new batteries, Jack used a brush from the toolkit to sweep all the dust he could from the electric motors attached to each of the Rover's wheels. He also rocked the Rover back and forth to break loose any corrosion that might have formed in the wheels or axles. There wasn't much else he could think of to do—except try the power switch.

He sat down in the port seat and toggled the switch. The gauges registered no change. He tapped them and the needles responded, swinging up into the green. Scarcely believing it, he eased the hand controller forward and the wire wheels dug in, the Rover lurching forward. He kept his eye on the gauges but all stayed in normal range. The Rover had been alternately baked and frozen for decades and all Jack had done was change out the batteries and kick the tires and it was ready to go. Jack had to laugh. Who said the USA couldn't build a quality vehicle?

Cernan had busted the aft starboard fender and fixed it with a map and duct tape. Then he'd taken the fender as a souvenir with him when he left. Jack fashioned another fender out of a folded map he found beside the Rover, used lots of duct tape, and hoped his fix would work. The Rover kept trundling forward and no spray of dust was hitting Jack in the back. His map fender seemed to be holding. He kept the controller eased back, not wanting to put any more stress on old fuses than was needed. He estimated it would take him six hours to travel down the path of *Apollo 17*'s second EVA, to Shorty.

Jack had brought along water and food. A drink port in his helmet allowed him to suck liquids, his food in the form of soups laced with vitamins. His most immediate problem was the need for sleep. Already groggy with fatigue, he knew he would have to rest soon or risk making possibly deadly mistakes.

Cernan and Schmitt had made stops along their journey to the North Massif, parking and hiking to interesting geological features. At the base of the mountain Jack found a parking spot and boot prints that led off to a huge boulder. It was then Jack realized his mistake. He had followed the track of EVA-3 to what was designated Station 6 on the maps. At the end of the tracks were two huge craggy boulders butted up against one another. Schmitt and Cernan had spent a lot of time at the site. Jack realized he hadn't made a disastrous miscalculation. He had enough air to backtrack to Shorty. The only problem was he doubted if he could stay awake long enough to do it.

He circled the boulders, noting where the astronauts had sampled, the scars on the rocks as fresh as if they had just been made. He spotted a scooplike device, one of the tools Cernan and Schmitt had used to pick up small rocks. The prongs were bent, probably the reason why it had been discarded. He walked around into the shadow of the biggest boulder and took in the view, the mounds of the Sculptured Hills off to his left, and the hulking South Massif across the cratered plain. The *Challenger* Lem and his Elsie were only about two miles away and in plain sight.

Jack chose the regolith in the shadow of the big boulder for his bed, calling and telling whoever was listening his plan.

Columbia was behind the moon. Houston answered. "We copy, Jack," Sam told him. "You want us to wake you?"

"Negative."

"Roger that. By the way, we're still working the rescue plan. Want to hear what we're thinking about?"

Jack smiled grimly, certain that whatever Tate was coming up with was about as useful as the rescue plan he had imagined for the *Titanic*. This was a done deal. "Thanks,

Sam," he said tiredly, "but I'll pass. I want to keep my mind on things here."

"If you stayed in one place, it would make it easier for us," Sam replied gently.

Penny broke in, *Columbia* apparently just coming around the rim. "Jack, there really are some things happening. We've been loading software for the last hour—"

Jack interrupted her. "You still here? Virgil, I thought I asked you to take off."

"Virgil's busy working to save your butt, Medaris!" Penny came back. "Be advised we're not leaving the moon without you!"

Jack sighed, wearily shook his head. "Whatever you say, Penny. Let me get some sleep now, okay?"

"Oh, God, Jack," she said, despairingly.

"Let me sleep, okay?"

She relented. "Okay, Jack."

Jack found it difficult to sit in the EMU suit, so he simply sprawled on his back in the shadow of the boulder. He looked up at a black sky strewn with stars and planets. *What a fantastic place for an observatory the moon would be!* The Hubble Space Telescope whizzed around the earth at five miles a second trying to focus on constantly moving targets while being knocked around by its own solar panels swiveling desperately to aim at the sun. Why hadn't NASA simply lofted a telescope to the moon? It was almost as if the agency had been afraid to go back to the site of its greatest triumph.

Jack wiped NASA politics from his mind, tried to get comfortable. He was so tired, he thought he would drop off immediately, but instead his mind kept turning. The suit's aluminum neckring hurt, and anyway, he had always disliked the moments just before sleep. It seemed a form of giving up and he hated to give up on anything. For some reason he thought of the Sinai Desert, where once he and Kate had dived the crystal waters and rainbow reefs of the

Red Sea, and explored the dry wadis and mountains of the surrounding desert. Now that he thought about it, those old brown hills and dry creek beds had looked a hell of a lot like the moon.

Go to sleep, Jack! he ordered himself.

His mind puttered on, then finally gave in to his fatigue. He had a final, fleeting thought: *Don't call me. Old not-quite-dead Jack will call you.*

MET 9 DAYS AND COUNTING . . .

High Eagle's Decision (3)
Taurus-Littrow

Jack lay on the moon and overhead there was nothing but stars. . . .

Kate was with him on a night dive, their two flashlights cutting the darkness, sweeping across the great reefs that lined the deep chasm of the Red Sea between the Sinai and Saudi Arabia. Creatures wandered in and out of the lights—great, sleek sharks, pulsating sea hares and nudibranchs, schools of darting squids, brooding lionfish. Phosphorescent fishes near the surface flitted about like underwater fireflies. Jack ascended with her. When they broke the surface, Kate's delighted laughter made him laugh too. "I love you, Jack," she called. "Thank you for bringing me here."

Her voice receded. Jack couldn't find her. "Kate!" Panicked, he turned in the water. "Kate!" He plunged underneath the surface, saw her far, far below. He kicked harder, heading down into the endless blue. He had to catch her, had to or she would die. . . .

Jack jerked awake. No fish swarmed over his head, only millions of stars, so many it was as if a dam filled with glitter had collapsed and flooded over the black sky. Stiff and sore, he groaned as he rolled over on his side. He reached back to rub his neck. When his gloved hand struck the back of his helmet, he remembered where he was and that this was the day he was going to die.

He rocked his head back and forth, scrunching up his shoulders, trying to work some blood back into his neck and upper body. Then he looked at his watch. "Dammit!" He had wasted four hours on sleep, hours that were counting down to zero for him forever. He struggled upright, moving his arms and legs, trying to work out the kinks. He gave Houston a call, just to let them know he was awake.

"Jack, good morning!" Molly Peterson, an astronaut, identified herself. In the background Jack heard the sounds of excitement in the Mission Control. "Great news! We've made progress on your rescue!"

Peterson's chipper tone reinforced Jack's dark mood. "I don't need rescue, I need coffee," he growled. He hoped there was some in the food pack he'd stowed on the Rover. He crunched out of the shadow of the boulder and pulled down his helmet sunshade. He looked out across a bouldered plain. If there had been a moon crow flying in a line from where he stood, the fictitious bird would have taken a straight shot across that plain for a distance of about four kilometers. In the interest of time that was the way to go, but it would mean crossing new ground. He eyed a possible path.

Peterson was doing her best to ladle good cheer. "Do you want to hear our plan, Jack?"

"No."

"Okay," she chirped, "we'll get back to you."

"How's *Columbia*?" Jack asked irritably, but trying not to growl.

"Super!"

He'd always hated trite astronaut chitchat. "Listen, Houston. Concentrate on *Columbia*. Get 'em home!"

"We copy!" Peterson practically bubbled.

Jack grumbled and clumped to the Rover, changed his air pack and scrubber, drank water when, despite a desperate search, he failed to find any coffee in his pack, took a satisfying leak, and jumped on board his trusty steed. The sleep had been too long by half but it had at least left him refreshed. He scrutinized his maps, made his decision on the route, and headed south by southwest.

Columbia

"Sam, that's the way it's going to be!" Penny stated flatly.

"Penny, I can't let you do it," Sam declared just as flatly. "I'm giving you a direct order. Elsie-2 will go down unmanned."

Penny was at the airlock hatch, already in her coolant underwear and cloth communications helmet. "In case you haven't noticed, Sam," she said, "we aren't exactly very good at following orders up here. Now, listen to me. Jack's getting low on air and there's no guarantee he'll be able to reach the supplies in the Elsie-2. Someone might be needed to carry them to him. I also know how everything is supposed to go together. I have to go down."

Penny was angry and determined. She was going after her man and nobody, not Virgil or Tate or every fudpucker engineer in NASA, was going to stop her. They either needed to help or get out of her way. She climbed inside the airlock, started getting into her suit. Since there was only one MEC-designed coverlet for the EMU suit, and Jack was wearing it, Virgil had fashioned something made out of a parachute shroud to protect her suit joints from dust. He'd used duct tape to wrap the pieces around the suit and the result looked as homemade as it was. "I must look like the first hobo in space," Penny complained.

"You look fine," Virgil said encouragingly, watching her through the airlock porthole.

"Penny, don't do this," she heard Tate in her earpiece. "An unmanned Elsie-2 will give Jack a chance and you'll still be safe. That's the way he'd want it."

"I'm going," Penny snapped. "Just get that through your head. Drop out if you can't take it."

There was a moment of silence. "Nobody down here is going to drop out," Tate said.

"Fine," Penny said sharply.

"Give 'em hell, Penny," Virgil said, grinning at her through the porthole. He'd done his share of arguing with Penny about her decision, too, but had ultimately seen the wisdom of it. He'd then argued that he should be the one to go but Penny wasn't having any of it. It was her idea and she was going to do it.

Penny finished her prebreathe, depressurized the airlock, and crawled through the hatch. *Columbia* was turned tail-forward to her orbital flight vector, her cargo bay turned down toward the moon. The RMS arm was stowed and everything else battened down except the tether apparatus and the Elsie-2. The spare moon lander was attached to the ATESS tether spool by a cable made out of the EVA guide wire that ran along *Columbia*'s starboard sill. The Italian builders of the ATESS in the Huntsville POCC had done their calculations and determined that the tether could take the load.

Penny worked her way up the ATESS boom and into the Elsie-2. Being a spare, the sphere had none of the controls in the Elsie Jack had flown down. Virgil had done the best he could to prepare it for its mission, stowing inside everything that Houston had ordered including the cabling and connections he had worked on for hours, mostly cobbled together from middeck experiments. It had all been packed away along with additional oxygen tanks taken from *Columbia*'s own air-system spares. The airlock primary oxygen system valve had been disconnected and attached to one of the tanks to allow replenishment of Penny's backpack supply. All of the equipment was secured tightly with heavy straps already inside the dome. It had been a quick engineering job, but a thorough one.

Virgil had also strung a web of straps for Penny. She zipped up the airlock tunnel and pressurized the dome. The

internal pressure gauge indicated no leaks. She clipped herself into the straps and stabilized her feet into the footloops.
"Ready," she said.

Tate came back on-line. His voice was resigned but
deliberate. "Penny, we're about thirty minutes away from
release. We're going through both the ATESS and the
OMS prefiring checklist now."

"Roger," Penny replied stolidly.

Houston had determined that the shuttle's standard
OMS rocket engines would be used for the maneuver, the
Big Dog engine in her tail held in reserve. Mission Control
knew all there was to know about the OMS propulsion system but Big Dog was not trusted. Virgil had told Penny that
he thought this was a mistake, that a "Not Invented Here"
syndrome was affecting the NASA troops because they
didn't know anything about the Big Dog. A message on the
SAREX told them that the MEC people had fed their calculations to *Columbia*, were standing by with Big Dog just in
case the OMS crapped out. Sally Littleton also said their
eighteen-wheeler was headed for Huntsville, flank speed.
MEC Control had been offered a back room in the POCC.

Penny trusted Virgil to sort everything out with Houston.
She had other things to worry about. "What will be the
command for me to pull the handle?" she asked Tate, refer-
ring to the loop of cable over her head that Virgil had attached through a port in the top of the dome (the port
meant for a UHF antenna). The cable led to three cables
attached where the landing spheres would have gone. By
pulling the loop, Virgil's design would cause the pins to
come out at the attachment points and the cables would be
released.

"We'll say it three times," Tate explained. "Release,
release, release. Got it?"

"Got it," Penny muttered, eyeing the loop. She could
only hope the untested mechanism would work. If it didn't
work, or worked poorly, Penny knew she could be flung into

an unrecoverable orbit, or to the lunar surface miles away from the target. That worried but in no way deterred her. She had her expedition hat more firmly on than ever.

A half hour passed like an eye blink. "Thirty seconds, Penny," Tate said.

"I'm here," she replied, pushing her feet into her foot-loops as far as they would go. "Ready to rocket and roll!"

Tate came back. His voice was calm, assured. "After you're down, Penny, your suit comm won't be powerful enough by itself to talk to us or *Columbia*. You'll need line of sight with the antenna on board Jack's Elsie to get back in touch. So get out and get oriented as quickly as you can."

"Roger, Sam. Understood." Penny looked through one of the port windows, saw Virgil standing at the shuttle aft flight deck view ports. It was his job to control ATESS. She could hear the background chatter coming out of Huntsville to Virgil. The Italian science leader, Dr. Emilio Broglio, was enabled for voice air-to-ground communications. "We are with you, Mr. Judd," Penny heard him announce as tether deployment began.

Penny couldn't feel it but saw *Columbia* move away through the ring of portholes in the Elsie-2. Her job at this point, besides pulling the release ring at the right time, was just to hang on.

The Drop Scenario
Columbia

Virgil watched the tether smoothly unreel until Penny's dome disappeared into the texture of the moon. He was going by feel, watching the tether length on the ATESS screen, keeping an eye on the numbers from the satellite as it automatically used its cold gas thrusters to keep the line taut.

The ATESS tether was eighteen miles long. *Columbia* was in a nine-mile-high orbit, skimming along at nearly

3,700 miles per hour. Virgil was going to let the tether out eight and a half miles. Then, after *Columbia* slowed, and after a scan by Starbuck to determine the Elsie-2's position over the lunar surface, Virgil would let the tether out a bit more and Penny would pull the pin and drop away. The Elsie-2 would hit the lunar surface at under a hundred miles per hour, the Elsie-2's braced aluminum lattice absorbing the impact. It would be a rough landing, but survivable.

At least that was the scenario advanced by Houston.

The first trick, Virgil knew, was to slow *Columbia*'s huge mass enough to allow a decent chance for the dome's survival but not so slow that *Columbia* herself would crash. Everything had to be balanced: the inertia lost by *Columbia* when the OMS put on her brakes; the dynamics of a nine-mile tether; and the boost in velocity the shuttle would need to get back up to orbital speed before it crashed. Tate had reported those calculations had taken the Cray in Houston more than several minutes to compute. It was going to be a near thing but it was, in NASA parlance, *doable*.

Doable. Virgil shook his head. He guessed it was *doable* for pigs to sprout wings and fly around the barnyard too. *Probable*, that was the question. . . .

SMC

Sam realized he was happy in his job for the first time in years. He had a free hand. The atmosphere in his Shuttle Mission Control reflected his electric mood, his controllers eagerly at their consoles. Huntsville had the show to control the tether, but Houston would control the orbital maneuvering system, the OMS, *Columbia*'s internal rocket engines. Tate got on the line with Starbuck at Farside Control. The word there was go, all the way. Starbuck reported he had a good view of both the ATESS satellite on the end of the tether and the lunar terrain underneath. He had plugged into the signal from *Columbia*'s Ku-band radar and between his own Farside data and *Columbia*'s, he could calculate the fluctuating distances to within at least a hundred feet.

A cheer went up from Tate's Turds when a picture appeared on their monitors, courtesy of Farside. There'd been no time to write a good virtual image program but Starbuck was giving Houston a fair representation. On the screen was a circle (Penny's dome) attached to a vertical line (the tether). A horizontal line beneath the circle represented the moon's surface. As Sam watched, the vertical line grew longer, the circle moving closer to the horizontal line. The horizontal line rose and fell as the terrain *Columbia* was passing over varied. In the upper right corner a six-digit number representing the meters between the dome and the lunar surface changed every half second. Sam thought Starbuck's work was crude but effective, amazing really considering the short time he'd had to develop the code. The truth was, Sam didn't see how Houston would've had a ghost of a chance of rescuing Medaris without Starbuck. But there he was, a miracle. He said a silent prayer that the miracles would keep coming.

There were two numbers Starbuck was providing that Tate's controllers were looking for: fifty meters for the release altitude, and two hundred for the velocity in miles per hour.

"Sam, we're not going to make it," the POD in Huntsville announced. "Dr. Broglio and Virgil are having trouble unreeling the tether. They've had to slow down the rate."

Sam grimaced. This was going to mean another lunar go-around. He called Penny, explained it to her.

"Okay, Sam," Penny replied. "I'll hang around."

Sam grinned at her joke. She was hanging, all right, from the shuttle toward the moon, on about six miles of pencil-thin tether.

With the extra time required for another orbit Sam made a decision concerning the media. The networks and the cable news were screaming for access, so he opened up the internal NASA Select television system. People around the world began to camp out in front of their television sets just to watch the mission controllers in Houston and Huntsville at work. No live television was coming from the moon, but cartoonists and model makers hired by the networks were getting rich.

Elsie-2

Penny hung in her straps, teeth chattering. She was freezing. She had turned down the suit coolant system but it didn't help.

"How's it going, Penny?" Sam asked.

"I'm cold," she admitted. "Anything from Jack?"

"Nothing," he answered. "We've been trying to raise him but no joy. I think he must have turned us off. Would he do that?"

"Yes. He can get arbitrary." Penny swore to herself. *Jack Medaris, I'd like to wring your neck!*

Montana (4)
The Perlman Plant

Perlman looked at the surveillance monitor with satisfaction. The crater that had been blasted in an attempt to open up the sand tunnel entry had turned into a huge, muddy pond from the water he and Charlie had pumped up into the ground beneath it. The men in black fatigues stood around the crater, pondering it. One of them jumped back when the edge started to crumble beneath him, and Perlman laughed. "You son of a bitch!" he said. "Serves you right!"

Charlie padded in behind him. "Doc, they're up to something again. I heard drilling topside and looks like they punched through. Ain't a big hole—it'd take a year of drilling to make one big enough for a man—but looks like they're threading something through it. You better come see."

Perlman swiveled around, grabbed his cane, and followed Charlie through the blast door, out into the concrete corridor. He looked nervously overhead. There was a lot of water sitting above them. Charlie saw his look. "Don't worry, Doc. This tunnel will hold the weight. It was built for compression in case of a direct atom bomb hit."

"If you say so, Charlie," Perlman muttered, hurrying as fast as his hip would allow.

They stopped at the end of the corridor, next to the elevator shaft. Charlie pointed to the floor in front of the door of the elevator. A spiral of steel lay there, apparently having fallen from a drilled hole far above. A scraping noise attracted Perlman's attention. He looked up at the elevator support structure and spotted a dangling wire, a black object attached to it, coming down at them. "I think we'd better get back to the plant, Charlie," he said nervously.

Charlie was studying the object. "Too small to do much if it's an explosive, Doc. Ah, I can see it now. It's a speaker, I think."

Perlman was glad Charlie had such good eyes because he still couldn't make out the object. A screech of feedback coming from it, however, convinced him Charlie was right. "Propaganda time, I think, Charlie. Warnings and threats."

"Yes, sir."

The speaker squawked, followed by a voice. "Dr. Perlman, the President of the United States orders you to vacate this site immediately. If you don't, we will have no recourse but to blast our way in. We cannot be responsible for your safety if that happens."

Perlman frowned. It seemed to him they'd already tried to blast their way in, down through the sand chute. What other way was there? Through the blast doors? How big a detonation would that take from the outside? The blast doors were six feet thick, built of tempered steel and re-inforced concrete. It would have to be a blast so huge, he thought, it would probably kill him and Charlie in the process, probably wreck the entire place, for that matter, all by itself.

Perlman shuddered. *They wouldn't do that, would they?*

He stared upward, looking at the dangling speaker. It sat mute, as if awaiting an answer. There was probably a receiver/transmitter in it. "What do you think, Charlie?" he whispered.

"We done okay not talking to the bastards so far, Doc. Don't see no reason to start now."

Perlman marveled at the machinist. He was starting to believe, even though he knew the best scientists in the entire world, that Charlie Bowman was the smartest man he'd ever met. A genius indeed!

The Letter
Taurus-Littrow

Jack was there. He'd gotten lost twice and nearly run into three deep craters, but he'd made it—Shorty Crater at last. To save Rover power he stopped at the crater's base and trudged up the slope. At the top he looked across the crater, estimating it to be a little over one hundred meters in diameter and perhaps fifty meters deep, a football stadium on the moon. Its walls were steep, much too vertical for someone in a spacesuit to climb out, so he kept his distance from the rim.

Apollo boot-prints led around to the northwest and stopped at a work site. Jack spotted the telltale hole left from a drive tube and walked to it. There, about three feet away, lying serenely, was the canister tube he'd wondered about practically from the day he had met Kate. Jack slowly knelt and picked it up. His heart pounded in his ears, as if he had found and touched a holy relic. He ran his glove down its side, savoring the moment so long in coming. The canister had a cleverly engineered latch made for the heavy gloved hands of an astronaut. The initials "K.S." were just below the latch—Katrina Suttner. He gently pushed the latch and it sprang open. He extracted what was inside—a sheet of notebook paper—and held it up to his helmet. There was her message, just as she had told him it would be, written in a girlish hand he still recognized as hers, sent to the moon by her adoring parents and uncles and the great Dr. Wernher von Braun himself. It was her message across space and time to him:

To my future husband—
My name is Katrina Suttner and I am ten years old.
But you know that. You know all the things I do
not.
I wonder—
Will you find this and bring it back to me?
Or will our brave astronauts of the future return it?
Or will I be the one to carry home my message to
you?
And I wonder—
Will you be handsome?
Will you be kind?
Will you be smart?
Will you always take care of me?
Will you always love me as I will love you, always
and forever?

A tear found its way down his cheek. "Yes," he whispered to her. "Yes."

The Elsie-2 Release
SMC

On the next flyby the word from Huntsville was go. The OMS boys also gave Sam the high sign. The OMS would be fired remotely from Houston, Virgil too engrossed in the ATESS to do it from *Columbia*. As planned, Starbuck would make the release call to Penny.

Sam stood. He simply could not stay seated. He hadn't felt such pride since *Apollo. No, damn it.* He felt more pride now. Those damn yuppies in the trenches were performing magnificently. No matter what happened, NASA was at least going out in grand style. Impulsively, he picked up the telephone and called his wife. When she answered, he said what he should have said long ago. "Geraldine, life hasn't been easy for you, I know. Me gone all the time over here, pulling these long missions, then all those hours of sims while you were at home with the kids. How have you ever put up with me? I can't figure it."

Geraldine laughed. "Well, it's simple, Sam. Kinda goes like this. From the moment we met, I have always loved you."

A crooked smile on his weathered face, Sam slowly hung up. His wife loved him. It shouldn't have been a revelation and it wasn't, not really. What it was was a goldurned *miracle* and so very nice to hear.

Low Lunar Orbit

Columbia came batting over the rim, gravity flinging it down the front side of the moon along what the mission controllers were calling the Taurus-Littrow corridor. Penny's dome swung a thousand feet above the surface. As the highlands approached, the distance began to decrease, not because the tether was being let out but because the terrain was rising. If all went according to plan, a small circular lava bed named Mare Crisium would come into view just moments before the landing site. Past that was the big circular Mare Serenatis, the dry sea that contained the landing site of the *Challenger* Lem.

SMC

"*Ignition!*" Sam cried.

Columbia poured out her inertia as her OMS fired for one minute, two minutes, then three minutes. Her velocity dropped to two hundred miles per hour. Her RCS jets fired, yawing her one hundred and eighty degrees. Gravity exerted its inevitable influence. *Columbia* began to fall. When the Elsie-2 dropped below nine miles altitude, the OMS fired again to lift it back up. It didn't work. *Columbia* kept falling.

"She's not holding!" one of Tate's Turds yelled. "OMS firing levels under the call."

"Huntsville?" Sam called smoothly. "Your MEC boys ready?"

"We got it," the POD answered. From the MEC back room Sally Littleton sent the command to Big Dog. It fired abruptly.

"Whooee!" Virgil called down. "That knocked me right out of my footloops!"

Columbia stopped her fall and held steady. But it was only a matter of moments before even Big Dog couldn't hold nearly one hundred tons in level flight at two hundred miles an hour, nine miles above the moon.

Farside Control

Mare Crisium was suddenly on Starbuck's screen and the computer blinking its demand. The small Mare had surprised him. "Release, release, release!" he screamed into his mike, a fraction of a second late.

The Elsie-2

Penny heard the call and pulled with all her strength. She felt two pins come loose but the third stuck. As the Elsie-2 dropped away, she kept pulling. Then she felt the cable give way and the lander go into a spin, probably imparted by the snagged pin. Penny was in the center, her feet and arms pulled outwardly by centrifugal force. She was going down and she was out of control.

The AG Visits the Veep
Vice President's Residence

When the vice president of the United States went to his residential office after lunch, he was surprised to find the attorney general waiting for him. "I just got the word somebody hired a private little army up in Montana to smoke out some sort of secret project. They used federal money to do it too. That's so illegal, it's not even funny. I've got FBI agents on the way to stop it."

Vanderheld eased into his chair. "How are you, Tammy? Or has common civility died since we last talked?"

Hawthorne sat up, smoothed her dress. She had been slumped into the chair as if somebody had poured her there. "Common civility doesn't attack private property, Mr. Vice President. You'll have to excuse me if I've got my panties in a wad. This outfit did a couple of other things too. Did you know they've shut down the space center in Houston?"

"Your intelligence is dated. Mission Control's back up. I ordered it so."

She nodded. "Have you ever heard of Puckett Security Systems, sir?"

Vanderheld looked thoughtful. "No. I can't say that I have."

"Not surprising. It's the kind of outfit that mostly operates offshore, an ass-kicker bunch for the oil companies."

Vanderheld felt very tired and old. "I see."

The AG scuffled her feet on the rug, looked down at her lap. She seemed to be debating something with herself. The veep waited patiently. At length she raised her plain face. As usual she had forgotten her makeup. "I had some visitors yesterday in my office," she said. "Jones and Rowe, couple of NASA comptrollers. You know them?"

The veep folded his hands on his desk. "No."

The AG looked dubious. "They came in on their own. They'd been ordered to do something that didn't seem right to them. They told me they got sent an order that opened up the floodgates on the Space Station account, about a hundred million dollars' worth. All that money's gone, vanished. Some of it went down to Belize, a private account down there. We saw a bunch of it heading over to Russia into the Russian Space Agency account, but it was after the fact. We couldn't stop either transaction. On paper it was all legal."

Vanderheld looked at the picture on the wall above Hawthorne's head. It was a painting of Harry Truman holding his fedora in his hands, standing in front of the Washington Monument. Truman was looking into the distance and slightly up, as if envisioning the future. That's what the future was supposed to be—always in the distance, slightly up. It was never supposed to be here and now and straight up. "Why don't you ask the comptrollers who sent them this order?" he asked placidly.

Hawthorne shook her head. "Not that simple, I'm afraid. The order came in to them electronically from NASA Houston. It looked like the JSC director had authorized it. They didn't know at the time Bonner was killed in that car wreck, so they let it go. All the charge numbers were correct, all the codes. Jones and Rowe had no reason to question it except it seemed damn strange to be spending that money on the Space Station during this shuttle crisis. Then they heard about Bonner and started to scratch their heads."

Vanderheld nodded. "Yes. I can understand why they might have questions."

Hawthorne crossed her legs, wiggling her foot. She was

wearing white sneakers. "You ever hear of an outfit called the January Group?"

Vanderheld tilted his head. "No."

She nodded. "Yeah, I didn't think so either. I looked it up, didn't see it on your list of memberships in *Who's Who*."

"I'm not a member," Vanderheld said.

Hawthorne pursed her lips. "Well, Mr. Vice President, from what I can tell, it's not the kind of outfit you pay dues to every year, get a slick magazine, anything like that. The January Group just kind of popped up on my radar screen. You know how? You'll like this, sir. You know the Russian breeder reactor that pooped radioactive crap all over Europe? Well, turns out the KGB, or whatever the hell they call it these days, decided somebody sabotaged that little old reactor. They asked us to help because they thought it was this January Group. We started looking into this outfit. It's big, sir, really big. The Russians supplied us with a long list of members."

Vanderheld sat stiffly. "I'm no longer part of the January Group."

"Why not, sir?"

"Because it changed," Vanderheld said quietly. "It used to exist to insure that at least some tranquillity remained in the world, and to end wars by ending want. And competition."

"Don't think I heard that last one, sir."

"And *competition!*" Vanderheld spat. "The January Group was dedicated to an orderly exploitation of the earth's resources for the benefit of all mankind."

"How'd it get its name?"

Vanderheld shrugged. "It's named after Janus, the two-faced god who looks forward and back at the same time. It also happened to be organized in the appropriate month."

"So you good old boys just got together every so often and figured out how things were going to run across the world as far as who did what with what? What did you have to do to be a member? Have some real clout, right? Be a senator or the president of an oil company? You'd sit there at one of your little meetings, look out across the broad old planet, and figure out how things were going to be run, I guess. Oil was your energy of choice, right? Anything else raise its head like solar energy, or nuclear, you'd make sure it failed, one way or the other, huh?"

"It wasn't quite like that. The nuclear energy industry did themselves in. It needed no help from us."

"But you'd make sure of that, wouldn't you, sir? You started out being all noble and trying to help your fellow-man but then you just ended up being in the pocket of the oil outfits, didn't you? You got used to their millions for your campaigns, all the little perks you got. And then, every so often, a million ended up in your bank account overseas, didn't it?"

"I never took a penny!" Vanderheld raged. "Twenty years ago I walked away from them." He shook his head. "That was when the drug cartels started to come in. They were blatant. They wanted stability above all else—not for peace, or to assist the poor, but so they would have a world they knew was safe for their narcotics. They didn't want anything to change."

"You know what else I've learned, sir? This came from your researcher, Shirley Grafton." At his surprised look she nodded. "She thought there was something strange going on, sent her information to me the same time she gave it to you, I guess. We already knew some things. Her research filled in pretty much everything. Did you know that the January Group funded an energy outfit in Montana? Dr. Perlman's the name. Maybe you've heard of him. Funny thing is we think the January Group's also behind this paramilitary outfit that's been trying to blow up Perlman's plant. Now, that's a mystery."

"Typical of them." Vanderheld shrugged. "They like to carry energy technology research as far as it will go, then pull back before it goes commercial. That way they'll have the technology when and if they need it. They know that someday we'll run out of oil. They want to be ready, be in the catbird seat when we do, bring it on nice and slow so the planet's not disrupted."

"Perlman got ahead of their curve," Hawthorne said.

Vanderheld nodded. "Something like that."

"Or maybe they're squabbling. What do you think, sir? Maybe there's an internal struggle going on? Some of these January folks want Perlman to succeed; others want him and the folks out at the moon dead. Got an opinion on that?"

"No."

Hawthorne peered at Vanderheld through her big thick glasses. "Who else could have sent those codes to the NASA comptrollers, sir, if it wasn't Bonner?" When he didn't answer, she stood up, walked to the window, looked out on Washington, the people going about their business, unaware of the struggle within their government. "Is the President a member of the January Group?"

"No."

"Who, then?"

Vanderheld shook his head. "Bernie Sykes."

Hawthorne turned. "How long has he been blackmailing you, Mr. Vice President?"

"Sykes?" Vanderheld shrugged. "It wasn't always him. Lots of Bernies over the years."

"What did they have you do?"

"Cajole this official or that. Argue for this bill or that. Whatever they wanted."

Hawthorne sat back down. "So you're a victim."

Vanderheld nodded. "I've done my best to resist them for the last twenty years. I brought up Mission Control in Houston when I realized it was probably them manipulating events. And, yes, I think there's an internal struggle. The old

Janists want to keep things as they are. The new ones are after something different."

"It's going to be nasty if I bring any of this out."

Vanderheld looked down, showing his shame. "Yes, I know. What are you going to do?"

Hawthorne shrugged. "Pursue it to the ends of the earth. What did you think?"

Vanderheld nodded. "I hoped you'd leave me out of it. I've tried to do my best."

"You let evil happen by saying nothing."

"I wasn't a Nazi or a Communist, Tammy. I wanted the best for the world."

"Sir, at least the Nazis and Commies were out front with what they wanted to do. You January guys did everything the sneak way. That ain't right."

Vanderheld twisted in his chair, let her see his humiliation. "But I just told you I'm no longer a member."

Hawthorne opened her briefcase, took out a sheath of papers, slid them across the desk to the vice president. He looked at them quizzically. "Bernie Sykes's deposition. We corralled him in Iraq. He opened up like a ripe cantaloupe after somebody tried to kill him in his hotel room. Lucky the Secret Service was around."

The vice president stared at the document. "Any surprises?"

"One. We found out the January Group knew about the *Columbia* hijacking well in advance. They weren't too worried about it, though. Sykes says he was told to do what he could to stop it but it was bound to fail, anyway. He said they had decided it was useful, that they'd use the incident to allow you to shut the entire shuttle program down. Put space out of reach forever—or at least until you wanted it."

"Me?" The vice president visibly gulped.

"Sykes says you were the one who's been calling the shots to him. Says you were blackmailing him, not the other way around. Had to do with some misappropriated White

House funds for his mistress. And I believe him, despite all your passionate denials. You are a very accomplished liar, sir. You know what I think? I bet you're vice president because those old January boys figured they owed you one after all these years of service. I guess that included shutting down old *Apollo*, too, didn't it, sir? You claimed everybody was bored with it, cost too much money, money that was needed for the poor, for education, all the usual eyewash. I've talked to Shirley Grafton. She helped me figure it out. The real reason was that stuff they found up there, that helium-3. The fat cats in the oil business knew what the hell that stuff could do to them."

"You have no proof of any of this, Tammy. It's all conjecture."

"Besides Sykes, I have another witness."

Vanderheld's eyes were twinkling with amusement. "Guess you might as well tell me who it is."

"Bonner's not dead. Somebody doped him up and then drove him in his Porsche like the devil on fire through half of Texas, attracting the cops. When they got out of sight of the County Mounties, they stopped, put him in the driver's seat, aimed the Porsche for the river, and wedged the accelerator wide open. Pretty slick. Only trouble was, they didn't quite have Bonner's seat belt attached. He got thrown out and lived. Pretty banged up but he's going to be able to testify that you *personally* sent the contractor—Panar Chemical Systems—to him that provided the gas canister that blew up in orbit. Turns out when we looked it up, it was just another name for Puckett Security Services. And we've been watching PSS, sir, ever since it tried to burn out Medaris down in Cedar Key. The local cop down there was a classmate of Hennessey at the FBI Academy and alerted him about it. It's a slippery outfit, and it's been a step ahead of us, but we've sorted it out, little by little. The latest is it murdered a group of young computer engineers in California. But I think you know all that."

Vanderheld let a smile play on his lips. "I guess this is where I jump up and make a run for it. Too bad I'm too old or I'd give you a helluva chase."

"No, you wouldn't, sir," Hawthorne said. "You're a coward and a liar. If you were younger, you'd just try to lie your way out of it. I guess that's what you'll do now. It's going to be your word against Sykes and Bonner. Puckett, when and if we find him, probably won't talk, too much of a pro for that. You're a world-class liar, sir. You might get out of this yet."

Vanderheld rubbed his chin. He was still smiling. "No. It's tempting but not this time. And I'll tell you why."

Hawthorne listened intently. "Well, I'll be damned," she said quietly but with enthusiasm. "God has Her ways, don't She?"

In Shorty Crater
Taurus-Littrow

Jack wandered over to a small boulder and leaned against it. He held the flimsy paper in front of his faceplate so that the big rock shaded it from the harsh sunlight. He was smiling. Every word was a jewel, each precious to consider.

You know so much.
You know how we met.
You know when we first kissed.
You know when you first said you loved me
And when I first said it back.
But I know something, even now
that I wonder if you know even then.
It is that I will always love you
And that I will always be with you
Across space and time.
You see, didn't I send you a message all the way to
the moon?

Love, love, love—
Katrina Suttner (daughter of Dr. Gerhard Suttner,
Huntsville, Alabama, USA)

Jack read the letter again, then rolled it up and put it back in its canister. He had no way to wipe the tears from his eyes. He turned his head, tried to put his eyes into the flow of air coming up around his neck ring. "Kate," he whispered. *Didn't I send you a message all the way to the moon?* "You did. Thank you." He leaned against the boulder, prepared to breathe the last of the oxygen he had remaining.

Somewhere Near the Moon

Penny had no sensation of falling but she could see the moon was rushing up to meet her Elsie-2. When the dome hit, the aluminum geodesic frame supporting the covering fabric bent violently inward. Penny was thrown against her web of supporting straps, her chest slammed painfully against the hard upper torso of her suit. Then the frame twanged like a plucked sitar string and she could feel liftoff, the Elsie-2 bouncing like a huge beach ball off a sand-packed beach.

Penny had no idea where the dome was going. All she felt was a confusing series of accelerations in nearly every direction, almost at the same moment. Her restraint straps jerked her, the hard places in her suit beating her body. She may have screamed, she wasn't certain, but her breathing came hard and fast at each impact. Then, for a moment, the Elsie-2 seemed to be moving smoothly, although still rotating. Then everything stopped. Penny gasped out thanks in the continuous prayer she realized she'd been chanting. And then the rotation began again. She'd apparently rolled up a hill, now was rolling back down it. "Oh, please, no!" She sobbed.

The dome began to accelerate again. Penny was spun,

her blood being pushed into her head and her feet. The sudden fluid shift made her stomach rebel but she fought the rising vomit. To throw up in the suit would be disastrous. Then the dome hit something, she wasn't sure what it was, but its geodesic frame flexed. With a *twang* the dome stopped spinning, then there was another flex of the frame and Penny guessed the dome had bounced off the surface again. She held her breath, hoping it was over. But it wasn't to be. The spin-up began again.

Taurus-Littrow

Nothing that had ever happened in his life had prepared Jack for the big white beach ball that suddenly fell out of the black lunar sky into Shorty Crater. It rolled across the crater, halfway up its far side, rolled back, wandered in a small circle, and stopped. Startled, he let the canister slip out of his gloves. He tried to catch it, juggled it momentarily, and then watched it fall on the edge of the crater, teeter momentarily, then tumble over, sliding halfway to the bottom, a little shelf of rock holding it.

Astonished, he clumped to the crater lip and looked at the dome. It was moving as if someone or something inside was trying to get out. He walked around until he could see the hatch. The zipper started to move, the flap fell open, and a helmet protruded from the opening. Someone in an EMU suit, wrapped improbably in what looked like parachute silk and duct tape, crawled out on gloves and knees. Jack turned on his suit-to-suit comm channel just in time to hear the call. "Houston," Penny said, "the High Eagle has landed."

"They can't hear you, Penny," Jack said. "You're in the bottom of a crater."

He watched her lift her head at the sound of his voice. "Jack?"

"Look up." He sighed. "You'll see me just to your left.

I'm not even going to ask what the hell you're doing here. Yes, I am. *What the hell are you doing here?*"

Shielding her eyes with her glove, she turned until she faced him. "Hey, Jack. Nice to see you too. I came down here to save your butt. What do you think?"

"Pull your sunshade down," he groused. "Do you think you can crawl out of there?"

"Maybe." Penny started to walk toward him, lost her balance, and fell to her knees.

"Take it easy. You've got to get the feel of it and plan each step."

"Okay." Penny struggled to her feet, shuffled over to the crater wall. She took two steps and slid back down. The soil of the wall was a mixture of pebbles and dust, the dust acting like a lubricant. "It's not going to be easy," she said, puffing. "And I've got a lot of stuff in the dome we need."

Jack took a moment, formed a plan. "Save your air, Penny. You're not going to be able to climb out of there. Did you bring a rope with you?"

"There's a lot of straps inside the Elsie. Would they do?"

"Go get them."

Penny crawled back inside the dome, brought out a bundle of straps and what looked to be an oxygen tank. "How's your air?" she asked.

"I'm in good shape," Jack lied. "Just take it slow and easy."

"What do you want me to do?"

"Tie enough of the straps together to throw one end to me."

Penny knotted three straps together, twirled one of the buckled ends, and threw it. It landed short of the crater lip. She pulled it back and tried again. Her second attempt was no better.

"It's too light," Jack observed. "Tie something heavy on it."

Penny went back inside the dome and pushed out two

aluminum boxes. She opened one of them and Jack could see it was a toolbox. She selected a wrench and tied it to the strap.

Jack coached her. "Hold the strap about a foot below your waist, Penny. Rotate several times back and forth until you're ready and then with all your might whip around and fling your arm up and let go of the strap."

She rotated and flung. The wrench and the strap landed about four feet beneath the rim.

"Good woman," he said. "Now wait." Jack crunched down the crater rim to the Rover, and grabbed a scoop with a telescoping handle from one of its stowage boxes. He held the scoop over the crater lip and tried to use it to drag the wrench up. As soon as the scoop touched it, it slipped down out of reach, taking the attached strap with it. "Dammit! You're going to have throw it again."

Penny pulled the strap back down, repeated her fling of the wrench. This time it landed only about a foot beneath the rim. Jack used the scoop again. "Got it!" he cheered. He jammed the wrench into the soil. "Wait, I'm going to go get the Rover."

"I'm not going anywhere." Penny sighed, leaning on the dome.

Jack made a quick Rover check. Battery power was down seventy percent. To get some momentum going he drove it away from the crater and then turned around. He was aimed at the rim. He goosed the Rover's throttle, the wire wheels dug in, and the Rover shot forward, lunging up the slope. Momentum carried it all the way to the top. Jack got out, picked up the strap, untied the wrench, and tied the strap onto the pole that held the Rover's moribund television camera.

"Penny," Jack called. "Grab the strap. I'm going to pull you up."

She tied on the toolkit and the other aluminum box.

"These need to go up first." She puffed. "They're the reason I'm here."

"How did you get down here, anyway?" Jack asked, and then made a guess. "You used the tether as a skyhook!"

"Bingo. Film at eleven. Now, pull these boxes up. They contain what we need to get back to *Columbia*."

The boxes came up with a bundle of extra straps and two oxygen tanks. He threw the strap back down to her. "Tie yourself off. Be careful. Don't struggle. Just lean back and walk on out. I'll hold you."

Penny started up. Her boots, without the extra traction of Jack's tire tread overbooties, slipped and she fell twice. Each time Jack kept the strap taut for her. At the rim she made a churning run and fell against him. Their helmets touched. "Thanks for pulling me out," she breathed.

"I had to," he said. "You had the oxygen."

She started to tell him the NASA plan. He listened, then said, "I'm going to collect the thirty kilos of fire beads according to our contract. And there's something I dropped. I'm going to go down and get it." He pointed to the edge of the crater.

Penny followed his hand, looked over the edge, and saw the canister. She clumsily turned back to him. "Is it what you came after?" When he nodded, Penny said, "Medaris, come on. We don't have time. We've got a lot to do to get out of here."

He led her to a boulder, something to shade her and to lean on. "Stay out of the way."

Her eyes widened at what she perceived an insult. "Go to hell."

He patted her shoulder. "I didn't mean that the way it sounded. I'm sorry."

She shrugged, subsided. "I know, Jack."

He moved the Rover to Schmitt's orange soil and used the long-handled scoop to fill the sample bag he had brought with him. If the calculations on earth had been correct, a full bag would be in the range of the needed thirty kilos, or more than sixty earth pounds. It would weigh around ten pounds on the moon.

When Jack finished filling the sample bag, he set it on a boulder and then clumped over to look down at the canister holding Kate's letter. It was below the orange soil, which consisted of tiny red and orange glass beads. Beneath them, Jack knew, there was another layer of beads, black and even smaller. They were, in effect, miniature ball-bearings. He'd have to be careful.

Jack tied the strap connected to the Rover around his waist and backed over the rim. The orange soil slid under his feet, sending a wave of pebbles cascading down the slope. He moved to one side, to keep the slides from hitting the canister.

Then the glass beads, under the weight of the Rover and the pounding from Jack's boots, gave way.

He looked up and saw the rim of the crater suddenly seem to wash toward him. Behind it came the Rover, surfing on a wave of orange and black soil. It just missed him and kept going down. The strap tied around his waist went taut and jerked him off the wall. His feet flew into the air and he landed on his backpack and slid all the way to the crater floor.

Penny carefully crawled to the new rim formed by the collapse of the orange soil. Below, she could see the Rover, upside down, its wheels the only thing protruding from a pile of dirt. Jack was lying on his back beside the pile, his legs covered. "Jack, are you okay?"

He was motionless for a moment, then she saw his hands move to push himself up to a sitting position. He raised the sunscreen on his helmet. She waved at him. "Throw me down the scoop, Penny. I'll need to dig myself out. Did you see where the canister went?"

She thought for a moment to lie to him but she didn't. She crawled around the rim, looked for it. She couldn't see it. "Maybe it's under the Rover," she told him, and then looked around until she found the sample bag and the scoop. She aimed and tossed the scoop to him. It landed within reach. Jack dug around his legs until he had uncovered them enough to stand.

Penny watched him look at the slide. She knew what he was thinking. "Jack, the canister's gone. Come on," she begged. "We're almost out of time."

He ignored her and started digging, but digging into the loose orange soil was like trying to scoop a hole out of water. Penny finally tied the wrench to another long strap and threw it down to him. "Jack, please. Please come up."

She watched as Jack knelt, jammed his glove into the dirt. He lifted a handful. It poured like a black waterfall through his fingers.

The Vice President Stands Before the Nation
The Senate

The vice president was late. The Senate was in full session, waiting for Vanderheld to gavel them into order for the WET vote. Some senators had brought in small television sets to keep track of the events on the moon. Just like the entire country, they were switching between two events. CNN and Fox Cable stuck with the moon story. C-SPAN1 and CNBC went with the President's historic trip to Iraq for the signing of the Iraqi-Iranian peace treaty. The Senate's vote on the World Energy Treaty was on C-SPAN2. The networks tried to work everything, bouncing back and forth.

Fox reported that the risky rescue attempt had begun on the moon but no word had come back yet as to the success of the landing of what was being called the Skyhook Scenario. Mission Control in Houston had advised the media that no inference could be drawn from the silence from the moon. CNN showed graphic cartoons of the planned rescue.

One question kept being asked by the correspondents but no answers were provided: Why had *Columbia* gone to the moon? The answer came back when *The Washington Post* and *Washington Times* simultaneously broke the story, the details leaked by "a source inside the President's cabinet." MOONWALKERS TO PICK UP SECRET FUEL ON MOON! the *Times* headlined. And in subtitles, *Fuel of the future, researchers say*. The *Post* went with MOON MISSION FOR ENERGY. Both articles outlined the story of fusion power and helium-3.

There was a buzz in the Senate. The president pro tem gaveled the chamber to silence and then steadied the microphone in front of him and cleared his throat. Standing beside him was the attorney general of the United States. The president pro tem introduced her, recognizing that it was highly irregular for the AG to address the Senate. "I believe this is pertinent to the question at hand, however. If we could have your attention."

Hawthorne stepped to the mike. Although the Senate chamber was nearly cold with air-conditioning, she felt hot. Sweat trickled down her cheeks and her back. "In every nation's life," she began, her voice cracking, betraying her nerves that were stretched nearly to the breaking point, "there come those moments when choices have to be made." She stopped, took a drink of water, screwed up her courage. "Usually such choices are based on stark reason." She fought to eliminate the quiver in her voice. "At other times emotion, hope, and daring are the basis for our national choices. The *Apollo* program was not based on logic but was the fulfillment of a dream. So was the opening of the western frontier by Lewis and Clark, the purchase of Alaska, our expeditions to the South Pole, the world's first underwater circumnavigation of the globe . . . these things were done by this country not because they were necessarily logical and certainly not because they were safe, or easy, or painless. They were done in the spirit of adventure and for the advancement of the world."

She stopped for another drink of water. Her voice had steadied. There was utter silence in the assembly. "Now we have the World Energy Treaty. The President, as you know, has asked that it be approved by this great body, made into law. He asked the vice president to shepherd it through, see that it was approved. But I must tell you that the vice president has resigned. The President, against my advice, has nominated me for that position."

There was a startled grumble from the senators that rose in volume. Hawthorne waited until it subsided, began again. "I have had time in recent days to study this treaty and I believe that it would ultimately restrict our freedom as a country and a people. It would substitute a form of cooperation that smacks to me of the cooperation that occurs between slave and master, the American people the slave to the masters of oil, the masters of trade, the masters of economic manipulation. I have heard the argument that cooperation is always desirable. But isn't *competition* more the American way? Isn't it through competition that great strides are taken? Isn't competition, in fact, the driving impulse of the human race, the inner stirring that makes us creative and daring? I believe that it is."

Hawthorne pointed skyward. "I think I see in the heavens tonight signs that we must become competitive again. There is a new gold in the sky, a gold for which we must make our rightful claim. We can pass this agreement and gain energy and perhaps economic stability for the next fifty years, while bowing to a world organization that will control our destiny as a nation. Comfort or independence, that seems to be the choice. My choice is for independence. That is why tonight I have decided, as acting vice president, to ask the sponsoring senators of WET to withdraw this bill from the floor of the Senate."

A rolling wave of voices seemed to rise up from the old chamber. The new acting vice president of the United States braced herself against it.

The *Challenger* Scenario
Taurus-Littrow

Jack and Penny staggered across the dusty, boulder-strewn valley, dragging the priceless dirt from Shorty, two boxes of equipment, and two oxygen bottles in a web of straps, following the old tracks of the Rover back to the *Challenger* Lem. It was not easy going, especially for Penny. Jack, appreciative that she hadn't blamed him for losing the Rover, stopped long enough to screw several sheet-metal screws from the toolbox into the bottom of her boots for traction. That helped but she was already exhausted.

It took three hours to reach the Lem. Beside one of its landing pads Penny dropped to her knees and then rolled over on her back and just sucked air. Jack checked her readouts and turned on her emergency oxygen supply. All the O_2 he had brought was buried with the Rover. The two bottles Penny had with her was all there was. He used one to refill her backpack.

He checked in with Houston. "Do you understand what you need to do, Jack?" Sam asked.

"Yeah, sure," he replied grimly. Jack had studied the plan and gave it about a one in ten trillion chance of working. Still, it was all there was to do. He dropped to his knees, and then crawled under the Lem platform, working his way underneath until he could see the descent engine oxidizer tank. He put his helmet against it and whacked it with the handle of a wrench. The tank rang hollowly, as he'd expected. In the intervening decades the oxidizer surely had evaporated through minute leaks. He put his shoulder to the tank and pushed it and was surprised to hear a sloshing sound. He did the same with the fuel tank. More sloshing. "What do you know?" he muttered. "Houston, there's liquid in both tanks. I can't tell how much."

Sam came back immediately. "Outstanding, Jack. Our records show *Challenger* made a quick descent. The descent stage should have at least half its fuel left."

"Okay, now what?"

"Start the wiring harness immediately."

Jack crawled out from underneath and picked up the toolkit and the other aluminum box Penny had brought with her. He placed them on top of the Lem and then used the ladder that went up one of the legs to climb up on it. The platform, constructed of sheets of bonded aluminum, gave a little under his weight but held. He searched out the electronic port used to command the descent engine. He found it scorched, no doubt from the ascent engine when the crew module had blasted off, but it seemed intact. He studied the plug Virgil had constructed and inserted it into the port, careful to line up the tiny pins. Then he used duct tape to hold it in place. He got out the circuit tester. "Joy," he said. "The plug works."

"Wonderful, Jack," Sam immediately responded.

Jack kept working according to the procedures Penny had brought with her, setting up the rest of the rig, ending up with the restraint straps.

"You have ten minutes to launch," Sam called, his voice calm, almost nonchalant.

Jack went back down the ladder and helped Penny to her feet. "Let's go," he said without preamble. There was no time for anything else. She was panting. He suspected her scrubber was giving out, the carbon dioxide in her helmet rising.

He led her across the platform and strapped her to the

deck. Then he did the same for himself and his precious sample bag of dirt. "We're ready, Sam," he called.

"Stand by," Sam answered.

Columbia

Virgil sat in the cockpit but he was not piloting *Columbia*. She was being flown from Houston. He was in reserve, in case communication was lost. Fuel cell number two had finally crapped out. Only number one still worked. If it failed . . . well, it simply *couldn't* fail.

Virgil braced himself for what was about to happen next. Big Dog was the propulsive unit of choice this time. Mission Control had seen what it could do and they wanted it. Sam had agreed but expressed worry to Virgil about its remaining propellant. Virgil's best estimate indicated only a few minutes firing time.

Virgil heard Starbuck's voice. "I've got my commsat in position, Sam."

"Thanks, Starbuck," Tate answered. Virgil knew Starbuck's part was critical to the success of the pickup. He had never met either Sam Tate or Starbuck, knew next to nothing about them, but now his life and the two lives far below him depended on what they did next.

"All right, boys and girls," he heard Sam say. "Let's begin the final countdown at my mark."

"I'm ready, Sam," Starbuck said.

"*Mark.*"

"Godspeed, Jack and Penny," Virgil muttered, gripping the seat.

Challenger Base Stage

Penny was trying to reach across the base stage to touch Jack but he was too far away. He looked at her. "You okay?"

"I can't seem to get my breath."

He knew why. Her scrubber was gone. Carbon dioxide was nearly to a deadly level. "Just relax."

"Jack, I have to know. Was there a chance for us?"

"More than a chance. Stop talking, High Eagle. Breathe easy."

"I'm sorry about Kate, Jack. I never told you that. You loved her so much and to have her taken away like that . . ."

He looked straight ahead, at the stars. This was what Kate had wanted. Humankind, back on the moon. "Just breathe, Penny. I've done what I needed to do for Kate. She can rest now and so can I."

SMC

"*Go!*" Sam stabbed the return button on his console. The signal he sent flashed across the Armstrong Sea from Houston, struck the transceiver attached to the Lem, and continued down the wiring harness into the plug to the engine.

Challenger

Jack felt the vibration of valves that had been shut for a quarter of a century opening beneath him. Oxidizer and fuel were surging into the combustion chamber. The stars were suddenly washed out from a burst of flame that licked around the platform, met in a plume of orange and scarlet above him. Then the hot gases were swept aside and the stars lunged at him. The Lem was taking off like a scalded cat. The wind gushed out of Jack's mouth from the kick of the engine. He turned his head and for an instant saw the Taurus-Littrow Valley and the surrounding hills, and then they were gone. Then he turned to see Penny lying in her straps, trembling from the engine vibration. Some color in the corner of his eye caught his attention. It was earth, a distant blue island in the sky.

Farside Control

Starbuck's Farside comm satellite picked up the truncated Lem when it was a mile high, still accelerating. It was displayed on Starbuck's virtual panel. "Got it in my sights, Sam!" he cried at Tate's prod. "*Challenger*'s flying straight and true."

SMC

Sam crisply acknowledged Starbuck, then received the FIDO's trajectory analysis. The *Challenger*'s ascent engine was going to take the Lem into a high, extremely eccentric orbit around the moon. *Columbia* had a chance to catch it.

Sam ordered Big Dog punched up, firewalled to the max. Then it was shut down. The Lem engine had also stopped, out of propellant. Sam sweated out the call from *Columbia*. If the Crays knew what they were doing, somewhere high above the moon, about thirty miles out, the two lines describing *Columbia*'s and the Lem's trajectories would intersect. Then it was up to Virgil.

Columbia

Virgil climbed out of the cockpit and took up station at the aft ports, activating the RMS arm. A small white speck floated up out of the darkness. "I see it!" he whooped.

Columbia shook as if in response to his call. It was Houston firing the OMS, making an orbit adjustment. The white speck grew. The Lem was falling but so was *Columbia* at the same rate. At least that was the plan. Virgil could only hope the Houston computers had made the correct calculation.

Gradually, the lunar surface growing nearer by the moment, the shuttle slid underneath the Lem, her payload bay like a huge catcher's mitt. Virgil maneuvered the arm, reaching toward the Lem.

"Come on, darlin'," Virgil crooned, cajoling the odd-looking contraption to come nearer. It was turned so all he could see was its base, the silent nozzle of its rocket engine, and its legs sticking out as if on a frozen insect.

The Lem stayed tantalizingly just out of reach. There was no grappling fixture on *Challenger*'s truncated base so all Virgil could do was jam the arm's end effector between the Lem's side and one of the landing legs. He stretched the arm out. If he merely bumped the Lem, he would send it tumbling out of reach. He only had one chance. He hauled the arm back, bending it at its elbow, and then slammed the stick forward. The arm pushed out at maximum velocity, struck the Lem, pushed the end effector past one of the legs. It jammed and held.

Virgil watched the strain gauge numbers on the arm's monitor go off the scale, then subside. Torrents of sweat flew off his face, collecting in sparkling beads around his head like a halo. He waved them away, gingerly moved the arm's joystick to slowly pull the *Challenger* into the cargo bay.

"Got 'em, Houston," he said when he saw the top of the Lem. There, strapped down, were Jack and Penny. One of them waved. The other one was motionless. "Houston, I've got two passengers!" Virgil crowed. "Rock me on out of here!"

One and a quarter seconds later Big Dog fired, just enough to circularize *Columbia* and all her cargo into a stable lunar orbit.

Virgil waited anxiously at the airlock. By the time it opened, Penny had started to regain her color. She crawled out first, dressed only in her coolant suit. Virgil hugged her and then helped Jack out of the airlock. He saw the worry on his face. "She's had a rough time," he said, nodding toward Penny. Then he hugged Virgil. "Thanks, old son. You saved our lives."

"Aw, twarn't nuthin'," Virgil said, hugging his boss back.

Then he helped Jack secure Penny in a sleeping bag and strap an oxygen mask on her.

Houston was calling and so was the SAREX. Virgil answered Houston. Jack went to the SAREX. The message was from the men and women of MEC.

DID YOU GET IT?

ON BOARD THIRTY KILOGRAMS OF THE FINEST DIRT ON THE MOON.

The laptop paused, clicking.

AND DID YOU FIND WHAT YOU WERE REALLY LOOKING FOR?

Jack stared at the screen. Had he?

YES.

Jack looked at Penny, gulping oxygen but asleep, and then turned the SAREX off.

7

Inbound

Out ride the sons of Terra,
Far drives the thundering jet,
Up leaps the race of Earthmen,
Out, far, and onward yet—
We pray for one last landing,
On the globe that gave us birth,
Let us rest our eyes on fleecy skies
And the cool, green hills of Earth.

—*Robert Heinlein*, The Green Hills of Earth

Bed of Air
SMC

Sam wanted to get *Columbia* the hell out of lunar orbit and on her way back but his controllers gave him two pieces of bad news: (1) Fuel cell number one, the only functioning source of electrical power on the shuttle, was failing, and (2) Big Dog had pretty much shot its wad, the remaining propellant not sufficient to get the shuttle back into earth transit. Sam created two tiger teams—one to work on the fuel cell problem, the other on the earth transit situation.

The answer for earth transit came back to him within an hour. He went into the back room, where the leader of the team awaited him with a diagram of *Columbia*'s propulsions systems on a Vu Graph. Her finger shaking nervously, she traced the systems, then replaced the transparency with another, this one filled with equations. "This is it, Sam," she said. "We've done the math. If the Big Dog engine and the OMS jets fire at the same time, and if we keep Big Dog powered up until it runs out of fuel, we think that will be enough to get *Columbia* up to escape velocity."

Sam peered at the equations. They looked credible. "What's the downside?"

The team lead adjusted her glasses, looked around the room for help, but when no one spoke up, she plowed on. "It might not leave enough OMS propellant to slow *Columbia* when she gets back to earth. Depending on how she hits the atmosphere, she'll either burn up or bounce off it, keep going into an orbit around the sun. We'd never get her back."

The room was deathly quiet, all eyes on Sam. He rocked

back and forth in his chair, his chin in the palm of his hand. "Do it," he said finally. "We'll worry about slowing her down later. We've got some time for that."

The room immediately emptied. Sam saw Shirley, picking up her notebooks and pens. He had all but forgotten she was there. "What's new from Washington?" he asked her.

"WET got voted down." She clutched her things to her chest. "My boss—my ex-boss has resigned." She glanced at the ceiling. "What are their odds, Sam? I mean really."

Sam gave Shirley his best Clint Eastwood squint. "I ain't gonna lose 'em, Shirley. I'm gonna get 'em home."

Columbia

Jack received Houston's solution and got to work on it. Two hours and two lunar orbits later, he'd plugged in all the parameters. He helped Penny up from the middeck, gently strapped her into the mission specialist's seat. She was pale, confused, but Jack had checked her blood pressure, breathing, and heart rate, and her vital signs looked good. Virgil joined him in the cockpit. *Columbia* would be behind the moon, out of contact with earth, when the engines were to be fired. Jack waited until the onboard computers gave him the go-ahead and fired both the Big Dog and the OMS. *Columbia* vibrated from the combined propulsion of the two rocket systems. It had been estimated that Big Dog would have enough propellant to fire for thirty seconds. It managed nearly a minute. The OMS kept going until the computers turned it off. *Columbia* came bursting around the rim of the moon and flew on, into what Penny had named the Armstrong Sea.

"We're inbound, America!" Jack announced.

"America here, *Columbia*," Sam responded, taking Jack's lead on his call sign. "Come on home!"

"I like that call sign," Jack replied. He had heard cheering, pandemonium, in Mission Control, and was caught up in their apparent joy. "Let's go with that. You're America, the country of our birth, home of the brave, land of the free."

Sam came back. "You know, Jack, I guess a lot of people across the country will wonder why we haven't always called ourselves that. America it is from now on." He paused. "Got some information from Huntsville. Stand by."

Jack waited. "Huntsville thinks it may have a solution to your fuel cell problem, Jack. The tether can provide power if you'll reel it out as soon as *Columbia* enters the magnetic field of the earth. We'll let you know when you get there."

Jack was familiar with past shuttle tether experiments. One of them had generated so much power, it had burned the tether in two. The ATESS tether experiment on board was beefed up to avoid that, the electrical current generated flowing into electron accelerators in the cargo bay. Jack listened to all of Huntsville's plan, pronounced it sound. He admired its raw seat-of-the-pants engineering and then explained it to Virgil. Someone would need to go into the bay and attach a cord from the accelerators to the power pallet. "My turn, boss," Virgil volunteered.

Using the last of the suit oxygen, Virgil successfully accomplished the relatively simple EVA, plugging the cord into the power pallet. Then he came back inside and unreeled the ATESS tether, stabilizing it a mile from the shuttle.

Jack watched the electrical power distribution system numbers. A surge of new power began to come in from the power pallet. There was so much power through the tether, Jack decided to power down the remaining fuel cell, hold it for emergency use only. *Columbia* sailed on, bright and warm. Since it was not known how the tether might react to the constant barbecue turn, the ship was stabilized, her black-tile belly toward the sun.

* * *

By the end of the first day of earth transit, Penny felt well enough to eat something. Within a few more hours she felt normal. Virgil was exhausted, had taken a sleeping pill, gone to sleep in the middeck, secure in his sleeping bag. Paco was with him. For the first time since their walk on the moon, Penny and Jack were alone, their panorama only stars, both the moon and the earth out of view. Penny snuggled in his arms in the cockpit, and they kissed, long and tenderly. "I still love you anyway," she said, teasingly.

"I still love you anyway too," he said, teasing back.

She put her hand on his chin, ran it over the scar, down his neck. He shuddered as she kissed the scar, her hands roaming along his shoulders, along his back, to his hips. He unstrapped them both, taking her with him as he pushed out into the clear air of the flight deck. He began to undress her but she couldn't wait. She pulled off her shirt, chucked her shorts away. While she was stripping, he was too. She admired his readiness, reached out, put her hands around his back, pulled him to her. She tucked her feet inside some footloops, and welcomed him inside her. When she arched her back in a spasm of pure pleasure, her long black hair sprayed into a zero g ebony blossom.

One hundred thousand miles above both earth and moon, a man and a woman, naked to the universe, clung to one another, no bed possibly softer than their cushion of molecules of air.

Panic in the Streets?
The White House

Vanderheld made his way through the dark, empty hall to the Oval Office. Sykes's office was empty, stripped. He'd turned himself in to the attorney general upon his return from Iraq. In the outer waiting room, only Secret Service agents waited. Vanderheld went inside. The President of the United States was waiting for him. He sat in a high-back swivel chair, its back to the door. The President didn't bother to turn around.

"Good evening, Mr. President. Thank you for seeing me. I'm sorry this worked out the way it did. But there are things you may not know, or understand."

"Please," he said grimly. "There's nothing you could say that would matter."

Vanderheld sat in one of the green wing-back chairs placed in front of the President's desk. "Nevertheless, I would ask you to carefully listen to me. Without the approval of WET everything I predicted is coming to pass. There's anxiety in every capitol in the world. In the Middle East there's panic in the streets, threats of war, rumors of war."

The back of the chair wobbled, as if the President was considering turning around. He didn't. "That much, at least, is true. The Iraqis and Iranians betrayed the treaty almost as soon as I was out of their airspace. With oil about to become obsolete, and their billions no longer at stake, they just decided to go at each other again." The chair rocked again. "Every mullah, sheik, and tin-pot dictator seems to have gone nuts over this thing, saying we've betrayed them. They're talking about cutting us off from their oil if we don't renounce fusion. I can't do that, so I suppose we're in for some very long, cold winters in this country if fusion doesn't work."

"I fear the country will be ruined."

The chair stopped rocking. "This country is going to be fine. You're a coward, Stuart. A piece of slime. I agreed to see you because you begged for it. If this is all you have to say, get out."

Vanderheld sagged. "I'm sick, Mr. President. Cancer. Doctor thinks about two, three months at most."

The President turned, narrowed his eyes at the bent old man looking for sympathy. "Good. I hope you rot in hell," he said. The days of peace, tranquillity, and compassion

were over, at least for a while. There was a race to get the
gold of the moon. The President, as much as his country,
was going to have to be tough and ruthless. He had tried out
his new persona, the New Frontier personality of the nation.
It felt good, *damn good*.

Vanderheld stirred, pulled himself erect. "One thing
more. While I'm rotting in hell, Mr. President, I'll at least
be warm. Did you think we in the January Group would
leave this to chance? *Columbia*'s mission is doomed, has
been from the moment it lifted off. There will be no test of
the fusion reactor. And do you really think the Middle East
leaders are going berserk on their own? Elements of the
January Group control them. But you can save yourself and
get everything back to normal. Immediately denounce
fusion."

The President blanched. "I can't!"

Vanderheld sneered. "Then you've sealed your own fate
and that of this country. This is a country that has been too
powerful for too long, a shameless country of racism, pollution, out-of-control capitalism, and disregard for the poor
and afflicted. Now I can say what I've always believed: it will
be a great day for the world when this country gets a boot
shoved in its face, is made to kneel before the peoples of the
world."

Edwards shook his head. "You're a traitor, always have
been."

Vanderheld shrugged, and walked to the door. "Call me
whatever name you like. The historians are the only ones I
care about now." As he went out, he flicked off the light
switch, left the President sitting in the dark.

MET 10 DAYS AND COUNTING . . .

Penny's Log (3)
Columbia

Penny looked up from the pilot's seat and smiled at Jack as he somersaulted over the back of the commander's seat and settled in beside her. Paco followed him, trotting along the spongy surface of the cockpit ceiling and curling up on it, purring. Ahead of her was earth, cocked on its side, the North Pole on her right. It would have made an acrobat dizzy, but orientation of things didn't mean much to Penny anymore. Wherever her feet were, that was down. Everything above her head was up. It was that simple.

"What are you doing?" Jack asked her.

"Writing in my log."

"Am I in it?"

She shook her head. "Isn't it just like a man to think anything a woman writes is about him!"

Jack shrugged, looked up at Paco, who reached a languid paw out to him. "I figured it was either about me or Paco."

Penny sighed, turned back a page in the spiral notebook. "Would you like to hear what I've written?"

Jack settled back. "You bet!"

"All right, Jack. But don't laugh or make fun. This is just a first draft."

Jack looked stunned. "Me? Laugh or make fun? I'd never do that!"

She gave him a knowing glance. "How very sensible on your part. Okay. Here goes." Penny took a breath and began reading:

"We are on a course for home at last. America called—"

"America. I like the sound of that."

"Jack, don't interrupt." She watched him out of the corner of her eye and then continued:

"America called with the word that only a short burst of OMS would be needed to put us on our final approach for earth. Jack was in the cockpit—"

"You see? I knew it was about me!"

"Jack Medaris, I'm going to stop reading if you interrupt me one more time!"

Jack put a finger to his lips, winked at Paco. "Paco. Be quiet while Penny's reading."

Paco opened his eyes, gave a little meow, and Penny could not help laughing. She wagged her finger at both her boys. "Not another peep!"

"Okay, okay."

"Jack was in the cockpit but the whole thing was done from the ground. I sat with him, and Paco came up too." She petted the cat's head. Paco responded with a deep, soulful purr. "The earth is peeking more and more into view. I've looked for the moon several times but it seems to have disappeared."

"It's behind us," Jack said.

"I know. May I continue? Thank you.

"Virgil is as happy as I have ever seen him. He is soon going to be with his family and that is all that he needs to know. I heard noises in the middeck earlier in the day and went down to see what was going on and he and Paco were doing zero g gymnastics. I wonder how Paco will do back on earth. I think he'll miss life on board the shuttle. Not me. I'm ready to let my hair down and have it actually come down."

"I like that line," Jack said.

"My editor won't."

"Why?"

"I don't know, but he won't. He'll want me to come up with a more emotional reason than just having my hair go in the right direction."

"Like what?"

"I don't know, Jack." Penny sighed. "I guess he'll want me to bare a little of my soul. That's something men don't know much about. But I'll think of something. Maybe I'll say I can't wait to get out of this little aluminum box with two sweaty men who haven't had a bath in a week and smell like it, and a cat—one Paco Fuzzy-Wuzzy Black and White Creature—who forgets to cover up after himself after he uses his zero g litter box."

Paco pinned his ears back at the mention of his name. Penny suspected he knew complaining when he heard it.

Jack stretched. "Well, I think I'm going to miss old *Columbia*. She's been a good old girl." He patted the console in front of him. "She's the best damn spacecraft ever built."

Penny studied him. "Is that all you'll miss? This big machine? What about me?"

"Well, I was kind of figuring you'd still be with me."

Jack's placid expression told her nothing. "That's news to me," she said.

When Jack seemed to suddenly turn mute, as if realizing he'd said more than he meant to say, Penny hummed her deduction that he was fearful of commitment, cleared her throat, and continued reading:

"Messages have been coming in, both over the normal loops and the SAREX. The one that most touched me was from the chief of the East Coast Council of the Cherokee Nation. I have been made a full member of the tribe and have been asked to address the council in the fall. I'll be there! America Control has passed along dozens of offers for me to speak. I was most surprised by the number of pro-space groups! Have I found a new constituency?"

"I bet there's more wanna-be astronauts than anybody knows." Jack grinned.

She ignored Jack and kept reading. "I continue to monitor the cell culture experiment although any results that I see are now suspect, considering the number of accelerations that have been placed on them. The lamb and frog cell accretions have stopped growing, probably due to the lack of space in the chamber. I still do not know if I have accidentally found a way to grow nerve cells into nerve tissue, but the possibility is definitely there. There is no question, however, that my mistake has generated a lot of interest. It is all so exciting. I look toward earth and hear her sweet call."

Penny closed her logbook. "Well?"

"Well, what?" Jack asked.

"What did you think of it?"

"I think it's amazing how you can put two sentences together, and have them make sense. Like most engineers I never could do that very well."

"Maybe I could teach you," she offered. When he didn't immediately respond, she added, "Maybe, Jack, there's a lot of things I could teach you."

Jack turned to her, put his hand on her cheek. She nuzzled it against his fingers. "Yes. If you took the time."

She held his hand to her cheek. "If you gave me the time."

He petted her for a moment and then dropped his hand, went back to studying the earth. "If I could save time in a bottle," he began, singing the words of the old Jim Croce tune. Penny laughed and joined him, offering him her hand. In a spacecraft perhaps unable to avoid headlong, destructive impact into the dense air of the planet they were hurtling toward, Penny High Eagle and Jack Medaris sang, holding hands, their voices joyfully drowning the pain and hurt that still racked their hearts, of dreams and wishes that might yet come true.

MET 12 DAYS AND COUNTING . . .

The *Soyuz*

Cosmodrome launchpad 12-D, Kazakhstan

"Let's go!" Ollie Grant yelled as the deep rumble of the engines igniting far beneath her rattled her barely cushioned seat aboard the *Soyuz-Y* space capsule. The rocket engines sounded like a gigantic popcorn popper about to overflow.

Yuri Dubrinski laughed and started a running commentary in Russian with the ground controllers. Ollie laughed with him. Grant had just spent the best few days in her life, absorbing the quick lessons from Dubrinski on piloting the crude little spacecraft, while keeping out of harm's way. There had been occasional gunfights just outside the housing area of the ugly, bone-dry Cosmodrome, but the vodka and sex had been great!

At least the Russians were good at getting their rockets off on time, Grant thought, but that was about as much credit as she was going to extend their way. Two nights before, she'd been on her way to the communal shower, a thin towel over her shoulder, when the first gunfire had broken out. She'd thrown herself to the linoleum floor while doors burst open all around her and men and women, some naked, others in various pieces of camouflage uniforms, ran up and down the hall. One of the naked men carried an AK-47 submachine gun, kicked open a door beside her, and ran in, blasting through the window. While Grant crawled back to her room, she heard the sound of breaking glass, the rattle of machine-gun fire, and insane laughter. Her room stank of burned gunpowder and for the rest of the night she heard the whimpering of someone apparently wounded just out-side the fence. Dubrinski told her the next day that the Kazakhs had tried to storm the building. It was a form of eviction notice, he'd said. It seemed the Kazakhs had heard the Russians were getting a slug of hard currency for launching Grant into space and they wanted their share. A Russian paratroop battalion was stationed at the Cosmodrome for protection and they liked nothing better than shooting Kazakhs.

Even that morning she had heard sniping around the perimeter as she took the lift up to the *Soyuz*-Y. Before the booster was out of sight, Dubrinski told her, Russian air-planes were going to be swooping in to pick up the para-troopers. The Cosmodrome was going to be abandoned. Russia was opening another, far to the north and east.

Grant felt the g-forces building, an unfamiliar stress dur-ing launch. Space shuttle astronauts usually only took three g's at launch, and then only briefly, but the booster was powering up to give her five g's, perhaps more as each stage dropped off and new engines fired. She heard the noise of the first stage engines die away, the vibration in the capsule subsiding.

"Get ready," Dubrinski said.

"Get ready for—?" She was going to say *what*? but never got the chance. Somebody in the capsule hiding behind her swung a baseball bat as hard as possible into her back. At least that's how it felt. "*Oooomppph!*" is what came out of her mouth. The second stage blasted away. The crude switch panel in front of her turned into a shaken blur. Grant gritted her teeth, hung on. She cursed Carl Puckett. What the hell was she doing on board this made-in-Russia Spam can, anyway? Puckett had surprised her with a visit briefly in Baikonour, brought her presents, promises, cajolery. The only part she believed was when he told her she was a pa-triot for undertaking the mission. Puckett had been fuzzy about the rest, citing secrecy. He'd seemed to have completely forgotten the tale he'd told her once, about the nuclear weapons on board and the homegrown atheist or religious nuts, take your pick. To her credit she hadn't laughed in his face. She was going for her office and all the astronauts. Whatever was happening aboard *Columbia* wasn't right and she was going to stop it.

A stowage box above her flew open, dumping a heavy flashlight on her head. "Owww!" she yelled at the sudden pain.

"You are okay?" Dubrinski yelled over the noise of the engines.

Grant held the flashlight, started to swing at him with it out of frustration and anger, but the g-forces kept her arms pinned. Then, the engines cut off. She lunged against her shoulder harness. "I'm fine." She gasped, rubbing the welt on her head and slapping his hand away when he reached across with concern.

"Get ready," he said again.

"Oh, jeez!"

"Third stage ignition, *now*!" Dubrinski yelled happily.

"*Oooompppph!*"

Moscow

Carl Puckett was enjoying the serene, cool quiet in the special VIP box overlooking the *Tsup*, the Russian version of Mission Control located in a deteriorating concrete building in the Moscow suburb of Kaliningrad. He was wearing a fox fur coat down to his ankles, and a sable hat so huge and fuzzy, it looked as if he had three dead animals sitting on his head. Beside him, hanging on his arm, was a blowsy blond woman in a tight red polyester dress, who had been given to him by his new best Russian friends. Her name was Livia and as long as he kept her properly filled with vodka, he had discovered she would do anything for him, however kinky. Puckett had never properly shaken out his kinks, he thought, and Livia was the perfect young lady to help him in that regard. He especially liked it when she wore her schoolgirl uniform with the badges that had Lenin's face on them.

On Puckett's other side stood a huge hulking man named Boris. Boris was wearing a black suit cut from wool cloth as thick as baloney slices. Boris was the other person assigned by Puckett's new best friends, the ones who had picked him up at the airport and explained the facts of Russian economic life to him, how a man such as Puckett with money could have nearly anything he wanted in Russia, especially if he was properly appreciative of those who gave it to him. Puckett liked his new best friends. They treated him with the respect he had always thought he deserved, especially after he explained how most of his money was safely in a numbered account in Belize. Yes, he'd be appreciative, at the time and amount of his own choosing. A man, especially a rich one, could do well in Russia, he was starting to think. When he looked back at Washington, D.C., and especially at the attorney general, now the vice president, who was after him, Moscow and its young blond women were looking very good indeed. Still, the Man, the former vice president of the United States, had given him a job and he'd built his reputation on doing whatever job he'd taken. And this was for the January Group after all. Vice presidents came and went but the January Group was forever.

A patter of applause from below broke his reflective spell. "What's happened, Boris?"

"The *Soyuz* is in space, Carl," Boris rumbled with a voice that sounded as if the Moscow subway were bottled up inside him.

"That is very good."

"Carulllll," Livia squealed, "shall we play now?" She swung a big cloth bag out to show him. "I brought my nurse uniform."

Puckett gave Boris a look. The huge man's face was like a bulldog's, so full of flabby folds, it was hard to tell what he was thinking. "Hold down the fort, Boris?"

Boris fingered his earpiece. "There is a back room." He looked down, as if embarrassed. "It has a couch, some chairs . . . vodka."

"Oooooh!" Livia grinned. She said something in Russian that Puckett took to be lascivious to Boris. Boris showed no reaction, only held his arm out to show them the way.

Space

"I'm going to kill whoever thought this up when I get back," Grant snarled, taping a bandage to her forehead. She slapped Dubrinski's hands away again. "I don't need your help!"

Colonel Dubrinski eyed her. "Olivia, I am sorry. But don't fret. We will rendezvous with *Columbia*, assess her needs, and escort her back to earth. It will be a glorious mission."

Grant shrugged, gave him a smile. God, he'd been good in the sack and she'd needed that, desperately. "You are right, of course, Yuri. We will save the shuttle. And all the world will rejoice." She sighed, touched her forehead. It still hurt. She allowed herself a little misery and then got busy. This time she was going to make certain *Columbia* would not survive.

A Call from San Antonio
Columbia

Jack sat in the cockpit, took Sam's call. "Jack, there's somebody down here who'd like to talk to you. He's not here in Mission Control. He's actually in San Antonio. He's been begging and I think it's the right thing to do."

Jack heard the name. "Frank Bonner? Sure."

"He's pretty sedated, Jack. He was burned over fifty percent of his body. He has a lot of therapy to look forward to. Guess you know something about that."

"Put him on, Sam."

Jack listened. The voice was weak but it was Frank. "Jack, I want you to know how sorry I am—"

"Save your strength, Frank. Whatever you did, you did it because you thought it was the right thing to do."

"I have to know . . . did you find her letter?"

"Yes."

"And was it . . . ?"

"Wonderful? Yes. It was everything I'd hoped . . . and more. I'm afraid it didn't make it back, though. It's still on the moon."

Jack could hear Bonner's voice catch as if a wave of pain had struck him. Jack very well knew how that happened when you were freshly burned, how suddenly it felt as if somebody was stripping off your skin. "Take it easy, Frank."

"Do you remember . . . any of it?"

"Yes."

"Would you . . . ?"

Jack closed his eyes, took a deep breath. He could see the notebook paper clearly, and every word on it. He started to recite and as he did, he could hear Bonner sobbing.

"But I know something, even now
that I wonder if you know even then.
It is that I will always love you
And that I will always be with you
Across space and time.
You see, didn't I send you a message all the way to
the moon?"

Montana (5)
Perlman's Plant

The new vice president loved helicopters, loved their versatility, their design, the powerful sound of the *whop-whop* of their blades cutting through the air. The only thing she hated about them was riding in them, had an inbred sense that it was impossible that they flew, that they were always a thin cable's width away from disaster. Her face was a frozen expressionless mask but its paleness betrayed her fear. She kept her eyes on the back of the two pilots' helmeted heads as their UH-1 Montana National Guard helicopter banked sickeningly and came in low over the knoll that overlooked the fusion reactor site. "There it is, ma'am," one of the pilots called back.

Tammy Hawthorne forced herself to look sideways, out the open door. The site was unremarkable, a square of fence, a rectangle of concrete where the blast door covered the silo, another rectangle and a low gray building over it that was apparently the elevator shaft.

"We're going to land," the pilot said.

"Good idea," the veep responded shakily, and wondered if it was possible for someone to rent a car in Bozeman and come and get her without embarrassing either herself or the pilots.

The helicopter leveled out, slowed, and settled in beside the blast door. The sergeant who rode shotgun beside her helped with her safety belt and she climbed out, ducking under the viciously rotating blades. An Army National Guard major ran up to her. He had a bullet-shaven head, started to salute, then thought better of it. "Madame Vice President, I'm Major Todd," he said, his voice hoarse and gravelly. "You can talk to them over here, ma'am."

Major Todd took her to the elevator shaft, pointed at the microphone that dangled from the doorway through a hole about the size of a quarter. "The bad guys who were up here put this in, ma'am. It works. They've talked to us but they're not budgin'."

The veep nodded, walked up to the mike. She waited until the helicopter's blades finished their spin-down. "Dr. Perlman, this is the new vice president of the United States. Please come up the elevator and meet me on the surface. There has been a great mistake. *Columbia* is almost home, bringing with her the helium-3 you need for a full start-up of your fusion reactor. The President has authorized me to tell you that you will not be interfered with in any way. WET has been defeated and it looks like the United States might be having some trouble getting the oil we need. We need you, Dr. Perlman, the whole country needs you. Please come up."

Below, in the echoing hall beside the elevator shaft, Perlman and Charlie listened with interest. Perlman leaned on his cane. "What do you think, Charlie?"

Charlie put his thumbs under the straps of his bib coveralls. "I think there's a woman up there we can trust, Doc."

Perlman put his hand on Charlie's shoulder. "Let's go up," he said. "Let's have a look at God's own fusion reactor, feel its radiance on our faces."

"I'm there, Doc," Charlie said, grinning and leading the way.

The *Soyuz* Attack

Columbia

Jack sat in the cockpit and watched nightside earth grow. Dozens of thunderstorms raged across the planet, violent flashes punctuating the darkness as if a war across the hemispheres were being waged. Scattered here and there was the pale glow of cities. Since everything had quieted down for their long trip back, he had been in a strange mood. There was something missing and he couldn't quite put his finger on what it was.

Perhaps it was because everything was on automatic. He was only a passenger on board the ship that he had come to think of as his. He was happy that it was all over but still . . . He shook his head. What was he worried about? Sam Tate had called up with news that, after careful analysis, it looked as if there was enough OMS propellant aboard to slow *Columbia* down so that they wouldn't burn up when they hit the atmosphere. They would hit it over the Indian Ocean, he said, skip a little, and then come in over the Pacific. *Columbia* would be guided in by the automatic landing system (ALS) at Edwards Air Force Base. Edwards was flat and dry. Even if *Columbia* missed the runway, the hard-packed desert floor would give her a good landing. All Jack had to do was sit back and enjoy the ride home.

He tried to relax but his mind was swarming. What was it going to be like back on earth? From the messages he had received, Cecil had managed to get him and the MEC employees off all legal hooks. And the thirty kilos of dirt he and Penny had collected were being eagerly awaited by the nation, according to a personal message voiced up by the new vice president. Everything seemed resolved and yet . . .

What about Penny? Perhaps that was what was bothering him. What was he to do about his feelings toward her? And what was she thinking? She was an independent woman. Would she really want to tie herself down with him? What could he offer her? His company was gone. He wasn't even certain he wanted to try to rebuild it.

Jack peered into the darkness. He thought he'd seen a blinking light, alternating red and then green. He looked away, an old observer's trick, and then scanned the area again. Nothing. *You're seeing things, boy,* he remonstrated to himself. Part of his general unexplainable unease and anxiety, he thought. To his knowledge, no one had yet put blinking buoys out on the Armstrong Sea.

Soyuz-Y

Dubrinski finally assumed control of his spacecraft, much to Grant's relief. The radar blinked its solution. He fired the *Soyuz-Y*'s thrusters for a ten-second count.

Grant searched ahead. "I see her." She pointed at a smear of pale light. "There!"

"Exactly on schedule," Dubrinski replied crisply. He switched on the docking lights, red to port, green to starboard. "Shall I call them, Colonel?"

Grant held binoculars to her eyes. Her heart raced as she saw the familiar shape of *Columbia*. She'd flown on her once, and she was supposed to be aboard her now. She felt a twinge of jealousy. "Not yet, Yuri. I'd like to inspect *Columbia* first, starting with her belly. And turn off your signal lights!"

Dubrinski toggled the switches. "Yes, ma'am. If I have learned nothing else about being a capitalist, I have remembered one axiom: The customer is always right."

Grant didn't respond to his attempted joke. She lowered the binoculars, looked around the capsule. Its stick and controls were the same as used on the MiG-29 fighter-bomber and also similar to those of the F-15, an Air Force jet she'd learned to fly to perfection. A button on the side of the stick acted as the throttle with an analog readout on the console indicating accelerations. It was simple but effective. She watched Dubrinski deftly work the stick, the lateral thrusters responding. The *Soyuz-Y* whisked around the shuttle and came in underneath.

Grant studied the glittering shuttle tiles. "Can you hold us in this position?" she asked the Russian.

"Of course." He worked the stick and the capsule slowed until it matched the shuttle's speed and course. "What a beautiful spacecraft," he said, awestruck.

"Right, beautiful," Grant muttered. She turned away

from him, reached into her personal kit stowed in a strapped-down cloth bag beside her.

Dubrinski kept admiring the big shuttle. "It is just like Russia's own *Buran* shuttle," he whispered. "It is such a shame we only flew it once, and unmanned at that. A damned shame . . ."

Grant jabbed a spring-loaded hypodermic needle into his thigh. Dubrinski jerked, looked down, and then back up at her, a startled expression on his face. When she pulled the needle out, his suit still held pressure, the hole too small to cause a leak. He reached for her but his hand drifted up past her face and then hung there. He was already out.

"Sorry, Yuri," Grant said, tenderly. The syringe had been delivered to her by Carl Puckett with the admonition to do her duty, no matter what her personal feelings might be. That's what she had done, God help her, because no one else would.

Grant worked the stick, flew through a few practice loops, until she got the feel of the *Soyuz-Y*. She was the best pilot in the astronaut corps and was about to prove it. Grant came up over the lip of *Columbia*'s port payload bay door and flew down the sill, snapping the shuttle's Ku-band antenna off at its neck.

Columbia

Jack felt *Columbia* shudder. He came out of his seat and flew back to the aft view ports in time to see the *Soyuz-Y* fly down the length of the payload bay and then come back. It was a very distinctive spacecraft and Jack knew what it was at once. He could see two cosmonauts in the twin window panels.

He also saw that the Ku-band antenna, their primary communications link to America Control, was missing. Penny and Virgil came up beside him. "Jack?" Penny asked. "What is it?"

"Company. They hit us."

"A *Soyuz*, Penny," Virgil explained. "Russian. Why do you think they're here, boss?"

Jack watched the little green capsule maneuver. "I hope they're a welcome wagon, Virg. But somehow I doubt it."

The *Soyuz-Y* came up to the view ports and hovered in front of them. "It's Olivia Grant!" Penny gasped.

That told Jack enough to bet on trouble. He flew to the cockpit and strapped himself in, Penny sailing into the seat beside him. "What's she doing, Virgil?" he called over his shoulder.

Virgil was still at the aft flight deck view ports. "Nothing. Just sitting out there watching!"

Jack got on the comm loop, using the S-band. Before he could reestablish contact with America Control, *Columbia* shook as if she had run aground. "Jack," Virgil yelled. "Grant hit the port sill. I think she's after the tether."

The tether was *Columbia*'s principle power source. It was standing out like a gigantic yo-yo string straight out from the cargo bay. If Grant was after it, there wasn't much Jack could do to stop her.

Soyuz-Y

Piloting the *Soyuz-Y* was about as much fun as flying a turnip in space but Grant was a quick learner. She flew down the payload bay, accidentally bouncing off the port sill, and then up the tether, striking it with the capsule's docking latches. She backed off and came at it again. The tether vibrated but did not break. She flew around the cargo bay and came in from behind. The OMS rocket engines were on both sides of the vertical stabilizer. If she could damage those, the spacejackers wouldn't be able to slow themselves and would either bounce off the atmosphere or burn up. Grant no longer questioned herself as to why she was attacking *Columbia*. She was there. She had been given her orders. She was going to do what needed to be done.

She piloted the *Soyuz*-Y into a wide circle around *Columbia*. She could see no one at the view ports. She willed calm, studying the shuttle, deciding her next move.

While Grant sat and thought through her situation, she didn't see the shuttle arm swinging out. The *Soyuz*-Y was a sturdy ship, essentially overengineered, but it had one great weakness. Even with the larger windows put in on the Y-variant, the pilot was blind to everything that wasn't directly in front.

Columbia

Jack pushed the motion rate to the peg, unfolding the shuttle arm and turning the wrist to open the end effector. He could only hope that the grapple had not been damaged when Virgil had snagged the Lem.

The *Soyuz*-Y had an American-style grappling fixture on the side of its descent module, added for its application as a lifeboat with the International Space Station. Jack aimed the end effector, pushed its velocity to the red line. The end effector closed over the fixture. "Got you!"

The thrusters of the *Soyuz*-Y lit up. The arm strain gauge numbers soared into the red zone. Grant was tearing the arm apart, pulling the shuttle around with it. Jack had to get rid of the arm. He called up the contingency deorbit checklist, chose QUICK RESPONSE JETTISON from the menu, and clicked on it. A few seconds later the explosive bolts in the arm's base detonated. The severed trunk rose, cables trailing behind, and described an arc out of the payload bay. The *Soyuz*-Y went with it.

Soyuz-Y

Grant desperately worked the controls. When she tried to fly forward, the mass of the arm carried the spacecraft off at a tangent. Frustration filled her and she slammed her fist again and again against the cockpit wall. Then she saw *Columbia* in the window. Luck had carried her to the rear of the ship. Grant's face turned from a grimace into a sad smile.

Calling on all of her piloting skills, she began to sense the center of gravity of the grotesque craft she was flying. She poured on the main thrusters, using the laterals at the same time, sending the *Soyuz-Y* trailing the RMS arm flying straight ahead until the five nozzles of Big Dog filled her windscreen.

The *Soyuz-Y* slammed into *Columbia*'s tail, snapping off the Russian spacecraft's instrumentation module and swinging the descent module up into the starboard OMS pod. Smashing the pod also crushed the fuel and oxidizer tanks positioned there. *Columbia* shook as the tanks exploded, flames erupting into space. The *Soyuz-Y*, its pressure hull ripped open, kept grinding, its destructive path ending only when it plowed into Big Dog, tearing the engine apart.

The Face at the Window
Columbia

By the time *Columbia* managed to make contact with America Control on the S-band, there was only one hour until reentry. Jack told the story quickly.

"We copy all that, Jack," Sam responded. "Stand by."

Virgil hung over the seat. "Stand by, the man says. This time we've had it. One OMS left and that ain't gonna be enough to slow us down. When we hit the atmosphere, we're just gonna be one big fireball."

"Virgil, please be quiet. Let Jack think," Penny said. "Please think, Jack."

Jack was thinking. He attacked the problem, his mind flying all over the shuttle, probing everything on it for something to slow them down. Then he thought about what was in the cargo bay and snapped his fingers. "Got an idea."

"What?" Penny breathed.

He told them. "I think it'll get us at least through reentry.

Where we pop out, I don't know. And I'll have to land this sucker wherever it is, and the biggest thing I've ever landed before was a Cessna-150. Maybe I could do it at Edwards but on some short strip . . . and of course we might not even come in over land. Still, it's a chance."

Penny's mouth dropped open. "You told me you were a pilot and could land a shuttle."

"When did I say that?"

"I don't know. The first day, the second—you know, right after you kidnapped me, Medaris!"

Jack smiled sheepishly. "I guess I wanted your cooperation, High Eagle."

"I can't believe this. . . ."

"What about the wreckage hanging off our tail?" Virgil worried.

"We'll hope it burns off when we come in."

Jack called Tate, explained his plan. "Virgil and Penny will bail out as soon as we get low enough," he concluded after outlining what he proposed.

Penny grabbed him by his collar. "Forget it, Jack. Where you go, we all go."

Jack knew better than to argue with her. "Go check the RMS base," he said. "Make sure nothing is left that'll interfere with the bay doors closing. Quickly, now."

Penny saluted sardonically. "*Yes, sir!*" She pulled herself out of her seat, went hand over hand along the flight deck floor, and then up to the bank of consoles and switches. She looked out the view ports to inspect the shuttle arm base left after the explosive bolts had blown the arm away. She screamed when she saw the face at the window.

Reentry
Columbia

Jack pulled on his suit and headed outside, ignoring the requirement to prebreathe. There was no air in the main

supply of his suit, and there wasn't much in the emergency
supply, and the scrubber was all but dead. If he prebreathed,
there wouldn't be anything left to use to go outside. What
he had to do out there, he'd just have to do quickly.

Jack pushed open the hatch and climbed out of the airlock into the cargo bay. He looked up and saw what he
assumed to be the Russian pilot of the *Soyuz*-Y still at the
view port, carrying Grant with him. He grabbed him by a
boot, drew him and Grant into the airlock, slammed the
hatch shut, and hit the pressure lever. After ambient was
reached, Virgil opened the inner hatch and the cosmonaut
came out, turning to pull Grant out with him. She was
unconscious. Jack followed after doffing his suit.

Penny settled in beside the Russian. "What were you
doing with Ollie Grant?" she demanded.

"A rescue mission," Dubrinski said after introducing
himself. He had taken off his scorched helmet. "But then
your Colonel Grant saw fit to drug me. There is a needle
wound on my thigh if you do not believe me."

"We believe you, Colonel," Jack said grimly. "How did
you get out of the *Soyuz*?"

Dubrinski shook his head, as if amazed at what he'd
done. "I awoke in twisted wreckage, half hanging out of the
spacecraft. Colonel Grant, as you can see, was knocked out.
She is a great pilot but apparently has gone quite insane. I
had no choice but to disconnect the air umbilical from the
Soyuz and try to attract your attention. I was very pleased to
find the wire running along the side of your spacecraft. I
used it to come forward after I got over the shuttle's tail.
Then I saw Dr. High Eagle and used the handrails on the
bulkhead to come up so she could see me. I apologize for
frightening her."

"I'm afraid you've gotten out of the frying pan into the
fire," Jack said. "We'll be hitting the atmosphere in one
hour and it's going to be a close thing."

"You are the pilot?"

"I'm going to give it my best shot."

"I was trained for many years on simulators to be a *Buran* pilot," Dubrinski said eagerly. "Perhaps I can help."

Jack didn't hesitate. "I think maybe you can." He led Dubrinski to the cockpit.

The Russian settled into the pilot's seat, scanned the bank of switches and instruments, and pushed the rudder peddles. "Are your hydraulics activated?"

"The APUs are up," Jack confirmed. "We have full aero-dynamic control."

"Show me everything," Dubrinski said, clearly overjoyed at the prospect of flying *Columbia*. "Now I will have the chance to fly a shuttle to the earth from space after all!" He stopped, looked sorrowfully at Grant. "Will she be all right, do you think?"

Penny was beside her, the medical kit in her hand. "We'll do what we can for her," she said.

SMC

Sam reacted to Jack's announcement by raising his palms toward the ceiling. *What else could possibly happen on this mission?* America Control had fed all the information it had to *Columbia*. All that could be done had been done. Jack's idea of using the tether as an aerodynamic brake was a roll of the dice. Not much was known about how it might work except for a theory relayed down by the Italians in Hunts-ville as to the satellite's drag coefficient in the upper atmo-sphere. The computers had subsequently calculated that it might just be enough to slow *Columbia* to a velocity that was survivable. The likely effect of having a burned *Soyuz*-Y and a flapping RMS arm hanging off her tail was a com-plete unknown. If it burned off quickly enough, Tate's peo-ple told him, then perhaps there would be little effect. If it stayed attached, then *Columbia* would probably be out of control even if she managed to survive to the lower atmosphere. At least, the port OMS rockets were still functional. If they had been damaged, it would have been all over.

"Okay, people, heads up," Sam announced as the moment of reentry approached. "This is the hairy part."

He heard a low burble of laughter emanating from the consoles beneath him. When he looked sharply at them, Mary Cantrell, the GUIDO, let him know why they were all laughing. "Sam, how can you say *this* is the hairy part? This ol' thing's been like one of Dolly Parton's wigs from the get-go."

Despite his belief in the need for decorum during desperate moments, Sam had to laugh with them.

Columbia

Jack and Dubrinski sat at the cockpit controls, having worked out what each would do in the various stages of reentry, from the first moments when *Columbia* hit the atmosphere, until she got low enough to operate as a glider. They went through it again and then started their first checklist. They quickly lapsed into their own lingo.

"OMS TVC gimbal check," Jack called.

"Port only, yes," Dubrinski replied, his head swiveling between the checklist and the oddly familiar panels. "The *Buran*'s console looked very similar to *Columbia*'s, Jack," he added.

"A coincidence?" Jack smiled.

Dubrinski shook his head, embarrassed. "I do not think so."

"APU restart?" Jack called out from the checklist.

"Restart on-line."

Jack took a breath. "Check CRT two GNC fifty Horizon SIT and CRT three BFS, GNC five zero Horizon SIT, then return CRT two to GNC SYS SUMM one and CRT three to BFS. . . ."

Dubrinski scanned the monitor to his left. "Yes, I have it. RCS dump?"

"Roger but only fifty percent. We may need control in the nose. Exercise brake pedals."

"Yes. Nominal APU performance."

"Roger."

Jack turned to look over his shoulder. Virgil was in the footloops in front of the aft flight deck view ports. He was to control the tether at the critical moment. Penny sat in one of the two seats bolted to the flight deck behind the cockpit. She had Paco in his transit box bungeed between her feet, prepared to take him with her in case of a fast evacuation. She also had the kit that contained all her cell culture samples and film cans. "Ready, Penny?" he asked her.

"I was born ready." she replied, although her voice betrayed her nerves.

He gave her a thumbs-up. "Attagirl. We're gonna be fine."

Jack took another moment to consider their situation. One problem with using the tethered satellite for an aerobrake after the final OMS burn was that the cargo bay doors had to stay open to keep the tether out, but had to be closed for *Columbia* to enter the atmosphere. He thought he had resolved that problem by having Dubrinski fire the OMS, then rotate *Columbia* so that the tether, twenty miles long, was pointing toward earth. When it hit the atmosphere ahead of them, it would troll through the air and slow them down. Then when *Columbia* hit the first stray molecules of nitrogen and oxygen and ozone in the upper atmosphere, they would let it continue to drag through the denser layer twenty miles below. Then Virgil would cut the tether, Jack would close the doors, and Dubrinski would use the dwindling RCS jets to rotate *Columbia* again, put her tiles down toward earth. The Cray in Houston thought that might be enough for the shuttle to survive reentry.

After the OMS burn Jack called, "Go for it, Virg."

"Roger that, Jack."

Jack knew Virgil would let out just enough on the reel to keep the cable from breaking. He waited calmly for Virgil's report.

"ATESS is hitting the atmosphere," Virgil called. "She's dragging big time, Jack!"

Jack kept his eye on the accelerometers. "It's working," he breathed. He looked over his shoulder again. "Penny, it's working."

"That's my man."

Jack knew what was happening far below. The tethered satellite was heating up, its aluminum shell glowing and then sloughing away. When it finally burned up, if he'd done his calculations correctly, it would have slowed *Columbia* to a velocity of fifteen thousand miles per hour, just below orbital speed.

"She's gone, Jack," Virgil called, meaning the satellite had burned up. With it gone the tether would recoil back at them, perhaps to wrap around the shuttle. "I'm cutting the tether," Virgil continued, indicating that he'd eliminated that dangerous possibility. Jack heard him climb into the seat beside Penny. "You can close the doors, Jack," he said.

Jack gave the command. The great doors slowly rotated about their pivots, closing tightly. *Columbia* was ready to reenter.

Jack and Dubrinski had decided to reenter at a steep angle and then pull up when *Columbia*'s wings began to develop lift. This would give the shuttle time to cool, since her tiles weren't built for the temperatures likely at such a high velocity. It was a risky technique but Jack thought that *Columbia*, out of all the shuttles, could handle the stress of repeated reentries. Because she was the first shuttle, she had been built with thicker beams and heavier attach points than her successors.

Columbia made her first dip into the atmosphere, indicated by a blue haze coming off her nose. Jack could see they were over the mid-Pacific. Then the haze caused by the air friction turned into a fireball. A shudder and rattle aft indicated that the impact of hitting the atmosphere had torn off the *Soyuz-Y* and the RMS. Jack could feel *Columbia's* tail starting to yaw.

"Compensating with the RCS," Dubrinski said, working the controls. "No response. I will go with the OMS to flatten us out."

Jack felt the g's build, then they were staring at cool, dark space again. He ran his fingers across the keyboard, watched the numbers march. "We bounced back up twenty miles." He whistled.

Dubrinski guided the shuttle into a flat trajectory. The blue haze formed again and then turned into a white-hot fireball. "Give it more OMS," Jack commanded.

Dubrinski complied, using the last of the OMS propellants. *Columbia* flattened out and then bounced twelve miles high. She was now eighty miles mean altitude and neither Dubrinski nor Jack could pinpoint where they were.

Jack watched approvingly as Dubrinski keyed in the digital autopilot. Then the Russian dived *Columbia* again. She began a flat skid just as she caught denser air. A Klaxon alerted Jack that the DAP was losing aerodynamic control. "Full RCS, Yuri," Jack ordered.

Dubrinski made the manual firing. "I'm doing this by the seat of my pants!" he confessed.

Jack said nothing, let his pilot do his work. *Columbia* skipped, this time five miles high. But she was out of her skid. "The seat of your pants is better than any computer, Yuri," Jack said.

Sweat poured off the Russian. He mopped his face with his sleeve. "Thanks, comrade," he said.

"All right, Colonel," Jack said calmly. "Let's try it again."

Dubrinski took a deep breath and keyed in the DAP. He kept his hand on *Columbia's* controller, ready to take over as soon as she gave him aerodynamic control. A calm settled over him. The man who sat to his right had given him complete trust, a man as calm and collected in a crisis as any he had ever seen. It was not simply a matter of his own survival. Dubrinski burned to perform at maximum efficiency for this man.

Columbia hit the atmosphere with a flash and an audible thump. But this time the fireball was more of a glow and the DAP held *Columbia* steady. Automatic elevon trim began and then Jack called out what Dubrinski longed to hear. "Aerosurface control, q-bar at two dot zero."

Columbia was dropping like a brick with wings. Jack looked down and saw clouds. "We're in!" he exulted. "We're in!"

Dubrinski marveled at *Columbia*'s feel as her wings began to develop lift and she began to glide. He eased forward the rotational hand controller and felt the shuttle's wings bite into the air. When he eased back, she seemed to sigh under his touch, skimming frictionlessly over an invisible high lake of clear air. *Columbia* was magnificent, he thought. The love of an aircraft and her pilot seemed to flow between Dubrinski and the shuttle, her great heart and his mixing into one energy, one mind.

Jack called up a descent profile, snapping Dubrinski out of his metaphysical musing. "Energy management looking good, Yuri."

Dubrinski fixed his eyes on the eight-ball indicator. The wings were exactly level. He swiveled his gaze to the horizontal situation indicator. It was giving a readout, but any navigational information it was picking up was probably bogus.

Jack watched the mach meter and the vertical velocity indicator. On the screens above his head was the position of the flaps. Everything was on the money. Dubrinski was flying *Columbia* with consummate professionalism. *No, by damn*, Jack thought: *with genius!*

That was when everything went to hell. The first tile gave way on the starboard wing, stressed past all design limits by the wild reentry. When it tore away, it took four more tiles with it. A millisecond later two more chunks also ripped from *Columbia's* belly.

Dubrinski felt the turbulence in his seat a fraction of a second before it came through the stick. He struggled with it, *Columbia* almost pitching into a tumble. He managed to level her but she was shaking as if she were his grandfather's sleigh crunching over remelted ice while the big horse pulling it tossed its maned head.

Jack deduced the problem when he heard a big chunk let go beneath him. "We're losing tiles! Can you hold her?"

"I think so!" Dubrinski said between gritted teeth.

Jack turned to Penny and Virgil. "You're going to have to activate the pole! Go!"

The two stared at him. "Go!" Jack screamed at them again.

A sudden turbulence bowled them over just as they unbuckled their belts. Virgil went howling into the bulkhead, striking his head. He sat down, moaning, blood streaming down his face and soaking the collar of his coveralls.

"Jack." Penny gasped. "I think we're going to need help."

Dubrinski clapped Jack's shoulder. "Go, Jack. I have *Columbia*. Help them!"

Jack unstrapped, crawled to the side hatch jettison handle, and slammed it down. Four shaped charges blew the hinges, and three thruster packs drove the hatch into the windstream. A blast of frigid air filled the flight deck, a snowstorm of ice crystals exploding from the humidity in the cabin air. Jack fought the blast and tore open the aluminum cover to get at the egress pole. The pole—a curved, spring-loaded, telescoping steel cylinder weighing 240 pounds—was needed to get crew members safely past the leading edge of *Columbia*'s port wing. He struggled with the pole, pushed it through the hatch, and ratcheted it into its bracket.

Penny grabbed him. "Medaris, I can't do this!"

"What the hell are you saying, High Eagle?"

Her eyes were wild. She stepped back from the blast of air, *Columbia*'s gyrations throwing her off-balance. "I can't go out that door. I'm afraid of heights!"

Her illogic floored him. *"But you've walked on the moon!"*

"This is a hell of a lot scarier than that! I'm going to ride *Columbia* down!"

"The hell you are!" Jack advanced on her, grabbing the straps on her parachute pack and dragging her to the hatch.

"I see something, Jack!" Dubrinski called out. "An island!"

Jack snapped the lanyard attach ring on her pack to the snap hook on the pole. "Did you hear that, Penny? We've got a place to go."

"You mean to land?" she asked hopefully.

"In a manner of speaking." He slapped the top of her helmet, threw her out of the hatch, then helped Virgil to his feet, hooked him onto the pole, latched Paco's box to his belt, and shoved him out behind her.

There had been three parachutes left. Dubrinski had refused to wear one, reasoning that the pilot would be the last to need it. Grant, still unconscious, was strapped to the deck. Her only chance of survival was with Dubrinski. "Go, go!" he called to Jack. "I'll try a water landing. They need your help!"

"See you on earth, Colonel!" Jack saluted. He dragged the bag of moon dirt to the door, clipped it to his belt, clicked his parachute ring to the pole, and, picking up and holding the bag to his chest as tightly as he could, flung himself into the blue-gray hurricane outside.

On a Crystal-Blue Sea
The *Linda Joyce*

Gladstone Powery looked through the salt-smeared window of his shrimper *Linda Joyce* as the familiar scrub of his home island slid past. He had come in from the open sea after a month of working the banks to the north and had managed a decent haul, enough at least to pay off his men, clean his boat and make repairs, and perhaps break even. His crew, most of them teenagers, sat up on the bow, smoking and eagerly watching the coast and laughing with the excitement of coming home after being at sea for so long.

He had heard a strange thunder only minutes before, a pealing double clap. The sky was clear except for the low fog that always stood off the coast in the morning so Powery had dismissed the sound. Odd things were always happening at sea. Then he heard an excited call and saw one of his boys pointing off the starboard bow. He eased up on the throttle and peered into the morning mist. There were three orange objects bobbing on the light swell out there. Flotsam of some sort, maybe something that he could use, Powery thought. He'd take a look. He hoped it wasn't the marijuana or cocaine bundles that often drifted in to shore, brought from who knew where by the currents. When he found those, Powery either sank them or drove right past. To attempt to turn them in to authorities was to invite suspicion and probably a search of his boat. He carried no contraband but who needed the government delaying him and his catch? The *Linda Joyce* eased through the smooth ocean. "Gladstone, there be somebody wavin'," one of his boys called.

Powery told his boys to go fetch his rifle and then idled in beside the first life raft. Two other rafts were attached to it by bright yellow lines. A man with a scar along his jaw was in the first raft, holding a duffel bag close to him as if it contained precious gems or gold. A woman was in the second raft, a beautiful woman. She had long black hair and she was throwing kisses at the boys on the bow. A big bear of a man struggled in the third raft. He had a white box with him from which seemed to come meowing sounds. "Help them, boys!" Powery called, and cut his engines and raced on deck.

The woman was brought up first. She carried some kind of a helmet in her hand. Powery saw that a symbol was sewn on her coverall over her left breast. He knew that symbol. "NASA?" he asked in wonder. "You be a space woman?"

The woman grinned. "Captain, the High Eagle has landed again!"

The man with the scar climbed on board the shrimper carrying the duffel bag. One of his boys tried to help him with it but it was so heavy, he almost dropped it on the deck. "Careful," the man said. "It weighs thirty kilos."

The big man was also clutching the box. The boys pulled it up. The letters *F-L-E-A* were inscribed on its side.

"Captain, where are we?" the man with the scar asked Powery.

Powery wondered if he was dreaming. "Well, mon," he said, "you be on the planet Eart'."

"Yes," the man said patiently, "but where, exactly?"

Powery turned toward shore, gesturing dramatically. "I

don't reckon it be no secret. Where else you see such fine clear blue water? Why, mon, this be Grand Cayman."

Penny and Jack hugged. "We made it," she said, nuzzling his cheek.

"Jack?"

It was Virgil. He had taken the rifle away from the crewman. He held it on Jack and Penny. "Captain, how deep is the water here?"

Powery frowned at the big man. "We're over the Cayman Trench, mon. Couple miles, mebbe more."

Jack separated from Penny. She took a step away. Virgil kept the rifle leveled on Jack's chest. "Jack, pick up the bag. Throw it overboard. Don't move, Penny," he warned.

"Virgil—" Jack began.

"They got to me, Jack, a long time ago. Said they'd kill my family if I didn't do what they said."

"Who, Virgil?" Penny asked quietly. "Who got to you?"

"The January Group, the same people who paid Perlman to build his fusion plant."

Penny squinted at him. "That doesn't make sense. If they paid for the plant, why would they want to stop us?"

"I'll tell you why, Penny," Jack said, his eyes locked on the unwavering barrel of the rifle. "They want the technology, just not now. They want to keep things on an even keel, let oil be the energy choice of the world. They own most of it, one way or the other, so why not? But when the oil runs out, they'll be ready with fusion. Nothing will change. They'll still have a lock on energy. It will be a nice, pre-planned transition, maybe in a few decades."

Virgil blinked, nodded sorrowfully. "They've known everything right from the beginning. I disabled the security system that night they smashed *Prometheus*. They weren't supposed to hurt you but what could I do, Jack? They went away after that. I thought they'd leave me alone. Then when they found out what you were doing with this mission, they called me and said for me to help out. I think they were having an argument between themselves. They told me to call from the pad, get my last instructions. Use the pistol, they said. Stop the launch. But Hoppy surprised me, took the gun away from me. I couldn't hurt him or you, Jack."

"So what's changed, Virgil?" Jack asked softly.

"I promised them if they would leave my family alone, I'd make sure the dirt didn't get back. After we got into orbit, you kept pushing and I couldn't figure out how to stop you without killing you and Penny. Then Sally promised on the SAREX to call Lori and Dawn every day, to let me know how they were doing. I also got her to tell Lori to be careful, to hire some guards to protect herself and Dawn. She did but nobody tried anything anyway. I guess January figured I was their ace in the hole. They're right. I got to get rid of this stuff or me and my family will be running for the rest of our lives."

Jack tensed. "You won't kill me, Virgil. Not after seeing me safe all the way to the moon and back."

"Don't try it," Virgil warned. "Nobody's more important to me than Lori and Dawn." He nodded toward the deck. "Jack, pick up the bag. Pitch it overboard. I'm desperate. Do it, now!"

Jack looked toward shore, then out to sea. He sighed, picked the bag up, walked to the boat rail. He stopped. "This is wrong, Virgil. We can figure out a way to look after your girls."

"I can't take any chances." Virgil cut his eyes to the sea. "Throw it, Jack. Get rid of it."

Jack looked toward shore and then down into the gloom of the Cayman Trench. Sighing, he took several practice swings and then, with a mighty heave, threw the bag off the starboard side as hard as he could. It hit the ocean, then went under, a few bubbles all that was left of the treasure that had come back from the moon.

Columbia

Dubrinski looked toward the distant speck of land. After the Americans had left, he had managed to trim *Columbia* enough to maintain level flight. He dared not try to control her further.

The speck grew into a dark hump. It was an island, the white rim of surf defining its coast. Dubrinski could make out a few roads cut into red soil and patches of lighter colors indicating clearings, perhaps small farms. *Columbia* flew on, her airspeed dropping and her altitude decreasing surprisingly slowly. The air must be very humid, Dubrinski thought, to keep supplying the heavy craft with so much lift. He hadn't seen air like that since he had been stationed in Cuba. The ridgeline of the mountains he was soaring past almost looked familiar. He looked again. He could have sworn . . .

A tone sounded in the cockpit. *Columbia* was stalling. Dubrinski pushed the stick forward and her nose dipped. He still thought he recognized something familiar about those hills. *Can it be . . . ?* Dubrinski questioned himself. *Have I already crashed and this is some sort of cosmic joke by God? And to think I have just started to believe in Him!*

Dubrinski could see a town . . . no, it was a city! A mountainous cove slipped past and there it was, a huge city stretching into the distance. The big harbor was below, filled with anchored boats of every size and color.

Dubrinski recognized the harbor. He had flown over it dozens of times. Eagerly, he let *Columbia* bring herself in, flashing over the startled heads of sailors on the fishing boats. *Columbia* entered the ground effect thirty feet off the sea and then settled in. The Big Dog engine performed its final function, its weight pulling the spacecraft down by her tail so it hit the water first. Huge domes of water formed on both sides of the tail for an instant and then shattered into a wave of spray as *Columbia* collapsed on her belly. She slithered along, her wake a giant V. Then she stopped.

Dubrinski unbelted himself and Grant and dragged her to the side hatch. The shuttle was settling fast, so he did not hesitate. Holding Grant, he jumped into the water and then crawled up on the wing, pulling her to safety. A gray patrol boat appeared and circled the spacecraft. A big boil of steam suddenly erupted from the port OMS pod and the boat raced away and then came back, as if its driver was too curious to let fear keep him away. The Russian was laughing, cheering, jumping up and down. The boat settled in beside him, the boys on the flying bridge behind the machine guns pushing back their olive drab hats and looking at him as if he were a space alien. There were women on board the patrol boat, and children too. Dubrinski swam to the boat, pulling Grant along. The children, too excited to stay still, jumped in the water beside him, laughing and chattering, and supporting Grant's head.

Dubrinski looked up at the uniformed man standing in shock on the bow. "Cuba, ¿sí?" he asked.

"Cuba. ¡Sí!" the man confirmed.

Star City
In the Air Between Moscow and the Yuri Gagarin Training Center

Puckett rode the bench between Livia and Boris in the little *Hind* helicopter. Painted olive drab with the big red star of the dead old Soviet Union on its sides, it had swooped into the courtyard of the *Tsup* in Kaliningrad to carry Puckett to Star City, the gated and fenced complex east of Moscow where the cosmonauts lived and trained. When the *Soyuz-Y* carrying Grant and Dubrinski had stopped transmitting, it had been assumed that the mission had failed, perhaps proved deadly to the crew aboard. It was time to get out of Dodge, or in this case the *Tsup*, and Puckett's new best

Russian friends graciously saw to it. They thought Star City was the best place for him to go since they had recently purchased it, lock, stock, and neutral buoyancy simulator.

Puckett leaned against Livia, who was asleep. He wasn't entirely unhappy. True, every one of his hopes, plans, and schemes had been foiled, but new opportunities always beckoned. The Russian "family" that had adopted him was very interested in his welfare. After all, he was a veritable fount of knowledge of the interworkings of the federal government in Washington, D.C. That was potentially useful to them since they had expressed an interest in penetrating it, acquiring some of its machinery for their own use. Puckett assured them that he could assist them. A little money properly applied, Puckett had explained, went a long way along the banks of the Potomac River if one knew just the right place to apply it.

Puckett smiled. He was going to be all right. He would learn Russian, climb to a leadership position with his friends. They already controlled much of the Russian government. He had already discussed with them his insertion back into the United States after the present furor had subsided. Puckett settled back. Yes, he would be fine.

That was why it was such a shock when Boris nudged him and Puckett looked into the barrel of a 9mm pistol. "Tell me your Belize bank account number or you are a dead man!" the huge man rumbled.

Puckett looked from the barrel to Boris's tiny, sad eyes. "Don't be a fool," he shouted over the whining helicopter engine and the rushing air around its blades. "If you kill me, you won't have the number. If you let me live, I will pay you handsomely."

"You don't understand, Mr. Puckett," Boris replied stolidly. "I have been ordered to kill you in any case. I just want the number before you die."

Puckett could not fathom such a thing. Kill him? He was way too valuable for that. He decided Boris was bluffing. He swiped at the barrel. "Don't be an idiot, Boris. Put that thing away."

Puckett's move surprised Boris and the pistol went off. Both Boris and Puckett looked forward. There was a hole in the back of their pilot's helmet that Puckett swore hadn't been there before. To his dismay the pilot's head wagged to one side and the helicopter banked in the same direction. "Uh-oh," Puckett said.

The guards at the main gate at Star City leaned nonchalantly against their guard shack, smoking and talking while watching with boredom the empty road that disappeared into the darkness. A distant helicopter attracted their attention and they observed its running lights. The lights were dancing, as if the pilot had decided to emulate the moths that battered themselves against the helmeted lights on their shack, swooping and turning, rising and falling. Then there was a flash of light, a boil of orange flame that rose out from behind the black forest that lay in front of them. The guards estimated that the helicopter had gone down two kilometers away. They discussed among themselves whether to call anyone or to mount a rescue mission. When no decision was made, which was in itself a decision, they shrugged and went back to smoking and talking of women and football and hockey. Helicopters crashed all the time in Russia these days, after all. Airplanes dropped out of the sky. Trains jumped off their tracks. The economy of the country itself kept opening and folding like an accordion. Why should they trouble themselves because some fool had decided he was a helicopter pilot? Somebody would take care of the mess left out there, clean up the burned, blackened bodies. Somebody would care. All they knew was they didn't.

Off Grand Cayman

Virgil sat on a stack of shrimp netting, holding his face in his hands. Powery had taken the rifle away from him, stowed it. Jack touched Virgil's shoulder. "It's all right, Virg. You did what you thought you needed to do."

"I'm sorry, Jack."

"I know." Jack looked at Powery. "Can I borrow that scuba gear, Cap'n?"

Penny came over. "Jack, even you can't dive down two miles!"

Jack let the cocky grin spread across his face that had once made her hate him, made her love him now. "I don't think I'll have to go that deep."

Jack took a giant step off the starboard side, holding his mask and regulator tight against his face. Before he threw the bag overboard, he had been watching the *Linda Joyce*'s drift toward a line of demarcation, a place where the water turned from dark purple to faded blue. He had thrown the bag as hard as he could toward the line that marked the sheer, vertical wall, the famous Cayman Wall that came arching out of the Cayman Trench. If he still had any luck left . . .

Jack spiraled down toward the wall. A turtle swam by, spotted Jack, flippered hard to get away from the crazy diver laughing in his regulator. Jack swam up to a big piece of pillar coral growing on the wall. He admired that kind of coral, always had. It formed itself into giant fingers that were almost abstract art. Scuba divers usually were careful to skirt around their jagged stands. Pillar coral could snag anything that came into contact with it, even a strap on a bag of dirt from the moon.

8

A New Start

Who has known heights shall bear forevermore
An incommunicable thing
That hurts his heart, as if a wing
Beat at the portal, challenging;
And yet—lured by the gleam his vision wore—
Who once has trodden stars seeks peace no more.

—*Mary Brent Whiteside, "Who Has Known Heights"*

3 YEARS LATER . . .

Back to the Cape
Cape Canaveral

It was a perfect day for a launch. The Cape sparkled in golden light as the sun peeked above the dark blue horizon, illuminating a single white puffy cloud hanging high in the sky. The crowd of dignitaries stood at the base of pad 39-B and admired the rocket sitting on its own squared-off base. It looked larger than it was because it sat by itself on the concrete pad. The gigantic towers of the shuttle era were gone. Only a small portable gantry, now rolled back, was needed for this machine, the first of the operational single-stage-to-orbit (SSTO) fleet fielded in three years of intensive effort and remarkable economy.

A siren wailed and the crowd tensed. Launch was imminent. A loudspeaker crackled beside the stands. "Ladies and gentlemen, I give you the Medaris Engineering Company's single-stage-to-orbit vehicle, *Moondog!*"

Flames immediately erupted at the base of the rocket and it powered smoothly off the pad, swept up into the sky, and disappeared within seconds. A thin cloud of water vapor, its only residue, hung in the air and then began to disperse in the light winds. The crowd oohed and ahhed appropriately and applauded enthusiastically. The doors on a concrete hangar beside the pad opened and a rail car, carrying another *Moondog* SSTO, crept out and started trundling toward the pad. "The second *Moondog* will be erected and ready for launch in thirty minutes," the woman over the loudspeaker said. "Powerful, safe, and economical, *Moondogs* are available for immediate lease. Terms are available."

Jack Medaris shook some hands, stepped down from the viewing platform. He looked with pride at his accomplishment, the *Moondog* reusable SSTO. His company had gone public and accomplished the design and construction of the *Moondog* using funds from the sale of its stock. In effect, a vast number of Americans had decided to risk their capital on Medaris's enterprise. A cluster of five Big Dog engines provided the boost to get the composite aerodynamic shell and the heavy cargo aboard a *Moondog* into orbit. Once there and its payloads deployed, a *Moondog* automatically reentered and landed back at the Cape or wherever it was ordered, tail-first. A quick once-over and refueling and she was ready to go again. After a few more test flights the Federal Aviation Administration was scheduled to clear *Moondogs* to be launched from anywhere in the United States. Jack's plan was to keep a fleet of six of them at the Cape to take advantage of the trained work-force there.

Jack used binoculars to inspect the adjoining Pad 39-A. The tower there was in the process of being dismantled. No more space shuttles of the *Columbia* class would ever fly off either pad again. After the final flight of *Columbia* the space shuttles of NASA never flew another operational mission. They were used instead in a rigorous test program, pushed to the far edges of their flight envelopes, NASA learning everything they had to offer about maneuvering in space and working in the hypersonic range of velocity in the upper atmosphere. It was the test program the shuttles should have undergone from the beginning.

There had been many changes at NASA. The space agency had gotten out of the operations business and moved into the forefront of research and development, handing over its scientific and engineering knowledge to American commercial space operators. With the data it had gained from the shuttle tests, the agency already had a prototype scram-jet that could fly into orbit from Edwards Air Force Base, deposit a payload, and return. NASA had fielded the prototype for a half-billion dollars, ten times less than the original estimate. That estimate had been made before MEC, by taking *Columbia* to the moon, had demonstrated what could be done with a little money and a lot of engineering guts. The scram-jet looked good, and the older and larger aerospace companies around the world waited eagerly to get their hands on it. But Jack was convinced his *Moondog* design would beat the scram in head-to-head competition. Or perhaps there might be room for more than one SSTO spacecraft. The commercial markets that had opened up since his moon flight were going to be too big for a single enterprise. It was as if that flight had opened some sort of mental floodgate. The possibility that so much could be done if the will was there to do it was energizing not only to the aerospace field but in all the scientific and even political disciplines. There were new starts everywhere. Anything was possible. To prove it, NASA was also cutting metal on a prototype fusion engine using helium-3 as fuel. This was an engine that could scoot out to the moon in hours, Mars in days. The entire solar system might soon be within America's grasp.

Medaris watched the group of VIPs, all potential customers, excitedly watch the erection of the second *Moondog*. With cheap access to space just on the horizon, commercial enterprises were making plans to produce a great number of products in space—new materials, new medicines, and new concepts such as tourism, space sports, and even homesteading. Jack intended that MEC would be able to provide the transportation to space they required. Although Penny High Eagle had been disappointed to find that immersion in salt water had destroyed her unusual cell culture experiment, her description of the nerve cell growths she had observed had caused great excitement in the medical community. Attempts to repeat her serendipitous experiment became a top priority of pharmaceutical and medical companies the world over. Industrial Orbital Facility, Inc., a private joint

Japanese-American company that had taken over the old International Space Station, announced that it would launch a new man-tended laboratory the following year aboard an improved Japanese H-2D booster. Competitive bids were being taken from the clamoring companies for room aboard the module. There was renewed hope among people paralyzed by spinal cord trauma and disease that space research would deliver a cure.

There were mining outfits represented by the men and women filing into the stand to observe the launch. The interest in helium-3 had reached fever pitch as soon as Dr. Perlman had come up into the bright sunlight of the Montana summer. Using the thirty kilos of beads found at Shorty Crater and rescued from the Cayman Trench, Perlman had demonstrated the full power of his plant. Montana Power & Light was working overtime to string in lines to it for commercial use. Energy companies the world over were flocking to the United States to learn more. The President of the United States, a year after *Columbia*'s landing, had agreed to make the technology of fusion power available to the world. Helium-3 was the new gold of the solar system and mining companies were lining up to dig it out.

There were government officials from several countries observing Jack's *Moondog* flight. The moon treaties of a previous era had been revoked and governments across the earth had staked out claims. The United States and Russia made the first, based on their landings there, but other nations—England, Germany, France, Brazil, India, Japan, China, even Portugal, recalling a past history of exploration and colonization—asked for and received territory set aside on the moon. An international agency was organized at the United Nations to act as an arbiter of the claims. If the land wasn't secured by a manned landing within twenty years, it would be auctioned to the highest bidder with the proceeds going into an international spaceflight general pool. Some people were already calling this as yet unnamed international agency by a familiar name: Star Fleet.

Jack knew his company was in a good position to take commercial advantage of both the commercial and political activities. A *Moondog* could carry a Big Dog aloft and place it into a parking orbit. All a nation or a company needed to do was to put its mooncraft in orbit, dock with the Big Dog, and then use it to reach escape velocity. There was a great land rush coming a quarter of a million miles away from earth across the Armstrong Sea.

The January Group was no longer a secret society. It had moved boldly into the open, especially after its members were exposed and they had no choice. From their positions of power these men and women began to espouse their belief that the world would be better without spaceflight or technological development. A movement was formed called Janism. Janists already controlled governments of small countries and had their eye on big ones. Another struggle began on earth for men's souls.

Jack could only hope that Janism would never catch on. He couldn't imagine that it would, considering the excitement of rolling back the new frontier. Sam Tate had been appointed administrator of NASA. Shirley Grafton joined Tate as his assistant. When a new president was elected, Tate and Grafton were invited to stay on.

Former Vice President Vanderheld had survived his cancer, saved by a powerful new drug developed from protein crystal growth experiments in space. He had moved to Mexico and built a walled compound patrolled by guards twenty-four hours a day. President Edwards decided not to run for a second term. He was rarely interviewed and spent most of his days playing golf. There was some talk of Jack Medaris running for president but he refused to even consider it, stating that "engineers had more important things to do, such as building rocket ships." The new president was a Gulf War general who declared his most important job was getting the federal government out of the way of the American citizens charging into the heavens.

Jack and all the MEC employees had come under the general amnesty worked out by Cecil Velocci with the Justice Department. Cecil had then gone back to Cedar Key. According to what Jack had heard, Cecil had continued to prosper. The citizens of Cedar Key thought about making the MEC hangar a tourist attraction but then decided against it. The character of their town was more important to them. Former Vice President Tammy Hawthorne bought a lot on the Key and built a house. Within a month an itinerant fisherman named Pelican Pete had moved in with her. There were regular late-night parties at the Hawthorne house and enough rowdy behavior that Trooper Buck often had to visit to calm things down. His visits usually lasted several hours.

Columbia was raised from the Havana harbor by private donations and placed in a site of honor at the United States Space Camp in Huntsville, Alabama. Frank Bonner, retired from NASA due to his injuries, accepted the position of Space Camp Dean. Soon afterward a plaque dedicated to Kate Medaris was erected at the *Columbia* site with the story of her love letter left on the moon and found and lost again.

Yuri Dubrinski and Olivia Grant stayed in Cuba, married, and opened a scuba resort. Besides running the kitchen, Grant also gave piano and flying lessons until a week before she gave birth. She had a daughter and named her Katrina.

Jack had stayed too busy with his projects to accept all the accolades offered to him. As soon as he had gained the funds for his new SSTO concept, he plunged back into his work. The result was the great booster sitting proudly on the pad.

A short line of blue-suited pad workers marched away from the second *Moondog*, their work of checkout finished. Virgil Judd, leading the workers in his MEC coveralls, gave the crowd a proud wave and then saw Jack. He cupped his mouth and yelled something.

Jack couldn't hear so he left the stands and went to the line. He and Virgil clapped each other on the shoulder. "I said Paco is doing great," Virgil said, grinning.

"He doesn't miss zero g?"

"Well, sometimes he kind of launches himself off the couch and looks surprised when he drops like the fat rock that he's become, but otherwise . . ."

"And how's that little girl doing?"

"A miracle, Jack. There's still some work to be done but her lungs are as clear as a bell. The docs say she's gonna be fine."

Jack and Virgil walked together until they reached the gate.

The voice startled Jack. He hadn't expected to hear it. "Hello, Jack."

She was wearing a strapless sundress, her long black hair shimmering down around her shoulders. Her smile was radiant. Virgil kissed her on the cheek. "I think you children need to talk," he said, and went on his way after giving Jack a significant look.

Jack took her in. "Well, High Eagle," he said. "What brings you to the Cape?"

"You did, Medaris," she said. "To tell you the truth, all of a sudden I couldn't get you out of my mind."

"Aren't you missing a speech or something?"

"A world tour, actually. I was supposed to be in Tokyo today." She looked past him, toward the pad. "Are you going to ride in that thing?"

"Eventually. If it works out the way I believe, everybody on the planet will get a chance to go into space. Maybe see some of the things we saw."

"Ah, well, that would be grand." And then, "Do I get a hug?" He put his arms around her and she seemed to melt. He noticed a tear. "What's this?"

"I have so much I want to tell you," she said, the tear rolling down her cheek.

Jack held her quietly, breathing in the perfume of her. *Sage.* "Sometimes," he said, "especially on tropical islands, when the sun goes down into the sea, just as it sinks out of sight, its rays flash up through the water. If you look fast, you'll see it—a green flash. One of the most beautiful things there is to see on the good earth."

Her big brown eyes gazed longingly at him. "I wish I could see it."

"We could be in Key West by sunset," he said.

"What about your next launch?"

"They can get along without me."

"Now, there's a change," she marveled.

"What about your tour?"

"Maybe I've toured enough."

"Now, there's a change," he said, but the old irony in his voice was gone.

"Shall we?" she asked. She had taken a step away. "See the green flash, I mean?"

"They say you only see it if you're in love."

"Then I think we have a chance," she said, offering her hand.

He took it without hesitation. Sometimes, to do great things, a chance was more than enough.

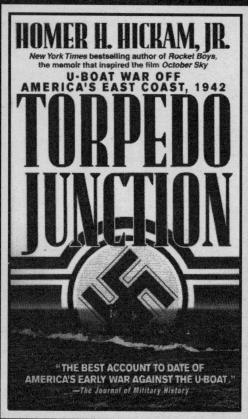